the diminished

KAITLYN SAGE PATTERSON

the diminished

HARLEQUIN TEEN

ISBN-13: 978-1-335-01641-6

The Diminished

Printed in U.S.A.

For everyone who's ever felt diminished,
and for Cody, for whom I've always been enough.

Part One

"Those who lose their twins shall join them in death, that
they are never without their other half. Some may cling
to unnatural life, and those shall be called the diminished—for
in their grief, they become less, and their violent breaking
shall scourge this land."

—from the *Book of Dzallie, the Warrior*

"Like the goddesses and gods, who are complete without a twin,
a blessed few shall be singleborn. You shall know them as our
chosen ones, for our divinity runs undiluted through their
veins. Raise them up, and let the wisdom that is their birthright
illuminate this world."

—from the *Book of Magritte, the Educator*

CHAPTER ONE

Vi

The first queen built the Alskad Empire from scorched earth and ash after the goddess Dzallie split the moon and rained fire from the sky. The god Hamil called the sea to wash away most of what was left of humanity, but the people who managed to survive gathered in the wild, unforgiving north, calling on Rayleane the Builder to help them shape an idyllic community that would be home and haven to the descendants of the cataclysm.

They failed.

I came up feared and hated for a thing I had no control over in a world divided. My childhood wasn't the kind of unpleasant that most brats endure when their ma won't let them spend all their pocket money on spun sugar or fried bread filled with jam. No. My days coming up in the temple ranged from lean and uncertain to hungry and brutal with shockingly little variation.

There were bright moments among the terrible ones, sure,

and my best friend, Sawny, was there for most of them. But even the shiniest days as a dimmy ward of the temple were tarnished. It had to do, I think, with the endless reminders of how unwanted I really was. Even Sawny and Lily, whose ma'd given them up, enjoyed a little more kindness than any of the anchorites ever managed to show like me.

One night, a month before I turned sixteen, I waited in my room, boots in hand, for Sawny's knock on my door. It had been about an hour since our hall's anchorite called for lights out. She was a rich merchant's daughter who'd recently committed to the religious life, and she slept sounder than a great gray bear. Though we'd be hard pressed to find an anchorite who cared that two brats nearly old enough to be booted out of the temple were sneaking out in the middle of the night, Sawny and I were still careful. Neither of us had the patience to endure even one more tongue lashing, halfhearted or not.

Keep them sleeping, Pru, I thought.

While I'd stopped praying to the gods and goddesses years ago, I kept up a sort of conversation with my dead twin, Prudence. Ridiculous as it sometimes felt, a part of me wanted to believe that she was looking out for me—that she was the reason I'd been able to keep myself from slipping into the violent grief of the other diminished for all these years. All Ma'd ever told me was her name and that she'd died a couple months after we were born. After that, it didn't take long for my ma to dump me at the temple in Penby, unwilling to raise a dimmy. Ma and Pa visited from time to time, bringing my new sisters and brothers to see me when they were born, but we never got close. Getting close to a dimmy's about as smart as cuddling up with an eel. Not even my ma was that dumb.

There was a soft tap on the door. I slipped out of my room and padded down the dim hall after Sawny.

We raced up the narrow staircase, our hushed giggles echoing through the stillness. Even the adulations were silent at this hour; the anchorites chanting over the altars of their chosen deities were tucked away in their rooms under piles of blankets and furs. At the top of the stairs, I jammed my feet into my boots and slid open the casement window, letting a shock of brisk night wind whine down the stairwell. Once I'd shimmied out onto the slate-tiled roof, Sawny passed me his knapsack and climbed through the window with practiced ease.

"Lily's asleep?" I asked, flicking my thick, dark braid over my shoulder.

"Snoring like a walrus," Sawny confirmed. "I put some of Bethea's sleep herb in her tea. No chance she'll wake up and rat us out."

It wasn't that Sawny's twin was a tattler—not exactly. Or that she hated me. She didn't. Not quite all the way to hate, anyway. But when you spend half your life being lectured about dimmys and how dangerous and unpredictable we are, you tend to not want your twin to go clambering across rooftops with one of us. Especially a dimmy whose twin's been dead as long as mine. Lily would've been a lot happier if Sawny would do as she asked, and stop speaking to me. She didn't want to become one of us, after all, and every minute Sawny spent with me increased the odds that he'd be around when I finally lost myself to the grief. Frankly, I didn't disagree with her. But she knew—as did I—that Sawny would never turn his back on our friendship. Not after all this time.

So Lily ran to the anchorites every time she caught us breaking the rules. It was all she could do, and I didn't blame her. But that didn't mean I wanted to get caught.

We scrambled from one rooftop to the next until we were well away from the temple's residential wing. Our favorite spot was next to a window tucked between two slopes of roof over a rarely used attic next to the temple's tall spire. It was safe, for one, but the view didn't hurt, either.

Though only a sliver of one of the moon's halves was visible, the early summer sky—even at midnight—wasn't black, but the same dark, cloudy gray as my eyes. I settled in, my back against the wall of the spire, and drew my layers of sweaters in tight around me. Summers in Alskad were merely chilly, not the biting, aching cold that sank into your very bones the rest of the year. But even though I hated the cold, I found myself wishing for winter, when Sawny and Lily and I'd nestle in close under a blanket and watch the great, colorful strands of the northern lights play across the sky.

"What'd you nick for us?"

"Couldn't get much, what with the kitchen buzzing with folks getting ready for tomorrow, but I managed a bit."

Sawny closed his eyes, smiled and stretched out next to me on his back, his long black lashes smudged against his dark olive skin. He was all heavy muscles and broad shoulders. Sawny's easy good looks drew appreciative glances from anyone able to see past the overly mended hand-me-downs we temple brats wore—which, to be perfectly honest, was a fairly small group. My pale, freckled skin and dark, unruly curls might've been considered pretty at one point, but my twice-broken nose, combined with a face that rested somewhere between furious and disgusted, made folks' eyes slip right past me. I couldn't say I minded. Being a dimmy brought me attention enough.

"Well?" I held out a hand expectantly. "I'm ravenous."

Sawny put his hand in mine and squeezed. "I'm going to miss you, Vi."

"Shut up. You'll find work," I said, but the lie felt sharp on my tongue even as I spoke the words. "You and Lily both. Though Dzallie protect whoever hires her."

"Vi," Sawny cautioned.

I threw my hands up defensively. "I didn't mean anything by it. You know as well as I do that your sister can be prickly. That doesn't mean you won't find work here in Penby."

"We've been looking for months now, and there's nothing. Nothing that pays enough to afford a room, anyway."

Sawny rummaged in his bag and handed me half a loaf of bread thick with nuts and seeds. I turned it over in my hands. Guilt over my thoughtless expectation that Sawny would keep putting himself at risk by stealing food from the temple kitchen, same as he'd always done, gnawed at my stomach. His position was so tenuous now that he and Lily had come of age.

"There's no way the temple'll get rid of you," I said, forcing assurance I didn't feel into my voice. "You make the best cloud buns and salmonberry cakes of anyone in the kitchens. Don't you think they see that?"

Sawny ducked his head. "Sure. If I was on my own, I might be fine, but Lily needs connections to get bookkeeping work, and we've none. The anchorites can't get away with letting us stay much longer. We've been of age for nearly a full season now. I'm surprised they haven't already kicked us out."

I looked out across the wide square at the palace. It was an old-fashioned, elegant thing, all clean lines and contrasting angles with none of the frippery and decoration that was the style now. It'd been built a generation after the survivors of the cataclysm had settled in Penby, around the same time the people'd built the temple where Sawny and I'd grown up. The two buildings were practically mirrors of each other, with the same tall spires and the same high stone walls and narrow windows. But somehow, even though it was a stone's throw away, the palace had always been impossibly out of our reach.

Sawny and I'd come to this spot for years. We'd look across the square at the lights glowing in the palace windows and imagine the people inside. The palace seemed so much warmer, so much friendlier than the temple. The lives of its inhabitants so much happier. I thought probably they were, but Sawny always reminded me that it only seemed that way because we couldn't see their dark secrets the way we could see our own.

I caught a flash of white fluttering in the shadows between the palace and the temple. I nudged Sawny and jerked my chin. "Shriven. Think they can see us?"

He shook his head. "Nah. Even if they could, what do they care?"

The whites of their eyes stood out against the background of the black paint they wore across their foreheads, mingling with their stark tattoos. I could almost feel the weight of their gaze settle on me, sending shivers down my spine. The Shriven were always in the background of my life. They patrolled the city, looking for people like me. Keeping the citizens of Penby safe from dimmys on the edge of breaking. They served as the spine and the fist of the temple, and no crime in the empire escaped the ever-watchful eyes of the Shriven. Everyone followed their orders, even the palace guards and city watch. And while everyone in the empire knew better than to cross them, their shadow fell darkest on people like me—on the diminished.

"At least the Shriven watchdogs don't track your every move the way they do with us dimmys." I shuddered, remembering the last time one of the white-clad Shriven warriors decided I was up to no good. They may've been temple-sworn, same as the anchorites, but I'd never believed they were holy.

Turning back to Sawny, I said, "You can get away with a few more weeks of looking. Maybe they'll hire you over there." I jerked my chin at the palace.

Sawny laughed. "Sure. And her Imperial Highness Queen Runa will take a liking to me and set me up with an estate of my own. Come on, Vi. The palace would never hire a temple foundling. Those jobs are passed through families, like heirlooms."

I wished there was a way to argue with him, but he was right. Folks like us had to claw our way up to the bottom of the heap, and dreaming of anything else was setting ourselves up for failure.

Us temple brats worked long, hard hours to build the temple's wealth and power with no praise, no pay and little enough reward, apart from the barest necessities to keep us alive. Meanwhile, the anchorites draped themselves in the pearls I harvested from the cold waters of the bay and wore silks and furs tithed to the temple. But even their indulgence was nothing compared to the Suzerain, the twins who led the religious order of Alskad. Their power was nearly equal to the Queen's, and it didn't take an overly observant soul to see the greed and corruption that colored their every move, like the silver threads that embroidered their robes.

Because of this, Sawny and I had our own brand of morality. It was fine for him to steal food from the temple kitchens because they were charged with our care, and we were always hungry. I wasn't above swiping the occasional crab that wandered by the oyster beds during my summer dives, and in the winter, when I worked in the canneries, few days passed when I didn't pocket a tin of smoked whitefish or pickled eel. I surely didn't feel an ounce of guilt over taking a bit of that work back for myself. None of us did.

Sawny and I took our petty crimes a bit further than most

temple brats, though. While most of them stopped at stealing from anyone beyond the temple, we'd no problem with
nicking baubles and the odd *tvilling* off the rich folks who
swanned around wearing furs and jewels and waving hand-
fuls of *drott* and *ovstri* at poor folks, like the fact that they'd
money to spend somehow made them special. We were smart
about it, and the likelihood we'd get caught was so slim that
the benefits always outweighed the risks.

But I'd gone even further than that over the past few years.
The way I'd built my own little store of stolen wealth was too
dangerous, so far beyond the line, that even knowing about
it would put Sawny at risk. I couldn't tell him. But I could
hint—especially if it convinced him to stay, at least until my
birthday.

"I'll be of age soon. We could go north, the three of us. I
can dive and fish—the two of you could work on some noble's estate. We'd find a way to make it work."

Sawny took the chunk of bread from me, broke it in two
and smeared both sides thickly with birch syrup butter from
a crock in his knapsack. He handed half back to me and eased
himself back onto his elbows, chewing thoughtfully.

"Lily wants to take a contract in Ilor."

I sucked in a breath, not wanting to believe it could be true.
Ilor was a wild, barely settled island colony, but there was work
to be had, and no shortage of it. The estate owners and the
temple's land managers there were desperate enough for labor
that they'd pay ship captains to bring willing folks from Alskad. All Lily and Sawny had to do was walk onto a sunship.

A part of me knew this had been coming. Lily'd talked
about leaving Alskad since we were brats. Their parents were
dead, and they'd no family left in Penby. What family they
did have had immigrated to Ilor before they were born, hop-

ing for a better life, more opportunities. It made sense that Lily had always seen their future on those hot, jungle islands.

"You can't actually be considering it. Haven't you heard the rumors? Just yesterday a news hawker was lighting up the square with a story about an estate burned to the ground by some kind of rebel group."

Sawny laughed. "And last week I heard one of them say that Queen Runa had taken an amalgam lover. Come on, Vi. You know better than to believe everything you hear."

"There's no such thing as amalgams, you oaf."

"You grew up with the stories, same as me."

The amalgam were the stuff of childhood horror stories, meant to scare children into good behavior. Twins who'd become one in the womb, they were said to have magic that let them see the future and control the minds of other people. They were supposed to be more ferocious, more bloodthirsty than even the diminished, willing to do anything to gain power and influence. Legends said they thrived on fear and power, like most monsters. I'd never believed they were real. If they were, they would've ended up under the temple's watchful eye, like every other threat.

Like me.

I made a face at him. "Stop trying to distract me. There's got to be something for you here. Surely you don't have to cross the whole damn ocean to find work."

"It's only a few years, Vi. We'll work hard and save our pay, and when the contract's over, we can start a new life. Maybe I'll open a bakery. Hamil's teeth, you could even come over with us."

I rolled my eyes. "Don't be an idiot. No captain would ever let a dimmy onto a ship planning to cross the Tethys, Hamil's blessing or no."

"You don't know that."

I tore a piece of bread off my chunk of the loaf and rolled it between my fingers, considering, before popping it into my mouth. The sticky butter clung to my fingers, and I licked each one, unwilling to waste even a ghost of sweetness and glad for a moment to think through what I'd say next.

"The only work you'll get is on a kaffe farm."

Sawny pushed a hank of black hair behind his ear and nodded. "We know."

"It's hard work. Backbreaking, and there's no law there. None to speak of, at least. Nothing to protect you if something goes wrong."

"Fair point," Sawny said. "But since when did laws ever do any good to protect folks like you and me? The work'll be hard, sure. Harder than anything we've had to do here."

"Maybe not harder than enduring Anchorite Bethea's worship seminars."

Sawny's laugh burst out of his chest, shattering the stillness of the night.

"No," he said. "Not harder than those. But there's no other option, Vi. And once we pay off our passage, we'll earn a wage. Can you imagine?"

I could imagine. I'd spent hours thinking about the day I'd be free of the temple and earning my own living. Free to live what was left of my life happy, or as close to it as I could manage with the threat of inevitable, violent grief looming over me. For a moment, my mind slipped away from thoughts of that life and pondered the path our friend Curlin had chosen. She'd—Magritte's teeth, it made me so mad!—gone and joined the Shriven. Broken every promise we'd ever made to each other and to Sawny.

That was the only other option for Sawny and Lily. It'd keep them safe and fed and earn them a kind of respect none of us could ever hope to gain on our own. We all knew it, but—unlike Curlin—we respected the promise we'd made each other, and we wouldn't break it. Not even if it was the only sure way to keep us together. It wasn't worth what we'd have to become.

I didn't need to say it. I could tell Sawny was thinking the same thing.

"When'll you leave?"

"Couple of days, I think."

I reached out and smacked his arm, hard, without thinking. "A couple of days? How long have you been planning this?"

He scowled at me, but when he saw the tears streaking down my cheeks, he wrapped an arm around my shoulders and drew me close. "Vi..." His voice trailed off, and I knew there wasn't anything he could say. Our friendship, no matter how important it was to both of us, was nothing compared to the bond between twins.

"You couldn't've told me sooner?" I asked, my voice barely above a whisper.

"Lily only settled the details yesterday. I didn't want to tell you until it was a sure thing."

I shoved my anger and pain down, cinching it tight into a heavy ball of misery in the pit of my stomach. Anger was dangerous, and I wouldn't let Sawny's leaving be the thing that broke me. Not after all this time. "I'll miss you."

"I'll miss you too, Obedience," he said, teasing me with the given name he knew I hated.

I elbowed him in the ribs. "I take it back. I won't miss you at all," I said, laughter slipping into my voice.

But we both knew that wasn't true.

Some days, there was no way to avoid the actual temple itself. On high holy days, the cusps of each season and the Suzerain's Ascension Day, every person who ate at the temple's table or was under their protection was expected to stop everything and haul themselves to adulations. Most folks in Penby made a show of attending adulations, even the Queen. Not many had so little to lose that they could afford to find themselves on the bad side of the Suzerain. Even folks like me, folks with nothing, weren't stupid enough to risk it. Because I knew that even with nothing at all, I might still have something to lose.

On the day the Suzerain celebrated their twenty-third Ascension Day, I sidled into the haven hall just after the adulation started, but—thank all the gods—before the Suzerain made their entrance. Lily and Sawny were perched on the edge of a bench on the far side of the hall. As I navigated my way through the crowd toward them, Lily caught sight of me first. She shot me an evil look, but I grinned at her and winked. Even though she'd never have to think about most of these folks again, the girl still couldn't stand to be seen with a dimmy.

"Scoot," I whispered.

Sawny passed me a cantory, and Lily heaved a sigh as he nudged her over to make room for me. I settled onto the long, scarred wooden bench next to Sawny just as the gathering sang the final note of the Suzerain's Chorale. The anchorites were at the front of the hall decked out in their finest, with pearls gleaming at their necks and wrists and their hair tied up in intricate braids, freshly shorn on the sides. Their silk robes, in shades of yellow and orange and red, whispered as they stood, and a hush fell over the crowd. Everyone's eyes turned to the two initiates drawing open the thick metal doors at the back of the haven hall. The high holiday adulations followed the same damned formula every single time, but somehow, folks still acted like it was some kind of glamorous and captivating performance.

The Shriven initiates entered the hall first, their white robes and freshly shorn heads gleaming in the light of the sunlamps. Their staves smacked the stone floor in unison with every step as they filed to the front of the hall and spread out to flank either side, leaving gaps at each of the altars. Sawny elbowed me.

"See Curlin?"

I shook my head. "Don't know how you could pick her out at this distance."

"She's the one with the black eye." He pointed, squinting. "She's gotten more tattoos since the last time I saw her."

I rolled my eyes. "Give it up, Sawny. She's one of them now. Our Curlin is dead to us, and starting tomorrow, you'll never have to see or think of her again."

My words struck a nerve in my own heart, and I knew they'd hurt Sawny, as well. I missed Curlin, and every time I saw her or one of the other Shriven, the thought of her betrayal poured salt water into the still-fresh wound. We'd promised years ago, in our spot on the temple roof, that we wouldn't join them. None of us. For a lot of temple brats, serving as one of the Shriven was the best option. The only option. But over the years, the four of us had seen what the Shriven did to dimmys—to people like me and Curlin—and not one of us wanted any part of that brutality.

Or so we'd thought. Until three years ago, the day Curlin turned thirteen, when she'd disappeared from the room she and I had shared. The next time we saw her, her head was shaved and her wrist was banded with the new ink of her first tattoo. She'd not spoken to any of us since, but where I held on to that betrayal like a weapon, Sawny'd always wanted to find a way to forgive her.

Steady me, Pru, I thought, leaning on the comfort I felt when I reached for my long-dead twin.

The catechized Shriven prowled into the hall on the heels of their initiates, all dangerous feline grace and coiled energy. They weren't the only people in the empire who had tattoos, but few bore so many or such immediately recognizable designs. The Shriven's tattoos favored stark black lines and symbols that evoked a time long forgotten. It was as though they'd inked a language all their own into their skin. Even in plain clothes, a person always knew the moment one of the Shriven came close. Everyone sat a little straighter on their benches and chairs, and their eyes flicked to the dimmys in the room, looking for a reaction, a sign, a threat.

I gripped the cantory in my lap and stared straight ahead, trying to calm my nerves.

At most adulations, Queen Runa was the last person to enter the haven hall. On Ascension Day, however, she shared her entrance with the Suzerain as a token of respect. They were an odd triumvirate. The Suzerain were tall, with porcelain skin and white-blond hair that, when combined with their white robes, made them look like a pair of twin icicles. Castor, the male Suzerain, was covered in grayscale tattoos of flowers that crept up his neck and onto his scalp, a portion of which was shaved to show off the largest of the flower tattoos. The female Suzerain was named Amler. Her hands were covered in a network of tiny black dots so close together, it looked as though she was always wearing gloves that faded up her arms and over the rest of her body, growing sparser the farther they got from her fingertips.

Before Curlin'd joined the Shriven, she used to joke that Amler looked as though she'd been spattered with ink.

Between them, Queen Runa was small and round as a teapot, the top of her crown barely clearing the Suzerain's shoulders. Every time I'd seen her on her own—mainly during her birthday celebrations, when she handed out sweets across the city—Queen Runa had been the very picture of imposing authority, wrapped in piles of furs and dripping with jewels. But when contrasted with the Suzerain's sharp faces and piercing blue eyes, the Queen looked positively friendly. Kind, even.

The Queen settled into a fur-draped chair in the place of honor at the front of the hall. The Suzerain stood shoulder to shoulder in front of the Queen and looked out over the silent crowd. Their eyes fixed on each person, taking stock, tallying. I kept my eyes on the cantory in my lap, avoiding their searching gazes. I knew it wasn't possible that they knew each of the folks who lived in Penby, but they certainly knew who I was. Maybe not on sight, but they knew my name. My story. They kept track of dimmys.

All I wanted was a life outside their line of sight. Outside their reach.

The rest of the adulation went as these things always did. The Suzerain lectured on the holiness of twins, giving particular weight to their own divine role as the leaders of the temple; the power of the singleborns' judgment and wisdom, Queen Runa first among them; and, of course, the role of the Shriven in protecting Alskaders from the violence of the diminished. Afterward, the Suzerain led the hall in an endless round of the high holy song of Dzallie, gaining speed and volume until the whole room echoed with the reverberations of their worship.

Sawny and I were silent, despite Lily's black looks and prodding elbows. Since our promise to each other that we wouldn't join the Shriven, neither of us had worshipped at adulations, either. We showed up when it mattered, of course. We weren't stupid. But we were always silent, much to Lily's everlasting chagrin. She worried that our silence singled us out, and the last thing any of us wanted was to be noticed.

After the adulation, the Suzerain stayed in the haven hall for hours, greeting, blessing and doling out advice to those folks rich enough to make it worth the Suzerain's time. Sawny, Lily and I filed out of the temple as quickly as we could and stood together in the square, soaking in the near-warmth of the early summer sun. The anchorites would expect us to report in for our various chores before long, but none of us seemed to want to be the first to break away.

"Tomorrow, then?" I asked. "What time?"

Lily shifted from one foot to the other. "The sunship leaves on the first tide."

"I'll come see you off."

"There's no need—"

Sawny cut her off. "Of course you will. But we'll have supper tonight, too. We're not saying goodbye. Not yet."

Anchorite Lugine strode toward us, scowling. Dozens of strands of pearls were wrapped around her neck and braided into her hair, glowing like fresh-fallen snow against the orange silk of her robes.

"I'd best get down to the harbor," I said, loud enough that the anchorite could hear me. "I'll be diving until sunset to make up for my lost time this morning. I've got to find Lugine some nice pearls if I want supper tonight."

Lily rolled her eyes, and behind her, Anchorite Lugine crossed her arms and glared. I gave her a cheerful wave, grinned at Sawny and darted toward the temple to get my diving gear from my room.

CHAPTER TWO

Bo

Like all great houses, the royal palace was a living, breathing thing, and the people who lived and served there shaped its personality. It was never entirely still. Even in the middle of the night, servants carried pots of tea and bottles of wine to guests' rooms; bakers kneaded endless rolls and loaves in the warm, steamy kitchen; and guards shifted and paced, warding off sleep. There were always books that wanted shelving, forgotten closets filled with the everyday relics of monarchs long dead that needed sorting and fires endlessly burning in the hearths of the palace—which, somehow, even in summer, never managed to fully drive off the chill that clung to those old stones.

No one so much as looked at me twice as I took the long way back to my rooms through the palace's wide stone hallways, my hands deep in my trouser pockets and a scarf wrapped tight around my thick Denorian wool sweater. I had a stack of books from Queen Runa's personal collection tucked under one arm, and a small journal full of scribbled questions and notes stuffed into the back pocket of my trousers. After I'd let slip the vast gaps in my knowledge about the shipbuilding industry in Alskad, the Queen had given me a pile of reading on top of my tutor's regular assignments, and I'd been up half the night trying to make some headway.

Alskad dominated the world-wide shipbuilding industry, and being a nation lacking many natural resources, we held that technology close. We were the first nation to perfect the solar technology that fueled the world after the cataclysm, and none of the rest of the world had managed to harness the power of the sun the way that we had. Denor and Samiria had ships, of course, but they weren't yet capable of the speed and distance that Alskad sunships managed regularly. Our sunships commanded the trade to and from Denor, Samiria and Ilor, and through our monopoly on ships and trade, the empire had become not only rich, but powerful, as well.

The great irony of a country that spent its winters in the blanket of northern darkness harnessing the power of the sun did not escape me. The sun's power lit our homes and sent great iron ships filled with hundreds of people hurtling across oceans, and while I knew the history—I'd been captivated by sunships when I was a child—the engineering details eluded me. Queen Runa would undoubtedly pepper me with questions throughout the day tomorrow as I observed her dealing with the monthly petitions from the people of Alskad, and there was little chance that I'd absorbed enough to hold my own under her sharp scrutiny.

There wasn't enough kaffe in the world to keep me awake through another chapter about the evolution of Alskad's shipbuilding technology, and I had to be up distressingly early, but there was a restless thread tugging at my mind. It was always like this on nights I spent in Penby, like the buzz of the city's energy pulsed through my veins, too, amplifying my emotions and keeping sleep just outside my grasp.

I paused outside my door, listening for my valet, Gunnar, and his telltale wheezing snore. In a few short weeks, I'd move from the comfortable, out-of-the-way guest rooms that had been mine since I was a child to a luxurious suite in the royal wing. I'd have to relearn all the creaking floorboards and fiddly sun-lamps, and while my new rooms would be closely guarded, the rooms I occupied now were so far off the beaten path that no one bothered to visit, a small boon I would deeply miss when my duties forced me to become even more social. I took a deep breath, bracing myself, and opened the door.

Gunnar sprang to his feet and, after rubbing the sleep out of his eyes, gave me an admonishing look.

"Lady Myrella's been looking for you," he said. "She's stopped in three times since dinner. I didn't know what to tell her, as you neglected to inform me of your plans for the evening."

I set the stack of books on the small writing desk in the corner, fished the notebook out of my pocket and added it to the pile.

"You didn't need to wait up, Gunnar. I'm sorry I put you out. I was in the library, studying."

Gunnar huffed. "You could have at least let me know where you'd be. I cannot be expected to adequately perform my duties if you refuse to tell me when to expect you and where you plan to spend your time. Your tea's gone cold, and I haven't the faintest clue what to lay out for you to wear tomorrow. What does one wear when speaking to the poor?"

I bit back a grin. Aside from cataloging the ways in which I'd wronged him over the course of any given day, Gunnar loved nothing more than reveling in his own snobbery.

"Clothes, I expect," I replied, pouring myself a cup of rich herbal tisane from the pot keeping warm on a trivet next to the hearth, despite Gunnar's hyperbolic warning. "It's still a bit cold for me to go gallivanting off to the throne room to greet my future subjects in my underthings."

Gunnar's jaw tightened, and he gave a stiff bow. His manners tended to become polite to the point of absurdity when he was irritated with me. Somehow, he managed to present a picture of perfect deference and simultaneously touch upon my every nerve. Even though I knew he would probably lay out something completely absurd—like a lavender silk suit— the next morning, I was altogether too drained to worry about the consequences of my sarcasm. Gunnar always paid me back in his own way, but I didn't have to worry about his feelings being too badly hurt in the long run. The man had practically raised me, and he, more than anyone, knew how difficult it was for me to endure these endless days at court surrounded by people who only ever approached what they wanted to say from the side.

Thanks to my sharp tongue and Gunnar's long memory, the maid woke me with just half an hour's grace before I was to meet the Queen. The clothes Gunnar had laid out for me were some of the most ostentatious and garish in my wardrobe, and he was nowhere to be found. Through the servant's sputtered protests, I stuck my whole head in a basin of freezing cold water left from the night before, scrubbed at my face and dried off with my shirttails as I stalked to the closet to find something else to wear.

Over my shoulder, I called, "I would be eternally grateful to you if you could manage to find me a cup of kaffe sometime in the next ten minutes."

When the young man didn't respond, I stuck my head out

of the closet, a pair of socks clenched between my teeth, to see if he'd heard me. There, lounging on the settee at the end of my bed, was my cousin Claes, with two enormous, steaming mugs in his hands and a grin lighting his gorgeous face. He, apparently, hadn't infuriated his butler, and was turned out in perfectly fitted navy trousers and a fine ivory sweater. The smattering of freckles across his high cheekbones stood out against his fawn skin more than usual, and there was a playful light in his angular black eyes.

"Good morning, dearest," he said, and crossed the room to hand me a mug and plant a kiss on my cheek.

I took a grateful sip, all the bitterness of the kaffe disguised by honey and cream. Claes knew me so well.

"Thank you. I'm afraid I may have annoyed Gunnar last night. All he's left me is that hideous mauve monstrosity, and I have to be in the throne room in twenty minutes. Do you think these will do?"

Claes looked down at the clothes I'd plucked out of the wardrobe, and his perfectly groomed black eyebrows climbed his forehead. He swept the clothes out of my arms and brushed past me into the closet.

"I swear, Bo, it's as if you've never dressed yourself. Do you pay absolutely no attention to what's fashionable?"

Ten minutes later, I was respectably garbed in a pair of gray trousers, a pale orange sweater knitted from soft Denorian wool and a long charcoal jacket. I stuffed a cloud bun filled with smoked bacon and caramelized onions into my mouth as I rushed through the palace halls to the throne room. I arrived with only a moment to spare and ran a hand experimentally through my riot of dark brown curls. I had no doubt that I looked a disaster, but there was nothing to be done about it now.

"Am I a total embarrassment?"

Claes smiled and drew me close in a warm embrace. "You're as princely as they come, my dear. Now go impress old Queenie with your vast intellect. I'm off to gather gossip from the maids. I hear that Lisette has taken a new lover, and I plan to learn who it is before your birthday invitations are sent."

Claes leaned in and kissed me, and I did my best to ignore the guards by the throne room door, who were covering their chuckling with coughs and exaggerated shifting of their weapons. It wasn't as though my relationship with Claes was a secret, but his public displays of affection drew more attention to us than I liked. Claes pulled away first, his implacable grin already in place as he winked at a guard over my shoulder.

"I'll see you tonight?" I asked.

"Of course. We've got to finalize the guest list, and I do believe that my dear sister has a whole collection of people she's planning to chastise and flatter with this event alone."

I sighed. It didn't matter that I'd been preparing myself to take the throne for most of my life: I would never get used to the social machinations and deceptions required by a life at court. They simply didn't come as naturally to me as they did to the other singleborn. Even my cousins, Penelope and Claes, had adapted much more easily to court intrigue than I ever had.

Claes brushed a bit of invisible dust off my shoulder.

"You worry about running the empire, my dear. Penelope and I'll be the ones to get our hands dirty controlling the nobility. Now scoot. You're going to be late."

Claes planted a final kiss on my cheek and nodded to the guards. When they opened the door, I was as ready as I could be.

Like the Queen, I entered the throne room not through the wide doors that the petitioners would use throughout the day, but via a small side door in the back. The Alskad throne loomed large on the dais. According to legend, it had been hewn from the upturned roots of an enormous tree, and the tangle of roots that fanned out over the head of the monarch reflected the Alskad crown they wore. The whole thing had been polished and waxed and varnished so often over the years, the wood had turned a glowing deep brown, almost black.

I rounded the dais and saw that the Queen was already seated on a pile of furs draped over the wide throne. Her eyes flickered to the clock in the corner of the room when she saw me, and her mouth turned down in disapproval.

"You're late, Bo."

I squinted at the clock. It was thirty seconds past the agreed-upon time.

"My most sincere apologies, Your Majesty."

The Queen crinkled her sharp nose and adjusted the crown of Alskad atop her graying hair. She was an intimidating woman, with skin that never lost its light brown glow, iron-gray hair and a habit of wearing wide-shouldered capes that made her body look nearly square. She was said to have been shockingly beautiful in her youth, though age had left her more arresting than lovely.

"You'll need a chair. These things tend to last for hours and hours, and you'll not want to be standing the whole time." She pointed at a cluster of chairs in an alcove between two sets of large casement windows. "Drag one of those over. Not the blue one. The cushion's as thin as a sheet—you'll be sitting on nails all day."

Three guards tried to take the chair from me as I crossed the room, but I waved them all off with a smile.

"You lot leave him be. He's a brawny young thing." Queen

Runa laughed. "No need to start coddling him until he's actually the crown prince."

I felt a flicker of unease at the implication, and—as if they could sense my discomfort—Patrise and Lisette swanned into the throne room, alight with jewels and draped in brightly dyed silks and furs. Though it was well known throughout the empire that I would soon be named Runa's heir, Lisette and Patrise nevertheless took every opportunity to remind me that they, too, were singleborn and eligible for the throne. Of all the singleborn in my generation, only Rylain, my father's cousin, refused to play this game, and I was forever grateful to her for that generosity of spirit.

Runa raised an eyebrow, and Patrise and Lisette bowed deeply.

"Sorry to be late, Your Majesty," Patrise drawled, his voice all lazy vowels and grandeur. "We were doing our best to decide what to get our Ambrose for his birthday."

"I wanted to get him a pony," Lisette said, pouting, "but Patrise insists that little Ambrose is far too mature for such things."

"A set of knives, perhaps, to protect him from his many enemies," Patrise said. "But we wouldn't want him to prick himself accidentally, now would we?"

"Enough," Runa snapped.

Patrise and Lisette collapsed into each other, giggling. I settled my chair on the dais, a step behind the throne on Runa's right, and glared at Patrise and Lisette as they waved for guards to bring chairs for them, as well.

The Queen turned to me, her tone low, but firm. "Ignore them. They only enjoy baiting you because you give them a reaction. If you are to lead, you'll have to learn to rise above the petty antics they use to entertain themselves."

I nodded, but a voice in the back of my head wondered how she could speak about the rivalries between the single-born so lightly, when they were so often punctuated by assassination attempts.

Runa continued. "I hope that you and I will have many more years to prepare you for taking the helm of this empire. But if there is one thing I'd ask you to keep in mind from the very beginning, it's that we, as monarchs, are here to protect our people. Remember that both the poorest urchin and the wealthiest merchant deserve our equal and undiscriminating respect."

"Of course, Your Majesty."

I tried to focus on the Queen's instructions, but it was hard with Lisette and Patrise looking over her shoulder and laughing behind their hands. I clenched my jaw and forced myself to look away from them.

"Too much of Alskad's idea of merit has become predicated on a person's wealth, rather than their character. As we hear petitions today, I want you to keep in mind how money plays into each person's story, and, more importantly, how it plays into your reaction." She glanced over her shoulder at the other singleborn and raised her voice. "And if the two of you could manage to resist teasing Bo while in the presence of our subjects, you might actually learn something worthwhile."

Without waiting for a response, the Queen signaled to the guards, and they flung open the throne room doors. A stream of people entered the room, each stopping to make their courtesies to the Queen as they entered. There were people from all walks of life: members of the nobility I recognized from the endless social engagements that were the norm when I was at court, merchants dressed in extravagant imported Samirian silks and common folk whose clothes had plainly been mended over and over again. Some of them came with petitions, others just to watch the spectacle and collect gossip with which to tantalize or lord over their peers.

The Queen's secretary bustled through the crowd, approached the dais and presented her with a list written in a neat hand. Runa scanned the list, raised her hand and waited for the room to fall silent.

"First, I will hear from Jacobb Rosy. Mister Rosy, if you would, please approach the dais."

The petitioners shifted and moved, and Jacobb Rosy came to bow before the Queen. He was a man in his middle age, of medium height and build, with unblemished light brown skin and dark, wavy hair. He was utterly unremarkable, but for the brilliant yellow suit he wore. The jacket was cut long, as was the fashion, ending just above his knees, and trimmed all around with black ermine. Embroidered bees climbed the legs of his slim trousers, and an enormous onyx brooch ringed with diamonds was pinned to his lapel. He spoke in a clear alto, loud enough to be heard throughout the entire room.

"Your Majesty, I am deeply honored that you have chosen to hear my petition today."

Runa raised one eyebrow, and I studied the man, looking to see if I could spot his tell. Most people did everything in their power to present themselves as the victim when offering their story to the Queen.

"I hear the petitions of all my subjects, Mister Rosy. What troubles you?"

"Your Majesty, I am on the verge of losing my shop. You see, for the last decade I have designed and created clothing for the fashionable people of your empire. My wife, with the help of a shopkeeper, ran the business in order to give me the freedom to focus on the creative side of the work."

"It sounds like you've created a comfortable and success-ful life for yourself."

"It was, Your Majesty. But now, without my wife's help, the burden of the business has grown to be too much, and with taxes due, I am likely to lose my livelihood."

Runa's face took on an expression of sympathy. "I'm sorry for the loss of your wife, Mister Rosy. How long has it been?"

The man squirmed, gazing down at the toes of his mirror-polished black boots, and fell silent. He hadn't walked to the palace, not with the gray slush of snow still clinging to the streets. He'd taken a carriage. So either he'd not yet sold off all the luxuries typically enjoyed by the merchant class—which was likely, given his clothes and the jewels on his lapel—or he had enough money to pay for carriages and jewels, but had squandered what he should have saved for taxes.

"How long?" Runa pressed.

Lisette snickered, and Runa shot her a hard look.

"She's not dead, Your Majesty. She left me."

"And she didn't see fit to remain a partner in your business or find a suitable replacement?"

"How could I trust her to have my best interests at heart if she was so willing to give up everything we'd built together?"

"This is not the haven hall, Mister Rosy. I am not in the business of arbitrating marital disputes. However, if your pre-dicament is due to neglect on the part of your business part-ner, there may be some grounds for leniency on the part of the crown. Will you give me your ex-wife's name, that I may call upon her for her side of this dispute?"

The man blanched. He seemed to be wilting. His shoul-ders drew inward, and he refused to meet the Queen's gaze. He muttered something unintelligible in the direction of his feet. All around the room, people were shifting and squirming, trying to get a better look at the man.

"What was that, Mister Rosy?"

"I told her she wasn't welcome in the shop after she left. I didn't want her running the business into the ground out of spite."

"I see." Runa looked at me out of the corner of her eye. "And what, exactly, would you ask of the crown today?"

"Humbly, Your Majesty, I ask that my tax burden be forgiven this year and the next, to allow me to rebuild my assets and business in the wake of this unforeseen tragedy. Additionally, I ask that my ex-wife be made responsible for the mess she left me in, and pay half of my taxes for the two years after that."

The Queen nodded slowly and shifted her focus to me.

"Your thoughts, Lord Gyllen?"

Runa had an incredible knack for putting on and taking off personas. In public, she was formal, even stiff, with me. She addressed me by my full name or title, a courtesy she didn't always bestow on the other singleborn, and she treated me with the respect of a monarch to her successor, despite the fact that I'd not yet been formally named. And while Rylain was allowed to while her days away at her northern estates, only emerging for the most important state occasions, Runa insisted I always be at her right hand.

Her demeanor in private was another matter entirely. She teased and cajoled and demanded that my mastery of matters of state be not just sufficient, but the best in the room. She was every bit the exacting and affectionate aunt, and though I'd not spent a great deal of time with her, the closer we got to my birthday and the announcement of my role as her successor, the more attention she paid me.

Despite all of this, I was shocked when she asked for my opinion. I took a moment to gather my thoughts, wanting to impress her.

"In most cases, I tend to believe that the duty of the crown is to assist and uplift its people. However, it seems to me that it is Mister Rosy's actions and choices that have led him to this vulnerable place. The taxes paid by the citizens of the Alskad Empire serve to provide basic services and resources to all the people of the empire. It seems that Mister Rosy did not plan adequately for his taxes this season, which is unfortunate. However, there is still sufficient time for him to liquidate some of his assets—such as the jewel he wears upon his lapel—and take in more work. He can hire a bookkeeper to help him as he learns to manage his business in the absence of his wife."

I paused for a moment, weighing my next words. "It is my belief that the crown should not forgive his tax burden. However, I do admire his excellent tailoring skills, and I will certainly pass some business his way, and I am sure my cousins Lisette and Patrise will do the same."

Queen Runa gave me a small smile and a nod. I'd done well. I breathed a sigh of relief and sat back in my chair. Mister Rosy's cheeks were burgundy, and his brows were so tightly drawn that it looked like he had an entire mountain range of wrinkles spanning his forehead. My answer, obviously, hadn't been what he wanted to hear. It would take a great deal of study for me to learn how to do this job without inciting the ire of my subjects.

"Lord Gyllen is right. The High Council and I have worked hard to ensure that taxes in the empire are not a burden on anyone's shoulders unless they simply do not plan. It is never any use to stick your head in the sand and ignore your responsibilities, Mister Rosy. That said, however, I appreciate that you sought my guidance and help, and I will have my secretary provide suggestions for bookkeepers with honest reputations to help you manage your business. Further, the royal treasury will pay the bookkeeper's fees for the time between now and when your taxes come due."

The tailor bowed, muttered his thanks and retreated into the crowd.

The rest of the day was much the same. We listened to troubles as large as a housekeeper accused of stealing a noblewoman's jewels—only to find that the noblewoman's husband had gambled away their entire fortune—and as small as an argument between two street vendors over a particular corner in a park.

Runa showed each of them the same amount of respect, and even made certain to include Patrise and Lisette in the consideration of certain petitions. She paid careful attention to the needs of the poor and destitute, and made notes of the bevy of ways in which the social services provided by the Alskad throne were failing. She frequently asked my opinion, and most of the time, she agreed with my assessments. When she and I were at odds, she explained her thinking to both me and the gathered petitioners, and every time, I saw how her logic was sounder than mine. There was so much I didn't know, and the plethora of ways in which the privilege of my wealth had coddled me and shrouded me from the everyday challenges of the Alskad people continued to shock me.

By the time the chamber emptied, we'd heard more than thirty petitions, and my brain felt like mush. That was the moment Queen Runa decided to begin quizzing me about the shipbuilding industry.

CHAPTER THREE

Vi

With only hours left until his departure, Sawny and I stayed awake all night, teasing and telling stories and remembering and acting like nothing would change when we were an ocean apart. Even Lily managed to endure my presence in their shared room with a bare minimum of complaints. She had, after all, gotten her way.

We'd planned to leave the temple quietly before first adulations, but the anchorites who'd taken the most responsibility in raising us—Lugine, Bethea and Sula—were waiting for Sawny and Lily in the entrance hall. They wore informal yellow robes and thick wool scarves in golden orange wrapped tight around their shoulders. The color flattered Sula's and Lugine's dark brown skin, making them glow. Unfortunately, for a woman committed to a lifetime wearing a very limited palette, yellow turned Bethea's thin, pale wrinkles sallow and sickly.

"You'll not sneak away in the night like thieves," Bethea

said grumpily, but she leaned one of her canes against her hip and pulled Lily in for a hug.

I pressed myself into the wall. This was their moment, and I wanted more than anything to become invisible. The anchorites had never hugged me. Not even once. Sawny and Lily and the other twins like them were, in their own way, the children these women would never give birth to themselves, committed as they were to their goddesses. Though we three were *all* wards of the temple, the fact that I was a dimmy made me a threat.

I couldn't help but wonder what kind of goodbye I would get when my time came.

Sula slipped a bulging satchel over Sawny's shoulder and stood on tiptoe to kiss his cheek. "We'd extra copies of some cookery books in the library. I thought you might find them useful in your new life."

Lugine cupped Sawny's and Lily's cheeks, one in each hand, a warm smile lighting her face. "Magritte protect you both. Write often, and let us know how you are."

"And get yourselves to adulations," Bethea added. "Just because we're not there to worry you into the haven hall doesn't mean you can stop showing up."

Lily burst into tears and flung her arms around Bethea. Sawny, chin trembling, bit his lip and nodded. I sank farther back into the shadows, tears welling in my own eyes. Even though we'd grown up in the same hall, in the same building, raised by these same women, our lives could not have been more different, and it had taken me until that moment to realize it fully. I would never be missed, never be wanted, never be anything but a burden.

We walked in silence through Penby's quiet streets in the faint glow of the waning moon, only one of its halves fully visible. I laced my arm through Sawny's, trying to burn him into my memory. He'd been my best friend my whole life, and it didn't seem possible that when I trudged back up the hill to the temple later, I would be alone.

The city came alive as we got closer to the docks, where the great iron sunships, Alskad's greatest pride, were moored. Sailors hauled trunks and crates up and down long gangplanks, officers shouted orders from the decks, and vendors pushed carts, hawking the kinds of trinkets a person might not realize they needed until they were on the verge of leaving everything they knew and loved behind. The whole scene was lit by the hazy, flickering light of sunlamps and the first rays of sunlight peeking over the horizon.

"The ship is called the *Lucrecia*," Lily said. "I spoke to a woman named Whippleston to arrange our passage."

We walked down the docks, scanning the names painted large on the backs of the ships.

"There's still time to back out," I said quietly to Sawny, fingering the small pouch I'd stuffed into my pocket after supper the night before. "The anchorites would let you stay a bit longer. Work's sure to open up somewhere in the city. If not, I'll be sixteen soon. I know there's work up north we can take."

But just as I finished speaking, the *Lucrecia* loomed up out of the darkness at the end of the dock, her name painted in bright white across the stern far above our heads. A brat couldn't grow up in Alskad without learning a bit about sunships. Even in the cheap cabins set aside for contract workers, Sawny and Lily would experience more luxury in the short trip across the Tethys than we'd ever imagined. There would be endless buffets, libraries and game rooms. They'd sleep on soft beds, and for the first—and only—time in their lives, they'd wake each morning with nothing to do. A part of me wished that I could walk onto the sunship with Lily and Sawny, just to see, but that would never happen. Not for a dimmy. Not for me.

An imposing woman stood at the end of the gangplank, a sheaf of papers in one hand, a pen in the other. The light gray fur of her jacket's collar set off her high cheekbones and deep, russet-brown skin. She eyed the three of us as we approached.

"Names?" she asked.

I turned to Sawny. "You're sure?"

"There's more opportunity there than we could ever hope for here," Sawny said, his eyes begging me to understand. "It'll be a better life. An easier life."

I retied the bit of string at the end of my braid. Lily reached out and squeezed my shoulder, and I started slightly. It was the first time she'd touched me in years.

"We'll take care of each other, Vi, and we'll write. All the time." She turned to the woman at the end of the gangplank. "Lily and Sawny Taylor. I believe I spoke to your sister?"

The woman laughed heartily. "My daughter. Though I'm grateful to you for the mistake. Let's get your papers sorted, shall we?"

I tugged on Sawny's arm, drawing him away from the gangplank and the sunlamp's glow. Once we were in the shadows, I pulled him close to me, like the sweethearts we'd never been. Never thought of becoming. People's eyes slipped away from sweethearts, cuddled up to say goodbye, and now more than ever, I needed to go unnoticed.

Sawny squirmed. "What're you about?"

"Shut up and let me hug you, yeah?" I said, loud enough for anyone passing by to hear. I stood on tiptoe and whispered in his ear. "If you're going to insist on leaving me behind, I have a going away gift for you. But you have to promise me you won't open it until you're well away at sea."

"Vi, you've nothing—"

"Don't be after arguing with me, Sawny. I've never had a scrap to give you for birthdays, high holidays, none of it. Let me do this one thing."

I dug into my pocket and fished out the little pouch, keeping my other arm around Sawny's shoulders. There were sixteen perfect pearls and a couple of dozen less valuable, slightly blemished ones inside the pouch I'd sewn from a scrap of a too-small pair of trousers. The pearls were some of the best of my collection, and enough to give them a start on their savings. It wasn't enough to pay off their passage or set them up with a shop of their own, but it was something. It was all I could give them.

A long time ago, when I'd first learned to dive from one of the anchorites' hirelings, she'd told me how pearls were made. The temple anchorites only had use for natural pearls, the ones that came of a tiny grain of sand or bit of shell irritating the oyster's delicate tissues. But, the woman had told me, there was beginning to be a market for a new kind of pearl, one that could be farmed on lines strung in the ocean. They weren't quite as valuable, but when you knew that almost every oyster would make a pearl, a bigger profit could be had.

That bit of information had sparked an idea, and as soon as I'd begun to dive on my own, I'd hung lines and baskets beneath the docks, where none of the other divers ever went. I tended them for four long years, and on my twelfth birthday, I opened the first oyster off my lines and slipped a pearl as big as the nail on my little pinky from its shell. In the three years since, I'd harvested close to two hundred pearls from

my lines, more than ten for every one natural pearl I'd found
and handed over to the anchorites.

That collection was hidden away beneath a floorboard in
my tiny room in the temple. I'd created a small cushion for
myself—enough to buy a cottage on one of the northernmost islands in the Alskad Empire, where folks were said to
keep to themselves.

When I lost myself to the grief, I'd be far enough away
from other folks that I wouldn't be able to do much harm.
I'd be alone. It was selfish of me, wanting to spend whatever
time I had left in the company of my only friend, but still
I'd thought about offering Sawny and Lily my whole stash—
everything I'd ever saved, everything I'd ever created—just
so they wouldn't leave. Wouldn't leave me alone. But in the
end, I couldn't have lived with the guilt of it. My friendship
with Sawny was the only real, honest relationship in my life,
and I couldn't bear the thought of holding them back from
the life they'd chosen just because I was so desperate not to
be left alone.

Pressing the pouch into Sawny's hand as stealthily as I could
manage, I pulled back from our hug just far enough to fix
him with a hard stare. "Don't say anything."

Sawny's dark eyes were wide. "Are these…?"

"Don't. You know the law. You know the consequences.
Sell them when you can. Take your time. Be careful."

"Vi, this is, far and away, the stupidest thing you've ever
done."

"Shut up," I said.

"Sawny," Lily called. "It's time."

Sawny threw his arms around me and squeezed me tight,
and a part of me shattered, knowing it was the last hug I was
ever likely to feel.

"I'll miss you," he said, and I tucked those words, his voice, deep into my heart.

"I'll miss you, too."

I watched as they boarded the *Lucrecia* and disappeared. As I stood there, the sun crept slowly up behind the ship, lightening the sky from navy to violet to lavender, and a sharp cacophony of pink and yellow and orange. Tears streamed down my cheeks as the sunship was tugged out into the harbor, as the tugboat disconnected and the enormous solar sails unfurled and turned to greet the rising sun.

Watch over them, Pru.

I waited until the ship was a mere speck, a memory traveling far across the sea. I watched, careless of the time, of the stares I gathered from passersby, of the tongue-lashing Lugine was sure to give me the moment I showed my face in the temple, empty-handed and having skipped my morning dive. I didn't care. I was alone in a city full of people, and nothing at all mattered anymore.

Without Sawny around to fill my spare time, I wandered through the temple aimlessly, counting down the days left until my birthday, when I would be free of this place and all the unpleasant memories of my childhood that frosted its walls and stained its floors. Whenever I wasn't diving or off on some errand for an anchorite, I found myself in the library, revisiting the books I'd read over and over as a child. I'd always been fascinated by the stories about the world before the cataclysm.

It had been so vast and varied, and yet so isolated at the same time. But, as the Suzerain would have us believe, its people had grown too bold, too selfish. Dzallie the Warrior asked Gadrian the Firebound to make her a weapon that would split the moon. As moondust and fire rained down upon the world, Hamil the Seabound washed away the dregs of the corrupt civilizations that had so angered the gods. Rayleane the Builder took the clay given to her by Tueber the Earthbound and reshaped the remnants of humanity, splitting each person into two, so that everyone would go through life with a twin, a counterweight—a living conscience. Those few precious to Magritte the Educator remained whole, becoming the singleborn.

There were dozens of religious texts that told the story of the cataclysm, but I think the thing that drew me back to the library again and again were the stories from before. Stories about a time when losing your twin didn't mean losing your life, your whole self.

It didn't take long for one of the anchorites to find Anchorite Sula and tell her I'd been lurking around the stacks, failing to make myself useful. One evening after supper, when I'd found an empty corner of the library where I could read in peace, Sula came bustling up to me, her orange robes fluttering behind her and a pained look of concern plastered onto her face.

"Obedience, child," she said. "Do you want for tasks that will better allow you to serve your chosen deity?"

I shut the book I'd been reading and uncurled myself from the sagging armchair, already exhausted by a conversation I'd had a thousand times or more over the course of my childhood. Every child was encouraged to choose one of the gods and goddesses on whom they could focus their worship. I'd chosen Dzallie the Warrior, not that it mattered much to me either way. I'd long since given up any pretense of believing in the gods and goddesses. Growing up in the temple had shown me time and again that the Suzerain's goal wasn't actually the salvation of the souls of the empire, but rather power over those souls and their wealth. If the gods and goddesses were real, they would have given us leaders immune to corruption.

Much to my chagrin, my lack of faith didn't stop the anchorites from forcing me to attend adulations and questioning me about my devotion.

"I don't want for anything, Anchorite," I said, grating against the fact that she'd called me by my given name. "I only had a bit of time and thought I might read."

"You've been downcast since Sawny's and Lily's departure."

I raised an eyebrow. "I'm surprised you noticed."

"I don't appreciate your tone," Sula said, her voice flat with a familiar, weary warning. "Because you seem to have found yourself with so much free time on your hands, I have notified the Suzerain that you will assist with their equipment and cleaning needs during and after the Shriven initiates' evening training."

My fingers tightened around the book in my lap, and I fixed my eyes on the stone floor between our feet. The worn flagstones were dark with age and centuries of boots. Someone had mopped recently, not bothering to move the armchair. There was a ring of dust surrounding it, the line between Sula's feet and mine; I, fittingly, was on the dirty side of the line. I took a deep breath and tried to force my anger down to a manageable level. If Sula heard even a hint of it in my voice, it'd mean overnight adulations in the haven hall for a week at least, and I didn't think I could stand the oppressive silence or being left alone with my thoughts for that long.

"As I'm sure you're aware," I said, taking the time to choose my words carefully, the lies like barbs on my tongue, "my daily service is in the harbor and canneries under the supervision of Anchorite Lugine. And while I would surely be honored to serve the Suzerain in whatever capacity they desire, I know Lugine can't afford to be left shorthanded during the warm months when we're able to dive, and I'm in the midst of training my replacement. My sixteenth birthday is just around the corner."

Sula sniffed. "Your assignment to aid the Shriven initiates' training is in addition to your service with Anchorite Lugine. There's no reason you shouldn't fill every available hour that remains to you as a ward of the temple by repaying the generosity that has kept you fed, clothed and housed for the first sixteen years of your life."

I bit back the sharp response that threatened to explode from my throat and simply nodded. There was no real use arguing with her. I'd do as they asked and count the days until I could leave, just like I'd always done.

"Go on," Sula said. "They're expecting you."

My head snapped up and I stared at her, bewildered. "Now?"

"Yes, *now*. Go!"

I managed to keep the string of curses running through my head from making their way out of my mouth until I got into the hall, where I launched into a dead sprint. The last thing I wanted was to be noticed—especially unfavorably noticed—by the Suzerain.

I vaulted down the stairs and tore through the maze of corridors that led to the Shriven's wing of the temple. I'd made it a point to stay as far away from the Shriven as I possibly could manage over the years, but I'd been sent on errands for them often enough that I knew my way to the large training room.

I paused outside for a moment to catch my breath before easing the door open, hoping to enter unnoticed. But the old hinges squealed, and I winced as every pair of eyes in the room turned to glare at me. There were maybe twenty of the Shriven initiates, all sitting cross-legged and silent. One of them grinned, baring newly sharpened teeth at me. Out of the corner of my eye, I saw Curlin, her face flicking from surprise to a callous sort of amusement as she realized that my being there had nothing at all to do with her. I managed to keep my expression neutral, looking instead to the Suzerain. They stood at the front of the room, their arms crossed over their chests, identically impenetrable looks clouding their faces.

"Obedience," Castor said, his voice at once familiar and disconcerting. "Anchorite Sula suggested that you might consider joining the ranks of the Shriven and would be well served by observing and assisting with the evening training sessions as we saw fit. In the future, do attempt to arrive in a timely manner so as not to disrupt our proceedings."

Amler's head cocked to the side, like a bird trying to decide if the creature in front of it could be eaten. I kept as still as I was able and did my best to fade into the wall. Standing there, with the full weight of their attention fixed on me, made me feel like they could see through to my very core and riffle through every secret I'd ever kept. My mind kept slipping to the loose floorboard beneath my bed and the box hidden there—my collection of pearls, waiting, glowing like so many miniature moons, still unbroken, inside.

"She doesn't want to join the Shriven, brother. She wants to be rid of the temple as soon as we'll consent to her leaving."

"I simply stated Anchorite Sula's suggestion," Castor observed. "I didn't say that she was correct."

Amler nodded. "A fair point, well made, but we've lost two full minutes to this disturbance, and I would not like to divert from our schedule any more than absolutely necessary.

Obedience, please remain in the back, out of the way. We'll let you know when you're needed."

I bowed my head and shrank farther into the corner. As the evening passed into night, I found myself strangely fascinated by the Shriven's training. I'd seen them at work in the city, of course—I somehow always managed to find myself nearby when one of the other dimmys fell into their violent grief, and the Shriven inevitably appeared to put a stop to their violence. But it'd never occurred to me that to become that capable, that deadly, the Shriven would have to work very, very hard.

The Shriven initiates mimicked the Suzerain in an endless series of exercises that inverted, balanced and stretched them in ways that didn't seem to translate into combat at all. They practiced the same movements again and again, so many times that even I, in the corner of the room, could see their muscles quivering.

Eventually, the initiates separated into pairs, the dimmys in the room silently finding one another, and the twins turning to face their other halves.

"The staves, Obedience," Castor called, not bothering to hide the exasperation in his voice. "Bring out the staves."

I glanced around the room helplessly. Blunt clubs hung in clusters in one corner. Racks of blades—everything from throwing stars to swords almost as long as I was tall—decorated the wall behind the Suzerain, but I saw nothing that remotely resembled the deadly, metal-tipped staves some of the Shriven carried on their prowls through the city.

Finally, rolling her eyes, Curlin peeled off from the group, darted across the room and shouldered me out of the way. She slid open a door that I'd completely overlooked, despite the fact that I'd been standing right in front of it. Blushing,

I helped Curlin heave the padded staves out of the closet and distribute them to the rest of the initiates.

The Suzerain exchanged a cryptic glance as I shrank back into my corner, fuming at myself and Curlin in equal parts.

"You're dismissed, Obedience," Amler said. "Remember, when you plan your day tomorrow, that to be on time is to be late, and to be late is to be an embarrassment to your faith."

With no need for an excuse beyond my burning cheeks and the terrifying attention of the Suzerain, I turned on a heel and fled.

CHAPTER FOUR

Bo

After a solid week of cold, gray rain, the skies cleared and the sun finally came out. Queen Runa suggested to my tutors that I might be allowed an afternoon dedicated solely to relaxation. While I would have been more than content to while away the entirety of my rare free time reading a novel, Claes and his twin, Penelope, insisted that we take advantage of the beautiful day and go for a ride. Just after lunch we took off across the city on horses borrowed from the Queen's stables.

We three had grown up riding, and all of us were as comfortable on horseback as we were on our own two feet. Nevertheless, it had taken a great deal of wheedling and pleading to convince the stable master to give us mounts with a bit more spirit than a hay bale. We'd still ended up with a set of stodgy, dependable Alskad Curlies that made me desperately miss the horses I'd left behind at my estate in the country.

Penby had grown up around the palace and temple, and as such, there were almost no palace grounds to speak of. However, there were wide swaths of parkland across the whole city—acres upon acres of green lawns, cultivated forests and trails that dotted the city like emeralds scattered over a field of ash. The parks had been a gift to the people from one of my queenly ancestors, and Queen Runa had recently declared that their upkeep would henceforth be entirely funded through a tax on luxury items like fur, kaffe and imported Denorian wool and Samirian silk. Just when I thought my mother was finished ranting about the subject, she brought it up again, appalled that the rich be punished "for having good taste."

The memory made me wrinkle my nose in disgust. For someone who had as much wealth and privilege as my mother to be upset by a tiny uptick in the cost of her unnecessary luxuries felt ugly, especially when that money went to providing all of Penby's citizens with something as lovely as free, public green space in the middle of the capital city of the empire.

"Smells like rotting fish, doesn't it?" Claes asked, misinterpreting my expression.

Penelope glanced over her shoulder and shrugged. "Better to suffer the stench of the wharf than chance getting our pockets picked by the riffraff in the End."

"Oh, please, Penelope," I said with a sigh.

"What? Didn't you hear what happened to Imelda Hesketh three weeks ago? She was robbed blind coming home from a party. I've no idea why, but she decided to walk through the End. A gang of miscreants jumped her—they took her wallet, her jacket, her shoes, even her hairpins. Fortunately, she wasn't hurt, just embarrassed by the whole affair."

Claes raised an eyebrow at his sister. "Are you certain that's what happened?"

"Of course. Imelda told me herself."

"I heard that she's been spending more than a little time

in the gambling dens in Oak Grove, and she used the story
about the End to get herself out of trouble with her wife. Patrise told me she's in debt up to her eyebrows."

I kneed my horse forward, up a hill and away from the
wharf, and let the rest of their gossip drift away behind me.
I focused instead on the city, watching the people I would
someday rule as we rode into Esser Park, the most fashionable neighborhood in Penby. Tall brick houses, their doors
and window sashes painted in bold colors, ringed the largest
and most carefully tended of Penby's parks. The houses were
trimmed with ornate stone fripperies and built so close together, their occupants could open their windows and gossip
without raising their voices. My father had owned one of these
houses, but my mother had closed it up after he died. I tried
to pick out which one had been his, but it had been too long
since I'd visited. None seemed more familiar than the rest.

Alskaders had thronged to the park, drawn by the lovely
weather. The benches and pavilions were full of picnickers
popping bottles of fizzy wine and laughing. Vendors hawked
their wares from colorful carts, and people crowded around
them, buying fry bread dusted with sugar, flaky meat pies
and baskets of steamed, spiced crab, shrimp and clams. Children played on the rolling lawns, and their parents watched
from blankets as they tumbled down hills and tossed balls to
one another. There were other riders out, too, and I nodded
at the familiar faces we passed.

Despite the fact that this park was free and open to the
public, the only people enjoying it were the nobility—the
same nobles who attended the parties and dinners at the palace. Who visited our countryside estate. Who sent me birthday gifts year after year, not because they knew me, but for
the simple fact that I was a Trousillion—and though the an-

nouncement would not come until my birthday, everyone knew that I would be the next king.

It was as though there was some kind of unspoken rule, more effective than walls, that made this space inaccessible to the poor.

"Why is it that the only people out on a day like today are the same ones we see at court all the time?"

Penelope and Claes exchanged one of their infuriatingly meaningful twin looks, and Claes shrugged.

"Did you give Gunnar the afternoon off before we left?" he asked.

The heat of a blush crept up my neck as I realized my mistake. I hadn't thought to give him time off. Of course I hadn't. I was a fool to think I had any idea what it was like to be poor in Penby—or, for that matter, to be employed. It suddenly made perfect sense that the park was crowded with the nobility. We were the only people who could afford the time to enjoy these green spaces.

The entire sum of my life had been devoted to work and pleasure in nearly equal portions. The work I did in preparation for the duties of kingship was challenging and extensive, but if I took ill or needed a day off to rest, I could have that. Queen Runa had always emphasized that the role of a monarch was to be a servant to their subjects, but the reality of my life was such that I rarely interacted with people who were actually poor. Those people I knew who worked for a living, by and large, worked for *me* in some capacity or another.

Penelope tapped my thigh gently with the end of her riding crop and said, "There's no reason you ought to have done, Bo. With your birthday around the corner, he hasn't got the time for gallivanting around a park all afternoon. And frankly, neither do we. We must decide on the menu for your birthday party, not to mention the entertainment..."

I stopped listening, and my eyes drifted to the edge of the woods, where a group of the Shriven stood, their white robes stark and austere against the dark evergreen tree line. I glanced around, looking for the city watch, but there were none in sight. Like the rest of us, the watch depended on the Shriven to protect us from the diminished, but it was odd to see a group of them standing there, as if waiting for something.

"Bo? Bo. Are you listening?" Penelope's voice snapped me back to the present, and I tore my eyes away from the Shriven.

"Obviously not," Claes drawled.

A hunk of grass exploded a stride to my left. Then another, closer. I looked over my shoulder, confused. A sound like a thunderclap reverberated through the park, and my horse sidestepped, flinging his head up and snorting anxiously. It was the most activity I'd seen from the beast since I'd mounted. I glanced at Claes, but before I could say anything, something whizzed by my shoulder, and this time, I recognized the sound. Gunshots. One voice rose up in a scream, and in no time, it was joined by a chorus of panicked yells.

I'd hunted for sport all my life. I knew the sound of a rifle, but it was so out of place here, so unexpected in this beautiful park in the middle of the city. There was no game to hunt, no reason for a person to come armed. I was as baffled as I was frightened; it simply didn't make any sense.

Realization dawned on me suddenly. Someone was shooting. At me. There'd been attempts made on my life before, but they'd been flashy, easy to identify and avoid. Poisonings, cut stirrups, clumsily hidden explosives. It was tradition more than anything—a show of strength and power. The single-born threatened each other with assassination all the time, but never with firearms, and people rarely actually died unless in some kind of horrible accident.

The horse jigged beneath me, and I knew he was on the verge of taking off. It took nearly all my focus to stay in the saddle, but even still, I saw the Shriven streaming up the hill toward the copse of trees at the edge of the bluff. They moved like silverfish streaking up a stream, silent and focused. Something about their coordinated movements, and the way they'd been waiting—it left a bad taste in my mouth. An overwhelming wrongness, like biting down on a copper *tvilling*.

Another shot rang out, and this time my horse wheeled and started to bolt off down the hill. I sat deep in the saddle and tightened my grip on the reins, murmuring soothing nonsense and slowing his pace. Out of the corner of my eye, I saw Penelope and Claes catch up to me as people dashed out of the park, leaving hampers and blankets behind in their rush to get away.

"We have to get back to the palace!" Claes yelled over the din of the crowd.

"Follow me," Penelope called. "Side streets will be faster."

We rode at breakneck speed through the city, dodging street vendors and pedestrians. Our terrified horses needed no encouragement, and they only gathered speed as we rounded the last corner and finally caught sight of the palace.

Startled guards threw open the gate, and we thundered across the courtyard, finally slowing as we neared the stables. Claes leapt off his horse, snarling, and stalked off toward the palace without a second look for Penelope or me. I dismounted more slowly. As the rush of danger faded, my hands shook, and my knees felt like jellied eels.

"Are you all right, Bo?" Penelope handed her horse's reins off to a groom and looked me up and down.

Dry-mouthed and weak, I ignored Penelope, pressing my forehead against the curly hair on the horse's thick neck, petting him automatically. He was shivering, too. Without thinking, I started to run my hands over his body, looking for injury. When I reached his left flank, my hand came away damp with blood. The poor beast had been skimmed by a bullet.

"Bo?" Penelope put a hand tentatively on my shoulder.

"He's been wounded. Call for the stable master. He might need stiches."

A groom gently took the reins out of my hands and led the horse away.

"Bo?" Penelope asked again, peering into my eyes. "Do you need to sit down?"

"I don't know, honestly. I'm not injured. That poor horse, though…"

Penelope sighed in exasperation. "Honestly, Bo. Worried about a horse. The beast will be fine. It was only a scratch."

"Do you think the Shriven will make a report to the Queen?"

"Why would they? They deal with the diminished all the time." Penelope drew my arm through her crooked elbow and led me back toward the palace. "They must've gotten a tip that one of the dimmys was on the verge of breaking. We were in the wrong place at the wrong time."

I stopped and drew back. "Why would you assume that it was one of the diminished? Those bullets were aimed at me. They hit my horse. It was an assassination attempt."

"The Shriven were there. What more proof do you need that a dimmy was holding that rifle? It was, in all likelihood, simply an unfortunate coincidence, and one of the diminished lost control while we were in the park."

"Why would Claes run off like that, then?"

Penelope's eyes flicked down the path, and though Claes was inside the palace and well out of earshot at this point, she lowered her voice. "You know that coming into contact with the diminished has always upset Claes, but ever since our father..."

Her voice trailed off. There was no need for her to finish the sentence as we continued down the cobblestone path that led to the palace. The twins' father was my mother's eldest brother. When his twin died, the family had gathered to say their goodbyes, but their father didn't do as was expected of him. He didn't die. In fact, he seemed healthier and more full of life than ever. After several weeks passed, the family was caught between relief that they wouldn't lose him as well, and fear of what would happen to their standing in society. Unfortunately, their fear was well-founded. They stopped receiving invitations and visitors, and before long, their social stock had fallen so appallingly low that the only place they were welcome was the palace—and there were whispers that even the Queen, with her liberal views on all social rules, would refuse to allow them to court, if only as a way of keeping herself safe should he lose his grip on the grief.

Not long after, Penelope and Claes had come to live with my family, and their parents immigrated to Ilor, where their social status would no longer threaten their children's prospects. Claes lived in constant fear of learning that his father had finally succumbed to the grief and done something horrible.

I ducked my head. "We still don't know if it was one of the diminished that fired that rifle. Surely the Shriven will tell Runa that much at least."

A guard held open the side door, and Penelope paused,

waiting for me to go first. The dimness of the inner hallway after the bright day was temporarily blinding. I stopped, blinking the starbursts of darkness out of my eyes.

"We shouldn't mention this at the dinner tonight," Penelope said. "Just in case."

"In case I'm right, and it wasn't one of the diminished?"

"In case it panics your already overwhelmed mother."

I scoffed. "Mother is absolutely fine. A meteorite could demolish our house on the same day a tempest strikes Penby, and the only thing that would make her bat an eye is the potential impact on our profitable interests."

"It isn't a bad thing to be concerned about, Bo. Her careful business strategizing is the reason you're kept in books and horses."

I sighed in defeat. "I know. I ought to go study before dinner. Queen Runa is sure to quiz me about the kind of metal used to make the pipes on the sunships or something equally obscure, and I'd rather not be embarrassed in front of the rest of the singleborn. Check on Claes for me?"

Penelope nodded, a knowing smile playing around her eyes. "Of course. See you at dinner."

State dinners were held in the same cavernous great room where all of the important royal ceremonies and celebrations had taken place since the cataclysm and Penby's founding. That evening, with most of the Alskad singleborn and nobility in attendance and fires burning in the wide hearths, the room was warm and bright and full of jewels glittering in the light of the solar lamps. I peered through a crack between the doors and watched as Claes moved through the crowd, all dark, perfectly mussed hair and bright blue silk. His jacket was embroidered with silver thread and crystals in a pattern that made it look as though there were raindrops clinging to his shoulders. He was, by far, the most handsome young man in the room.

The whisper of footsteps snapped me out of my reverie, and I stepped away from the door just as the Queen said, "We can't be spending the whole night in the doorway, mooning over some pretty young thing, Bo."

"Apologies, Your Majesty." I bowed.

The Queen adjusted the golden cuff bracelet on her wrist and made a face.

"You'd think that after all these years, I would have grown used to the ceaseless gossip and small talk these kinds of functions require. Yet every time I come to stand outside this room and wait to be announced, I find myself desperately wishing for a quiet night in the peace and comfort of my rooms."

I nodded, grateful that I wasn't alone in that feeling. Before I could respond, she went on.

"It's the meaningless, petty gossip that I find intolerable. Most of the people in that room have no idea that the seemingly scandalous behavior of a wealthy member of the nobility will have mind-bogglingly little effect on the struggles and triumphs of the greater population. Sometimes I wish that the first queens of the empire had quashed the ambitions of the noble class in the very beginning. It's those most innocuous and seemingly necessary things that will do the most damage in the long run." She paused and looked at me wearily. "There's a lesson in there somewhere, Bo."

Queen Runa took a deep breath, and before I could reply, she asked that I be announced. The butler called out my name and titles, and as I entered, I realized this was the last time I would hear the titles I'd been given at birth spoken into a room in just that way. In a couple of days, I would turn sixteen, the Queen would declare me her true and rightful heir, and all of my titles would change. When the room quieted, the butler blew a triplicate call on the long, twisting horn, a relic of some long-extinct animal, and announced the Queen.

Runa swept into the room, all smiles and cheerful greetings for the courtiers who approached her, the irritation of moments before washed from her face. It didn't seem to matter at all that she loathed these kinds of events—she played along beautifully. Waiters swept through the crowd, offering the guests flutes of sparkling wine, snifters of ouzel and appetizers as complex and intricate as they were small. The long table was laid with gilt-edged dishes and gold-plated flatware. Exotic hothouse flowers overflowed from tall vases, and each place setting had no less than five matching crystal glasses.

I snagged a glass of sparkling wine from a passing waiter and searched the room for the brilliant blue of Claes's jacket. Before I spotted him, Patrise and Lisette descended on me. They wore matching looks of predatory delight, and with them came a cloud of rich perfume. Patrise's dark brown eyes were crinkled in amusement, his sepia skin bore almost no wrinkles and his black hair was perfectly arranged, as usual— I'd never seen a single lock out of place on his head. But where he was all languid grace, lithe muscle and smoldering looks through suggestively lowered lashes, even I could appreciate that Lisette's beauty was sumptuous: all elegance and not a hint of the deceptive and brilliant political maneuvering that came so easily to her. Her tawny skin and auburn hair glowed like amber in the soft light of the sunlamps. Claes had often made a great point of reminding me that there wasn't a man or woman at court who wasn't entirely under Lisette's sway.

"Darling Ambrose," Lisette trilled. "How are you? We

heard about the unfortunate incident at the park this afternoon. You must be terribly unsettled."

Patrise laced an arm through mine and leaned in conspiratorially. "You don't believe it was a coincidence, do you?"

"Isn't it odd that Rylain hasn't yet arrived for your party?" Lisette asked, sending me a look full of meaning. "We've always suspected that she was up to no good, haven't we, Patrise?"

Spotting Claes, I squirmed out of their grasp, only barely managing to keep a civil tongue in the process. Of all the singleborn, Rylain was far and away my favorite, the one with whom I felt comfortable enough to be myself. She was a historian who'd devoted her life to researching the cataclysm and its fallout. She had visited our estates often when my father was still alive, and always brought with her huge numbers of books for my father and me. After my father's death, Rylain had been a great comfort, always ready to lend a sympathetic ear.

I refused to give weight to Patrise and Lisette's ridiculous accusations against her.

Well-meaning members of the gentry stopped me over and over as I tried to make my way across the crowded room. The questions on all of their lips were about the incident in the park that afternoon, and I had no answers for them. None at all. By the time I reached Claes, the butler had just announced that dinner was to be served. I laced a hand through his and leaned in close to whisper in his ear, my false smile beginning to make my cheeks and jaw ache.

"How is it that every soul in this room has heard about what happened this afternoon?"

Claes squeezed my hand. "It did take place in Esser Park, darling."

"Do you know anything else? Was it an assassination attempt?"

"Bo, honestly. How often is there an incident with the diminished in Penby? Once a month? Twice? The Shriven wouldn't have taken action had the violence been committed by anyone not diminished. It had to be a coincidence."

The assumption didn't sit right with me, but I wasn't about to argue with Claes in the middle of a dinner in my honor. The guests were beginning to find their ways to their seats. I glanced over at the Queen, flanked by the singleborn of her generation—Zurienne, Olivar and Turshaw, all wearing matching expressions of mild annoyance. Runa eyed the seat to her right, the place of honor I was meant to occupy. I took a step in that direction, but Claes kept hold of my hand and leaned in once more.

"An attempt on the heir apparent's life, so close to the ceremony? Think of the scandal such a thing might cause. It would look as though one of the other singleborn was so desperate to usurp your place that they would try anything. No one is that stupid."

Claes dropped my hand, and I sat down to my last state dinner before I became the heir. But his words sat like lead in my belly, and for the first time in my life, I wasn't quite sure if I trusted him or not.

CHAPTER FIVE

Vi

The tide was low and the fishing boats not yet in the water as I walked, shivering, into the sea. Though the weight of the whole ocean pushed me back toward the shore, I slogged through the icy water as fast as my legs would propel me. The wind whipped black curls loose from my braid and into my eyes, but I kept my focus on the red marker bobbing in the water and the salty musk of the ocean. Five more strides before I could dive.

I checked my knives, my nets, my ballasts. I tried to breathe deeply, to get ready. *Focus, Vi*, I thought. This cold summer morning would be the last time I dove for the temple, and glad as I was, I wanted the ocean to myself to say goodbye. I knew the memory of this last dive would stick to me like a barnacle I'd carry with me forever.

I wondered what Anchorite Lugine would say when I left. She'd be glad, more than likely. I certainly wouldn't get the tearful goodbye that Sawny and Lily had been given.

Four more steps.

My feet slicked around smooth rocks and sank into the sand. The seawater was as gray as the clouds. Gray as my eyes. Scummy foam laced the tops of the tiny waves and lapped at my shoulders. The chill would cling beneath the waves for months yet, turning lips and fingertips blue after a few minutes. But not mine. Not anymore. Not after today.

Three more steps.

Something sleek and scaled slipped past my calf in the cold water, breaking my reverie. I shuddered. It didn't matter that I'd spent most of my nearly sixteen years in this same harbor— until I got underwater, the unseen creatures that swam past my legs still set my teeth on edge. My oil-slicked body had grown almost used to the cold.

Two more steps.

One last time, I checked that my tools were securely tied to my belt. As I pulled my goggles into place, I started taking deep breaths. Today's dive would be easier than usual, with the water low and the tide nearly imperceptible.

One more step.

I took a last, long breath and sank beneath the waves.

The sea was never silent. The hushing crush of the water, the clicks and squeals of the few hardy sea creatures and the soft thud of my heart finally drowned out my racing thoughts. My goggles were older than me, issued by the temple when I first began to dive. The leather was cracked, and tiny bubbles in the glass left my vision hazy at best, but they kept the seawater from stinging my eyes and made it a little easier to see below the surface. I found the red rope net that surrounded the underwater bed of oysters the temple's divers were harvesting this month and swam toward it. I had to focus.

When I reached the marker, I swam back to the surface

and treaded water for a few minutes, breathing in the pattern I'd learned many years ago. A deep breath in followed by many little gulps of air.

Good luck would go a long way today, Pru. See if you can't manage a bit for me? I thought.

Finally, on the third breath, I dove toward the ocean floor. I couldn't hold my breath for as long as some of the older divers—only about seven minutes—but I was faster than most and a strong swimmer. I dug my fingers into the sea floor and yanked the rough shells of startled oysters from their sandy beds, my mind settling into the rhythm of the work. By the time my chest began to burn, my net bag was half-full. I ascended slowly, like I'd been taught, and as I caught my breath, I pulled my ballasts back up by the long lines that attached them to my belt.

I went down three more times, and when both my bags were full, I swam back toward the wharf, where I'd hidden my clothes. I had one last thing to do before I steeled myself to get out of the water. I tied the net bags, heavy with oysters, to a rusted iron ring that had long ago been sunk into the wood of one of the pilings halfway between the end of the dock and the shore. I swam back out toward the bay, keeping myself hidden under the dock.

I turned sixteen the next day, and I could finally bid farewell to the city, the temple and the anchorites. It was time to harvest the last of the pearls I'd been so carefully cultivating beneath the docks all these years. Since I wouldn't be returning to the harbor again, I cut the ropes, after pulling the oysters from my lines, and watched them drift to the ocean floor.

When I got back to shore, I set my bag of oysters apart from the others before I dried off and dressed with numbed fingers gone blue and wrinkly in the cold water. The cool air was a shock after having gotten used to the water's chill. Even in the summer, Alskad was never hot, especially early in the morning before the sun had baked away the mist and fog.

I stuffed my braid under my wool cap, kneeled on one of my folded sweaters and set to work. I needed to move fast. The others would be making their way to the shoreline soon, and they'd have questions if they saw me shucking oysters on the beach rather than under Anchorite Lugine's watchful eyes. I could already hear the news hawkers on the docks, calling headlines about the declaration of the heir and rebel groups disrupting trade in Ilor. I thought of Sawny, hoping that he and Lily had arrived and settled safely as I slipped my knife into an oyster shell and twisted, popping it open.

After I pulled the pearl from each of my oysters, I tossed its meat to the seagulls gathered around me. My stomach was talking at me, but even that wasn't enough to make me eat the pearl oysters. Unlike the oysters we gathered to sell to the nobility for pricey appetizers, pearl oysters were tough and tasted of seaweed and slime. I wished I'd had the foresight to steal a couple of scallops from their seabeds.

I worked fast, leaving a heap of shells in the sand next to me. By the time I finished, I'd harvested sixty-three pearls, my biggest haul yet—and of them, twenty were some of the biggest I'd ever seen, oysters I'd left undisturbed since I put them on the lines nearly ten years before. I dug a quick hole in the wet sand and buried the shells that had housed my small fortune. By the time the ocean pulled them back up, I'd be long gone.

Pearls tucked safe in a pouch beneath my shirt and sweater, I hauled the bags of the anchorites' oysters up and over my shoulder. If I could get back to the temple before the end of the morning's adulations, I might be able to sneak a sugar-dotted cloud bun from the anchorites' tray before it went up to their buffet. I didn't just miss Sawny for the treats he'd pocketed for me, but I would've been lying if I said I didn't wake up thinking about cloud buns and sweet, milky tea on mornings like this.

I picked my way across the gray puddles that littered Penby's streets. The merchants and street vendors had just started stirring as I stepped into the market square. Bene's bakery windows were misted over with the fragrant steam of rising dough. My mouth watered at the thought of her spiced pigeon pies, which I'd tasted a few times but could rarely afford to buy on my own. Shopkeepers leaned against doors just opened and sipped their tea as their assistants chalked specials and sales onto display boards. Early risers bustled down the streets, shopping baskets hooked over their arms. A farmer set bowls heaped with the first salmonberries of the season onto his cart next to jars of bright pickled onions and the cabbages and potatoes we'd seen through the winter. I nodded to Jemima Twillerson as she flipped the sign to open her apothecary shop, but her eyes—no great shock—slid away from mine.

No one wanted to be seen associating with a dimmy. Worse still, a dimmy like me—penniless and a temple ward. In all my life, Sawny'd been the only twin willing to call me friend. Others, like Jemima, might do me a kindness from time to time, but not where they might be seen—and worse yet, judged—.

I pushed away the familiar sting and adjusted the sack of oysters balanced on my shoulder. A bright slash of red caught my eye, and I turned on a heel to see a girl I recognized streaking through the market square. She clutched a long, curving Samirian knife in each white-knuckled hand, and her feet were bare on the stone road.

Her name was Skalla. I'd only met her the once. She was some Denorian merchant's daughter, and he had enough *drott* to dress his girls in imported silks and brocades. Her twin sister had died a couple weeks back, and when the girl didn't seem to be succumbing to death herself, Anchorite Lugine dragged me on a visit.

"Vi," Anchorite Lugine had said, "it's important that she sees the glorious contentment that your faith has sustained, even after all these years of being diminished."

The implication—that the grief would inevitably catch up with me—had lingered in the air unsaid all through the painfully silent visit with Skalla and her family. What could I say to her? That I was sorry for her; for what she'd become? What we'd both become?

I hated those visits. They were such a lie. I had no faith, and I certainly hadn't kept myself from violence all these years through prayer and piety. I was a fluke: I would eventually lose the tight hold that kept my anger from turning to violence. Just because I'd lasted this long didn't mean I would be able to avoid the grief forever.

Skalla's silks were damp with sweat, and her arms prickled with gooseflesh. Her eyes were blank with rage. She was gone; lost to the grief she felt for her twin.

Before Skalla, it had been at least a month since another dimmy was lost in Penby. There'd been rumors of an incident in Esser Park, but I'd overheard a group of the Shriven saying that it'd been a ruse. Folks did that from time to time. Used dimmys as an excuse, as an explanation for their bad behavior.

I clenched my jaw and sidled toward an alleyway. I didn't want to see what happened next. Sometimes it seemed like I always managed to find myself nearby when a dimmy lost their grip. When I was younger, I'd tried to stop one of the temple brats, a dimmy, when she attacked Lily in a dark corridor in the middle of the night. I got between them right before the Shriven arrived and threw me off the other girl. That was the first time I'd broken my nose.

Skalla's bare feet smacked slush from potholes, and, in a moment, she was across the square, dragging the baker from her doorway before the woman had a moment to think. Still frail from a bout with the whispering cough, Bene never stood a chance.

Blood spattered across the bakery's steam-covered window.

I froze in horror. Skalla smeared Bene's blood over her porcelain pale face, screaming. The sack of oysters was an anchor, tethering me to the walk outside the apothecary's shop. No one moved. We sank into the shadows, took shallow breaths, willed ourselves to become invisible. The Shriven'd appear soon, all tattoos and white robes and swift, deadly action. We'd be safe once they arrived. As much as I hated them, they were good for that much, at least.

A high, keening wail poured from deep inside Skalla's body, and then she screamed. In a language that had to be Denorian, her voice filled the square. She'd be cursing the gods and goddesses. They always did. Even the Denorians, who placed an irreverent amount of value on science over religion, spent their last, raging breaths cursing the gods for condemning us with grief.

The names of the Alskader goddesses spurted from her rant as the Shriven slipped silently into the square. Magritte the Educator. Rayleane the Builder. Dzallie the Warrior. I couldn't parse all her words, but I knew that feeling of vitriol. It rose in my chest, the anger, and I bit down hard on my

cheek. I couldn't afford to feed the slow burn always smoldering next to my heart.

Not a day went by when I didn't bite back fury. Every moment was a fight against the close heat of rage when I caught
someone's eyes staring, and I knew from that one look that
all they saw was a dimmy. I stopped being a person and was
reduced to danger wearing the skin of a teenaged girl in a
hand-me-down sweater. But the anchorites' chorus of voices
in my head reminded me that anger loosened my grip, and I
couldn't let that happen. I wouldn't be like Skalla.

The Shriven descended on her like a shroud. Their long
staves whipped through the air, fast and dangerous as eels.
I lost sight of her for a moment, then dark crimson spurted
over one of the Shriven's white-clad shoulders. He collapsed
in a heap with Skalla on top of him, and I gagged as I caught
a glimpse of her face. Blood streamed out of her mouth and
down her neck—she'd torn the man's tattooed throat open
with her teeth.

A moment later, it was over. Skalla's wrists were held behind her back at vicious angles by two of the Shriven, another
two stood at her elbows and a fifth had his hand wrapped tight
around her throat. She wasn't but a slip of a thing, but dimmys were unnaturally strong, and it looked like the Shriven
were going to be extra careful with Skalla. They didn't often
lose one of their own—they were trained for this work.

As they hauled her away, I tried not to picture the inevitable scene on the wide square between the palace and the
temple. I'd seen it so many times—before I was old enough
to know to hide, one of the anchorites had always taken it
upon themselves to drag me and any of the other dimmys in
the temple's care to the executions. As though it would help.
As though anything would help.

They would chant Skalla's name as the tattooed Shriven led her through the crowd. *Skalla. Skalla. Skalla.* The Shriven would pull her onto the platform, still writhing and wailing. They used to hang the diminished, but the day before my twelfth birthday, the Suzerain had declared hanging immoral and cruel. So violent dimmys lost their heads these days—as if that bloody death was somehow less cruel.

All of us in the temple knew the truth. Donations poured in after those executions. Folks were so grateful to be protected from one of the diminished, they'd increase their already steep tributes. There was money in fear, and money in blood, and there was nothing the Suzerain liked better than a fat tribute and a city that remembered who kept them safe.

Waiting for the Shriven to clear the market square before I headed back to the temple, I could imagine Skalla standing on that platform, fighting like a wild thing. They never went quietly. Her fiery red hair would be tangled and matted with blood, her fingers raw from scraping the stone walls of her cell. There would still be blood on her face, dried and flaking.

They'd wait a day. Let the story spread. Drum up the crowds. The Suzerain'd be there at the back of the platform, all calm and beatific in their white robes. The benevolent guardians of everyone in Alskad—except for the people who needed them most.

People like me.

The yeasty warmth of the day's bread baking swirled around me when I opened the kitchen door. Perhaps tomorrow, on my birthday, Lugine might slip me a thin slice of ham or a cheese rind with my dinner roll. She'd never hugged me like she had Sawny and Lily, but from time to time, if it was a special occasion, she'd give me a small treat. After all, I'd been with the anchorites longer than any other dimmy but Curlin.

As I turned to close the door, I was startled to see Sula, Lugine and Bethea sitting at the kitchen's long slab of a table, their faces grim. They shouldn't have been back in the residential part of the temple yet—adulations were barely over. Moreover, it was more than a little strange for all three of them to be in the same room together like this. What would bring them all here at this hour?

My hands trembled as I dumped the sacks of oysters into the tin trough at the end of the table and shrugged out of my sweaters. I sent up a silent prayer to my twin. *Watch my back, will you?*

"Before you say anything, I know I should've gone to adulations this morning, but I hadn't yet had any luck this month, and I wanted to find at least one pearl for you before my birthday." I gave the women my best smile, which none of them returned.

They were each powerful within their orders. Anchorite Sula supervised all that went on in the trade library and made certain that each of the temple's charges were assigned a craft or else made our way into the Shriven. Anchorite Lugine oversaw my work as a diver in the summer and in the canneries in the winter. Long-suffering Anchorite Bethea, the eldest of the three, was responsible for the spiritual education of us brats the temple took in. They were the closest thing I had to real parents. Though, to be fair, they were collectively about as warm as an ice floe. I'd spent my whole childhood with their eyes on me, watching me with the same wariness they'd use with a rabid dog.

Once, when I was barely seven, a gang of grubby urchins cornered me in a back alley. One of them managed to break my nose before I fought my way free. I ran through the streets, blood and tears streaming down my face, and sought comfort from Lugine in the kitchen. She'd taken one look at me, thrown me a dishrag and set me to scrubbing pots. From then on, when the other brats came after me, I scrambled up onto the roof of the nearest building or into a dank corner to hide.

That was how Sawny and I'd found our spot on the temple roof.

Sula sighed. "We've long since given up on forcing you to attend daily adulations, Obedience."

My jaw clenched. I hated being called by my given name, and she knew it. The name "Obedience" had always seemed like a cruel joke. "I'd prefer you call me Vi, Anchorite." I fetched a plain ceramic bowl and a spoon from one of the shelves that lined the walls of the cavernous kitchen. "My birthday's not 'til tomorrow, and before you ask, I already sent my ma a birthing day note. Did you come to tell me you'd miss me when I leave?"

I lifted a ladle from its hook and started toward a pot of rich broth studded with root vegetables and chunks of lamb. Before I got close, a low, disapproving sound from Lugine stopped me. I turned to the half-congealed pot of pea and oat mush on its hook at the edge of the hearth instead and filled my bowl, and settled myself on the rough bench across the table from the anchorites to eat. Diving was hard work, and trouble or not, I was ravenous. I shouldn't have provoked her with the stew, though. Not when she already looked so angry.

"Tell me, Vi. What are the rules of the pearl trade?" Lugine asked.

I swallowed my spoonful of lumpy mush and recited the rules I'd been taught since I began to train. "All the fruits of the dive must go toward the betterment of the temple and its occupants. The meat to feed the servants of the goddesses and gods, the pearls to glorify the goddesses and gods by making their home and their servants beautiful."

"And why are laymen allowed to partake in the bounty of the sea?" Bethea asked.

"So that they, too, may share in the glory of Hamil's gifts." Sula nodded. "And how do the laymen honor the god's gifts to them?"

"I don't plan to stay here and keep diving, Anchorite," I said. "I'll look for work in the North, near my ma's people."

"Answer the question."

I sighed. "Laymen must offer their bounty to Rayleane, Hamil's partner, to thank him for his gift. They can keep what the goddess doesn't want and be paid for their service besides."

The anchorites stared at me in silence. I set my spoon on the table, the pouch of pearls burning between my breasts. A wave of cold ran over me, and I tried not to shiver.

Finally, Bethea asked, "What is the penalty if a layman is found to be giving the goddess less than her due?"

"What is this about?" I asked, though the answer weighed heavily on a thong around my neck. They'd found my stash. That was the only explanation for this interrogation.

They waited, unblinking. Lugine's brow furrowed. Bethea bit the inside of her cheek. Sula's face was implacable, as always.

"They suffer the same penalty as any thief, time in jail and half of their earnings until their debt is doubly paid."

"And what is the penalty for a thief who is diminished?" Sula asked.

Lugine stared at her lap, and Bethea cleared her throat. So. This is how it would end. Just shy of sixteen years, and not a day without someone's terrified glance. I'd long ago accepted that no one would ever hold me, kiss me, love me, but I had hoped that I would at least have one day when no one looked at me with fear in their eyes.

"Death," I whispered.

"Do you know why we are here?" Sula asked quietly.

I nodded, studying the table, tears hot in my eyes. I wasn't ready to let go. I'd held on for so long.

"We sent Shriven Curlin to pack your things in preparation for your birthday. She brought us this." Sula slid the wooden box full of cultured pearls across the table toward me. My pearls. My savings. Of course Curlin had known where to look for my secrets. She'd shared the room with me for years. "You know, if you were to join the Shriven, you would be exempt from any penalty."

Fury flooded me. Nothing, not even the threat of death, could make me become one of those mindless, soulless murderers. The people of Alskad might think that the Shriven were righteous, holy even, protecting them from the atrocities of the diminished, but I knew better. I'd grown up in the temple. I knew the kinds of poison that ran through their veins.

"Over my rotting corpse," I snarled.

Lugine drew in a sharp breath, but Sula put a calming hand on her arm.

"We assumed you'd say something of the kind." Bethea laid a stack of papers on the table.

"What's that?" I asked warily.

"A choice," Sula said. "We care for you, as much as you may not believe it. We've not brought this matter before the Suzerain. Instead, we've decided to let you choose your own path. You may either join the ranks of our holy Shriven, or you will be sent to Ilor, to spread the word of our high holies to the wild colonies by helping to construct temples there.

You'll serve one month for each pearl you stole from the temple through your deceit. Twenty-five years."

My breath caught in my chest. It wasn't a choice. Not really. Either way, I would be forced to spend the rest of my life in service to a pantheon of gods and goddesses I didn't believe in, couldn't bear to worship.

I would be no better than a prisoner in Ilor, but I knew deep in my bones that I could never join the Shriven. I could never be like Curlin.

And there was a bright spot of hope in a future in Ilor: the only person who'd never been afraid of me. While I knew I would never see freedom if I accepted the temple's twenty-five-year sentence—the grief would take me long before those years were up—but at least in Ilor, I would be close to Sawny. I would see him again. Missing Sawny was an ache that went all the way to my bones.

I met the eyes of the three anchorites and took a deep breath, rising to my feet. "Ilor. I choose Ilor."

I stalked out of the room, visions of space, of time to myself, of freedom crumbling in my mind, leaving my bowl of half-congealed mush uneaten on the long-scarred table—and my hard-earned fortune in the hands of the anchorites.

CHAPTER SIX

Bo

My bedroom was warm from the large fire crackling in the hearth, but I was ice all the way to my bones. I'd been cold since I woke up, probably due to nerves at the thought of what the day would bring. I smoothed my jacket's embroidered cuffs and stared out the window. I turned sixteen at midnight, and the Queen would declare me a grown man, singleborn of the Trousillion line and successor to her throne. The thought of that heavy crown and the responsibility that came with it nauseated me.

I wanted to be King. I wanted to be a *great* king, but I'd never felt the easy entitlement the other singleborn flaunted. And after the incident in the park, I'd never felt so unsure of myself, so afraid. I'd spent my whole life preparing for this day, yet still feared that I would trip over some part of the ceremony and embarrass myself—or, worse, my mother.

The soft din of the party drifted through the palace. The fashionable quintet my cousins had hired seemed to play only fast, reeling tunes. My feet ached at the idea of another night spent dancing, but I'd do, as always, what was expected of me, though the stack of books Rylain had sent for my birthday called to me from my bedside table. There was a history of trade dating back to the cataclysm that I ached to dig into.

Outside, in the dark night sky, the two halves of the fractured moon were full, and so close they looked like they might crash into each other. My tutor, Birger, said this interaction of the moon's halves was a rare and good omen: the reunited twins. He claimed that when the halves of the moon were close, the goddesses and gods forgot the evil our ancestors had done when they split the moon in half. I'd always thought they looked more like twins conspiring in a corner than a pair long lost and reunited, and personally ascribed to the theory that the halves were always the same distance apart—it was our perspective that shifted.

No great wonder Birger was so fascinated by the moons. He and his twin, Thamina, were always whispering in each other's ears and exchanging those infuriatingly weighted looks twins gave one another. Nothing made me feel more alone than standing in a room full of twins, steeped in the knowledge that I ought to be grateful for the fact that I was single-born. I knew it was a blessing, but the constant reminders that I'd been born with a greater conscience, a keener sense of justice, a powerful birthright—they had never helped me see those things in myself.

A knock at the door brought me out of my reverie, and Mother swept into the room, not waiting for my response. Rather than her usual well-cut breeches, silk tunic and jacket, She wore a floor-length, lavender-gray gown that sparkled with silver embroidery and accented her olive skin. Her brown hair had been curled, and it brushed the immaculate white

fox-fur stole wound round her neck. Huge hunks of raw di-
amond set in creamy gold cuffs decorated each of her wrists,
but her bare arms and sleeveless dress made more of a statement than those jewels. She was the living personification
of Dzallie, invincible and immune to the chill of the early
summer night.

She narrowed her dark eyes and looked me up and down
and adjusted my jacket. "That color suits you, Ambrose. It
brings out the gray in your eyes."

"I thought it was a little garish, but Claes insisted I choose
something bright." I felt like a pigeon dressed in peacock
feathers. The purple silk jacket was festooned with scads of
embroidery; colorful birds and flowers exploded from my
shoulders, trailing down the sleeves and to the wide hem
that brushed the floor. At least my trousers were plain—if
very fine—gray wool, with embroidery only along the cuffs.

I was waiting for someone to notice how out of place I really was.

"You look so like your father, Ambrose."

She wasn't exactly right. I saw him in the line of my jaw
and the stubborn set of my mouth, but my eyes were gray
where my father's had been hazel, and I'd grown taller than
both my parents by the time I was twelve. Four years later,
and I still hadn't filled out the promise of that early growth.
Though my shoulders were broad enough, I was tall and
skinny, where the rest of my family was small and muscular.

I coughed, not knowing what to say. I never knew what
to say about my father. His absence was like a gaping hole
in our lives, and Mother had an uncanny knack for bringing
him up at times when feeling the enormous emptiness of his
loss would be crippling. I didn't think she did it on purpose.
Even after four years without him, the specter of my father's

death was a constant weight my mother carried. Her grief followed her everywhere, and his memory colored every private moment we shared.

Mother perched on the edge of a gilt-legged settee piled with furs and patted the seat beside her. I sat obediently, careful not to wrinkle my jacket or sit on her skirt. She ran a hand through my newly shorn curls. She used to cut it herself when my father was still alive, as she'd done for him. We'd had the same dark brown curls, unruly and difficult to style. But since his death, she'd left the task to my valet and was ever critical of his work.

"I have something for you."

I looked at her questioningly. "I thought we were going to wait to open gifts until tomorrow. The spectacle's half the ceremony, or so Claes and Penelope are always telling me."

"You'll get the rest of your gifts tomorrow, but this is between you, your father and me. He and I decided long before his passing."

She pulled a small cedar box from her skirts and handed it to me. I untied the crimson ribbon. Inside the box, a long, brass key rested on a velvet cushion.

"A key?" I asked, bewildered. There was no door in our house I had any reason to unlock, and the only time I left our estate was in the company of my mother and our ever-present cadre of servants. There was never a need for me to unlock anything at all.

"To your father's house here in Penby. You'll need a place to get away from the chaos in the palace as you spend more and more time at court. Your father's house is perfect for a crown prince. We'll have to hire a staff to open it, but that shouldn't be any trouble. I'll even give you an allowance to redecorate it to your taste. Do you remember it?"

Strange that, after years without thinking of it, the property had come up twice in one week. I hadn't been there often— since Father's death, we'd always stayed in the palace when we went to court. Before his passing, I'd only been a child, and rarely visited Penby—children of the nobility were raised in the countryside, where they could breathe clean air and learn genteel sports. But, much to my mother's dismay, Father had taken me to see the sunships launch when I'd been briefly fascinated by them as a little boy. I'd wanted to become a ship's captain in the royal navy, to spend my life at sea, exploring the vast swaths of land left unpopulated and destroyed by the cataclysm. I remembered sliding down the banister of the grand, sweeping staircase in the front hall and hiding on the landing long past my bedtime, wrapped in blankets and listening to my parents laugh with their guests.

The reality of what lay ahead of me curdled my stomach. The responsibility of guiding the empire, of working hand in hand with the Suzerain—it was daunting, especially when I felt so very alone. I wished, as I so often had, that I was normal; that I had a twin like everyone else. And seeing the expectation, the eager hunger for my accomplishment and success in my mother's eyes inflamed me.

The old argument, the one that tangled our every interaction lately, took hold before I could stop myself. "Mother…"

Her jaw tensed. "Don't start, Ambrose. You are the Queen's choice. It's your duty to serve the empire. To become its next King. You will show Queen Runa that you are, without a doubt, the best choice to lead the succession, just as your father or I would have done, had we had the luck to be single-born." She tucked the key and its box into an end table drawer.

I bit the inside of my cheek and tried to extinguish the anxiety rising in my chest like a flame. If only I could escape from that word. My whole life, I'd been told I was special because I'd been born alone. Singleborn. The conscience of the empire. Every move I made was lauded, commented upon. My interests became trends. I was deferred to, admired and praised at every turn. But Mother's eyes never rested on me for a moment without the expectation that I could do more, be better.

As if she could read my thoughts, Mother reached out and cupped my cheek. "You know that I'm proud of you? You know that I love you?"

I sighed. "I know. I know you want the best for me. I love you, too."

Before the heaviness of the moment could weigh me down more than my anxiety already had, I changed the subject.

"Has there been any more news about what happened in the park?" I asked.

Mother dropped her hand into her lap, exasperated. "There's no need for you to continue to bring that up," she said, annoyance sharpening her words. "It was a coincidence. One of the diminished. Honestly, if there were something to tell you, I would. Now, tonight is a momentous occasion, and I want for you to remember it fondly." She glanced at the clock on the mantel. "We should go down. Your cousins are doing what they can to keep Her Majesty occupied, but Claes may run out of gossip if we don't relieve him soon." She laughed, a sound like a burbling spring that did nothing to soothe my frayed nerves. "Worse, Penelope will be in a state trying to keep him from saying something out of turn."

I grinned, knowing she was right. I offered her my arm. "Best make my entrance, then. Into the den of foxes, as it were."

Mother swatted at me as we left my room. "Hush, you. You mustn't make jokes about the other singleborn where someone might hear you."

"It's Father's joke," I protested.

"I know." Mother stretched up onto the tips of her toes and kissed me on the cheek. "But those foxes hold your fate in their jaws."

Outside the great room, I stared at the enormous, ancient doors. Doors I'd seen so often during our many visits to court, but never truly looked at. I wondered what had crossed the minds of each of the other singleborn chosen to wear the crown, who'd all waited outside this very door on the night of their sixteenth birthdays. It was a sobering thought, and all my jokes and nervous giggles fled my body.

Gunnar, my valet, knocked twice on the carved panel beside the great room door. I took a deep breath, and three bass notes from the horn just inside the great room reverberated through my bones. The musicians went quiet, and an anticipatory hush settled over the crowd inside. Gunnar looked to Mother for her signal. She wound her arm through mine and looked up into my eyes searchingly.

"Ready?" she asked.

I nodded and set my jaw, forcing a slight smile onto my lips. Gunnar heaved against the doors' polished bone handles. Inside, a uniformed servant took up the Trousillion horn, curling and carved, and blew a long, clear note. Silence hung heavy in the room, and the weight of hundreds of eyes fell upon me all at once. The solar lights were dimmed, and they cast a golden glow over the nobles dressed in their best silks and furs. Their jewels shimmered as they waited for the ceremony to start.

Penelope, Claes and I had spent months shaping the guest list. In addition to the ambassadors from Denor, most elite Ilorian merchants and the highest-ranking members of the nobility, the guest list included a number of my more irritating relatives who had to be invited, despite their tendencies to hoard all of the attention in a room. The three other singleborn of my generation were like that, captivating and dazzling all at once. Even Rylain, despite her hatred of public appearances, was the kind of person who could enchant a crowd with a single word.

I felt drab standing next to them, like a baby puffin before its plumage fills in. I should have been brimming with excitement, but instead I was blinded, unable to move, like a fish frozen in a streambed. My eye landed on a woman draped in austere black wool, her dark brown hair threaded with silver, and a serene look on her unlined face: Rylain. My heart lifted slightly—I hadn't thought that she would be willing to make the trip to court, even for such a significant event. I was relieved to see her—perhaps her presence would stop Patrise and Lisette from spreading their bizarre notion that she'd had something to do with the shooting in the park.

Patrise lounged on a chaise nearby, flanked by a beautiful, red-haired woman. I wondered if the accusations he'd leveled at Rylain were a thinly veiled attempt to hide his own involvement in the most recent attempt on my life. He'd tried to have me killed more than once, or so Mother claimed. It was a fair concern—if something happened to me, the Queen would likely choose either Patrise or Lisette to succeed her. Patrise's companion whispered something to him, and he threw back his head and laughed. His hearty guffaw became the only sound in the room, and he turned to grin at me before leaning in to reply to the redhead.

For a moment, everything I'd learned to prepare for this moment disappeared. I started to turn, to flee, but Mother's elbow dug into my ribs. My eyes darted around frantically, and I finally found Claes standing with his sister. He smiled at me, his face a beacon in the crowd. His grin lit me like a torch, and warmth blossomed in my belly. When I looked at him, it felt like he and I were the only people in the room, and suddenly, I cared about doing this right.

I wanted so badly for him to be proud of me. I wanted to show them all that I deserved to be King.

I blinked and looked away before I could start blushing. Beside him, Penelope looked at me with the impatient urgency that seemed to be the natural set of her face, and my hours of practice flooded back to me. I stepped forward, smiling the solemn smile that my cousins had cajoled me into replicating for hours on end until it was more natural to me than any other expression.

Our guests parted, creating an aisle that led to the dais where Queen Runa waited. Tonight, her cape was black sealskin trimmed with gray fox fur. She wore the Alskad Empire's ceremonial crown, a hefty circlet of hammered gold studded with raw jewels and pearls. Her hands rested on the Sword of the Empire, a weapon nearly as tall as she, forged in folded steel so keenly sharpened, it could cut a whisper in half. It was a weapon made to shed blood, though the empire's rulers had expanded their borders by exploration rather than force.

Queen Runa was flanked by the Suzerain. With their pure white robes, pale skin and blond hair, they looked like twin towers of salt. Aside from the Queen, these were the most powerful people in the empire. While the Queen controlled the nobility, and had the final say on all laws written in the noble council, the common people looked to the Suzerain and their ranks of the Shriven for religious justice and protection from the diminished. The Queen never made a decision without considering the opinion of the temple.

Seven of the Shriven, all clad in the purest white, stood like statues against the wall behind the dais, their eyes glittering amid the black paint that bisected their faces. Tattoos crept up their necks and across their knuckles, and one of them bared her teeth, sharpened to spikes, at me. It took everything in my power to keep from grimacing. I wished they'd take their hands off the long knives in their belts, even only for the duration of the ceremony, but I knew it didn't matter. They were as deadly unarmed as they were if they bristled with weapons.

Wrenching my gaze away from the Shriven, I was grateful for the kind faces of the anchorites, with their brilliant yellow-and-orange silk robes and the ropes of pearls that draped their wrists and necks. They stood before the dais, the emblems of the empire in a chest at their feet. The anchorites showered me in approving nods and warm smiles as I approached them. We stopped before the first step, and I leaned down to kiss Mother on both cheeks. She took her place next to her twin sister, to the right of the anchorites, and I knelt before the Suzerain and the Queen. I inhaled deeply and focused my thoughts on the ceremony at hand.

Together, their solemn voices filled the room, as rich as kaffe and sweet as honey. "Why do you kneel before us, Ambrose, son of Myrella and Oswin, descendent of the Trousillion line?"

I paused, took a breath and let the responses I knew by rote flow. "For I am worthy of the Trousillion crown."

"By what right are you worthy?"

The words caught in my throat, and I coughed before saying, "By right of birth. I am singleborn, chosen of the goddesses and the gods."

"Why were the singleborn chosen to rule their lands?"

"When the moon split and the people corrupted the earth, the goddesses and gods chose to split their souls in twain, that the consciences of the people be doubled. They decreed that each person be born with a twin they would love above all others, to whom they would be responsible for all their deeds. The goddesses and gods chose a family from each land, one who had demonstrated great honor, compassion and intellect. The descendants of those families would bear a number of singleborn in each generation, and from those, the next ruler would be chosen."

Silks rustled as the crowd shifted from one foot to the other. The Queen nodded to my mother, who joined her on the dais. They each took hold of one end of the long Sword of the Empire, hefting it above their heads to form an archway. The female Suzerain, Amler, stepped through the archway, carrying the empire's golden wheel. The male Suzerain, Castor, followed her, a delicate gold net stretched between his hands. Finally, the Queen nodded to me, and I stepped beneath the sword, ducking to clear my head. I was grateful to kneel once again on the other side and hide my shaking legs.

The Queen handed the sword to my mother and came to stand before me, to perform her role in the ceremony. She faced the crowd. "Do you swear to uphold the honor of the singleborn of the Trousillion line?"

I looked into her deep brown eyes, feeling the enormous magnitude of the vow radiating from the depths of her soul. "I do."

The weight of the net, surprisingly heavy for all its delicacy, settled over my shoulders like a ballast, and my heart sank. I admonished myself silently—I'd spent my whole life preparing for this, and it would be years yet before I took the throne. The weight of the responsibility need not feel so wildly overwhelming yet.

"Will you guide the people of the empire with your conscience, serving them with justice and grace, putting their needs before your own?"

"I will." I accepted the wheel, and the Queen gave me the barest hint of a smile.

"Will you wear this cuff as a daily reminder of your duty to your crown and your country, and swear in the name of your chosen god that you will serve the people of the Alskad Empire for the rest of your days?"

I held out my left wrist. "I swear on my honor and in Gadrian the Firebound's name that I will serve the people of the Alskad Empire for the rest of my days."

The Queen snapped the hammered gold bracelet onto my wrist and locked it in place. The crown-shaped bracelet was fitted to my wrist, loose enough to move up and down my forearm, but too tight to slip over my hand. There was no way for me to take it off without the key unless I was willing to break my hand. As the weight of the bracelet settled on my arm, I wondered if any of the other singleborn had ever tried to remove the cuff.

The Queen held out her hand to me, her own bracelet gleaming in the low light. "Stand, Ambrose, son of Myrella and Oswin. Stand in the knowledge that you are my chosen successor to the throne of the Alskad Empire."

I took the Queen's hand and stood, heart pounding in my chest, raising the wheel over my head. The room erupted in cheers and whoops, and the musicians struck up a fast, reeling war song. Queen Runa squeezed my hand reassuringly as we descended the dais together.

★ ★ ★

There were several comfortably furnished chambers adjacent to the great room, where guests could rest or talk quietly during the epic gatherings that were the social centerpieces of the empire's nobility. I followed the Queen and my mother into one of these rooms, and they waited in silence as two anchorites lifted the golden net off my shoulders and relieved me of the wheel.

When the anchorites had gone, closing the door behind them, the Queen settled into a wide chair, plucked the crown off her head and set it on a side table. The regal monarch disappeared, and in her place was my great aunt, all sharp wit and convivial smiles.

"Myrella, be a dear and pour me a glass of something strong, will you?"

Mother went to the sideboard and filled a glass with clear ouzel from a crystal decanter. She took a sip from the glass, to show it wasn't poisoned, before handing it to Runa. The Queen accepted it and downed it in a gulp, holding the glass out to be refilled.

"Sit, sit, both of you," she said.

Mother poured a cup of kaffe, doctored it with cream and sugar and took a sip before handing it to me. I sank gratefully onto a divan, and Mother took her place in the room's other chair, an ouzel glass of her own in hand.

"Now, tell me. Whom will he marry?"

"His cousin Penelope, though we haven't made the formal arrangements yet."

I choked on my kaffe. This was news to me. My heart fluttered. What would Claes say? Did he know? There was no way Penelope would agree to the match, not when I'd spent the last year kissing her twin. Even the Queen had seen me kissing Claes. Never mind the fact that I had no desire to marry her. No desire to marry a woman at all. And why should I? Even as King, the heir to the throne would not necessarily be *my* heir, but the singleborn I deemed most suited to the role. Runa herself had never married, never had a child. She ruled the empire alone, and while I didn't entirely understand why she'd chosen me out of all the singleborn, I didn't think it was purely due to our close line of descent.

When my coughing fit subsided, I looked up to find Mother glaring at me.

"When was this decided?" I asked. I tried to keep my voice level.

Queen Runa laughed, ignoring me. "It's a good match. She's smart and will continue your good work with the estate with no great trouble. Poor Oswin would have been destitute without you. Poor man didn't have a practical bone in his body." She bit her lip, eyes softening. "My apologies, Myrella. I miss him so, as I'm sure you do."

Mother nodded. "It has been exceedingly difficult, but we've made do."

"The Suzerain think we should see Ambrose married within the next two years, and for once, I don't disagree. It will lend him more weight with the nobility if they know he has a strong partner."

I sputtered, "Excuse me?"

They ignored me.

"And the other matter?" Mother asked.

A muscle in the Queen's jaw twitched. "Still safely in the hands of the temple. Magritte's wisdom keep her."

"Magritte keep who?" I blurted, knowing as soon as the question left my lips that I should've kept quiet.

There was no point in asking questions that wouldn't be

answered. It seemed like they were intentionally speaking in riddles, throwing out one incomprehensible statement after another in order to infuriate me. It wasn't as though they didn't know better. It wasn't as though they weren't the ones who'd taught me my manners, and here they were. Acting like I wasn't even here.

The Queen waved her hand dismissively and shot Mother a look cold enough to freeze mulled wine. "No one you need ever worry about. Now, before you leave, I'll have a chat with the tutors about the topics they'll need to cover in Ambrose's and Penelope's curriculum. We'll correspond soon about announcing the engagement and planning the wedding. Meanwhile, he should spend more time at court, and Penelope will be able to assist you in running the estate."

The music died away in the great room. My mind raced, trying to process the last few minutes of conversation.

Queen Runa lumbered to her feet and replaced the crown on her head. "Time for toasts. Come along." When she got to the door, she turned sharply. "You do have someone tasting for him, don't you, Myrella?"

I looked at my mother, one eyebrow raised. My valet, Gunnar, was ostensibly my taster, but I rarely bothered with the pretense at home. It didn't seem necessary.

"Of course," Mother said.

At the same time, I replied, "Sort of."

The Queen closed her eyes and inhaled deeply through her nose. "Not a drop, not a *crumb* passes his lips before a taster has sampled it. Not. A. Crumb. I will not lose my heir to something so easily preventable. Not after everything I've done to secure his place. Do you hear me?"

Mother bowed, her knees nearly dropping to the polished marble floor. "Yes, Your Majesty."

They swept out of the chamber together, leaving me to wonder what, exactly, the Queen had contrived to make me the heir to the Alskad throne.

Part Two

"The knotted, tangled cord that stretches between twins serves as both lifeline and tether. Your twin exists to be your counterweight, to balance you as you balance her."
—from the *Book of Rayleane, the Builder*

"When my earth was rent apart by the mothers and fathers who came before, Dzallie spilled her fiery fury upon my land, already so broken by the shards of the moon. Steward this second chance well. Use and care well for my gifts, for you will find no mercy in my arms again."
—from the *Book of Tueber, the Earthbound*

CHAPTER SEVEN

Vi

A single day was not enough time for me to find my balance after my whole world had turned upside down. The anchorites tasked Curlin—her shaved head, seemingly ever-multiplying tattoos and newfound piety still startling, even after all this time—to be my shadow in the hours before I was to board the ship at dawn. I didn't like to think about how they'd managed to get a captain to agree to give me passage, or what that would mean for me on the journey ahead, so instead, I focused my ire on Curlin.

I suppose the anchorites thought I might've tried to run, despite the fortune they'd taken from me and I from the sea. I might've, too—the weight of the secret pearls in the pouch around my neck whispered to me of escape, but I knew all too well how far the temple's reach extended. How far the Suzerain could see. There was nowhere I could hide if they wanted to find me. My stash would have to go with me to Ilor.

Curlin shifted from one foot to the other in the doorway of

my bedroom, her arms crossed over her chest. The new tattoo on her knuckles was red and tender-looking. Yet despite the vast chasm that'd opened between us since she'd joined the Shriven, I could still read Curlin's face as easy as any book.

"Dzallie's eyebrows, Curlin. Come in or don't, but stop looming there like an ass. We're alone now."

Curlin made a sour face, but came in and sat on my bed. Her eyes avoided the side of the room that'd once been hers. I shoved my spare set of clothes and the few small bits and trinkets I'd collected during my childhood into an ancient bag and sat back on my heels, glaring.

"Now what?" I asked. A long day and a longer night stretched ahead of us, and I'd nothing else to occupy my time until I left to board the ship that would take me to Ilor. There was no one who'd care to hear my goodbyes, no one who'd care that I was gone. The only person in the world who'd ever given me a second thought was on the other side of the ocean.

My heart beat a little faster at the possibility of seeing Sawny again. I wouldn't hate seeing Lily, either, though I could only imagine the look on her face. She'd thought herself rid of me, after all.

Curlin's dark blue eyes searched my face. "There's still time, you know."

"Time for what?" I asked.

"Time to change your mind, idiot," Curlin snapped. "They'd still take you. It's not so bad. Better, at least, than what you're walking into. Do you really want to spend the rest of your short life hauling stones until your fingers bleed or your back breaks? You'll never make it twenty-five years. I bet you'll hardly last one."

I ran my hands through my still-damp hair, working out

the snarls and doing my damnedest to stay calm. "Do you have no recollection at all of the promise we made?"

"Of course I do, but—"

"I'd rather die than break it," I said, cutting her off. "I would rather die than turn into a monster like them. Like you."

Curlin's brows furrowed, and she set her jaw. I'd gotten under her skin. I couldn't help but dig a little deeper.

"At least in Ilor, I'll be near Sawny. Near someone whose word actually means something."

"Actually," Curlin said slyly, her voice taking on a cruel, musical edge, "you won't. They're sending you to the far side of the islands. They know the kind of trouble you two get into together. They'd never chance letting you see Sawny again. You don't deserve a reward like that after what you did."

Bile rose in my throat. There was no one in the temple who could possibly care that much about my only friendship. "Horseshit," I said. "They're sending me away to die quietly. Where I won't embarrass the Suzerain when the grief breaks me."

Curlin scoffed. "If the Suzerain knew what you'd done, that you'd stolen pearls from them, you'd be waiting for an execution block, not a ship. Count yourself lucky that the anchorites care enough to protect you. Though I'll see Hamil dry the seas before I understand why."

"Are you going to tell them?" My nails dug into my palms, suddenly wondering if Curlin had truly changed that much.

It would be the right thing for her to do. Her loyalty had been to the Suzerain since she'd taken her vows. There was a part of me that hoped some flicker of our friendship still warmed her, though. Just a little.

"I could. One more dimmy given over to the gods and

goddesses to excise in their mercy," she pondered, her voice icy and distant.

"Don't talk like that," I said, my voice a hoarse whisper. "We were friends once, Curlin, and you're a gods'–cursed dimmy, too. Remember?"

"No," Curlin said. "I'm Shriven now. Shriven of all sin. Past and present. No more rules. No more holding back. My only task is to protect the faithful. I am not cursed, but forgiven. Each time I do violence, I bask in the glory of the gods and goddesses, for I act as the arms of the Suzerain, and they are the embodiment of the gods and goddesses."

Curlin crouched in front of me, looked me in the eyes and raked her sharpened nails across my face. Pain shot through me, and even as I forced myself not to flinch away from her, the tears that'd welled in my eyes snaked down my cheeks, mixing with my blood.

"You could have been saved, Vi. But you're too stupid to save yourself."

"Get. Out," I snarled.

She smiled at me coolly. Unable to contain my fury for another moment, I spat in her face. Shock played over her features like wind over the ocean, and before I could even process what I'd done, she'd stood, lifted one booted foot and kicked me in the gut, sending me sprawling backward. Air gusted out of me. It had been a long time since someone'd caught me and given me a proper beating, but the red-hot blaze of pain was uncomfortably familiar.

She was gone, with the door slammed closed behind her, before I'd gotten my breath back.

In the gray light of the predawn, I walked the foggy streets of Penby for the last time, surrounded by the women who'd colored and shaped my childhood. Sula and Lugine flanked me on either side. Bethea walked in front, her two canes clattering on the cobblestones, and Curlin trailed behind. No one had remarked on the three slowly scabbing wounds on my cheek where Curlin'd scratched me, but I was well aware of them, especially as the icy air stung the tender skin.

I would've left Penby on my sixteenth birthday anyway, but instead of heading toward a freedom I'd chosen, clouded though it was with the threat of my own unstoppable violence, I trudged toward twenty-five years of hard, never-ending physical labor—and the inevitable loss of myself in a land impossibly different from the one where I'd grown up.

I knew a little about Ilor, but only what we'd been taught in our history lessons. After the moon split and the goddesses and gods rained their vengeance down on the world, little land was left habitable. The virtuous chosen who survived fled to the places not pocked by falling moon shards or covered in fiery rock spewing from the fragmented earth, splitting into three settlements.

Samiria, a distant, mountainous land, had closed themselves off from the world. Even now, everything we knew about them came through their ambassadors. Trade ships were forced to dock in their harbors and wait for the Samirians to come to them. There were rumors of magic, but, much like the stories of the amalgam, hardly anyone believed them. Denor's people were said to have little fear of the goddesses and gods, instead living their lives guided by the murky principles of science. And in the Alskad Empire, all gray and frozen drizzle, lived the only people brave enough or stupid enough to venture out to explore and colonize the unsettled lands decimated by the rage of our goddesses and gods.

When Alskad's explorers had harnessed the power of the

sun and built the first sunships, they set off to explore the land left empty since the cataclysm. It was in these explorations that Ilor had been discovered. Its wild jungles, high mountains and deep harbors had lured some sailors to stay, and thus, the first settlement on Ilor had been born.

The crowd on the docks hushed and parted in the presence of the anchorites. The great hulking masses of the sunships, nestled into their places along the docks, took on new meaning this morning, though I'd seen them almost every day for the past ten years. We approached the ship that would take me to Ilor, its portholes like black sores lined along its lower levels. The decks that ringed its upper third were already half-full of folks flapping their handkerchiefs at the lives they'd chosen to leave behind.

Irony of all ironies, it was the *Lucrecia*. Tears pricked my eyes at the thought of Sawny and Lily, but I fought them back. I wouldn't let Curlin see me cry.

"I don't suppose I'll see any of you again," I said. "Let my ma and pa know what you've done with me, yes? And Curlin..." I smiled sweetly at her. "I hope you rot and die."

Curlin glowered, and I could see the effort it took to keep her trap shut. She deserved it—her vindictive prying had gotten me into this mess in the first place. I'd never forgive her for that, never forgive her for becoming one of them. I was glad to be rid of her, even with the short, hellish life that was laid out before me.

Anchorite Lugine tsked at me and handed a slip of paper to the familiar uniformed woman at the end of the gangplank. I recognized her fox-collared coat and the humor crinkling the corners of her dark brown eyes. She was the same woman who'd arranged for Sawny's and Lily's passage to Ilor. She examined the paper and rifled through a box before handing me a ticket. She didn't seem to recognize me, but why would she? I'd just been one in a sea of unremarkable faces she saw every day.

Lugine pulled a parcel from the pocket of her wide skirts and pressed it into my hand. "Rayleane bless you, child."

Sula exchanged a meaningful glance with Bethea before saying, "Remember what we've taught you. Only devotion can save you from the burden of your diminishment."

I did my best to keep from rolling my eyes. These women had raised me from a babe, but they'd forget me before I'd been gone a month. My ma certainly had. Da'd come to see me from time to time, plying me with sweeties when I was little. Later, after some brat had broken my nose the first time, he'd taught me how to climb walls and find hidey-holes. He'd even taught me how to throw a punch, the idiot. Not many in Alskad were stupid enough to encourage a dimmy to violence.

I shook away the thought. I didn't want to think about Da. The man, as much as he'd tried to be kind to me, had still abandoned me to the temple. All those memories brought with them were darkness and pain. No matter how many times he'd come to see me, no matter how many times he'd told me he cared, at the end of every visit he still left me there, alone in the temple, and went back to my brothers and sisters in their warm house on the good side of the End. And not once did he hug me. Not once in all those visits had he held me close, like he did his other brats.

I was far better off without him. Without any of them.

I didn't look back as I climbed the gangplank. Not once. Not even a glance. I'd forget them as quick as they'd push me out of their heads.

See if I don't, I thought petulantly to Pru.

By the time I made my way to the railing on the third-class deck, the tugboats had begun to chug us out toward the open ocean, where the sunship's sails would unfurl. The folks around me wept and laughed and talked in nervous whispers about the lives they had to look forward to in Ilor. They talked like they'd never heard about the way folks treated their contract workers. No one mentioned the temple's demands on the folks they hired to manage contract workers like these folks, and the length those managers would go to to see those obligations fulfilled.

It was like the news hawkers on the streets of Penby never once hollered a story about rebel groups destroying crops or workers so mistreated they ran away, only to be hauled back, the terms of their contracts doubled. The world we were chugging toward wasn't any better than the one we were leaving behind, but I understood the impulse to escape. Sawny and Lily weren't the only folks who'd had trouble finding work in Penby. Outside fishing and shipbuilding, jobs were hard to come by. At least in Ilor there was a chance, albeit a vanishingly small one, for a person to make something of themselves. To change their station.

That chance existed for some people, anyway. But not for dimmys. Not for me.

I raised a hand to my brow to protect my eyes from the icy drizzle and watched the capital of the Alskad Empire disappear into the fog of the early summer morning.

Good riddance, I thought.

I took one last look across the frigid gray waves and spat into the water. Hoisting my bag over my shoulder, I elbowed my way through the folks peering over the railing as if they could still see their kin on the docks. I wanted to claim a bunk in the cabin where I'd sleep for the next two weeks. I didn't plan to do much more than sleep there, though. The ship was filled with so many things I wanted to see, so many rooms and luxuries I'd only ever imagined, and I planned to savor every moment of freedom I had left. I never thought I'd get the chance to explore a sunship, much less live on one for any length of time.

Free of the crowd, I rested my bag on an empty bench, blew on my numb fingertips and tried to get my bearings. It'd gotten colder on the deck as the ship picked up speed, even in my sweaters and scarves, and I wished that I had thicker leggings and another pair of woolen socks on under my worn knee-high boots.

Someone tapped me on the shoulder.

"Excuse me, miss." The deep voice still held the nasal vowels of the End, though softened and disguised. Anyone who got out of that poor, shabby neighborhood always tried to leave it as far behind them as they could.

I assumed my most polite expression before turning around. "Yes, sir?" I asked, gray eyes wide and innocent. That look worked on all the anchorites, even Bethea, unless she was in a particularly foul mood.

"See your ticket?"

My face masked in a feigned, sweet smile, I fished the slip of paper out of my pocket and handed it over to the bald, pinch-faced man, his chapped skin red and peeling. His eyes lingered on the scratches Curlin had left on my cheek.

He scanned my ticket and his mouth twisted in a cruel smirk. "Temple worker, are you? Miss Obedience Violette Abernathy. Cabin 687. You'll need to find E deck with the rest of the trash. Walk down there a ways, and take the staircase on the left down six flights. Follow the signs in the corridor from there." His rough words grated on my nerves.

"Thank you, sir," I said as politely as I could manage, heaving my bag over my shoulder.

"Where's your twin, girl? Ought not get separated, even on the ship. It's an easy place to get lost." There was a dangerous glint in his pale eyes.

"I'll keep that in mind, sir."

I started walking toward the staircase he'd pointed out. I knew where this conversation led.

"Where's your twin, Obedience? Mayhap you need some help finding her?" His thin screech carried over the din of the ship and the ocean beneath us.

I continued striding across the deck and fled down the stairs as soon as I reached them. I'd have to be more careful. Some people could smell dimmys from a mile away and took special pleasure in torturing us. The scratches on my face didn't make me any less conspicuous, either.

I shuddered, remembering Gil, a little towheaded boy who'd been left on the temple doorstep when he was maybe five years old. There was a note pinned to his sweater, explaining that his twin sister had died, and his parents couldn't be burdened with a dimmy. It wasn't unusual; dimmys were left on the temple steps all the time. Curlin and I used to take them under our wings a bit. Us being the dimmys who'd lived in the temple longest, we knew how to skirt the rules. Make things more comfortable.

Gil'd been practically silent during the day, but every night he'd shown up in our room, asking for a story before bed. One day, early in the spring, Gil hadn't come back from an errand. The anchorites fussed for a night or two, but after that it was like they'd forgotten him. Sawny, Curlin and I had combed the streets for days, driven by some invisible force. None of us wanted to give up on him. He was too little to fend for himself, and too sweet. I'd finally found him, shivering in an alley, covered in burns and blisters, his arms and scalp cut to ribbons.

He'd never spoken another word, and soon after, he'd tried to set the temple ablaze. The Suzerain had forced all of us temple brats to watch his execution. Curlin, Sawny, Lily and I had stood there, shivering in the first snow of the fall, our tears cutting icy paths down our cheeks, as the Shriven hauled Gil onto the platform. One of the anchorites stood behind me, hands on either side of my head, so that I wouldn't be able to look away when the Shriven hangman tightened the noose around his slim neck. That was the day we'd sworn, on our lives, that none of us would ever become one of them. We promised not to join the Shriven, and three of us kept that promise.

The people who'd targeted Gil hadn't been dimmys, just cruel folks who knew a lot more about hate than love.

I followed the signs through a maze of corridors, looking for my cabin. Turning on to the final hall, 680–690, I saw a young man with dark brown skin that glowed under the hall's sunlamps leaning against the doorjamb outside what looked to be my cabin. His shoulders were broad beneath his deep purple livery. Another of the ship's crewmen, and likely as not, this one'd hold the same prejudices as the other. I stepped quickly back around the corner, hoping he'd not spotted me.

I didn't know if I could manage to hide myself from the ship's entire crew for the whole of the journey. It didn't seem possible. I gritted my teeth and tried to push down the fear, anger and exhaustion that brought tears to my eyes. I'd hardly slept the night before, and the idea of dealing with another ignorant, aggressive idiot was almost too much.

Steady me, I thought, reaching out for Pru, and strode down the hall with every bit of confidence I could muster. The young sailor straightened when he saw me, drew his hands out of his pockets for a brief bow and watched me with clear, golden brown eyes.

"May I see your ticket, please?" he asked pleasantly. His voice was warm and carried a faint lilt I didn't recognize.

"It's already been checked," I said. "And you're blocking my way. Excuse me." I tried to shoulder past him, but the young man was all lean, hard muscle, and my head barely came to his chest.

He very gently placed his hand on my shoulder and nudged me out of the door frame, which he now fully occupied. "I'm sorry to bother you, but I'm required to check the tickets of everyone who's been assigned to this room."

A cluster of middle-aged Denorian men dressed in beautifully dyed and intricately knitted wool whispered at the end of the hall. Their broods of children swirled like storm clouds at their feet. I eyed the young man standing between me and the cramped room lined with bunks. It was empty, thank all the gods. I didn't think I could bear to have one more person witness this exchange.

The young man's amber eyes refused to leave mine, not even to linger on the scratches on my cheek, and I was grateful to him for that small kindness. Heat crept into my cheeks, and I could've kicked myself for blushing. His wide mouth seemed unable to contain its smile, and with his high cheekbones and those eyes, he was easily one of the most handsome men I'd ever seen. It was a pity he was a sailor—a good-looking fellow like him could make a fair match in the city. He looked to be about the right age for marriage, perhaps five years older than me.

I glanced at the Denorians and weighed my options. The

part of me that knew better than to cause a fuss outweighed the urge to run—though only because the young sailor had some of the longest legs I'd ever seen and would surely catch me before I made it back to the stairs.

I fished in my pocket and handed my ticket over. "See? 687. Now may I please pass?"

He studied the paper for a moment and handed it back to me. "Miss Abernathy, would you come with me, please?"

"Why? This is my room. Haven't you got to check the other tickets?"

His jaw tensed and his voice softened, like he was talking to a frightened animal. "Your cabin assignment has been changed. If you'll come with me, I'll escort you to your new room."

Alarms sounded in my head like the horns that blew each time some hovel in the End caught fire. I took a step back and my eyes flashed to either end of the hallway. This felt like a trap.

"I'm fine here. Promise," I said.

"I must insist you come with me, Miss Abernathy." He put a big hand on my shoulder, but I ducked out of his grip, thinking fast. He didn't seem threatening, but I'd learned the hard way that looks were often deceiving. I didn't trust anyone.

"I'd rather wait for my twin," I lied. "Don't want to get separated. It's a big ship, you know."

The young man leaned down close to me, careful not to touch me again, and whispered in my ear. "I know you're traveling alone, and I think it's for the best if we keep that knowledge as quiet as possible. Don't you agree?"

His breath tickled my ear, and fear roiled in my belly. I hadn't been on the ship for an hour, and two people already knew I was a dimmy. But how? I hadn't given this sailor any indication.

"There you are, girl," the deep, nasal voice of the crewman from earlier echoed down the hall. "Good thing you caught her, Whippleston. There's something squirrelly about this one."

Whippleston. His name was familiar, but I couldn't quite place it. I adjusted my bag over my shoulder to keep my hands from shaking. The young man stepped between me and the crewman and put up a hand in warning, stopping the other man's advance.

"I'll handle this, Hicks. Go about your business."

"I don't remember passenger safety being included in the duty of—what was it they were about calling you this time? A steward?" Hicks scoffed. "Why don't you let someone who actually earns his keep see to the ship's safety, yeah? You can go fluff your uncle's pillows or stir your daddy's pot, hear?"

I remembered. Whippleston was the name of the woman who'd arranged Sawny's and Lily's travel. A family business, then. Maybe this was her son.

Whippleston drew himself up, and even though the other man was nearly as tall, he cut a much more intimidating figure. "If you'd like to clarify the range of your duties versus mine with the captain, I'd be happy to have that conversation—after I've seen to the task I've been assigned. Out of our way, Hicks."

Hicks scowled at Whippleston, but stepped aside, vibrating with malice. He was clearly outranked and not at all happy about it.

Dangerous.

Whippleston strode past the other man, who glared at me. Given that my choice seemed to be to follow Whippleston or stay in the hallway with the now-seething Hicks, I fled down the hallway behind Whippleston, feeling the crewman's eyes following me like baying hounds.

We climbed three flights of stairs in silence before the young man stopped and turned to face me.

"I'm sorry. I never offered you my name. I'm Mal. Mal Whippleston. Welcome aboard the *Lucrecia*." He put a hand over his heart and bowed his head, the amused smile still playing across his wide mouth.

I stared at him for a moment, flabbergasted, before blurting, "What was his problem?"

Mal twitched his eyebrow up at me. "Hicks doesn't appreciate the fact that my brother and I outrank him, and he has a rather nasty way of showing it."

Every lesson in good manners the anchorites had tried to cram down my throat in the first fifteen years of my life was gone, sacrificed to fear and a healthy dose of self-preservation. "Where are you taking me?"

"Like I said, your cabin assignment has changed. My uncle, the captain, asked me to take you to your new lodgings. The anchorites alerted him of your, erm, status, and he thought it in everyone's best interest that you bunk alone."

How very strange, I thought, *for a man to be a captain*. I knew men worked on ships—men did all kinds of work, and it would be a bad idea for their female twins to leave them behind, given how out of sorts twins seemed to get when separated for too long—but women were usually heavily favored to become officers. We women were the ones linked to the moon and the stars, after all. Our bodies, like the tides, were controlled by the moon's twin halves. Or at least that's what we'd been taught by the anchorites. Nevertheless, there was no doubt in my mind that what I didn't know about shipboard life could fill volumes, and now was not the time to ask questions.

"But why?" I asked, still wary. "Shouldn't I be staying with all the other temple laborers?"

"I'm sure you'll be much more comfortable in your new cabin. Trust me?" He smiled at me again, all white teeth and warm golden eyes, and for a moment, I almost did.

"I don't, but you can call me Vi."

Chuckling, Mal led me out into the corridor and through the maze of halls that was the interior of the vast ship. His silence was a blessing, as my mind had set off racing. Sawny and Lily had left on this ship a month ago. Maybe Curlin had been wrong. Maybe I could find out where they were. Maybe I'd be able to get close enough to see them again.

The hallways on the upper decks were well lit by brass lamps that hung from the walls every few paces. Plush carpets quieted our footsteps, and the people we passed wore elegant, fashionable clothes. Mal made frequent shows of respect to them, and they nodded back at him, but pointedly averted their eyes from my damp, threadbare wool clothing and disheveled hair. A gaggle of anchorites, the sides of their heads freshly razored and the rest of their long hair elaborately braided and oiled under tall, fluted orange hats, swept by us in a whisper of orange silk robes and heavy perfume. We both bowed deeply as they passed.

At the end of the long hallway, Mal unlocked a door with an enormous brass key and ushered me inside. He crossed the room to fling open the shades while I stood, rooted in place, just beyond the room's threshold.

The room was nicer than anything I'd ever seen. An ornately carved four-poster bed was bolted to the floor and ceiling, covered in pillows and blankets and thick, lustrous furs. A sofa and two armchairs done in blue upholstery were clustered around a small hearth. A delicate table and three matching chairs sat next to a large window. A glass-paned door opened onto a deck that was the size of the room I'd shared with Curlin in the temple. Walls on either side of the deck enclosed it, ensuring privacy, and a pair of chairs held brightly dyed wool blankets for those brave enough to face the arctic air of the passage before we turned south.

I took it all in, miserably comparing it to the room I'd seen over Mal's shoulder. Guilt prickled up my arms. I didn't deserve this kind of luxury.

Surely, I thought, *this must be a trick of some kind. What am I missing, Pru?*

Mal, who'd been lighting the lamps, saw me gaping and grinned at me. Laughter colored his voice as he said, "Best come all the way in and shut the door."

I did as he said, but had a hard time finding the right words. I didn't want to offend him, but surely—surely!—this wasn't simple generosity. I couldn't see his play, his angle, but I knew it felt all wrong.

"You look as wary as a cat over a bathtub. Speaking of, the washroom's through that door there," he said, pointing, "and there's a tap for hot water in the tub, but don't crank it all the way. Comes out near to boiling. One of the benefits of a sunship, I suppose."

"What's the catch?" I asked.

"The catch?"

I raised an eyebrow at him. "I'm guessing you know what I am, and there's no reason I can think of that a body would put a dimmy in a room so nice as this."

Mal pressed his lips together and slumped into one of the armchairs. "Would you like to have a seat?"

"I would not."

"Will you at least put your bag down? No one is going to jump out of a closet and steal your things, I promise."

I realized I was crushing my bag to my chest, so I set it at my feet and stared at him. "It's not like I've anything worth stealing," I grumbled, knowing the only thing I owned of any value was safely in the pouch around my neck.

"My uncle wanted you to have a room to yourself in order to keep you safe," Mal explained. "A ship like this may seem big, but it isn't—and if people find out that you're a dimmy, they're going to want you off the ship, land beneath your feet or not. They'd rather throw you overboard than risk storms and sea monsters, and loudest among those that'd speak up are a gang of superstitious crewmen."

"Why would your uncle agree to give passage to a dimmy like me in the first place?" I asked nervously.

"Because the anchorites paid well, very well indeed, and my uncle worships nothing more than a bit of coin." He sounded grim and a little sad.

I perched on the edge of the sofa and narrowed my eyes at him. "So your uncle decided to risk the lives of all these people to make a few *tvilling*?"

"It's likely more to do with money owed than earned. My uncle's not always so good at remembering his tithing." Mal coughed. "And it's not much of a risk if he manages to limit the number of people who see you."

"What do you mean?"

"I mean, as deplorable as I find this whole thing—and trust me, Vi, I do—I'm going to have to lock the door when I leave."

My hands knotted into fists and rage boiled in my belly.

"I've gone sixteen years without hurting anyone. I think I can make it two more weeks."

"I'm sure you're right. You seem about as harmless as a shark," he said, eyes twinkling. "But you've been on the *Lucrecia* for less than two hours, and Hicks already has you in his sights. Imagine what'll happen if the whole ship finds out there's a dimmy onboard."

I could imagine it quite well, and I found my own concern reflected in his eyes. "You won't survive the trip," Mal said with a pained look. " It's for your own safety as much as anyone else's. Besides, the anchorites said your twin died when you were still an infant. I think if you were meant to succumb to the grief, you would've done it by now."

I gaped at him. No one, not even Sawny, had ever considered aloud the possibility that I might not turn to violence like every other dimmy.

Seeing I'd apparently lost my ability to speak, Mal went on. "My brother and I'll bring you meals and anything else you want. Do you read?"

The hidden insult snapped me back to myself, and I said, "I was temple-schooled. Of course I read."

"I don't mean to offend you," Mal said, that infuriating smile never leaving his wide, lovely mouth. "Not everyone does. I'll bring you books then, too. Novels, histories, whatever you like."

"Fine."

"Can I ask you a question?"

"You just did."

Mal snorted. "Why would the anchorites send you all the way to Ilor, and you diminished?"

My pearls felt heavy around my neck, and I thought of what Anchorite Sula had said in the kitchen. Anger had so clouded me in that moment that I hadn't seen the truth of what had happened, of what they'd given me. Tears welled in my eyes, and I fought hard to keep my voice from trembling. "They saved my life. They gave me an impossible, horrible choice, but they saved my life."

Mal cocked his head to one side, sympathy on his face. "May I ask what the choice was that they gave you?"

I swiped my eyes with the back of my hand and snapped, "No. But I'll tell you that twenty-five years hauling rocks for the temple was far and away the best option."

I didn't know why there was so much of me that wanted so desperately to confide in him. Perhaps I needed to feel heard by a real person, and not just the specter of my long-lost twin. It'd been only a month since Sawny left, but I still felt like there was a hole in the world next to me where he ought to've been. Maybe there was some idiotic part of me that hoped Mal might become something like a friend, at least for the short time we were both on this ship.

Mal let out a long, low whistle. "I'm so sorry. That can't have been easy."

"Wasn't much of a choice anyway."

A bell sounded, and Mal got up to leave. He stopped at the door. "I'm going to do everything I can to make this passage easy and comfortable for you. It's the least I can do."

I sighed. He seemed sincere, but I'd seen sincerity worn and discarded like a mask many times before. Still, it wouldn't hurt me to be polite. "Thank you, Mal."

He beamed, and his white teeth gleamed against his deep umber skin. "You're quite welcome. If there's anything you need, don't hesitate to ask. I'll do my best."

With that, he left. I waited until I heard the key turn in the lock before examining the rest of the room. I unpacked the few things I'd brought with me from the temple quickly, burying my little pouch of pearls in a drawer beneath my few extra pieces of clothing. I sat on the bed, regarding the package Lugine had given me. I didn't want to open it, didn't want to know how she'd chosen to say goodbye, but curiosity got the best of me. I untied the bit of twine, unfolded the butcher paper and opened the box.

The scent of cedar and argan hit my nose, and I lifted a tin of the healing salve the anchorites made for the Shriven out of the box. I smoothed a tiny bit of the salve onto the scratches on my cheek and stowed the tin on my nightstand, the sting of the scratches fading almost instantly.

On the bottom of the box, there was a plain, leather-bound book. At first, I assumed it was a cheaply printed copy of the holy books, the words of the gods and goddesses, but when I flipped it open, my breath caught in my throat. It was a novel taken from the temple library, the book I'd been reading when Sula sent me to serve the Suzerain. I took a deep breath and clutched the book to my chest. It was proof that they'd cared about me, these women who'd raised me. The plan I'd so carefully constructed for the rest of my life had been ripped away, but at least I was alive.

A wave of exhaustion washed over me, despite the sunlight shining through the windows of my cabin. I had no idea what the rest of my days would bring, but for now, I could at least get some more sleep.

Sinking deep into the cloud-like feather bed, warm for once beneath thick down blankets, I closed my eyes and thought of my twin. *Happy birthday, Pru.*

CHAPTER EIGHT

Bo

I worried the gold cuff on my wrist, twisting it round and round. I hadn't yet gotten used to its weight or the way it fell heavily against the joint at the base of my thumb. Birger, my tutor, was currently engaged in drawing a dining chart on the blackboard he'd wheeled into the parlor, his low voice droning like the buzzing of a well-smoked beehive. Queen Runa had decided that my engagement to Penelope ought to be announced as soon as possible, and a date only a few months away had been set. No amount of protest on my part had swayed Runa, my mother or even Penelope. It was like I was a puppy yapping at their ankles, better ignored in polite company than chased down and quieted.

In the two days since my birthday, everyone—Mother and Penelope included—had swirled into action. No one in the household had been given time to recover. We'd packed up and left the capital in favor of the country estate where I'd grown up to escape the distractions of court. I was rather relieved by this—I certainly had no desire to stay in Penby. I was furious with everyone, and I didn't think that I could keep a civil tongue in my head around Queen Runa at this point. Her duplicitous manipulations were the kind of thing that I'd expect out of Patrise and Lisette, or even Penelope, but from a woman who had dedicated her life to serving the people of the empire, these deceptions were outrageous. I knew that I ought to look past it, to assure myself that the Queen and my mother knew best. I should focus on my duties, on learning to be the kind of ruler I wanted to become.

Instead, I was consumed with thoughts of Claes.

He was inexplicably placid about the whole mess. He'd spent this morning cheerfully discussing the politics of seating charts and deciding on the arrangement of the high table at my engagement party, despite the outrageous fact that my engagement was to his twin sister and not to *him*, the person I'd been kissing for the past year. Loving, even.

"How does none of this bother you?" I asked him, whispering to keep Birger from hearing. It felt like the thousandth time I'd voiced the question in the last two days.

Claes smiled lazily at me and slung his black hair out of his eyes. It didn't matter how I approached the question; Claes managed to slip away from it every time without so much as grazing the topic.

"Your Royal Highness, do you have a question?" Birger snapped. "I know you're still excited from your birthday, but I should think that I need not once again explain the importance of the arrangements for this party. Your engagement, more even than the announcement of your ascension to the throne, will be the singular event that solidifies your reputation in the eyes of the nobility."

I drew in a breath, still unused to my new title, and said, "No, sir. I understand, sir. My apologies."

Birger raised a bushy eyebrow, but continued his stentorian lecture on the politics of seating charts. I glared at Claes. He picked at his nails and pretended not to notice me.

When Karyta, the butler, ducked in to announce the noon meal, Claes leapt out of his chair, grabbed my hand and dragged me from the room, giving Birger only the briefest of courtesies. The door closed behind us before Birger could assign extra lessons for the afternoon. We sprinted halfway to the dining room before slowing to a walk. Claes grinned, and his dark brown eyes crinkled above his cheekbones like twin crescent moons.

"Let's go for a ride this afternoon. Maybe we can filch a couple of rifles and bring home some game for tomorrow's supper. How does that strike you?"

I clenched my jaw and scowled at Claes. My burning need to confront him about my mother's plan to marry me to his sister threatened to erupt at any moment. He *had* to have an opinion. There was no way that he was simply fine with the idea of my marriage to his sister.

"Are you really going to ignore this?" I snapped.

"Ignore what?" He paused by an end table and idly hefted a gold paperweight.

"Ignore the fact that we're planning my engagement to your sister!"

"What about it?"

I wanted to throttle him. How he could be so easygoing, so cavalier, was entirely beyond me. "Are you playing dull on purpose, or do you not care that I'm meant to marry Penelope?"

Claes tossed the paperweight back onto the table and closed

the distance between us. He ran a hand through my hair and kissed me on the cheek. "Don't be cranky with me, Bo."

I shrugged out of his embrace and pushed his hand away. "I'm not cranky. Don't try to make me sound like a petulant child. I'm a grown man."

He pursed his lips and looked out the window.

"How long have you known?" I asked, heart pounding in my chest. I almost didn't want him to answer, but I had to know. Had to know if everything I thought we had was a lie.

"Honestly, I don't understand how you didn't see this coming. It's the right thing to do, strategically. It strengthens your power base among the nobles. Everyone knows Penelope is brilliant. Everyone respects her. There isn't a bit of tarnish on her reputation anymore." He stilled for a moment, and I knew he was thinking of his father, far away in Ilor, out of the public eye, but then his face masked into a smile. "You'll have a strong business partner who can, with any luck, bear you a singleborn child." He giggled. "Do you find her attractive? I don't think I've ever asked if you like girls, too."

"I… But… I don't know. No," I sputtered, my mind racing. He was the only person I liked. The only person I found attractive. The only person I trusted. I corrected myself—had trusted. The fact that he'd known about this mess, had been part of its plan all along, made me regret every secret I'd ever shared with him.

"I didn't think so. I do." Claes smiled, and something deep in my chest cracked as I realized that the relationship I'd imagined between myself and Claes had little to do with the reality in which he and I lived. "Penelope likes power," he continued. "I don't think she's attracted to anything else. She'll make a wonderful consort."

"But what about us?" I snapped, asking the question almost out of spite.

"What about us? Nothing has to change. Penelope knows what we are, and honestly, it wasn't as though this romance was built to last a lifetime. You're sixteen. I'm not yet eighteen. Can you imagine how much we'll change in the next five, the next ten years?"

My throat constricted. I willed myself not to cry. He may not have thought we were meant for a lifetime together, but I'd imagined a life with him beside me often enough for it to feel very real.

He went on, chipping further and further away at the dreams I'd had for us. "We're young. We'll drift apart. I'll marry, or I won't. You'll have affairs. Penelope will have power and renown, and that's all she cares about. She's perfectly happy with this arrangement." Claes wrapped his arms around my waist and smiled into my eyes.

His nonchalant smile was the last hammer tap that sent my heart shattering. While I had been busy falling in love and dreaming of a future with Claes, he'd been engaged in a meaningless dalliance. He hadn't reacted to the news that I was to marry his sister because he didn't care. The only things that mattered to Claes were power and pleasure, and with his twin married to the King, he would have plenty of both.

I couldn't believe that I hadn't seen it before. All the lies and half-truths and wiggly excuses that I'd forgiven because I'd believed that we were in love. I'd believed that Claes wanted the same things I did. Wanted a life with me.

A cloud of flowery scent surrounded me, and something sharp poked me in the ribs. The telltale heat of a deep blush rushed into my cheeks. I stepped back out of Claes's arms and turned to face Penelope. Taking a deep breath, I silently cursed my blushes. Every minor embarrassment, irritation or pleasure was always painted plain on my face.

She was older than Claes by just three minutes and shared his features, though they were soft and feminine on her. The twins had the same thick black hair and fawn complexions; the same angular brown eyes, small noses, high cheekbones and full mouths. They were two sides of the same coin, but where I found Claes achingly attractive, those features didn't hold the same draw on Penelope.

Penelope winked mischievously at her brother and put her hands on her hips. "Your ears are as pink as seashells, my dear. Has Claes been telling you raunchy stories from one of his novels again? I'd hate for him to ruin your innocence before our wedding night."

I forced my face to impassive stillness as Claes chuckled and clutched his hands over his heart, wearing an exaggerated look of shock. "Your accusations cut me to the core, dear sister."

I looked from Penelope to Claes and back again and threw up my hands in frustration. "How is it that you are both content with this? How can such a political *arrangement*—" I spat out the word like a bitter seed "—not bother you?"

Penelope arched an eyebrow at me and said, "Don't be so melodramatic, Bo. Why do you think we stayed when our parents immigrated? This has been decided for as long as we've all been alive."

"Could we please move on?" Claes asked. "I'm bored of going 'round and 'round in circles. What's more, I'm starving."

Penelope wove her arm through her twin's and led the way into the dining room, leaving me spluttering and furious in the hall.

★ ★ ★

Mother, austere and imperious in a crisp navy shirt, high-waisted trousers and fur stole, swept into the room as I took my seat. She motioned for Claes and me to remain seated and continued to dictate instructions to her secretary, a mousy, obsequious woman who skittered in Mother's wake, scribbling notes. After several minutes, she finally waved the woman away and turned to me.

"Ambrose, darling, I hope you haven't planned another of your elaborate luncheons today," she said, settling into her chair at the head of the table. "I've gotten word that there are some issues that must be settled at the mill this afternoon."

I clenched my teeth. I had never been able to predict the tides of my mother's desires. When I planned sumptuous meals, I was berated for my extravagance, but if the meals I chose were simple, they weren't considered appropriate for entertaining guests—not even Penelope and Claes, who'd lived with us for years.

"Just four light courses today." Her lips began to purse, and I quickly added, "But that includes dessert."

"Hold it until tomorrow."

I waved for Karyta to begin the luncheon service. She would make sure the kitchen knew to keep back dessert. Servants flowed around the table pouring water, iced tea and wine. In unison, they set the first course in front of us. Gunnar, my valet, leaned over me and tasted everything in front of me. I forced myself not to roll my eyes. I'd practically made the soup myself the night before.

After a nod from Gunnar, Karyta introduced the meal. "A creamed soup of the first summer snow peas, with fried sage leaves and bacon."

I watched carefully as Mother took her first bite. Since I

had taken over the menu approval in the household, food had become something of a hobby of mine. The soup was a new variation on an old favorite of hers, made with herbs picked the day before and cream from our own cows. I'd asked Jasper, the cook, to add a single dragon fire pepper—a variety I'd acquired from a rare seed dealer and grown in the estate's greenhouse—to the large pot of soup. Mother closed her eyes and sighed. Pleased, I spooned a bite of the soup into my own mouth. The familiar creamy sweetness of the peas played well with the smoky bacon and crispy sage. I swallowed, and a mellow but notable heat filled my mouth. Perfect.

I looked up to find Mother's hawkish glare fixed on me. I glanced around the long table. Claes and Penelope, eyes fixed on one another, spooned up their soup with placid expressions on their faces but pointedly did not meet my gaze.

"Ambrose, darling," Mother said, her voice far too sweet.

"Yes, Mother?"

"What, in the names of all of the goddesses, have you done to this soup?"

I nearly batted my eyelashes and asked what she meant, but the vapid posturing that worked so well with my tutor only made Mother angry. Instead, I bowed my head to hide my smile. "I do apologize, Mother. I only thought to improve upon an already exemplary recipe. Do you find it disagreeable?"

"You know how I feel about overly spiced food. Your father would be disappointed in your inattention and neglect of the tastes of the people at your table." Mother placed her spoon back in her soup plate and waved Karyta over. "Bring me some of whatever the servants are having, please."

Karyta's usually implacable expression twitched. "It's cabbage and potato, but Jasper's added a heap of the same peppers to the broth. It's enough to make a body perspire, ma'am. Begging your pardon."

Mother's eyes flashed at me, and she said, "Fine. I'll simply have a lighter luncheon. I trust you haven't similarly contaminated the remainder of the courses with your culinary experimentation?"

Karyta whisked away the soup plate and glowered at me over Mother's head. I would feel the harsh side of her tongue later, no doubt, but she wouldn't chastise me in front of my mother. Jasper, the head chef, was her twin, and the two of them had practically raised me, along with Gunnar. The three of them had always treated me like I was their own child. Normal. They'd never allowed me to self-aggrandize, and I loved them for it.

In a calm voice, I said, "No, ma'am. There will be a vegetable terrine, followed by roasted pheasant, and I'd planned a meringue and fruit for dessert."

"That will do. Serve the dessert, if you please, Karyta. I apologize for the confusion my son has caused."

I returned to my soup, which I quite enjoyed, triumphant. Something about irritating my mother, who'd so upended my life recently, was delightful.

As the servants cleared the first course, Mother said, "Queen Runa wants you married within the next two years, and I think if we select a date for the summer after this, that should provide a sufficiently long engagement. It will give you both an excuse to spend time in the capital between now and then, cultivating your relationships with the merchants and the nobility."

"Do you think that will be enough time to plan the wedding?" Claes asked. "Given the circumstances, shouldn't it be rather ostentatious?"

Penelope laughed, sharing a meaningful look with my
mother. "It's a wedding. How much work could it possibly
be to plan? A ceremony and a few days of feasting. Done."

Claes rolled his eyes. "You don't know anything about
what it takes to move through high society, do you? A wedding like this will take ages to plan. It's got to be damned
near perfect. Bo and I'll handle everything."

"We will?" I asked in a choked voice.

"Don't be petulant, Ambrose," Mother said. "Now, enough
about the wedding. We haven't even had the engagement
party yet." She turned to Penelope. "Would you care to ride
with me to the mill this afternoon, dear? I've gotten word that
there is an issue with the foreman and a manager that must
be resolved immediately. It will be yours soon, and you've a
lot to learn before you're prepared to take over the running
of the estates. No time like the present to begin."

For the rest of the meal, Penelope spoke with Mother about
the various businesses we held, and I counted the minutes
until I could excuse myself and get to the barn. They spoke
about a perfumery—obviously, a sort of code for something
else, as Penelope chose her words altogether too carefully, but
I let my mind wander rather than focusing on their conversation. I kept thinking about the person Mother had asked
about after I was named heir. It wasn't as though her keeping secrets from me was unusual, but she was almost never
so open about it.

I watched the clock on the wall, willing the seconds to
pass more quickly. Nothing could bother me when I was on
a horse.

After lunch, Claes followed me down the rocky, heather-
covered hill to the stables. He had to know I was annoyed

with him; I hadn't said a word since we left the dining room, and he'd spent the whole time trying to make me laugh. Carrying the two long fowling pieces he'd snatched from the safe by the door, he mimicked my mother in a high, proper accent, "Your father would be gravely disappointed."

I glared at him. "She did not say gravely. She would never have made a pun about Father. She isn't that horrid."

"She's right, though, in a way."

"What do you mean?" I stopped walking, and Claes turned to face me.

"You've been testing your mother's patience these last couple of days. If I didn't know better, I'd say you were acting like an amalgam, two-faced and fearsome, not the blood-of-the-empire singleborn you are. What's gotten into you?"

"We aren't children anymore. There's no such thing as amalgams, and you know it. Anyway, I've no idea what you're talking about."

"You've been cross since you learned about the engagement. I don't understand, Bo. It makes perfect sense. Once you marry Penelope, you'll be the richest singleborn in the whole of the Alskad Empire, and the crown prince besides. Before you know it, you'll have every noblewoman and man in the empire slavering at your feet, begging for favors."

I bit my lip, blushing. I knew I had to get used to the idea of all that attention focused on me, but it didn't come naturally. Not like it did to the other singleborn. I'd never felt like I could live up to the expectations of the people around me, much less those of an entire nation.

I reached for something to say. Anything. "It is incredibly rude to discuss the intimacies of my finances, Claes."

"Gadrian's hammer, Bo. Why wouldn't I talk about your finances? When you and Penelope are married, they'll be my finances, too. All we want is to see you become the best King you're able to be. Why does that make you so uncomfortable?"

I knelt to tighten my bootlaces. I didn't want him to see me blush again. When I stood, Claes took me by the hand and led me into the leaf-draped privacy of an ancient willow tree. He leaned our guns against the gnarled trunk and took my face in his cold hands. "You don't need to be frightened of the succession. You're singleborn. You were born to rule."

He pressed his lips to mine, and I did my best to relax into his kiss, but I couldn't. I saw Claes in a different light now. It was one thing for him to resign himself to the fact that a political match between his sister and me made sense. It was another thing entirely that he'd pursued me, that he'd *romanced* me, knowing that I would someday be asked to marry his twin. Worse than that, though, was the thought that he might've been responsible for what happened in Esser Park. That kind of recklessness was terrifying—innocent lives could have been lost in a rash bout of political scheming.

The overwhelming weight of his lies battered against my love for him, chipping away chunks and shards, and left me with nothing. Worse than nothing. I was incomplete, like I'd forever misplaced a piece of myself.

I stepped back, cold with the knowledge that I would have to guard my tongue around Claes from now on, would have to keep my own secrets. So I simply said, "The Queen is healthy yet. It'll be a long time before I sit on the throne."

"Perhaps you're right, but we'll have you ready either way. Now, then, are we sorted?"

I nodded, and Claes patted my cheek before retrieving our rifles and holding the branches of the willow aside to let me pass. "Let's go. I've a craving for goose, and I had the juiciest letter from the capital yesterday. I simply cannot be asked to keep this much delightful gossip to myself."

We were close to home—dirty, drenched in sweat, with geese slung like grim saddlebags over our horses' backs—when Claes toppled off his horse and landed in a clutch of bracken. I thought for a moment that his mare must have spooked, but rather than galloping toward home, she stopped and nuzzled him, clearly puzzled herself.

"Claes? Are you all right?"

His back arched, and a low wail came from somewhere deep inside his chest. He screamed and tore at the grass, his howls reverberating through my body. His horse jigged away from his thrashing form, eyes rolling back in her head. Terrified, I kicked my feet out of the stirrups, but before I could dismount, Claes had collapsed, heaving, into the mud. I slid down from my horse, unsure what else I ought to do.

Claes beat his fists into the muddy ground. He tore at his hair, his clothes. He was wild, ferocious. When he finally turned to look at me, there were tears streaming from his eyes. Slowly, hesitantly, I approached and knelt down beside him. The cold gray Alskad sky had spit rain all day, and the damp seeped through the knees of my trousers. I shivered and took Claes's hand in mine. He was clammy, as though with fever, when only a moment before, he'd been hale and joking.

"Something's happened," he said, jerking his hand out of mine. "Hamil save me, I have been so faithful. Please, Hamil, by your oceans, make it false."

"What is it? Claes, you're scaring me." I touched his cheek, but he shrank away from me.

"Don't touch me." His voice was choked, hollow. "Something's happened to Penelope."

"What do you mean?" My anxious mind whirred with awful possibilities, like a cloud of screaming beetles flying through my thoughts. All my irritation and mistrust melted away as I watched him, fear gripping me. I reached for him again, but he pushed my hand away.

"For the love of all the gods. She's gone. I can't feel her anymore."

"That doesn't make any sense. She's at the mill with Mother. Why would you be able to feel her at all?" My voice trembled and threatened to crack—something it hadn't done in ages. I wanted so badly to hold him, to kiss him, to do *something* to make whatever this was right.

"She's my twin, Bo. I can always feel her. She's there, like a weight—" a sob, like a songbird dropping from the sky, stopped him mid-thought "—in my head. She's there all the time. She *was* there. Now, she's just gone."

His face flooded with another wash of tears, and he curled around his wet, muddy legs. Our horses, no longer perturbed by Claes's low moans, grazed peacefully in the light of the dying sun. I pulled his head onto my lap and stroked his hair. We sat there for hours, and even as Claes wept, I tried to make myself believe that nothing had happened, that nothing was wrong. But I knew, deep in my bones, that everything had changed.

When the sun sank below the horizon, I pulled Claes to his feet, got him onto his mare and took the reins from him once I'd mounted. I led him back to the barn, and in the soft glow of the solar lamps, I could see that the servants already knew something was amiss.

The stable hands supported Claes up the hill toward the house. I trudged behind them, dreading what I would find inside.

★ ★ ★

Karyta ushered me into the sitting room as soon as my boots clacked onto the hardwood in the wide entrance hall. Birger and his twin, Thamina, were seated side by side on a sofa next to the fire. Thamina's dress, a too-small indigo thing that was three years out of fashion, clashed with the saffron upholstery and wallpaper in the room and turned her long face sallow. Each of the twins clutched a tumbler of clear liquid—ouzel, if I had to guess.

I cleared my throat. When Thamina's eyes met mine, tears rushed down her cheeks, as if at a signal. I'd never seen her cry, and I didn't quite trust it. Birger motioned to an armchair, and I sat, fists clenched on my knees.

"What happened to Penelope? Where's Mother?" I asked.

Birger refused to meet my eyes, and Thamina sipped from her glass, grimacing.

"Tell me. Will she recover? I know something's wrong. Claes collapsed on our ride."

"You tell him," Thamina commanded. "Get him a drink first."

Something inside me went cold as I watched Birger and Thamina, still as stone. A servant appeared and pressed a glass into my hand. I thanked him automatically and took a sip, realizing as soon as the liquid was in my mouth that no one had tasted it for me. I swallowed it anyway, careless, and my throat burned as the ouzel slid into my belly.

Birger's lips compressed, and he said, "I'm so sorry to be the one to tell you this, but there's been an accident." He laced his fingers through Thamina's and kept his eyes trained on the flames in the hearth. "Your mother and Penelope were killed at the mill today. One of the turpentine stills exploded, and the building caught fire. There was nothing to be done. I'm so sorry, Lord Ambrose."

I watched numbly as the glass fell from my fingers. It took a curiously long time to land, as though time had ceased moving forward at its usual pace. As it rolled across the carpet, the spilled liquid seeped into the pattern, darkening it from burgundy to black.

CHAPTER NINE

Vi

I forced myself to stop pacing and stared out the window at the endless waves. The temple's maps had shown me that the sea between the Alskad Empire and the Ilor colonies was enormous, but the reality of water as far as the eye could see made me itch, and we'd only been sailing for three days. Being locked away in my cabin didn't help one bit. I was so close to things I'd never dreamt I'd get to see, and yet still impossibly distant from them—there was a heated swimming pool on this ship, a room designed for dancing and innumerable gambling halls, all done in different themes. The ship was filled with the kinds of entertainments that only the stupidly wealthy could manage to contrive, and while I might not've been allowed in those rooms, I could've peeked through the doors. I could have at least *seen* them.

Beyond those extravagances, though, I wanted to climb the masts and see how hot the solar panels on the sunsails got at midday. I wanted to see the enormous pantry full of enough food to supply so many people for the voyage. I wanted to peek into the hold and see all of the luggage and trade goods destined to make these people a bit more comfortable as they started new lives in Ilor.

I wanted to do anything but let myself obsess about my own uncertain future. A deep, heavy sadness had settled over me like a dark blanket I couldn't shake. It was worse than the grief that possessed me in the depths of winter; worse than anything I'd felt before. Without a goal to work toward, without something driving me, I had nothing to live for. I couldn't stop thinking about Sawny, and the life he was building in a place he'd not yet been in long enough to call home. I hoped the pearls I'd given him had helped. Even a little.

Sighing, I picked up one of the books Mal'd brought for me and took it out to the private deck. If I was stuck inside the confines of the small cabin, I could at least have some fresh air. Really, it wasn't as though I *couldn't* leave my rooms—I'd long since planned a handful of escapes. Over the rail and between the private decks, down to the decks below or—if there was time—picking the locks and simply walking through the door. Just in case. It was simple good sense to know a couple of ways out of any room, especially a room meant to keep a person locked away.

But Mal had gone out of his way to be kind to me. I didn't want to give him a reason to distrust me, so I stayed. Not because I was locked in, but because Mal was right, and keeping the danger on the other side of that locked door was the smartest thing I could do for myself.

The air was still brisk, but warmer than when we'd left. Despite my presence onboard, our luck had held, and the weather had been fair. I wondered what it would be like to

feel the island heat of the Ilor colonies every day, instead of
the constant chill of Alskad.

The horizon was empty as far as I could see, and the blue
of the sky blurred into the sea's shining waves. It was almost
as if, alone in my room, I was the only being in an oceanic
world. I set the book aside and went to the small deck's railing. Mal had said we'd be turning southward today, into a
warm current that would carry us to Ilor. Soon, he'd said,
I would be able to see beasts swimming alongside the ship.
The kind of great, fierce creatures I'd read about in the temple's library, staring in awe at the drawings of beasts with
horns growing from their heads and creatures that thirsted
for the blood of sailors. In the old days, when we sent raiders
to Denor and Samiria in wooden ships—before we'd dared
to explore as far as Ilor—the beasts would overturn ships to
feast on the crews, leaving nothing but wee scraps of wood
floating on the waves.

I leaned over the rail, searching the sea for dark shadows
and beasties. I'd spent my whole life in the ocean, but the
harbor was a nursery compared to these waters. In the depths
beneath this ship, there were worlds I would never see, creatures that I couldn't even imagine. Even if I could hold my
breath for an hour, I'd never make it to the dark ocean floor
beneath us. No one would ever see the mountains and gullies
and coral cities down there, preserved beneath those waves
like precious jewels on blue velvet, caged in water.

I'd seen the jewels of the Alskad Empire displayed like
that once. Sawny'd heard they were to be pulled through the
streets of the wealthy neighborhoods in the capital to celebrate Her Majesty's thirtieth anniversary as the ruling monarch, so we'd found Curlin and dashed off to see them after
my morning's dive. Some in the crowd whispered that they

were replicas, but the glittering sapphires and diamonds and the rich, creamy gleam of the metal in which they'd been set had more than convinced me.

Sawny. He would have loved to be trapped in a room this luxurious. He'd have reveled in it, pretending to be some sort of fur-draped aristocrat.

A spout of water erupted from beneath me, and I caught sight of a pod of whales, something I'd only ever read about in books. I leaned so far over the railing that the wind caught in my loose curls, whipping them around my face. They didn't look ferocious at all. They were beautiful, playful, and their antics brought laughter bubbling into my throat. Seeing them weave through the waves elicited the first real joy I'd felt in what seemed like years.

Catching sight of a baby whale, I leaned even farther, straining to see more. Suddenly, strong arms closed around my waist, and I was hauled off my feet. In a moment, I was back in my room, having hardly had time to blink. As soon as the arms let go of me, I whirled around snarling, and found myself face-to-chest with a man who could only be Mal's twin, Quill. Fury curled through me, and I glared.

"What the bloody hell do you think you're doing?" I spat.

Quill laid a broad palm over his heart and looked at me askance, a startled smile crinkling the corners of his eyes. "Me?" he asked, and the laughter in his voice set my nerves ablaze. "What am I doing? I just saved your life. What the bloody hell are you doing, leaning over the rail, fit to leap?"

"I saw a pod of whales! I'd never imagined I'd see such a thing in all my life. I was in no danger, thank you very much."

My cheeks felt hot, and fire danced along the half-healed scratches Curlin had laid into my cheek. I was startled to realize how it must have looked—like I was thinking about jumping—but that'd been the farthest thing from my mind. I'd only wanted to revel in that one gleeful moment and watch those enormous, graceful beasts play in the waves.

Quill'd never come to my room before, but Mal had mentioned that he would bring some of my meals when Mal couldn't get away. Mal and his brother had the same golden eyes and wide mouth, though Quill's hair was twisted in long locks and tied back from his face. I wondered if their personalities were as alike as their faces. My interactions with Mal had been so straightforward, honest to a knife's edge. He was as earnest as a person could be, but he had the easy laugh of a person who'd spent his whole life well loved. But as I glared at Quill, I realized that his smile held something more, a kind of mischief I hadn't seen in his brother.

"Mal's gone on and on about how civilized you are, especially for a dimmy, but I see the truth," he teased. "You're quite the nuisance, aren't you?" He closed the glass door that led to the deck and pulled out a chair at the little table, gesturing ostentatiously for me to sit.

"A nuisance?" I sputtered. "I didn't ask for any of this! I'd've been just fine in a cabin with the other temple laborers." I yanked out the chair opposite the one Quill held for me and sat, trying to slow my pounding heart. "You didn't need to pull me off that railing, either. I wasn't in any danger. I'm probably a better swimmer than you by half."

I didn't know why I was still talking. Quill made me nervous. Under my breath, I muttered, "Son of a goat."

He quirked an eyebrow at me and went to the liquor cabinet, still smiling. "I think my father would be insulted that you called him a goat."

"Your father?" I asked. "Why would he care what some worthless dimmy thinks?"

"Jeb Whippleston's our da. He's the one who's been providing this grub for you, and he'd be right hurt to know how
ungrateful you are. Though I imagine he'd be more concerned that you think yourself worthless."

I bit my lip. *Magritte's tongue, Pru*, I thought. *Send me guidance. I've no idea how to read this one.*

"I need a drink," he said, opening the cabinet door. "What's
your poison? Wine, ouzel, cider?"

"Isn't it a bad idea to drink when you're on duty?" I asked,
eyeing Quill's neatly ironed uniform. I wanted him out of my
room. His easy confidence—the way he'd so quickly made
himself at home with me, in this room—made me antsy, and
I couldn't stop blushing.

"I'm done with my shift as soon as you're fed, and frankly,
I think saving someone's life deserves a bit of celebration,
even if you won't earn me a single *twilling*. Wine then, yes?"
He pulled a bottle out, examined the label, then replaced it
and took another. Seemingly satisfied, he plucked two crystal
goblets and a corkscrew from one of the shelves and closed
the cabinet. Seeing my expression, he laughed. "Best close
up that flytrap, Vi. You look as dull as a porgy fish, and not
even the kindest of the temple's farm managers'll be inclined
to do you any favors if they think you'll let them pull one
over on you."

I blinked at him, struck by an idea. "How much do you
know about them? About the temple's farm managers, I
mean."

Quill shrugged. "My ma runs an import and export business that Mal and I've been helping with for some years now.
She sends a lot of contract laborers from Alskad to Ilor and
works fair closely with the temple. I'd say I've met most everyone who hires contract labor in Ilor, temple included. Why?"

"I wish I knew a bit more what to expect. This wasn't exactly my choice, you know."

Quill studied me, his mouth compressed into a thin line. "You're not alone in that. It doesn't happen often, but we've taken more than a handful of folks to Ilor to serve long sentences laboring for the temple. No matter what they might've done, it's not a mercy. I can tell you that much."

I stared down at my hands, knotted together on the polished wood tabletop. "Does anyone…" I hesitated. I didn't know what it was that made me want to trust Quill—Pru's guidance, or gut instinct—but either way, I forged ahead, reckless. "Does anyone ever manage to find their way out of serving that sentence?"

Quill's expression turned uneasy. "What do you mean?"

I shrugged, doing my best to look noncommittal, but my heart was pounding in my chest like waves against a seawall. "I mean, do you think it would be possible for me to take another contract, rather than going to work for the temple? I'm no one, a dimmy. The temple's got no reason to look for me or care now that I'm away from Alskad. Do you think someone would take a dimmy's contract?"

He studied me thoughtfully. "It'd be a risk, defying the temple that way."

"How would they ever find out?" I asked. "The anchorites' orders are here on the ship. If they just…got a bit lost…" I gave Quill my most winning smile.

He grinned back at me. "You're even more trouble than I suspected." Quill popped the cork out of the bottle and sniffed it appreciatively. "There's something to be said for the idea, though. It might surprise you, but there's a bit of a market for oddities in Ilor. Our percentage on a contract for one of the

diminished would be more than we'd make on all the laborers on this ship right now."

My mouth fell open. "Gadrian's fiery breath. Why?"

He handed me a glass of ruby liquid and shrugged. "Some
folks have more money than sense." He grimaced. "No offense intended. It's the fashion now, see, for folks in Ilor to
use their wealth to show their rich friends how brave they
are. The Ilor colonies are new, you know that. Almost none
of the empire's nobility have immigrated, but more than a
few wealthy merchants have, and they've used the resources
in Ilor to create vast fortunes. But those rich folks don't have
any system in place to decide who's the most important the
way the nobility does. So it's become fashionable to collect,
well, oddities, to show the others how brave and interesting
they are. Some collect dangerous animals, like long-toothed
cats, wild dogs and bears, but others—"

I finished for him. "Collect people. Dimmys." An idea
began to crystalize in my brain.

"No one's been able to yet, though I know more than a
few who'd pay a fortune for the privilege. There aren't exactly scads of dimmys on the docks advertising themselves for
hire. Some recruit Denorian poisoners to tell stories at their
dinners—others bring in Samirian chefs to slice up puffer-
fish for their guests to taste, even though it kills one in every
hundred or so folks that eat it. I even know a man who's gone
and married an amalgam. I've heard people call him brave,
but I think stupid's probably a better fit."

The word amalgam struck me like a bolt of lightning. I'd
never believed the stories about the amalgam were true, but I
found myself wondering—briefly—if maybe I'd been wrong
all along.

"You can't hornswoggle me!" I said. "Everyone knows there's no such thing as an amalgam."

"Sure there are!" Quill protested, laughing. "Vicious creatures, too. I've heard they can do magic. People say their eyes are two different colors, and that they have the power to force anyone to do whatever they want."

"I suppose I'll be sure not to look any of them right in the eye then," I said wryly. My tone more serious, I asked, "But, Quill...would you consider it? Helping me?" I looked down, nervous. "The only thing I've ever wanted was control over my own life. And, like you said, you stand to make quite a profit."

Quill raised his glass to me. "To profit and freedom, then. Let's hope Mal can be convinced."

I smiled at him, daring, for the first time in a long time, to hope.

"Take a sip. That's a carmenere from northern Denor. My da sure does know a good bottle when he sees it. I'm surprised you haven't done more damage to that cabinet."

I sniffed the wine experimentally. It smelled tart, and the alcoholic fumes burned my nose. "Never saw the point of drinking piss to wind up acting a fool and clutching my head come morning."

Quill laughed, a deep belly laugh, and swirled the wine in his glass with expert grace. He sipped and sighed contentedly. "The worst thing my da ever did was give me a taste for good wine. Go on. Try it. It tastes like cherries and chocolate and spice."

I took a cautious sip, and the flavors exploded in my mouth. I tasted cherries and spices, as he'd said, but no chocolate. "Won't your father be angry that we're drinking this?"

"No, not at all. What's in this room is his private stock.

He's got a soft heart, my da—thought that if we were going to keep a person locked in these rooms for the whole passage, they should at least have something nice to drink. He always says that good wine's meant to be drunk and shared."

There was a brief tap on the door, and Quill rose. He produced the long brass key that was now familiar to me, slid it into the lock and unlocked the door. The shipboard locks were the old-fashioned kind that required a key to lock and unlock the door from either side. Easy to pick, if you had the right tools. Mal entered, carrying a tray that held three plates covered with silver domes. He smiled at me, and I wondered if he could be convinced to go along with my idea as easily as his brother had been.

Quill said, "About time. I'm starved. I'm glad you insisted I come. Vi is a delight."

"Nice to see you, Mal," I said, cool as I could manage with so much of my future hanging on the line. "I've just been getting to know your brother."

Quill's eyebrows shot up. "There are the manners I've heard so much about. I half thought Mal was lying to me!"

"Nice to see you, too," Mal said to me, shooting an exasperated look at his brother. "Allow me to apologize for Quill. He does mean well, but his own manners are atrocious. May I set this on the table?"

I nodded and moved the bottle of wine to make room.

"I see you've already opened the wine, and no idea what our supper will be, eh, brother?" Mal turned to me. "That is, if you don't mind us having our supper with you. I thought you might like the company."

I glanced at Quill and felt that inevitable blush curling up my cheeks again. "Of course not. I'd love it."

Quill grinned. "I'd put heavy odds on stewed goat and rice.

I heard Da cursing about one of the nannies having gone dry. I've opened a carmenere."

Mal whipped the covers off two of the plates, and fragrant steam filled my nose. My mouth watered. Flaky golden pastry encircled a thick slice of pink meat. There were root vegetables, gleaming like gems in their glaze, and next to them, a swirl of white fluff that promised to be potato or turnip.

Quill gasped and let out a low whistle. "Are you being fed like this every day?"

"It's the best food I've ever had," I said, tucking my feet up under me. "Though if I keep eating this way, I'll burst my seams and have to go about in a robe all the time, like some kind of gadabout noblewoman."

The twins exchanged a look and burst into gales of laughter. Mal went to the cabinet and retrieved a glass. When he was settled in the empty chair, Quill poured more wine, distributed plates and discarded the tray.

"We should have been volunteering to take meals with you all along. Da never feeds us this well. This is first-class food," Quill said.

Mal grinned wolfishly at his twin. "She's not half so ferocious as you thought, eh?"

Quill's face darkened. "Not to you maybe, but she's no innocent lamb. She was trying to hop the railing when I came in. Girl has a taste for the ocean."

I put my fork down with rather more force than was necessary. "I certainly was not. I saw a pod of whales. I bloody told you that."

Mal scrutinized me, and exchanged another of those infuriatingly meaningful looks with Quill. It seemed that these two were another pair that could nearly read each other's

minds. I wondered if my twin and I would have been so ob-
noxious if she'd lived.

"I wasn't!" I insisted. "I only wanted to see if I could catch
another glimpse of the baby."

The twins snorted, and I forced myself to breathe. If I
pretended that I'd known them as long as I'd known Sawny
and treated them like they were old friends, perhaps they'd
begin to see me that way. But as we ate, I found myself relax-
ing more and more in Mal and Quill's company—they were
so easy to be with. Where Mal approached every sentence,
every gesture with earnest thought and consideration, Quill
was sharp-witted and vocal about his deeply seated opinions.
Though they were identical twins, they were so very clearly
their own men that I would've been able to tell them apart
after a single sentence, even if not for their different hairstyles.

After supper, Quill produced a deck of cards and suggested
that we play a hand of brag. I forced my expression to impassive. Sawny, Lily, Curlin and I had learned brag when we
were bitty little things, and it hadn't taken long for one of the
older temple wards to teach us how to cheat well enough to
take a good bit of money off unsuspecting folks in the End
who'd had a few too many. The trick was, we'd learned, to
make them believe you were just learning the game.

"I've nothing to stake on a game. You could sell everything
I packed, and you wouldn't get more than a few measly coins.
Not even enough to buy your sweetheart a poesy," I said, and
paused, doing my best to contain the smile that so often accompanied my lies. "Plus, I don't know brag."

"That's fine. We can teach you. And Mal will lend you a
few *twilling* to get you started. Just promise that you'll pay him
back when you make your fortune in Ilor. Shake on it?" Quill
offered me his hand, and Mal shot his brother a confused look.

"I suppose I could try," I said, pushing reluctance into my words.

Quill shuffled. By the time he'd dealt, he'd explained the rules of brag fairly thoroughly and set a stack of copper *twilling* in front of each of us. "Think you understand the basics, Vi? We can have a practice round, if you'd like."

"No point in playing a game without stakes," I said. "If I win, I'll pay you back what you lent me, but I get to keep any profit. Sound right?"

"Sure," Mal said, laughing. "Do dimmys have beginner's luck, or is it negated by your bad luck?"

Quill punched his brother's arm. "Rude," he said. "Just rude."

I laughed and looked at my cards, then drew from the pile. "Don't worry, Quill. At least he's not trying to throw me overboard."

"No," Quill quipped, laying down a set. "You did that yourself."

I lost the first few hands on purpose as we bantered, getting a feel for how Mal and Quill played.

"Did you know that there are sixteen places to sit in this room, if you include all the tables?" I asked suddenly.

Mal blinked at me. "What?"

"I haven't had much to occupy my time. A girl can only read for so many hours in a single day." I drew another card.

"I could stop by in the afternoons when I finish my duties, if you like," Mal offered.

Quill arched an eyebrow at him. My heart beat hard in my chest. They were both so handsome, the thought of it made me blush, and Mal had been so kind to me, had taken time out of his days to bring me little comforts. He was the softer of the two, the more straightforward. And yet somehow, despite all that, I wished it'd been Quill who'd offered to spend his time with me.

"I'm all in," I said, dodging Mal's comment.

"Are you sure?" Quill asked.

I nodded. A bell sounded, and the twins both sighed in resignation.

"It'll have to be our last hand," Mal said. "I fold."

Quill eyed me, a light in his golden eyes. "I'll go all in, too. No sense in leaving money on the table."

He pushed his *twilling* to meet mine in the center of the table and laid his cards down. I screwed up my face, but couldn't help grinning as I showed them my hand.

"Looks like I win," I said, winking at Quill. "I guess dimmys do have beginner's luck after all."

Mal, laughing, started to collect our dishes and glasses and arrange them carefully on the tray he'd brought.

Quill took a long, betrayed look at his cards before gathering them up. He stood and walked over to the deck door, locking it with a long brass key. Seeing the annoyance on my face, he shrugged apologetically. "You were nearly over the railing when I came in earlier. I'm sorry to lock you in, I am, but Uncle Hamlin would have my head if I let you out there alone after a stunt like that. It's for your own good."

A surge of anger swept over me like a wave. My jaw clenched, my eyes narrowed and I bit my lip to keep a string of curses from spewing out of my mouth. "I see," I gritted out. I could pick the lock, of course, but I didn't want to sacrifice a couple of pins for the sake of fresh air. Not if I didn't have to.

"Sorry, imp. That's the way it is," he said. "By the way, tomorrow's laundry day. Do you have any that wants doing?"

I grimaced. "I'd love that. Everything I have is in need of a good cleaning."

"All right, then. I'll come by in the morning to get it." Quill grinned broadly at me and plucked a book I'd been reading off the end table. He shuddered. *The Pirates of Cala-vance. That one gave me nightmares for weeks."*

"I like adventures," I said. My heart fluttered in my chest as I gathered up my courage. I'd have a better chance of convincing the Whipplestons to help me out of my temple sentence if I could get both of them on my side. "And, Mal, I would like it if you visited in the afternoons. If you have time, of course."

He grinned at me and started toward the door. "I'll see you tomorrow, then."

I smiled, and pulled two leather billfolds from my pocket. "Might not want to leave without these."

Quill's and Mal's faces contorted with an identical series of emotions—confusion, recognition, anger—before they both erupted in peals of laughter.

"How did you do that?" Mal asked. "I never even got close to you!"

"You think that, you need to pay closer attention. I'm not even a half-decent pickpocket. Never had anyone to teach me the trade."

Quill guffawed and clapped me on the back. "I'll pay you a *drott* if you show me how to do that. For now, though, we need to be off to bed. We've an early shift tomorrow."

Mal smiled warmly and wished me a good night. Quill held the door for his brother. When Mal had gone through, Quill smiled rakishly at me and saluted. "Pleasant dreams, Vi. I'll see you soon."

When they'd gone, I undressed, turned off the lights and crawled into the big, soft bed. I tried to hold on to every detail of the evening—every taste, every word, every look. I wanted desperately to fix all the luxury of this journey in my mind, for fear that these memories would be the only bright spot in the coming years. But the wine made me sleepy and unfocused. I kept drifting from the bits of conversation that were important—like the man Quill had mentioned so causally, the one who'd married an amalgam—to the patently irrelevant, like the long, straight bridge of Quill's nose. His slow, warm smile, and the broad expanse of his muscular shoulders.

I pinched my arm hard. On my way to a short life of hard labor, and here I was, all soft-eyed and swooning over a handsome face and a bit of witty banter. But even as I silently scolded myself, I wondered if he had a sweetheart.

CHAPTER TEN

Bo

The funerals were a blur of indigo crepe and sympathy. I followed Claes as he drifted from room to room, neither of us hearing the whispered condolences of our guests or the murmured platitudes of the anchorites. He held tightly to my hand, and I was as unwilling to let go, even for a moment, as he seemed to be. The house overflowed with the nobility of Alskad, including all of the singleborn. Even the Queen had come for the funerary rites. Some faraway part of me was grateful that she was there, grateful for the support of my family, no matter how distantly related.

The hurt and betrayal I'd felt at Claes's flippant acceptance of my betrothal to his sister had all but disappeared now, and as I watched him fade before my eyes, I fought desperately to keep from clinging to him, from begging him to hold on to his life for my sake.

On top of the aching pool of grief and fear was the question of how this had happened. Most people might easily accept that it was an accident, but that felt too simple to me. Too coincidental. It had been only a few days before the explosion that those shots had been fired at the three of us—Claes, Penelope and me—in the park. I found myself wondering if the assassination attempt hadn't been meant for me at all, but perhaps for Claes or Penelope. Retribution for some wrong they'd committed during their endless rounds of blackmail and political maneuvering.

I was so preoccupied that I didn't notice Queen Runa at my side until she placed a light hand on my arm. With an apologetic look at Claes, she pulled me away to an alcove, leaving my cousin behind.

"This is an unfortunate turn of events, and I'm sorry to lose so much of your family at once," she said. "Your mother and her sister were very dear to me, as was your sweet Penelope. You'll have to be strong now, Ambrose, but look at this as an opportunity to show the nobility that you can manage your own affairs." She reached out and squeezed my hand. "Feel free to look to your mother's solicitor for help. She has access to your finances and records and has been apprised of your situation."

"Thank you, Your Majesty, but…" I trailed off. How could she expect me to think about managing an estate when I'd just become an orphan, when Claes was succumbing to his sister's death before my eyes, when all too soon I would be all alone in the world—and none of it looked at all like an accident? It was too much. I'd already cried until there were no more tears—all I felt now was emptiness. I was hollowed out, and I wanted desperately to curl in around the gaping pit in my chest.

"You ought to come to court, and soon," Runa continued. "Do your mourning publicly. Allow your parents' acquaintances in the city to offer you their condolences without making the trek out here." She squeezed my hands again, this time with an iron grip, and tapped the cuff on my wrist twice. "I mean it, Ambrose. Take charge of your finances. Go through your records. I'd hate for you to find yourself caught unawares by something you might have otherwise been prepared for." She met my eyes, giving me a meaning-ful look that I couldn't quite interpret, and said firmly, "I'll expect you in the capital before the Solstice."

Before I could reply, she'd swept across the room, leaving a path of bowing nobility and scraping servants in her wake.

Though the Queen's command echoed through my head like a never-ending reel, I couldn't bear to leave Claes's side. He stood next to his sister's pyre for hours after the funeral, still as a statue. By the time I managed to get him back into the house, his cheeks and mine were both chapped from the wind and our tears.

After our well-meaning guests departed, Claes retreated upstairs, saying he wanted to be alone. He stopped coming down for meals, stopped leaving his room at all. He refused to bathe, refused to speak to anyone. I recognized in him the way my mother had grieved after my father's death, and his suffering impressed upon me how rare my parents' love must have been. It was as though when Penelope died, she took hold of the cord of Claes's life and began dragging it through the halls of the gods with her, pulling him toward death with every step she took, every second they were apart.

One morning, two days after Penelope's funeral, I found Claes in his room, curled in his bed under a pile of blankets, the drapes all drawn. A sour smell hung in the air, like dirty laundry and curdled milk. The flame guttered in the hearth, so I plucked a log out of the basket. Before I could add it to the fire, Claes's voice echoed from the bed, startling me.

"Don't waste the wood."

I jumped and dropped the log on my toe in the process. Teeth gritted, I did everything in my power not to curse and stirred the coals before adding the wood to the fire anyway.

"I came to see if you wanted to go for a ride," I said.

"I'm too tired. I'm sorry, love." Claes seemed like a thin, brittle sheet of paper that was being folded over and over. This folding, I knew, would continue until he was simply gone.

"A short one, then. We'll go down to the river and back. It'll do you some good to get some fresh air." I drew back his bed curtains and opened the window's drapes before returning to his side.

Claes turned away from me and pulled the covers up to his chin. "Don't you understand, Bo? I'm dying, and I certainly won't stand in the way of it the way my father did. I won't become a dimmy. You have to let me go."

My stomach twisted, and I looked away for a moment, trying to come to terms with what he was saying. I knew he was dying, but his insistence on it infuriated me.

"You're just giving up? You'll leave me without even saying goodbye? You selfish prig."

Claes sat up and swung his legs over the side of the bed, anger written all over his face. "I didn't choose this, Bo! I would never choose to leave you. You couldn't possibly understand what it's like. When Penelope died, I died, too. I cannot be me without her. I cannot live in this world if she is gone. You don't know how it is, having someone be a part of you like that. I feel her calling me away, calling me out of this world, and even as much as I love you, Bo, I can't leave her alone in death."

It was like he'd slapped me. I stumbled back and collapsed heavily in a chair, trying to sort through my thoughts. At least he'd been whole for most of his life. I knew I was supposed to be grateful to be singleborn, but all I could think was that he was lucky to have had a twin at all. All I'd ever wanted was to not feel so alone. I'd had that with him, or at least I thought I had. Now I knew that I'd always come second to Penelope. And I'd never hated myself so much as I did, thinking that. I knew it was selfish. Knew that I was a terrible person for warping his grief that way. And knowing how terrible I truly was broke my heart even more.

"So that's it, then. That's our goodbye?" I whispered, tears hot in my eyes.

Claes crossed the room and knelt in front of me. His voice was resigned, weary. "No, Bo. You're right. It isn't fair to you to say goodbye like this. I don't know how much longer I have, but I'll ride out with you."

My tears fell like the curtains at the end of a play, heavy and final.

My eyes were still swollen when we reached the stables. Claes sent the stable hands to polish the fittings on all the carriages and sleighs so that we could tack up our mounts in peace. Though most gentlemen relied on their staff to take care of their horses, Claes knew that I found the chores cathartic, and I wouldn't want to try to explain my tearstained face. I was grateful to him for being so thoughtful of my needs and feelings even through his own grief. It wasn't like him to put my needs before his own.

Claes was quiet as he groomed his glossy chestnut mare, Allera. She was a Turkmene, and her name meant "gentle wind" in the language of the Samirian mountain traders who raised the breed. She was a beautiful creature, and Claes whispered fondly to her as he curried dust from her shining flanks. I didn't try to hear what he said—there are some secrets that are meant only for horses' ears.

My own mount, a long-legged dapple gray Trakhener I called Laith, stamped in the cross ties, anxious to move. Laith lived to run fast and jump high. We made a good pair, Laith and I, and as I groomed him, I began to feel some clarity for the first time since my mother's death. The tasks I'd completed hundreds of times—combing his mane and tail, brushing the mud from his hips (he, like every light-colored horse I'd ever known, loved nothing more than rolling in mud), picking small stones from his hooves, cinching his girth—opened up space for me to think.

Though the day was cold and gray, and storms threatened the sky, we warmed up in the small ring by the barn and took off across the pasture, all without saying a word. I let Claes lead, and when he gave Allera her head, she streaked off toward the river like a vein of copper. Laith soon overtook her, and I laughed with the simple joy of riding fast on a horse I trusted. We drew rein and slowed our mounts to a walk when we reached the rocky shore of the river that marked the manor's northern border. We often swam in its deep, slow pools in the heat of the summer, but now, the thaw had only just begun in earnest, and chunks of ice still floated in the currents.

Claes's eyes were narrowed, but not against the sun; the sky was still a mass of roiling gray that promised rain by supper. I waited for him to speak.

Finally, after several long minutes, Claes asked, "Will the Queen push you toward another engagement soon?"

My mouth fell open. "You've barely spoken to me in two days, and *that* is what you want to talk about?"

Claes's brows furrowed. "This is what my life has been, Bo. Everything I've ever done has been to make your ascent to the throne as seamless as possible."

Rage washed over me, and I kneed Laith toward the icy river. I wanted to scream. Claes would focus on the damn throne now, as he was dying, of all times. On some level I knew that I could never understand the pain that had enveloped him since Penelope's death, but that he still found the energy to consider political maneuvering was altogether too much. My ribs seemed to squeeze my heart, caging it in ever-smaller spaces.

"Why are you being so selfish?" he asked me. "What's gotten into you?"

"Selfish? How, in Gadrian's own name, could you call me selfish?" I tried to keep myself from screaming at him and spooking one of the horses. Tears stung my eyes. "You're the one leaving me all alone."

"I don't have a choice!" Claes exclaimed, wheeling Allera in front of me. "This is how it works. Penelope is dead, and soon I will be, too. You'll have to accept it."

"Accept it? Just like that, I should accept that you're giving up?"

"I'm not giving up. I'm letting nature take its course. I don't want to fight it." He sighed.

Thunder echoed off the mountains in the distance, but I didn't want to return to the house yet. I swung off Laith and led him to the riverbank. I could feel Claes's eyes following me as I squatted by the river and splashed icy water on my face. Laith drank, and pawed playfully at the river with one hoof. I wished that his playing would lighten my mood, but I felt like

I was about to collapse. I stood and laid my head on his neck. He whickered and nudged my hip with his velvety black nose, begging for the lump of sugar I always carried in my pocket.

Claes led Allera to the water and stood quietly beside me as she drank.

"Why do you work so hard to hide from your fate? You were born alone for a reason. The Queen chose you, declared you the singleborn best able to succeed her, and you're telling me you don't want that? You don't want to be King of the Alskad Empire?"

"I never said I didn't want it, Claes. I just don't know if I deserve it."

I scuffed the dry grass with the toe of my boot. When I looked up, Claes was studying me thoughtfully.

"Why not?" he asked. "You're singleborn, and from a long line of singleborn, aren't you?"

I toyed with the cuff at my wrist. Less than a week ago, I would have kept my mouth shut. I would have kept my anxieties and the self-doubt that was on constant loop in my head all to myself. I had known then that he would run to tell Penelope anything I told him, and I didn't want anyone to know how little I believed in myself. In my ability to rule. I had thought that I trusted Claes, but looking back, I'd always known that there were some things I couldn't tell even him. His first loyalty had always been to Penelope, and, in the cold light of our goodbye, I realized that was the reason I'd been so mad about his reaction to our engagement. My feelings didn't matter nearly as much as Penelope's, and being married to the future King was a great triumph for her.

But none of that mattered now. For the first time in my life, I could give voice to the fears and doubts that clung to me day and night.

I scrubbed a hand through my dark curly hair and said, "I've always felt out of place. I've never felt like I belonged. I feel unmoored, like I'm just following the currents of a life set before me. There's never been a moment in my life when I knew with any kind of certainty that I was the right choice to be King." I sighed. "I don't think I'm capable of living up to the job. I don't think I'm smart or kind or compassionate enough to hold that responsibility in my hands."

I waited for him to say something, to tell me I was wrong, but he didn't. He looked at me, like he was weighing my worth and finding me wanting.

Finally, he broke the silence. "Maybe that's the burden of being singleborn. You have to find a way to steer on your own. There are people who say that Queen Runa only chose you because your father was her nephew. People who'd rather see you dead than see another Trousillion on the throne." I flinched, but I knew he was right. Still, it made me uneasy to hear him give voice to it. "Your mother was positive that Patrise tried to have you killed, and more than once. You've lived through how many known assassination attempts now? How many times has one of the other singleborn whispered, just loud enough for you to hear, that you were a bad choice for the throne?"

More than I could count—and being reminded of those things didn't exactly help soothe my nerves.

Claes met my eyes squarely. "Don't you want to show them the kind of King you can be?"

I looked away and shrugged. Wanting to have that kind of motivation and actually having it were two very different things. Claes's comment about the assassination attempt bit into me, and I cocked my head to the side, studying him.

"What?" he grumbled.

"Did you do it? Did you stage that assassination attempt in the park last week?"

Heaving a great sigh, Claes jerked Allera's head up rather more harshly than was necessary. "I'm exhausted. Let's go back to the house before it rains." He led Allera up the riverbank, sniffed and wiped a hand across his eyes.

I called after him. "Claes! Wait." I led Laith up the hill and stood in front of Claes, drawing myself up to my full height. "I won't blame you. I just need to know. Did you do it?"

Claes tapped his crop against his boot, and I could almost see him weighing his answer.

"Please, Claes. The truth."

Rolling his eyes, Claes sneered. "You may make a great king, Bo. Honestly, I think you will, but you don't always focus your attention on the right questions. What happened in Esser Park doesn't matter. What *does* matter is what happened to my sister and your mother. Do you actually believe that was an accident?"

My heartbeat quickened, and I stared at him. I'd had the same suspicions, but it was different to hear someone else voice them as well.

"For what it's worth," Claes said, "I wasn't behind the attack. I think it was Rylain, personally, but there are any number of people who would benefit from your death." I winced, and he sighed in exasperation. "Honestly, Bo, you have far too much faith in her. In people in general. You need to realize that most will try to take advantage of you now that your mother and Penelope are gone—especially once I'm gone, too." I swallowed hard as he continued. "I don't know that it matters who killed them, if anyone, or if it was only a terrible accident. But Bo, your next move does matter. You have to show the rest of the nobility that you won't be broken by this loss. You have to stand up to them."

Tears welled in my eyes. This was all too much. Too overwhelming. I wasn't strong enough to make it through all the gossip and intrigue and the endless things I'd yet to learn. Not by myself.

I swiped at my eyes and took a steadying breath. "The Queen commanded that I get to the capital before the Solstice. Come with me, please?"

Claes squeezed my hand and lifted it to kiss my knuckles. "I'll make you no promises, but as long as I last, I'll stay by your side. But you must learn to keep a wary eye about you, especially with Thamina and Birger. You know that they're working for Patrise, don't you?"

I gaped at him. "How do you know?"

He rolled his eyes, and for a moment, I could almost see the arrogant boy I'd loved for so long. "He bought them off years ago, Bo. It's half the reason your mother kept them around. Easier, after all, to keep an eye on the spies when you know who they are."

I leaned in and laid my head on his shoulder. "I don't know what I'm going to do without you, Claes."

"You'll fend for yourself. You'll become the King we all know you're meant to be. You'll make us all proud as we watch from the halls of the gods and goddesses."

Fighting back tears, I kissed him on the cheek, trying to memorize the salty tang of his sweat, the musky cologne he wore and the dusty smell of the horses that clung to him. Memories would be all I'd have left of him before long.

CHAPTER ELEVEN

Vi

A sharp knock on the door registered in my dream as a cadre of drummers appeared rather suddenly. They beat a sharp tattoo as they followed me through the winding alleys of the End. The motion of the enormous boat was hardly perceptible when I was awake, but something about it lulled me into the deepest sleep of my life, a sleep remarkably hard to come out of. The drummers disappeared as quickly as they'd arrived, and I opened my bleary eyes to see a grinning face looming over me.

I shrieked and sat up, pulling the covers to my chin. Narrowing my eyes, I made out the name stitched on his jacket and glared.

"Good morning, Vi," Quill said. "Quite the slugabed, I see. It's nearly seven o'clock."

I ran my hands through my hair. My dark curls were sticking up in every direction. I wasn't best pleased to be seen sleep-creased and crowned with wild tangles. I tried to tell myself I was just making nice to get where I wanted to go, but that didn't mean I couldn't appreciate the twins' charms for what they were. I certainly didn't want Quill to see me all puffy-eyed and looking a total mess.

"You're so chatty in the morning. Makes me wish I could stay and gab, but if I'm not on the bridge in ten minutes, Uncle Hamlin will hang me by my ankles from the sunsail rigging. I brought some more books for you, and pen and paper. Also—" he tossed me a bundle of heavily embroidered silk "—Mal and I found a trunk that's been sitting in storage since some rich woman left it onboard a few months ago. She was about your size, and her clothes are a lot nicer than the lot you brought. We usually sell those kinds of things, but as you're here…well, we thought you could use some new things. He'll bring up the rest later."

I unwrapped the bundle. It held a pair of sheepskin slippers, a silk shirt, an absurdly soft sweater and loose wool trousers, all of the finest quality. "This is too much. You can't give a wharf rat like me a getup like this."

Quill tapped his foot impatiently. "Shut up. You've never had something so nice in all your life." He winked at me. "Just take it and be grateful, yes?"

I grimaced. "I'm grateful, but you've all done so much for me since I boarded the ship. I keep waiting for the catch."

"No catch, imp. Uncle Hamlin put you in the only empty room he had. Pa feeds you what's left over, and I've given you someone else's forgotten clothes. No one's gone out of their way. At least not yet." Quill gave me a little shove. "Scoot on out of bed and change. I'll take your kit to the laundry."

Incredulous, I climbed out of bed and darted into the washroom. Before I stripped off my old, ratty nightshirt in favor of the new things, I smoothed a touch of ointment onto the scratches on my cheek. They'd faded away to almost nothing in the days I'd been aboard the ship, thanks to Lugine's gift.

I was pulling on the trousers when Quill knocked. "Vi? Hand your things out. I'll bring them back as soon as they're done, all right?"

Blushing, I opened the door a crack and passed my night-shirt out to him, embarrassed that it was still warm from my body. "The rest are in the drawer. I can get them if you wait a moment."

"I'll grab them and go. See you at dinner."

I pulled the silk blouse on and burst out of the washroom, buttons half-undone, altogether too aware of my red face and wild, snarled curls.

Quill raised an eyebrow at me from where he knelt in front of the chest of drawers.

"I may be a dimmy, but I'll have you remember I'm still a person, and I'd rather you kept your nose out of my things." I dug my clothes out of the drawer, careful to keep the pouch with my pearls out of sight. There was a part of me that didn't trust this good fortune of mine, not one bit, and I was sure I didn't entirely trust Quill yet. I wanted to, desperately, but I had as many reasons to be cautious as I had scars.

Still blushing, I handed him the clothes. Quill set them in his lap, let his weight shift back and sprawled on the carpet, graceful as a cat. He propped himself up on an elbow and re-garded me with the deep-set gold-brown eyes he shared with the other men in his family. I noticed that he'd missed a spot when he'd shaved that morning—there was a patch of coarse stubble under his chin.

"What're you hiding, then? What's in the drawer you want to keep hidden so bad you're willing to sit out here half dressed? Not," he added quickly, "that I'm complaining."

"Oh hush," I said, cold as the sea in winter. "I'm a dimmy. You know as well as I do that I could snap at any moment. I once heard about one of us, a noble girl, who was praying in temple for her salvation when the grief overtook her. She ripped out an anchorite's throat with her teeth."

"Hogwash. I've heard that story told ten different ways by ten different people. You'll have to do better if you want me scared of you. Meantime, I brought you breakfast, and you don't want that tea to get cold. Eat up, and read your books. I brought you a few to choose from, plus a pamphlet on the rules of brag. Best study up, aye? No telling how quick beginner's luck will fade." Quill rose and was out the door before I could say another word.

I was counting the pressed tin ceiling tiles and doing my damnedest to figure out how to convince Mal to help me ditch the temple's sentence and take a contract of my own when he arrived with an enormous steamer trunk. Mal hefted the trunk into my room, set it down with a huff and retreated into the hallway. When he returned a moment later, he was pushing a wheeled tea trolley laden with enough food for all the temple brats back in Penby. My mouth watered, and I longed to dig in, bare-handed like a wild thing. I didn't want Mal to think I was entirely without manners, though, so I restrained myself. He grinned at me, pulled a handkerchief from his pocket to mop his sweat-damp brow, and bowed deeply.

"Afternoon. Hope you've got an appetite."

"Have you invited half of the crew for tea?" I asked, brows raised.

"They're leftovers. Da won't let food waste. Mind if I stay? I'm famished."

"Yes, please. My mind is going to mush stuck in here, and there's not a chance I'll finish all that on my own."

"What are you doing with your time? Have you been reading?"

I had just crammed a pasty into my mouth, so I shrugged and chewed. Around a mouthful of spiced meat and flaky crust, I said, "Some. It's hard to focus on a novel right now."

Mal wheeled the tray over to my little table and poured tea for both of us. I sat down and took another pasty from the tray.

"Why's that?" Mal asked.

I pushed an escaped curl behind my ear. *To hell with it, right, Pru?* I thought. "I know we've not known each other long, and you've no reason to do me any favors, especially not after all the kindness you've shown me."

"What can I do for you?"

I shook my head and studied the tea tray, avoiding Mal's golden eyes. "Never mind. I shouldn't ask."

Mal reached across the table and took my hand. His long, elegant fingers closed over mine, and his palm was warm against my skin. It felt comforting enough to near take my breath away. The last person who'd so casually touched me had been Sawny, before he left.

"Tell me what it is you want, Vi, and I swear I'll do my best to see it done," he said.

There it was again, the sincerity I'd heard from him when we'd met for the first time. I looked him in the eyes, searching for some kernel of a lie, for the fear and mistrust I'd seen looking back at me every day of my damned life. But it wasn't there. All I saw in his eyes was blazing, incomprehensible sincerity and fathomless warmth.

I took a deep breath. "I want you to help me avoid the temple's sentence. When we get to Ilor, I want you to help me find a contract. Quill said there were people who'd take a person like me. A dimmy."

Mal jerked his hand away from mine and looked at me like I'd set myself on fire.

"What?" I asked. "Quill said you'd make a fortune off a dimmy's contract. I thought you'd be pleased."

"Ignoring entirely the fact that we're to deliver you to the temple, and I've no interest at all in a quarrel with the Shriven, what on earth would make you think that life as a contracted servant would be any better than what you've got waiting for you in Ilor?"

I rolled my eyes. "You can't honestly think that being some rich ass's plaything for a few years would be worse than half a lifetime of hauling rocks, can you?"

Mal bit his lip. "I don't know. Those contracts are ironclad, and they don't allow any rights for the workers themselves. The folks who hire out that kind of labor think nothing of exploiting the contracts for everything they're worth." He paused, and said quietly, "I don't think it should be legal. It makes me sick."

Mal picked up a sandwich, studying it, carefully not looking at me. "No one tells folks when they sign up that they may never see the end of their contract. Uncle Hamlin's even had some reports that say there are groups of folks who've run out on their contracts and are revolting against the worst of the rich folks. You don't want that life, Vi."

"Maybe I do, and maybe I'll live to regret it immensely. But at least it'd be my choice," I said. I hesitated for a moment, and decided to be honest. "My only friend in the world is in Ilor. He and his sister came over on your ship. *This* ship. This could be a chance for me to see them again. Spend the rest of my life close to the only people who care about me."

Mal's brow furrowed. "I know what it is to want to be

around friends, but there're risks involved, Vi, things you haven't considered. I don't want to see you in a situation that could erupt into all-out violence at any moment. And that's even if we could get Hamlin to agree to this."

"But you'd ask him? For me?"

The muscles in Mal's jaw clenched, and he stared me down, unblinking. "Vi, before I bring this to him, I need you to understand what a difficult life you'd be setting yourself up for. I'm sure you've heard the rumors about the unrest in Ilor. They aren't just rumors. Estates have been burned to the ground, whole farms abandoned when their laborers run away from their contracts. And if the runaways are caught? The law is cruel at its best. Plus, it's not like you'd be getting out from under the temple's thumb anyway."

My stomach twisted. "What do you mean?"

Mal looked away and finally took a bite of the sandwich he'd been holding. He chewed slowly, avoiding my eyes. Finally, he said, "Most of the people who hire contract work in Ilor are in debt to the temple in some way or another. Either they themselves are growing things on the temple's behalf—fruit, kaffe, linen, that sort of thing—or they're folks who pay enormous tithes to the temple in order to be overlooked in some way. They don't take care of their employees the way they should, and the temple doesn't care as long as their goods are delivered on time. You wouldn't believe how much of what we export is owned by the temple. They collect nearly all of the profits from Ilor, and all of the goods are produced by underpaid and overburdened contract workers."

"But five or ten years of that kind of work is still better than twenty-five years of hard labor. Twenty-five years of being forced to adulations and watched by anchorites waiting for me to give them a reason to slice my head off my neck."

Mal grimaced. "But you'd still be signing your life away, agreeing to years working beneath someone you don't know at all. You've no idea the kind of people who'd pay money to have one of the diminished on their property. No offense."

"But you do. Quill does. You'd make sure I didn't sign a contract with someone awful."

Mal's eyes softened again. "Think this through, Vi. Even if we agreed to it, you're supposed to be fulfilling a sentence for the temple. Don't you think they'll be looking for you?"

"Who's going to tell them? You? Worst luck, Anchorite Lugine thinks to ask after my well-being, and they come looking for me. Someone will've paid a fortune for me. The temple doesn't care enough about me that a bribe won't send them on their way in a hurry."

I plucked a small cake off a silver tray and picked it apart. Bright red jam spilled across my fingers and onto the white porcelain plate in front of me, pooling like blood. I started to lick the jam off my finger, but stopped when I caught Mal's amber eyes watching me. I used my linen napkin instead, wincing at the stain it created.

"So. Will you help me?"

Mal studied his hands for a moment. When he looked up, he said, "I'll talk to Quill about how to approach Uncle Hamlin. I'm not making any promises, but I will try. For you. If you're sure it's what you really want."

I smiled at him. No one had ever thought twice about what it was like to walk in my shoes, and yet here was this young man—so empathetic, so kind that he'd put himself at odds with the temple to help me.

"Why aren't you scared of me?" I asked.

Softly, Mal said, "I guess I can imagine what it would be like for me, if I lost Quill. He's a bothersome cad, but I can't imagine my life without him." His eyes looked sad at the thought. "I've never been able to blame the diminished for what they do. It's not as if any of them can help it. And you— you've been alone your whole life, and somehow, you're still strong and smart and, well, whole. I admire you for that."

I bit my lip, looking away. "I'm not so strong as all that. I'm terrified of what's coming next. All I wanted was to find a little cottage somewhere up north and wait out the violence. I know it's coming, and I can't stand it. It's like I walk every day under the shroud of a crime I've not yet committed." I gestured at the remains of our tea, at the room. "And now there's all this. I can't afford to forget what my life was like before—"

Mal reached across the table and laid a hand over mine. I let myself appreciate the warmth of his calloused fingers, the memory of what it was to have a friend for a moment.

"I wonder," I said, "if I could ask you for one last favor."

"Why not?" He laughed and took his hand away to refill our teacups.

"No matter what happens with me and the temple, I wonder if you might help me find my friends before you leave Ilor. I'd like to know where they are—maybe see them again if I can."

Mal looked at me in confusion, then grinned.

"You don't know!" he said. "I thought that's why you'd asked for our help, but of course, we haven't told you yet."

"Told me what?" I asked.

"Quill and I are finished with sailing. Our mother and aunt have an import and export business in the capital, and we're going to run their office in Ilor. Quill and I both like the islands, and there's money to be made there. Chances that don't exist in Alskad."

"And give up the adventure of the high seas, traveling the world, for the life of a merchant trader?" I quipped.

Mal looked at me quizzically. "It's what our parents have always planned for us. I'll manage our exports. Kaffe, precious metals and gems, some weapons, wine."

"And Quill?"

"Quill's running the import side."

"Contract labor? Working with the temple?" I asked, but I already knew the answer. I went to stand near the glass door that led to the deck and stared out at the ocean. Quill was funny and charming, and something about him made me want to melt into a puddle of blushes. But for all that, the fact that he planned to make his livelihood from negotiating labor contracts when he knew how badly the folks who took those contracts were treated set my teeth on edge.

But I couldn't let my feelings show—I'd asked for Mal's help in doing just that. I wanted to contract myself out, and not as a laborer, as an oddity. And if I did everything right, I might be able to land near my friends, spend the rest of my days with Sawny and Lily. I might get close enough to find a bit of happiness for myself. If I wanted a chance at that sliver of joy, I had to keep myself in check.

Mal crossed the room, took my hand and said, "He's not a villain, Vi. He does everything in his power to see that the folks who choose this path are treated fairly. He does more than you know, more than I can tell you, to change the system from within."

"Maybe my contract will help you make a name for yourselves," I said, forcing my voice to be airy and light. I wondered, though, what Mal meant about Quill changing the system.

"Vi..." His voice was strained.

"Honestly, Mal. Don't think about it for a second. I'm sure you're right. Quill would never let someone be taken advantage of. Not if he could help it." Despite my best efforts, I sounded exhausted, frustrated. I plastered a smile across my face and looked up at him. "I've lived my whole life under the temple's thumb. Any life would be better than what I'm facing."

A bell sounded in the hall, and Mal started.

"I'm sorry, but I've got to get back." He squeezed my hand once before letting go. "I'm happy to know you, Vi."

"Talk to your uncle?" I asked.

He nodded, and in a moment, he was gone, the tea cart with him. I collapsed on the bed, all the pieces of my plan spinning themselves into place like so many gears. I imagined my twin, a mirror of myself, and wished she could be here to share this with me. But then, if she'd lived, I wouldn't be here, wouldn't be so thrilled to find a pair of friends like Mal and Quill. If she'd lived, we might have been scheming to start a business of our own, or giggling over what it might be like if Quill tried to kiss me. I imagined kissing Quill, how his lips would feel against mine, how his arms would feel around me, his hands on my waist.

I shook my head to clear away those thoughts—I couldn't indulge my growing feelings for him. Instead, I fetched my pearls from their new hiding place between the mattresses. I spilled them out onto the blue bedspread and counted them, one by one. Sixty-three pearls. I'd thought they might serve as a bribe for the Whipplestons, to help me out of the temple's grasp, but I hadn't yet needed to add the extra incentive. Maybe instead, they could do something even more important. Maybe they could buy me a future after my contract, if Mal and Quill could convince their uncle to go along with our plan.

I poured the pearls back into their pouch, put the pouch back in its hiding spot and went back to counting ceiling tiles. There were 194.

CHAPTER TWELVE

Bo

Several mornings later, a thick envelope bearing the Queen's seal waited for me on the breakfast table, along with a stack of condolence notes. Though I couldn't hope to keep anything a secret from them for long, I slid Runa's letter under my chair. I didn't want to give either of them the opportunity to read any correspondence that might prove to be sensitive over my shoulder. Claes might be sequestered in his room, but his warning about Birger and Thamina burned bright through the fog of sleep and grief that lay heavy on my mind.

I drank two cups of strong kaffe and read the bulk of the letters before the heady smell of bacon cooking awoke my appetite.

"How kind of you to wait for us," said Thamina as she strode into the room. Birger stumbled in close on her heels. The dark smudges under his eyes and the cloud of tafia fumes that surrounded him belied his clean shirt and damp hair. Birger had always been fond of drink, but the stench of cheap tafia was a new one, and until now, he'd not let his drinking interfere with my lessons.

I noted, with growing ire, that Thamina wore the third new indigo mourning jacket I'd seen on her this week. I wondered if she thought I was too blinded by grief to notice all her new things, or if she just didn't care. I certainly hadn't increased her salary since Mother's death, so she had to have found a new source of income—and even if Claes hadn't warned me, it wouldn't take much to imagine who'd bought her services.

Though it had not been their custom before Mother's death, my tutors had taken it upon themselves to have their meals with me in the days since. Presumably they meant me to think they were there to ensure that my grief did not overwhelm me. But it was obvious that Thamina, at least, had other priorities.

She eyed my stubbly face and rolled sleeves with distaste, and said, "I believe that we ought to begin to discuss your plans for the coming year. Without the assurance of an alliance with Penelope, it is imperative that you are an irresistible candidate for marriage when you reenter society. Therefore, we must spend some time working on smoothing your rougher edges."

Birger drained a cup of kaffe and eyed his sister warily. Perhaps there was still a shred of loyalty beneath his corpulent, tafia-soaked exterior. I wondered if I could trust Gunnar enough to see if we couldn't sway Birger back to our side.

"They've not been gone two weeks," I said, tapping my cuff nervously on the wooden table. Since Mother's death, memories of my family, especially my father, had screamed for my attention through every moment of every day. This familiar conversation about my future and my marriage—

I could feel it chipping away at the floodgates. My eyes felt hot, my throat tight, but I did my best to keep my tone level. "I'd like to abstain from discussing my marriage prospects until I've had sufficient time to grieve. The Queen wishes for me to make an appearance at court before the Solstice. Please make yourself ready to travel tomorrow if you wish to accompany me."

"As you wish, my lord, but I'm afraid we mustn't put off this conversation. I feel it is my duty to see that you make an appropriate match."

"Thamina..." Birger stopped at the derisive look his sister shot him and went back to moving food around on his plate.

"Your duty is to see to my education in preparation for becoming the King of the Alskad Empire. It certainly is *not*—" I bit out the word, making it as sharp as the anger rising inside me "—your duty to think about or plan for my marriage. If you continue to presume duties outside those you've been hired to fulfill, I'll see that your time as my employee comes to a quick end."

Thamina's mouth fell open, and even as I maintained my glare, I berated myself. It would do me no good at all to let Thamina know what she could do to get under my skin. Any advantage she was able to find over me would inevitably be passed along to Patrise, and he undoubtedly knew too much already.

I cleared my throat. "As I said, we'll leave tomorrow. See that Claes's things are packed for him."

Both Birger and Thamina looked at me with horror in their eyes.

"Surely Claes will not agree to return to Penby. Not with his...condition," Birger wheezed.

"I've no idea what you mean by that," I said coldly.

"He's diminished," Thamina said, looking as if she couldn't believe she had to spell it out for me. "You cannot mean to bring one of the diminished into the capital. What will the Queen think? What if he were to do something? The Shriven would take him. Behead him. You cannot want that."

An image of Claes, pale and weeping softly in his darkened bedroom, flooded my brain. My stomach clenched, and bile rose in my throat. I bit my lip, forcing the contents of my stomach back down.

"Claes is not diminished. He's dying. The Queen has summoned me to court, and I will not leave him alone. Not in his final days. Let the Shriven try. No one but the gods will take him from me." I rose and pushed back my chair in one swift motion, reaching for the Queen's letter. I didn't wait for a response before grabbing up the rest of my correspondence and stalking out of the room, slamming the heavy wooden door behind me.

I raced up the stairs to the library, tossed the letters into an armchair and collapsed on the floor, trying to slow my racing heart and force the tears from my eyes. I couldn't think about Claes slowly withering away in the rooms below me. I didn't want to face the fact that in almost no time at all, I would be really, truly alone, with no one in the world who knew me as well as my mother had, or Penelope, or Claes. It was too much. Too much loss, too much sadness, too much heavy, overwhelming responsibility.

Father had once told me that lying on the floor changed a man's perspective, and whenever he'd felt overwhelmed, he'd simply lie on the floor, breathe deep and stare at the ceiling. It sent Mother into hysterics when, out of nowhere, Father sank to the floor and lay still for several minutes. She always tried to get him up, giggling and calling him an improper heathen.

He ignored her, and eventually the silvery peals of her laughter rang through the house. The servants grinned and nudged one another, unable to keep their placid masks in place.

Though I never followed my father's example in front of Mother, I often retreated to my room or the library, locked the door and lay on the carpet, staring at the ceiling. In those moments, my father came back to life, and the idyllic time before he died didn't seem so very far away.

My mother had always been an ambitious, well-respected woman. Her intelligence and business acumen had seen my father's bedraggled—though royal—estate grow into a flourishing enterprise with scads of holdings. Before my father's death, she'd been warm, affectionate. But his loss had broken something in her. She'd been stricken, keeping to her bed and avoiding everyone. She emerged a month later, hollow-cheeked and sallow, with an edge of anger that had made her capable of lashing out at any moment.

Though I had never had the gall to ask her about it, my mother's fury confounded me. It was as though my father's death turned her into an entirely different person. Then Claes and Penelope came to live with us. Our games and manipulations consumed me, and Mother continued to ignore me as best she could.

I didn't want to think ill of the dead, but as I listened to the clock tick, I found myself wishing that she had been a different sort of mother in recent years. I studied the clouds that had been painted on the high, domed ceiling. They were great, puffy white things—the type of clouds rarely seen in the rain-drenched countryside of the northern Alskad Empire—and the ceiling's painted sky was nearly always at odds with the gloomy gray one currently visible through the library's tower windows.

I picked myself up, went to sit at the desk and tore open the Queen's letter.

My dear Lord Ambrose,

I have taken the liberty of having your house in Esser Park opened and refurbished for you. Now that you are the heir and a man grown, it's only right that you occupy your own property when visiting the capital. The nobility will respect you more if they see you operating outside the palace and away from my constant oversight. That said, I expect to see you in court before the Solstice. Let me once again reiterate the importance of your taking an interest in your finances and records. Power is gained not through blood or right, but through knowledge and control. Be thorough and keep yourself well-guarded.

With fondest wishes, your great-aunt,
Runa, Queen of Alskad, Empress of Ilor, Singleborn Chosen of the Goddesses, First of the Trousillion

I read the letter twice more, committing the Queen's words to memory, and went in search of my mother's ledger. Perhaps there was a kernel of truth in the Queen's commands. I resolved to arm myself with knowledge. Perhaps, if I knew enough, could learn enough, other people would stop presuming to make decisions for me. Perhaps I could become the kind of King that my parents had so wanted me to be. Perhaps I would find a way to stop the churning anxiety that ate away at the pit of my stomach.

At the very least, it would stop me ceaselessly considering every person I'd ever met and wondering whether or not they were capable of plotting a murder—mine, my cousins' or my mother's. It hadn't taken much to entirely demolish my sense of safety in the world.

It was full dark and the clock on the mantelpiece had chimed ten when I finally flipped to the last section of the ledger. I was driven by a kind of unstoppable energy to make my way through the enormous book, which covered the estate's financial transactions for the past seven months, before I went to bed. The silver pot of kaffe the cook had sent up with my supper—confit goose leg, roasted vegetables and fresh bread—had long since gone cold, but I gulped down another cup anyway. My elbows and shoulders crackled when I stretched, and I rolled my neck before I read the final entry.

Much of the information in the ledger had been familiar to me. It detailed the expenses associated with each of the houses we kept. There was the townhouse in the capital, the cottage by the sea and the grand manor house where I'd grown up. Also in the ledger were personal budgets for each member of the family. My heart ached when I saw the line that documented the yearly allowance paid to the household for Penelope and Claes's upkeep by their parents.

Grief washed over me in waves. It seeped deep into my body and settled there, a dark and silent weight. As quickly as it came, it evaporated, and I was able to move on for a little while. I focused on the work in front of me once more.

I already had a general understanding of the house's budget for food and entertaining, since I'd taken charge of running the household after my father's death. However, Mother continued to pay the staff's salaries, and as I flipped through this final section of the ledger, I was shocked to see that each maid was paid less per year than was allotted for new clothing for me each season.

Buried in a column of payments to craftsmen—clockmakers, tailors, cabinetmakers, cobblers and the like—was a line I couldn't explain.

X.A.—G.O.A.T.—200 *drott* per annum.

It was strange. Every other entry in the column had some explanation of the expense after the name, but this only had letters. I stared at it for a few minutes, but I couldn't make heads or tails of it. X.A. might be someone's initials, but what could G.O.A.T. stand for?

Rubbing my eyes, I added a note about the line to my list of questions for my mother's solicitor and closed the ledger. I stacked my notes on top and locked everything in the safe built into the floor beneath the desk. I turned off most of the lights and crept downstairs to my rooms.

The next morning, I wrestled all of my questions into a letter to my mother's solicitor, a woman called Gerlene, and, letter in hand, went to look for Gunnar.

"I'm planning to go to the capital this afternoon," I said when I found him. "Will you see that mine and Claes's things are packed and the carriage is made ready?"

"I assume Thamina and Birger agreed to this?" he asked.

I cringed inside, but managed to keep my face impassive. I was determined to be treated like an adult. "I don't believe I need my tutors or anyone else's permission."

He raised an eyebrow. "You'd best ask them before you go making plans."

I gave him a doleful look. "They've been informed," I said dryly.

"And Mister Claes? He's willing to travel with you? Even in his condition? What of the temple? The Shriven? Oughtn't you make arrangements for him to spend his final days here instead?"

I rubbed my temples, willing myself calm. "Gunnar. Am I, or am I not, your crown prince?"

"You are, sir."

"And am I, or am I not, a grown man and master of this house?"

"Well, sir, you are, of course, but…" I sighed, and he suddenly became quiet, gazing into my face. He shook his head ruefully and patted my shoulder. "Sometimes, sir, it's hard to remember that you're no longer a wee little tyrant running about the house in nappies, wailing for your father to stop his writing and take you riding. I'll do my best to show you the respect you deserve." He held his hand out. "Would you like me to see your letter posted, sir?"

I'd nearly forgotten about the letter I was holding. I passed it to him, with thanks. Gunnar bowed, and an idea skittered into my head. "Do you, by any chance, happen to know where my father's journals were stored after his death?"

Gunnar cocked his head to one side and tapped his lips. "If I can't put my hands on them, Karyta will be able to find them, surely. Would you like me to pack them to take with you?"

"Please. And, if you would, I'd like the last of them in with my things for the carriage ride. I've been missing him so terribly lately. Perhaps if I know what he was thinking before his death, I can be more of a comfort to Claes."

It was an easy lie, or perhaps not even a lie at all. Just the truth stretched and folded to look like a swan, when it was more like a great gray bear.

CHAPTER THIRTEEN

VI

As the days passed and we drew nearer to Ilor, the twins seemed to relax, just as my nerves seemed to fray to the point of collapse. Hamlin Whippleston had agreed—albeit reluctantly—to our scheme, and Mal and Quill had been dual whirlwinds of planning and preparations ever since. But when I was alone, I spent as many hours pushing my muscles to the point of trembling exhaustion as I did studying the map of Ilor Quill'd brought me.

The colony was small, situated on three islands so close, they were nearly touching. All told, a person could walk from one end of the string of islands to the other in just under two weeks. Or rather, they could if not for the enormous mountains that ranged up the center of the islands and spread like sand dunes from coast to coast. In the century and a half since Alskad had sent its first settlers to Ilor, the colony had grown exponentially. Between the three major towns—one on each island—small villages had sprung up, and around them, vast estates where kaffe and other goods were grown. The only land that hadn't yet been claimed and settled was the range of mountains that were the spine of the island chain, dominating the great majority of its acreage. I'd never seen mountains, apart from illustrations in books, and I had a hard time imagining them as anything but snow-capped, even though I knew Ilor's climate was far too warm for snow.

One evening, after supper, Quill'd lost early in our card game and had made himself comfortable as I did my best not to beat Mal too handily. He was convinced I'd been cheating, and while he was right, I didn't want him to know it—not yet, at least. Didn't mean I'd let him win, I just let him take longer to lose.

"How do you feel about someone religious?" Quill's boots were off, and he was sprawled out over the small settee, jacket unbuttoned.

I didn't know how he could possibly be comfortable like that, and yet, there he was. "Have you found out who holds Sawny and Lily's contracts?" I asked.

As Quill put together the list of people who'd be invited to interview me when we arrived in Ilor, I'd marked each of their estates on the map, but he'd not yet told me where Sawny and Lily were. I refused to make a decision that would land me clean on the other side of Ilor from them.

Mal looked up from the cards in his hand and glared. "Do we have to talk about this now? The records aren't on the ship. We'll find them as soon as we get to Ilor."

I rolled my eyes and slid another *twilling* into the middle of the table. "I don't think it's outrageous for me to want to be as close to the only two people I know in the whole damn colony. Fold or call?"

"You'll know us," Mal said, and stared at his cards for another moment before folding.

"You know I'm fine with whichever rich fool's willing to pay the most for my contract," I said to Quill. "So long as they're close to Sawny and Lily."

Quill lifted his head to grin at me, eyes sparkling. "Oh, they'll pay. Never you worry about that, imp. They'll pay."

"I think you're missing my point—" I said, but Mal was already talking over me.

"Who are you thinking of?"

"Mehitabel Long. She's got some kind of flower farm. Makes essential oils that sell for a fortune in Penby. We've got a small bit of her export business, and she's contracted workers from us in the past. Close ties to the temple."

Mal, shuffling the cards, made a face. "She's awful. Don't put Vi through that. She built that horrible haven hall on her property, and she makes us sit through endless prayers every time we have to go over there to do business."

"I don't want her to end up with the contract, you ass," Quill said. "I want her to drive the bidding up."

Mal dealt the cards. "This'll be my last hand. Do you mind, Vi?"

I looked at my cards and gave him my most wicked smile.

"Only if you don't mind handing over the rest of your coin."

My cards were garbage, but half the point of the game was to bluff, and I excelled at bluffing. Mal took one look at his cards and pushed the pile of coins across the table to me.

"They're all yours. I can't play with a pair of twos."

I raked the money to my side of the table, grinning, and laid my cards on the table faceup. A seven and a two. Possibly the worst hand a person could be dealt in brag. Mal gaped at me for a full moment before a smile spread over his face.

"I can't decide if you're the most foolish or the most brilliant woman I've ever met. Either way, I'm off. Quill? You coming?"

Quill looked up from the *ovstri* he was flipping back and forth across his knuckles.

"In a bit. I want to run a few more potential candidates by Vi."

Mal nodded and gathered the dishes from our supper onto the tray. I went to help him, but he shook his head, smiling. "I've got it. See you tomorrow, Vi."

As the door closed behind Mal, Quill stuck out his tongue at his brother's back, rolled to his feet and began to pace.

"We should invite more people than we need to be there. We've already got four—I think three more."

Quill tapped a finger against his lips, and for a moment, all of my thoughts were replaced with a bone-deep wish that I could, for a moment, know what it was like to kiss Quill. As if he could read my mind, he settled himself on the small settee next to me. His thigh brushed against mine, lighting me on fire and burning away my every thought.

"There's one who springs to mind. He's got the money, and he's expressed interest in similar hires before, but I don't know if he'd be a good fit."

"Why not?" I tried to focus, but I couldn't tear my eyes away from his long fingers, absently brushing my leg as they drummed against his knee. I so wished I had the courage to take his hand, lean into his touch.

"For one, his wife is an amalgam."

I groaned. "There's no such thing, and you know it."

"I've seen her. She's like two people in the same body. She's half redheaded, half blonde. Half freckled, half pale as porcelain. One eye is green, the other violet. I didn't believe it myself until I saw her. You wouldn't want to be in a household with an amalgam, would you?"

I dropped my head back, resting against the couch, and stared at the ceiling.

"I can't go about my life afraid of something out of a bedtime story when I'm that same kind of horror myself."

"Vi…"

Quill's tone was frustrated, defeated, and I felt the muscles in his leg tense as he started to stand. I put up a hand to stop him without thinking, and he relaxed back onto the couch. I pressed my lips together, willing myself not to blush, and spoke, if only to cover the silence. "It's the plain truth, and you know it. What's the fellow's name?"

"Phineas Laroche."

I ran my hands through my curls casually and grinned at Quill, as though it was easy. As though I was thinking of anything but kissing him. "That's quite a name."

Quill laughed. "He's got an estate called Plumleen. They mostly grow kaffe, I think, but he has an eye for oddities, and he and his wife breed and train some of the best horses in Ilor."

"I've always wanted to learn to ride a horse."

"Then onto the list he goes."

Quill stayed in my room for another hour, teasing and laughing. When he finally left, I collapsed onto the floor and stared up at the ceiling, wishing for my sister and thinking of all the secret thoughts I'd pour into her ears if only I could.

CHAPTER FOURTEEN

Bo

The only way Claes could be coerced into the carriage was if he were allowed to ride alone. Rather than upsetting him, I had another carriage made ready and spent a bumpy, uncomfortable day and a half making tense, uncomfortable conversation with my tutors and wishing that I could be reading my father's journals instead. I wanted to dismiss them both, quite frankly, but I preferred to have known spies in my household than ferret out whomever Patrise sent to replace them. So I spent much of my time staring out of the carriage window while Birger snored and Thamina nattered on about the possibilities she saw for a potential match for me.

When we arrived, I found a letter written on thick green paper waiting for me. It was from the solicitor, Gerlene, and I was fairly shocked at how quickly she'd managed to not only receive my letter, but respond. While procuring more information about the property in Ilor would take a considerable amount of time, she'd given me clear answers to many of the questions I'd had about the estates in Alskad, except one. The large sum paid to X.A.—G.O.A.T. was as much a mystery to the solicitor as it was to me. All she could tell me was that a woman came to collect the *drott* once a year, on the Solstice, and it was to be paid without question as long as she continued to appear.

I'd ruled out the idea that it could be a pension, as the records of all the pensions we paid were kept alongside the salary ledger. But even though the amount was negligible in the grand scheme of things, I couldn't shake the need to get to the bottom of the whole mess. The Solstice was fast approaching, so I wrote to Gerlene to inform her that I planned to be there when X.A. came for her money. This, at least, was a mystery I could solve.

I didn't know if I would ever learn who, if anyone, was responsible for my mother's death, but the looming question of X.A. gave me somewhere to focus my attention. Something outside of my grief, outside of myself, that could occupy the dark, empty pit in my heart. If I kept myself occupied, perhaps the overwhelming weight of loss and responsibility that had slammed down on me since my mother's death would disappear. I knew there would be freedom in this new, lonely future of mine, but I wasn't yet ready to begin building a vision of how that future might look. This strange little mystery was a way for me to escape.

Claes had drifted upstairs, into one of the guest suites, the moment we'd arrived and had refused to see me since. Rather than dwelling on the hurt that his stubbornness caused, I chose instead to dive into my father's journals. My father had written almost religiously throughout my life, taking time every evening right after dinner to sequester himself in his library. Those journals had always seemed sacrosanct, but with the

Queen's words echoing in my head, those pages seemed as good a place as any to learn more about my family's history. Thus far, the most interesting thing I'd learned was that my father had called my mother "Rellie," which I could only imagine she had hated, and that the only time he called me by my given name in the pages of his journals was when I'd committed some sort of truly heinous childhood offense. On most of the pages he'd called me his darling monster, a nickname I'd long forgotten.

After yet another trying supper with my tutors, I settled in with one of my father's journals. I'd worked my way back to the time just after I was born, when my father was in his late thirties. It seemed as though his relationship with my mother became more and more tense as I traveled back in time. The closer I got to my birth and their wedding, the less my father seemed to like his wife, and the more arguments and scuffles he described, sometimes in excruciating detail.

I'd read almost as much as I could stomach when I stumbled upon a passage that made my hair stand on end.

Myrella's spies brought something to her attention today that both astonishes and bewilders me. I'm not entirely sure if I believe them, but the evidence they present seems more than compelling. It would seem that there is some question as to the truth of my and my brother's parentage. An old nurse has, on her deathbed, confessed to these spies of my wife's that before Runa was crowned, she spent a great deal of time here at our estate with her elder sister, my mother, in the months before my brother and I were born. This nurse said that she was the only servant still living who'd been in attendance here at the time. The implication being, of course, that Runa is our mother, and for whatever reason—perhaps because she would have been what, sixteen, at the time?—decided to pass us off as belonging to her sister.

I read the passage again, and then again, aghast. Did that mean that the Queen was my grandmother? Why would she have kept this a secret? And if this was true, why hadn't she had more children?

I scanned the rest of the journal, looking for more explanation, further exploration of what must have been the strangest discovery of my father's life, but there wasn't so much as another word. In his whole life, the only words he'd written about this enormous secret were in the short paragraph staring through the years at me from a midwinter day when I was still a babe.

I wondered briefly if there were some way that I might bring this up with Runa, but quickly dismissed the possibility. If it were true, surely my father would have written more about it. Or would he? I'd no way of knowing, and no way of verifying what might well have been the bizarre fancies of a dying woman. Once again, I was left with more questions than answers—and an early appointment with the solicitor the next morning.

I asked Gunnar to wake me at dawn.

"I would like to go for a walk in the morning," I said. "Set out the wool trousers, please. It'll be chilly. I won't take breakfast. Just kaffe, please."

"As you wish, sir. Though I wonder if you oughtn't ask one of your tutors to accompany you. For propriety's sake, I mean."

I answered his question with a glare. He nodded, turned off the lights and left, wishing me pleasant dreams.

I lay in bed, tossing and turning for what felt like hours. I must have eventually drifted off, though, because when I woke to Gunnar's rather violent shaking of my bed, my room was no longer bathed in darkness. I opened my eyes a crack, took one look at Gunnar and closed them again, despite the smell of strong kaffe filling the room.

He cleared his throat. "You asked me to wake you at dawn, sir. You said you were going to take the air."

At that, my eyes flew open and I leapt from bed. I was dressed and out the door in less than a quarter hour, the solicitor's address secreted in my pocket.

Just past dawn, the streets were busier than I expected. Nobles stumbled arm in arm, singing bawdy songs and swilling the dregs from fat-bottomed bottles of sparkling wine. They looked like wilting flowers in their wrinkled silks and bedraggled hats. Street sweeps followed them, collecting the shattered remains of the nobles' merriment in dustbins. Paper girls ran from house to house, depositing newspapers on doorsteps.

Having a secret errand of my own, I felt the most kinship with the filthy street urchins who darted from shadow to shadow, pockets bulging with stolen and dropped finery. I had hardly ever been up so early in my life—social events ran late into the night, and even as a child I'd slept late. This morning, though, I buzzed with nervous energy.

Gerlene's house at 42 Hawthorne was plain, much like the others on the street, distinguished only by its green door. I knocked and waited for an awkward minute, shifting from one foot to the other and glancing up and down the street before I knocked again. The door opened a crack, and a steel-haired, green-eyed woman glared out from below the chain.

"Oh. It's you," she said. "You're absurdly early."

She slammed the door closed in my face. Bewildered and blinking, I raised my fist to knock again. The door flew open, and the woman I assumed was Gerlene yanked me into the house. She exerted a surprising amount of force for someone so small. With strands of gray hair escaping her braid and wire-rimmed glasses perched on her wide nose, Gerlene resembled nothing so much as a disgruntled porcupine. The olive dressing gown and slippers she wore set off her russet-brown skin, and, looking around, I saw that the green was a decorative theme that carried through the house, perhaps to the extreme. The entryway was all done in green and dark wood; a Clifton table held a green glass vase filled with light green flowers, and the chandelier's glass shades were in green, as well.

"I apologize for waking you. When you said seven in your note, I assumed I ought to come a bit early, to be safe, and it did not take nearly as long to walk here as I thought it would. Should I pop out and scrounge up something to eat? Or some kaffe? Tea?" My nerves made me babble.

Gerlene rubbed an ink-stained hand across her eyes and yawned. "More than an hour early?" She snorted at my blush. "No need for you to go out. I bought pastries last night and have tea in the kitchen. What if you make us a pot while I dress, and I'll meet you in the office?"

I pursed my lips and stared at the green floral carpet. "I'm sorry. I don't..."

The solicitor interrupted me with a sigh. "You've never brewed a cup of tea in your life, have you? Never mind. I'll do it. You can make yourself comfortable in the office. It's through there." She pointed at an arched doorway that led into a sitting room, also decorated exclusively in green and dark wood.

"I don't mean to be a bother, but do you have any kaffe? I've only had the one cup this morning."

"I might have some in a cabinet somewhere."

"Thank you. I do appreciate it."

"Certainly. Now, you know how to light the lamps, don't you?"

Gerlene's condescension put my teeth on edge, but I did my best to control my tone. I needed her on my side. "I'll manage."

"Good boy. I'll be down in a tick." Without waiting for my reply, she trudged up the stairs, and I wandered into the office.

After lighting the lamps, I ran my hand down the spines of the gilt-edged law tomes that lined the bookcases along the walls and peeked through the picture window behind an enormous mahogany desk. Gerlene's garden was meticulously tended, though small.

I took a seat on a small, spring-green sofa. Its silk upholstery matched the two armchairs planted in front of Gerlene's desk and the one behind. My fingers drummed an anxious rhythm as I played through all the possible scenarios for the thousandth time. I'd imagined this moment—meeting X.A. and solving the puzzle—so many times that every disastrous possibility turned my skin a little greener. Before long, I was sure to match Gerlene's decor.

Some little time later, Gerlene bustled into the office carrying a tray, heavy with an assortment of plates, pastries, cups, pots and silverware. She slid it onto the table and adjusted her crisp mint trousers.

"She should be here soon. She nearly always comes before eight, or so I'm told," she said.

"You haven't met her?"

"This is a task for a clerk, not a solicitor with clients like the crown prince. I've always given my most junior clerk the payment and had her spend the night on the sofa. Never had a problem. I take my tea with cream," she added pointedly.

I was on the verge of apologizing for my manners when there was a tentative knock at the front door. I jumped to my feet. Gerlene rose, as well.

"I'll get it."

She strode out of the room, and a moment later, soft voices murmured in the hallway. Gerlene entered first, a tall woman following close on her heels.

"Let's have it done, aye?" she rasped. Her accent was coarse and Northern, but bogged down by the lazy slur of the poorest section of the capital, the End. Her voice was harsh with years of tobacco smoke and cheap tafia, and her clothes were little more than rags—a shock given the sum she was about to receive. Her hair was tied back in a stained kerchief, but the few brassy curls that had escaped were laced with gray. Something in her face was so familiar to me, yet I couldn't manage to place her.

Gerlene retrieved a fat purse from a drawer in the desk and showed it to the woman before putting it back in the drawer. "Madame, if you don't mind, I would like to present Lord Ambrose Oswin Trousillion Gyllen. He has some questions for you."

"Ambrose?" The woman turned to look at me, and when our eyes met, she flushed bright red. For a moment, our eyes—identical, large gray eyes—stayed locked on one another's, and, without a word, she bolted for the door. She was gone before I had time to get my bearings.

"It's rather striking, isn't it?" Gerlene asked. "It's in the eyes, obviously, but your mannerisms are so similar."

I didn't bother to answer. Instead, I dashed out of the room

and down the hall. When I flung open the front door, I found
Thamina on the stoop, her hand poised to knock.

Her nose twitched in surprise, and she said, "Ah! Ambrose.
What a coincidence."

Clearly it was not. Gunnar must have taken it upon himself to let the tutors know that I had decided to go for an
early morning walk. I itched to push past her, to run after
the woman whose eyes were so similar to mine, but I simply
couldn't give Thamina that kind of ammunition.

"Come to see your solicitor, eh? And so early in the morning." Suspicion filled her every word.

Gerlene padded up behind me, her shoes muffled by the
thick green rug. Thamina inclined her head politely. I craned
my neck to peer over her shoulder, scanning the street for any
sign of the fleeing woman, but she'd disappeared from view.
Thamina would manage to ruin this.

"You're a patient woman to put up with our prince's questions at this hour. If your business is concluded, Ambrose,
allow me to escort you home."

Gerlene put a hand on my arm and gave it a warning
squeeze before she nodded politely at my tutor. "You're too
kind, Thamina. As for the matter at hand, Ambrose, I've all
the information required to follow up with the parties in
question, and I'll contact you when the budget is balanced.
Thank you for bringing it to my attention. Your mother
would be proud."

I looked at her helplessly. I had to go after X.A.—I had to
know who she was, and what she was to me—but I couldn't
risk rousing Thamina's suspicions. "Thank you, Gerlene. I'm
grateful you were able to take the time to see me. I'll be staying at my house in Esser Park. You have the address, I assume?"

Gerlene nodded, so Thamina and I made our goodbyes and turned back toward Esser Park. We walked for several long minutes in silence before she said, her tone blithe, "It's good to see you so engaged in your financial affairs, Ambrose. Up before dawn and in the solicitor's office. Your mother would never have believed it."

I had to tread carefully. I wondered how Claes might handle this situation. He was such a brilliant manipulator—most of the time his marks hadn't even realized they'd been had. "It was kind of you to come to collect me. I think it's necessary for me to take more of an interest in my affairs, now that I've officially been named the heir. Though I do, of course, still appreciate your tutelage and the care you've taken with me. Your service is invaluable."

Thamina preened with my flattery. "That's wise. Your mother often lamented your lack of interest in the succession. Perhaps, then, you are ready to return to your lessons?"

The city was waking around us. Merchants with bags under their eyes swung open the doors of their shops. Carriage drivers in stripped-down livery fed their exhausted horses. Flower hawkers took up their street-corner posts and halfheartedly called their wares. Servants guzzled tea in preparation for another day run on borrowed sleep, while last night's revelers lay safely tucked in their beds, blissfully unaware of the buzz of the waking city.

"Soon," I said. "I've been so focused on settling my mother's estate that I've barely had time to grieve." I paused and looked out into the park, willing tears into my eyes. "I think I need a bit of time to myself. You're so compassionate—I'm sure you understand. It's so hard with the servants and all of my social obligations…"

"Well, if it would help…" Thamina straightened her cuffs.

I bit the inside of my cheek, hoping my silence would push her to speak.

"No, it wouldn't do at all. Never mind," she said.

"What is it?" I asked.

"Birger and I had planned a visit with our parents, but in light of your recent losses, we decided we should stay close, in case you should need us."

Thamina might well want some time with her parents, but I would put good money on a visit to Patrise being much more likely.

"You should see them. Gods know, I don't want to keep you from your family."

"I wouldn't want to abandon you. We would be gone for at least two days."

We ambled up to the house, where Gunnar waited in the entryway. With the tutors gone for two full days, I'd have enough time to find the woman with my eyes—and uncover the reason she'd run from me.

"You should go. Take a week, if you like. Gunnar and Karyta will see that I'm taken care of, and you'll be back in no time at all."

I stepped into the dim entryway. The curtains hadn't yet been drawn back, and dust motes floated in the slats of light that came in through the gaps in the rich crimson fabric. The strange woman's gray eyes still haunting me, I went up to my room and waited for word from Gerlene.

CHAPTER FIFTEEN

V<small>I</small>

The next evening, Quill and I sat in the two chairs on my little deck, watching the ocean and talking long after Mal retreated to his own cabin for the night. The ship's bell rang, startling us out of our laughter at eleven—later than Quill'd ever stayed in my room before. He looked at me with an expression I couldn't quite read, eyes narrowed and brow furrowed, but smiling.

"What?" I asked. "Do I have basil in my teeth or something?"

"No. I was just wondering..."

My stomach knotted around itself. "What?"

"Do you want to go for a swim?"

"First you want me to keep out of the ocean, and now this?" I raised an eyebrow at him. "Make up your mind, sir."

Quill took my hand, laughing, and tugged me back inside. He led me barefoot through the quiet halls of the ship, our giggles caught behind lips clamped shut in giddy smiles. We twined our way through the ship until finally, Quill stopped. He pulled a set of keys out of his pocket and, hushing me, unlocked the door.

The smell hit me as soon as I walked onto the warm tile floor. Water. But not ocean water—it was cleaner, more controlled, like a bath, almost. I closed my eyes and breathed in the scent.

"Pretty, isn't it?" Quill asked.

The room was cavernous, with high ceilings and columns that surrounded a wide pool. Every surface gleamed with white stone or metal. A few dimmed solar lights twinkled along the walls, but most of the light in the room glimmered up out of the water, casting wavelike shadows on the walls and ceiling. Cushioned deck chairs were arranged in pairs around the pool, and between them, tables were stacked with towers of thick towels. At the far end of the room, a bar dominated one wall, the bottles and glasses on the shelves behind it glittering like jewels.

"It's astonishing. I've never seen anything like it."

"The excess steam from the solar panel system is piped through the floors and around the pool, so the whole room stays comfortably warm," Quill said. "There are bathing suits in the room over there. No one will notice if one goes missing. Meet you back here?"

"Bathing suits?" I tried to keep the laughter out of my voice, but I couldn't manage it.

Quill blinked at me. "Did you not wear a suit when you dove for the temple?"

I raised an eyebrow at him. "I might write a letter to Anchorite Lugine just to let her know that such a thing exists. I can't wait to see what this suit of yours looks like."

Without waiting for a response, I skipped across the warm

tile floor and into the changing room. Turned out, a bathing suit was more or less the same as my underthings, but cut from a thicker fabric. I found a drawer full of the things and rifled through until I found a pair that looked as though it would fit. I shucked out of my clothes and slipped into the striped top and bottoms. Untying the ribbon that held my braid, I shook loose my curls and left the changing room.

Quill hadn't yet emerged, but my whole body tingled at the idea of swimming. I shifted from one foot to the other at the edge of the pool, trying to be patient, but I couldn't wait.

I dove.

The water was startlingly warm after years of the freezing Penby harbor. It wasn't hot, not like a bath, but instead the perfect temperature. Just cool enough that I could have floated there happily for the rest of my life, and warm enough that I'd never start to shiver. I kicked down to the tiled bottom of the pool and turned happy somersaults there. It wasn't deep—maybe twice as deep as I was tall—and when I looked up through the water, I was startled to see stars overhead.

I floated back up to the surface and lay on my back, staring out through the glass roof of the pool and marveling at the vastness of the sky overhead. I'd never seen stars like that. Even high on the temple roof in Penby, the lights of the city drowned most of the stars. But here, in the middle of the Tethys, the sky was awash with pinpricks of distant, ancient light.

"How's the water?"

Quill's voice startled me, and I flipped my body beneath the surface, suddenly, inexplicably shy. Everyone I'd ever dived with back in Penby had seen me in a lot less than this bathing suit, and mine was a body like any other, after all. Quill stood at the edge of the pool, hands on the ladder, and dipped a toe into the water. His bathing suit, like mine, was nothing more than a pair of undershorts, and the sheer beauty of his strong, lean muscles and smooth brown skin made my heart seize in my chest. A smattering of tight curls of hair sprang up across his muscular chest, and I caught a glimpse of a tattoo on the underside of one of his arms.

Hot blushes burned across my cheeks, and I forced myself to look away. "You can't possibly be serious," I said teasingly. "Just jump."

"Not a chance. A body shouldn't take a shock like that."

He eased himself down the ladder, and the long, elegant fingers of one hand kissed the top of the water, making little ripples that reached out to me like invitations. I needed to get myself together—no good could come of indulging myself in this flirtation.

"You say that to the girl who spent the past fifteen years of her life swimming in the Penby harbor half the year."

Quill grinned at me over his shoulder and lowered himself another inch into the water. I had to do something. Had to stop staring. I swam toward him at the shallow end of the pool, made scoops of my hands and directed the biggest splash I knew how to make at his unsuspecting back. The water rushed over his head, soaking his long, twining locks and tensed shoulders. Quill froze, and a moment later, he let go of the ladder and flopped backward into the pool, laughing.

"I'm going to get you for that, imp."

"Try and catch me," I said, ducking under the water.

I swam to the other side of the pool. Not so slowly that it would feel like taunting, but slow enough that Quill could catch up. He was a strong swimmer, but it would take a lot of practice for someone to be able to keep up with me after my years in the water. When I surfaced, I saw Quill draw his hands back to splash me, so I somersaulted toward the deeper end of the pool.

I wanted him to catch me. I wanted it with every bone in my body, and I was a Dzallie-damned fool for it. Quill made me feel like I could be myself. Without apologies. Without restraint. Just me.

A hand closed around my ankle, but I slipped out of his grasp. When he wrapped his fingers gently around my wrist, though, I let him pull me to the surface. His eyes, like glimmering amber, were something other than playful as he laced his fingers through mine.

I knew better. I knew it wasn't right or fair for me to let the bubbling flirtation between us go any further. But when he pulled me through the water toward him, I let him. And when he brushed my long, dark hair over my shoulder, I met his eyes. And when his arms went around my waist, I let him pull me close. I'd never kissed anyone before. Never imagined what it would be like to kiss someone. I never thought I'd have the chance.

So when his lips met mine, damp with pool water, I didn't expect the electric need that ran through me like a bolt of lightning. I didn't expect to wrap my arms around his neck and bring him closer. I didn't expect the greed and the power and the flush of joy that threatened to drown me. He was gentle and acquiescent, like a slow-burning fire, to my overwhelming, hungry desire.

I never wanted to stop kissing him. I didn't think I could.

He held me close as he kissed me. His arms slicked around me, steadying, as I pressed him into the cool tile side of the pool. He drew back for a moment, only to lay a line of kisses from my jaw to my collarbone.

I wanted things from him that I couldn't even name. When

I pressed my lips to his again, he let go of restraint, whirled us around so it was my back against the tile wall and drew me deeper into the kiss. Filled with that unfamiliar, fiery need, I wrapped my legs around his waist and gave myself over to the burn.

Later, we lay side by side on deck chairs, wrapped in towels, our pruned hands interlocked, staring up through the glass ceiling at the sky. While we'd hauled ourselves apart before our scant bathing suits had come off, our wild, exploratory hands had roamed across the landscapes of each other's bodies.

The two halves of the moon hung huge and silver overhead, washing the room to shades of gray. I thought about the whales, those sleek gray creatures cavorting in the waves, racing the enormous ship. They were so playful, so happy. Seeing those whales leaping from the water had delighted me, and I found myself wishing I was as carefree as they were, flipping through the dark jewel of the ocean without a second thought for the monsters that lurked below.

I would miss the ocean. More than anything from Alskad, I would miss the ocean when I made it to Ilor and sealed my terrible fate. But even more than the ocean, I would miss this feeling. I was so glad for this night—for the one, precious memory Quill had given me. I'd finally had one normal moment in a lifetime of standing out.

"Will you miss the sea?" I asked.

Quill turned to me. "I've never felt entirely comfortable on the water. Swimming's a different thing than living on a ship. The fact that a ship made of iron can float—and not just float, but speed—across the sea feels like impossible magic. It doesn't matter how much I understand the science of it, I can never quite forget the weight of the ship and the fact that there's a whole, vast world filled with ferocious beasts we haven't even begun to imagine beneath us. It could swallow us at any moment."

"You're scared!" I teased, punching him lightly in the arm.

He gave me a wry smile. "I'm smart enough to know I belong on land, is all. What about you? Will you miss it? You likely won't end up close to the ocean. Most of the wealthy folk live farther inland, close to the mountains."

"Yes," I said simply. "I haven't ever been away from the water. I'll miss the challenge of diving and the way it sounds beneath the waves—but I won't miss numb fingers or jellyfish stings. I already miss the seals, though."

"The seals?" Quill asked.

I smiled. "They're almost like puppies. The ones in the harbor grew up with us divers, and they'd get in the water and play with us while we dove."

Somewhere, far across the ship, the bell tolled three o'clock in the morning. I bit my lip, not wanting the night to end. I knew I could count my future with Quill in hours, minutes. Like this perfect night, he and I would be over far too soon.

I sat up and swung my legs over the side of the deck chair. "We should get back. What if Mal's gone looking for you?"

Quill sat up slowly and pulled me across the gap between us and into his lap. "We should. But first..."

He kissed me again, and this time, he was the lightning, and I was the fire, and together, we burned.

CHAPTER SIXTEEN

Bo

Thamina and Birger left later that morning, due in large part to Gunnar's and Karyta's assurances that they would keep an eye on me. I heartily protested the necessity of such a measure, wondering the whole time if either of them had been bought, as well. If they had, it was likely that Karyta's brother had been, too, and then I'd have to hire a new cook for fear of poisoning. I didn't like to think of them in such a distasteful light, but Claes's warning echoed in my head. I had to be more vigilant. More aware.

A note arrived not an hour after they left.

Dear Lord Ambrose,
I've made several discoveries regarding the X.A. account we discussed earlier. However, I need you to verify some facts before I move forward. The necessary documents should be stored in your father's study and labeled X.A. or G.O.A.T. Under no circumstances should they be given to a messenger, as they are

the sole copies and cannot be lost. If you are able, please join me tomorrow at The Turnspit Dog, a tavern on West Riverton Road, between eight and ten in the evening. Dress plainly. You must go unrecognized. I am,
Your most humble servant,
Gerlene Vermatch

While Gunnar took most of the afternoon to finish a long list of errands I'd concocted, I searched the study for a file labeled X.A. or G.O.A.T. and came up empty-handed. I spent ages tearing through my father's desk drawers, to no avail, until I remembered that he'd had a safe built into the floor beneath his desk at our country estate. I lifted the rug and, sure enough, there was a safe, its face covered in dust.

Luckily, the combination was the same as the other safe at our country house, and it only took me two tries to get it open—my hands were shaking too much on the first attempt. Inside, I found the file Gerlene needed, along with a small sack of gold *drotts*. I so rarely had need for coin, as every merchant in the city simply put my purchases on credit and billed the household later. Still, I might at some point want the anonymity of physical money, so I tucked the coins into my pocket and the file under my arm.

Back in my room, I locked the door and settled myself onto the floor by my large, curtained bed. The papers inside the file were neatly organized into three sections, each sealed with wax and tied with a ribbon. Before I could begin to read, however, Gunnar knocked and announced dinner. Quick as I could, I slid the file and the money into a bag and tucked it away beneath my bed.

I desperately wanted to know the contents of the documents, but I also felt the burning need to be near Claes with what little time he had left. So after dinner, I pulled the file from its hiding place and slipped down the hallway and into Claes's room. He was asleep, the curtains drawn and his bed piled with blankets. He looked so gaunt. So pale. He was still refusing to come to meals and now would not even take broth or tea. I knew that he was ready for death, and I was glad for the fact that his door wasn't locked, glad to spend this little time near him.

I pulled an armchair up to his bed, opened the file and began to read.

Some time later, I rested my head against the back of the armchair, my mind reeling and my heart racing, like I was on the verge of a swoon.

"Bo?" Claes's voice was hardly more than a whisper. "You look as though the Shriven are knocking down your door."

I reached over and took his hand in mine.

Claes shook his head and wheezed, "Tell me what's the matter."

Everything that could have been, every lie I'd ever been told, every horrible moment since my father's death flooded through my shattered, splintering heart—and all I wanted was to have someone else share the burden of what I'd just read.

If it had been a month earlier, I would've put him off, knotted these secrets up inside me and lived with the uncertain ache of questions I could never ask. But between Claes's gaunt face and his every rattling breath, I didn't think he could possibly live much longer. And when he was gone... Well. I couldn't bear to think of it. In a rush, I told Claes all about X.A., about the things I'd learned in my father's journals and files. And while I couldn't yet manage to voice my suspicions,

I gave him all the pieces I'd put together myself, the facts that could only lead to one possible conclusion.

When I finished, Claes brought my hand to his dry, cracked lips and said, "The gods work in mysterious ways."

I sucked in a breath. "How can you be so apathetic? Not two weeks ago, you said that you'd spent your whole life working to get me onto the throne. I've spent my whole life training for something that—" I choked on the words.

"You cannot know the will of the gods, Bo," Claes said with a sigh.

The wire-taut anxiety that'd threatened to drown me flashed into anger, and it was all I could do to keep myself from punching through the damned bed frame. "When did you turn into such a flaming devotee?"

"I'll be meeting the gods soon, my love," he whispered. "I should not want to offend them. You should consider it, you know—finding your way back to the temple. We've been too lax in our worship."

A moment later, his eyes fluttered shut and his breathing slowed. I left him there, furious at him, yet even angrier with myself for the rage I felt toward him, whom I had loved so well. I found myself unable to face the possibilities I'd laid before Claes, and in some ways, much as it made me loathe myself, it was easier to be mad at him than to sort through my own mess of a life.

With the next day came an endless stream of visitors, and I found myself unable to tear my eyes away from the mantel clock as the day wore on. Whenever I managed to get away to check on Claes, he was asleep, and by the time I managed to extract myself from the last of my distant relations, it was well after seven in the evening.

I didn't know the tavern Gerlene had named, The Turn-spit Dog, but West Riverton Road was halfway across the city in Oak Grove. I'd never been there—the families in my social circle had moved closer to the fashionable parks long ago—but if I hailed a driver, I could be across the city in less than half an hour.

When the clock struck quarter to nine, I returned to my room, where I stuffed Gerlene's note into a bag with the files and money I'd found in my father's safe and hoisted it all onto my shoulder. I hadn't thought through how I would leave without alerting Gunnar or Karyta. They certainly wouldn't allow me to go out unescorted at night, so I would have to sneak out. There was sure to be a servant posted by the front door, so that was an impossibility. I couldn't go out the window; my room was on the fourth floor.

I'd never been properly grateful for the freedom and solitude of my life in the countryside. In the city, with the endless duties at court, the social calls and the propriety required of my position as the crown prince, I was hardly ever alone. Taking a deep breath and hoping for the best, I crammed an old knit cap I'd found in the basket of servants' winter things into my pocket, opened the door a crack and peered into the hallway.

"Anything you need, sir?" Gunnar's deep voice was slurred with sleep. He'd been slouched in the wing-back chair in the alcove outside my room, but leapt to his feet when he saw me.

I clenched my teeth. With a watchdog like Gunnar, I'd never get out of the house in time. "Nothing, Gunnar. You can go to bed," I said.

"I don't mind, sir. I'll stay out here in case you need anything."

"I'm fine, really. Just looking for a book to lull me to sleep."

I gave him what I hoped was a disarming smile. "Why not get some rest? I'll be asleep soon. Early morning and all. I'm exhausted. Please, go to bed."

Gunnar gave me a skeptical look, but bowed and said, "Thank you, sir. Sleep well."

After Gunnar disappeared into the servants' stairwell, I closed my bedroom door and watched five minutes tick slowly by on the clock on my mantel. I put my ear to the door and listened. Silence. I called Gunnar's name softly, and then again, a little louder. When no response came, I eased my door open again and crept into the dimly lit hallway.

The fourth floor was quiet. I snuck down the stairs, sticking close to the walls, where dark alcoves and potted plants might hide me should the need arise. I paused on the second-floor landing, peering down over the railing. As I'd expected, one of the servants was waiting by the front door, in case of a summons from the palace or some sort of emergency. The house's main staircase had been designed to descend dramatically into the front hall, so I couldn't go that way without being seen.

The grandmother clock in the hallway chimed nine o'clock. That only gave me an hour to get out and across town. I took a deep breath and scurried to the servants' stairs. I prayed to my chosen god, Gadrian the Firebound, that no one would be on them and eased the door open. I glanced up and down. Empty, thank the gods. I sprinted down the stairs two at a time, slid through the door at the bottom and dashed across the hall into the sitting room.

Fortunately, the room stood empty; the ashes were cold in the hearth. I eased a window sash up and froze, hearing a carriage rattle to a stop in front of the house. Voices and laughter rang merrily out. I strained and thought I heard Birger's distinctive cackle, but dismissed the idea. He and Thamina were half a day's ride away, and I had to move fast if I wanted to catch Gerlene.

I dropped the rucksack to the ground—a good five feet below the window—and swung myself over, as well. I nearly lost my footing as I landed. There was no time to struggle with getting the window closed, so I grabbed the rucksack and bolted down the narrow alley between my house and the next. I slowed to a walk when I reached the next block of houses and pulled the hat, which smelled rather strongly of sweat and unwashed hair, down low over my brow.

Three hansom cabs passed me before one stopped, and I had nearly given up hope of making it to my meeting. The driver, a broad woman with thick braids to her waist, said, "Where to, sir?" in the thick, clipped accent of the lower-class city dwellers.

"Do you know The Turnspit Dog? In Oak Grove?" I asked.

"And what's a gentleman like you going to a seedy place like that for, eh?" She twisted in her seat to get a good look at me.

"I'll give you a *drott* if you get me there before ten and don't ask me any more questions," I offered, showing her the coin.

Her eyes widened, and she turned back to her horses. "Just as you say, sir," she said cheerfully. I climbed inside, and she urged her team into a bone-rattling trot.

The Turnspit Dog occupied all three floors of a decrepit house that had likely been beautiful in its time. I tucked my cuff bracelet into my sleeve before entering. A symbol like that, and gold, too, would be noticed in a place like this.

The air inside was thick with tobacco smoke and the sour stench of stale beer and unwashed bodies. The booths and tattered couches on the first floor were unoccupied but for one enormous, bearded man. He stood when I entered, then sat again with a sneer on seeing me. I'd never felt so small in all my life and was sorely tempted to race back outside, flag down another cab and disappear back into my safe, cushioned world. Instead, I glanced around the dingy room, steeling myself.

A stout, smiling woman who was dwarfed by the mammoth wooden bar she stood behind asked, "Get you a drink, love?"

"Err, I'm, ah…" I cleared my throat. "I'm meeting someone, but I don't see her."

The bearded man snorted.

"Most everyone's upstairs," the barkeep said.

I nodded my thanks and headed for the stairs at the back of the dark room.

"Not those, love," she called after me. "Take the front stairs."

I did as I was told, feeling absurdly out of place. When I reached the second floor, I saw the reason for her suggestion. The other staircase led directly onto a dance floor, where several couples swayed to the sad whine of a lone fiola. There was a second bar on this floor, and several bedraggled characters hunched over their drinks, engaged in quiet conversation. It seemed clear to me that there had been some kind of mistake, some misunderstanding. For surely Gerlene—proper, business-minded, respectable Gerlene—wouldn't in a thousand lifetimes bring me to an establishment so thoroughly caked in disreputability. Just to be sure, I decided to climb the next set of stairs and make a hasty pass through the third floor before heading back to Esser Park.

I found Gerlene in a dim alcove beside the staircase. The third story of the building was essentially a balcony that looked down on the dance floor below. Mismatched tables snuggled up to the railing, and booths occupied the dim, stoop-ceilinged alcoves that ringed what must have originally been the building's attic. Gerlene, having naturally chosen the only green table in the room, had a pile of papers and the dregs of something dark and thick in a mug in front of her.

"Ah, good," she said. "I didn't think you were going to make it. Do sit down. Are you hungry? Thirsty?"

I slid into the booth and stowed my rucksack beneath the table. Eyeing the overflowing ashtrays and smudged glasses that littered many of the tables, I shook my head. "No, thank you."

Gerlene chuckled as she rose. "Don't look so worried. The kitchen's clean enough, and Mistress Vick brews the stout herself. You'll have a draft and a couple of pasties. A boy your age wants regular feeding. I'll find Ed and let him know."

She disappeared down the stairs in a flutter of olive serge, and I looked around nervously, fiddling with the buttons on my coat. Most of the alcove booths were occupied by hard-looking men and women. They leaned their heads together and spoke in low voices. The majority of their garments appeared well-made, if worn, and every person I saw wore a knife or pistol on their belt. The sight of so many armed persons actively seeking dark corners only increased my anxiety, and the sidelong glances they directed my way had me shaking by the time Gerlene reappeared with another woman beside her. I nearly jumped when I realized it was Queen Runa, dressed in drab trousers and a veritable collection of sweaters, her hair sloppily braided and dark circles beneath her eyes. She set a pitcher of dark brew on the table, along with three smudged stout glasses, and slid into the booth beside Gerlene, smiling fondly at the solicitor.

"What...?" I spluttered, but Gerlene interrupted me.

"Did you find the file?" she asked.

"File? Oh! Yes. Here. I, uh, I have it here." I pulled the documents out of the bag and handed them across the table. Gerlene took them and pointedly looked from me to the pitcher and back again, but I couldn't stop staring at the Queen. She stuck her hand across the table, offering it to me. I took it, my own hands shaking badly, and noticed that her fingernails were dirty. I'd never seen her anything less than perfectly put together. The sight was deeply unsettling.

"Is it safe for you to be here?" I asked, my voice a whisper.

"Try not to cause a scene," Runa hissed. "I've three of my most loyal guards here, but if these folks get wind of something untoward, we'll be in a bit of trouble." She grinned at me. "It's good to get out around the people every once in a while. Gives me a sense of what's really going on in the empire."

Gerlene nodded to her. "We've business to attend to, youngling, and quick-like. Can't afford to let all our hard work be bungled because you don't know how to handle yourself." She slid the papers to Runa, who leafed through them, nodding.

"I made it here with no trouble, didn't I?" My statement was made somewhat less convincing by my wavering voice. Belatedly, I realized that Gerlene still expected me to pour the stout. I hastily slopped the dark brew into one of the stout glasses, filling half of it with foam that oozed over the top. Gerlene put out a hand to stop me pouring again.

"That'll be yours." She took the pitcher and deftly poured a glass for the Queen and one for herself. "I suppose it stands that a man in your position needn't know how to pour for himself." She took a sip and sighed in irritation. "You should've dressed more plainly."

I looked down. I'd worn my oldest trousers and a plain shirt with far less embellishment than fashion dictated. Granted, my burgundy waistcoat was rather loudly embroidered with turquoise toads, but the jacket I wore covered most of the bold colors and I hadn't brought a fur, thinking all of mine would be too ostentatious. "Can we please get to the point? I don't see what my clothes have to do with anything."

Runa shot me an exasperated look. "Aside from the fact that you're quite young, quite pretty and dressed like the noble you are, you blush every time anyone so much as looks at you. You're hard to miss, and you'll be harder to forget. Have your tutors taught you nothing?"

I started to ask what the hell kind of lessons she thought I'd been given, but Gerlene put her hand up to stop me as the scent of spiced meat wafted over my shoulder. A scruffy man in his middle years, long hair pulled into a tail, set a plate of steaming pasties on the table.

"That be all for you, Miz Gee?" he asked in a thick city accent.

"Yes, thank you, Ed," Gerlene said, and added as an afterthought, "Ed, this is our great-nephew, Tiffin. He's a footman for one of the noble families down by the parks. He's been kind enough to spend his precious night off with his old aunties while his brother tends to their employer's needs. Tiffin, say hello to Ed."

The man cracked a gap-toothed smile at me and wiped his hand on the pristine apron tied around his scrawny hips before offering it to me. "Pleased to meet you, son," he said. "Your aunties are some of our favorite customers. Been coming in together as long as I've worked here, these two lovebirds."

I forced my jaw to stay closed as I wondered why, in the names of all the gods, the Queen of the Alskad Empire was known in a place as seedy as this—and why Ed implied she was Gerlene's lover—but now was not the time for such questions. I shook his hand, trying not to grimace at the clammy sweat clinging to his palms. "The pleasure's mine, sir."

"Ooh, look at the fancy manners on this one." He winked at Runa. "If y'all will excuse me, I best be getting back to the kitchen afore sissy skins me alive."

Ed nodded to us and ambled back toward the stairs. Gerlene pushed the plate to me, took the papers I'd brought from Runa and riffled through them, reading quickly in the low light and muttering to herself.

"It's all in order. These papers back the woman's story."

"What's her story?" I asked. "You're my family's solicitor. Shouldn't you know everything about my estates?"

Runa gave me a sharp look over the rim of her stout glass. "Manners, child."

I blushed, but neither of them seemed to notice.

Gerlene gestured at the papers. "This was all done in my mother's time. She died ten years ago now. Before that, I had my own practice. She wouldn't have kept notes about something like this."

"Like what?" I asked. I didn't want to believe what I'd read. What I'd told Claes. I was desperately hoping for another explanation.

"First, let me ask you two things. Do you have any birth marks?"

I nodded hesitantly. "A port wine stain on my thigh. Why?"

Gerlene ignored my question. "Did you ever hear your parents talking about someone called Ina?"

I racked my brain, but I couldn't remember hearing that name. All I could see was the woman who'd run from Gerlene's house, her gray eyes so like mine.

Bile rose in my throat. I didn't want it to be true. I'd prayed to all the gods, not just Gadrian, that it wasn't true. "Who was that woman, Gerlene?"

"Best have another drink, child. We asked you to come here rather than meeting you somewhere more respectable, because what we have to tell you shouldn't be overheard."

I did as she suggested, taking a hurried sip of my stout.

The Queen leaned in close and whispered, "She's your mother."

I swallowed hard and stared at Gerlene and Runa, horrified. "My mother is dead."

Gerlene looked at Runa, and at her nod, said, "I had an assistant posted at the corner in case she ran. He tracked her to a slum house in the End. When I went to see her, she told me a wild story that I had a deal of trouble believing, but your birthmark and Ru—erhm—these contracts confirm the claims the woman made.

"She said Myrella, your father's wife, had trouble falling pregnant, and when she did, she often lost the babes. The woman, her name is Xandrina—Ina—was a servant in your family's household. She and your father had an affair, and she learned she was carrying around the same time as Myrella. Ina was bundled off to Penby to avoid a scandal. It would have all been over then, but this time, Myrella carried the babe to term. He was singleborn, a boy they called Ambrose."

"Me," I said. My heart rose in my throat, and suddenly I realized the meaning of the acronym in the records I'd found—G.O.A.T. Those were my initials, scrambled. Ambrose had been my mother's choice. Oswin for my father, and my family names, Trousillion and Gyllen. Trousillion had been my father's last name before he'd married my mother and taken hers.

The pieces began to fall into a startling, horrifyingly clear picture.

Runa touched my cheek. "No, dear, not you. The birth was hard on Myrella, and she was very sick for a long time afterward. The doctor said she'd never have another child, so when her babe took ill, she was inconsolable. I suppose it occurred to Oswin that Ina's babes were the same age, and he came to the city asking after them. One was a girl, Obedience, and the other was a boy, Prudence. Oswin offered Ina a great deal of money and a yearly stipend to switch her healthy babe for Myrella's sickly one." Seeing the shocked look on my face, she added, "She was young and had few skills. It's a pitiful story, but she said she saw a better life for one of her babes."

"So...that woman. She's my real mother?" Cold spread from my gut to the tips of my fingers and toes. My father had loved nothing in the world so much as he'd loved my mother—except perhaps me. To know that he had been unfaithful, like so many other members of the court, shattered my memory of him. I'd always wanted to be like him, above the immoral indulgences of the nobles. I'd always imagined he was better than the rest of them.

"Ina gave birth to you," Runa said grudgingly. "But Myrella raised you. By my reckoning, Myrella's as much your mother as Ina, if not more."

Her words, their meaning, slammed home. "And I'm not singleborn?" I twisted the gold cuff at my wrist. I'd always known I didn't deserve its weight. I shouldn't have taken those vows. My chin trembled, and I fought back tears.

Gerlene poured more stout into my glass, refusing to meet my eyes. Runa, however, met my gaze, her warm brown eyes steady and unconcerned.

"No. You aren't. Though these documents are ironclad—we made sure of it. Gerlene's mother knew what she was about."

"What do you mean?" I asked.

"One is a secrecy agreement," Gerlene explained. "Ina is bound to tell no one about the circumstances of your birth, other than yourself or your legal representative—me. The other names you sole heir to your parents' estates. But the third is the most brilliant—a contract, signed by Runa and your parents, that names you Runa's chosen heir. It is irrevocable. You're the first twin in the history of the Alskad Empire to be the heir to the Trousillion throne." She paused, her eyes gleaming. "This could change everything."

The reality of what Runa and my parents had done bloomed like deadly jellyfish up from the treacherous depths of the ocean. "I have a twin?" I asked tentatively, wanting more confirmation. Gerlene and Runa nodded. "I'm heir to the Alskad throne and I have a twin? Hamil's watery damnation. A sister? Where is she? *Who* is she?" I stared at Runa, aghast. If she was my father's mother—if she was my grandmother, as I was nearly positive she was—then this cruelty was far, far worse. She'd taken away my other half. My balance. My conscience. "How could you?"

Runa's weariness disappeared, and she fixed me with a glare that held all the power and might of her years on the throne. "You do have a sister. Her name is Obedience, though she goes by Vi. When Myrella's babe died, we asked Ina to give her to be raised by the temple. It seemed to me that it would be a bit easier for Ina to let go if she lost both of you, and I have some friends among the anchorites who have kept me apprised of Vi's progress. We thought that if Ina could start over, could live without the burden of raising one of the diminished, her life would be more or less normal. It isn't easy to live with one of the diminished, much less raise one."

My heart thudded. It was as though everything in my life had been explained by one simple fact. I had a sister, a twin. No wonder I had always felt so alone. I ached with the knowledge that she must have spent her whole life knowing that she didn't belong and waiting for the grief to take her. My feelings of not belonging and estrangement were at least couched in wealth and love and a lie that would put me on the throne. Her childhood couldn't have been so easy.

I closed my eyes and imagined what my sister's life must have been to this point. Horror and disgust sweeping over me in turns. "But Ina knew she wasn't one of the diminished."

Gerlene took up the thread of the conversation. "She appeared to be, and with the stigma that entails, it was more than Ina could've handled on her own. I hate to say this, but Ina isn't a good woman. She's greedy, mean, a drunk. You're both better off without her."

"But, Ru…" I stopped myself. "But I can't be King if I'm a twin. It isn't right. I'm not fit to rule."

Runa rolled her neck and sighed deeply. "I've been the Queen of this empire for more than thirty years, and I can tell you with a great deal of certainty that my not having a twin does not make me any better than you are. It has broken my heart every day to keep you and Vi apart, and I'd never planned to keep up the ruse forever. So when your mother died, I thought it best you knew now rather than later. You needed to know all the ways you were vulnerable, so that you can protect yourself as we continue grooming you for the throne."

I couldn't fathom it. Everyone around me had spent every day of my life preparing me for a position that our religion—

that simple common sense—dictated I should not hold. "Why not Patrise? Why not Lisette? Why not one of the actual singleborn?" I demanded.

In a dangerous voice, too low for anyone but Gerlene and me to hear, Runa said, "You are the most direct heir to the throne. Trousillion blood runs in your veins, and I will not sit by and watch one of those pompous, lazy nitwits ruin my empire. I know better than anyone what it takes to lead this nation, and I chose you. You will sit on the Alskad throne."

My heart raced. This knowledge, that the Queen had chosen me for her heir, even though I was a twin, even though everything dictated that it was a role I should not hold—it bolstered me. She, at least, believed I would make a good king. And she was the only person who could say so, really. "Then why not tell me the truth?"

"And risk you telling someone? If the Suzerain find out who she is, they'll use her to control you. They've been looking for a way to take more power than they've already managed to steal from the throne, and I refuse to let those graspingly devout charlatans take any more control of this empire. You've not said anything to anyone, have you?"

I paled, thinking of Claes. Runa, her eyes sharp as a hawk's, must've caught my expression. She ran a hand through her hair, and a moment later a filthy, dangerous-looking woman sidled up to the table.

"Your contact in the Shriven. How quickly can you get information from her?" Runa asked.

"Before night's end, I expect," the woman said in a harsh voice.

"I need to know if the Suzerain have called a meeting of the Anchorite's Council in the past day. If they have, I need to know everything you can learn about that meeting. Also, find out if there's an Obedience Abernathy—Vi—on their list."

The woman nodded, and a moment later she was gone. Runa drummed her fingers on the table. "Who was it? Who did you tell?"

I swallowed. "My cousin, Claes. But he's dying. And he loves me. He'd never..." A pit opened up in my stomach, and my hands grew cold. I didn't know anymore. I didn't know anything. "Where is she? Where's my..." I choked, unable to say the word, that single, beautiful word. "Where's Vi?"

Gerlene coughed. "She's in Ilor. She was sent to do labor for the temple there as punishment for stealing. I'd planned to use back channels to see that she was released from her sentence as soon as possible. She could, at the very least, live comfortably in relative safety there with a share of your father's wealth, so long as no one knows of her connection to you."

Runa took a deep breath through clenched jaws. "We'll have to wait," she said. Rage and betrayal coursed through my veins like fire and ice, burning in equal measure. Seeing the expression on my face, Runa added, "I'd planned to reunite you eventually, Bo. We could have manipulated the laws, tempered the influence of the Suzerain. Their power comes from the people's terror of the diminished and the odd mix of fear and safety the Shriven bestow upon them. That, and their belief that only the singleborn can sit on the throne. Let's hope your Claes has kept his mouth shut."

We waited in tense silence, the pasties on the table growing cold. Our eyes burned from the smoke in the air for what may've been minutes or hours. I'd not thought to bring a timepiece, and in the dismal, endless anticipation, time seemed not to exist. The lateness of the hour, it seemed, had no effect whatsoever on the number of patrons occupying the filthy tables of The Turnspit Dog, for each rough character that left was replaced by someone dirtier and meaner-looking.

Eventually, after what seemed to be forever, the woman reappeared and whispered in Runa's ear. The Queen braced her fingers against her temples and let out a long sigh.

"According to Tove's source, the temple received a letter this afternoon. Soon after, the Anchorite's Council was summoned by the Suzerain for a meeting. Not even their secretaries or attendants were allowed into the chamber, and they've been sequestered ever since. Tove's source says the letter came from Claes." My heart sank as Runa continued. "So it looks as though your cousin could not be trusted after all. It will take some great effort for them to find the connection between you and Ina and Vi, but I have no doubt that they'll learn the truth eventually. You'll have to be extraordinarily careful."

"And Vi?" I asked desperately. "Do they know about Vi?"

Runa shook her head. "Her name isn't on the Shriven's list. Not yet."

"It's only a matter of time," Gerlene said. "I should leave immediately. Perhaps, with some luck, I can get her out of the temple in Ilor before they discover the rest of the story."

Runa nodded. "Get on the next ship. Do you have sufficient liquid capital to keep yourself from being traced?"

"I'll go," I blurted. "Let me go."

Gerlene looked at me aghast, but I saw a spark in Runa's eyes. As we'd waited, I'd considered my future. I'd thought about the heavy weight of knowing that my sister, my twin, was somewhere else. I'd thought about going the rest of my life without meeting the girl who'd been with me in my mother's womb. And I'd wondered if I could live with the guilt, the fear of being found out—and the aching loneliness that'd haunted me every day of my life.

"She's my sister," I said pleadingly. "I can't go my whole life without knowing her. Let me go. You said yourself I can't go home. Tell the world that I've sequestered myself in Denor or on your northern estates. Tell them that I'm grieving."

"And what of your tutors?" the Queen asked, eyebrow raised.

"They're on Patrise's payroll and at their parents' house outside the city. Have them arrested, tell them they've been dismissed. Hell, give them a minor title and a bit of land. That'll shut Thamina up in a hurry."

"You cannot mean to let him travel to Ilor on his own," Gerlene hissed at Runa.

The Queen gave her a look that would turn a shark into a quivering, fearful mass of gelatin.

"I'll go whether you give me permission or not," I said, reckless bravery going to my head.

"You are a particular kind of foolish if you think that's true, but be that as it may, I think you're right," Runa said. "You should go. See what kind of girl your sister has become. Find a safe place to settle her in Ilor until I think of what we will do with her." She turned to Gerlene. "See that he's given passage on a ship and has access to adequate funds once he reaches Ilor. Your mother—" She stopped herself. "Myrella bought land in the colonies. Perhaps that can serve as a refuge."

She leveled one last hard gaze at me. "There will be little we can do to help you once you arrive in Ilor. See that you make it back in one piece."

PART THREE

"There is joy that can be found in ignorance, but true bliss, true
freedom may only be found in the profound knowledge of self.
In the peace of total self-awareness, fear fades into nothingness.
It is in this fearlessness that true power may be found."

—from the *Book of Magritte, the Educator*

"In the wash of the ocean and the caress of the rain, you will
find my strength. In the rivers and lakes and springs—therein
lives my forgiveness. Each time you bathe your face, each
drink you take, let it cleanse you of anger, fear and regret.
With my water, start each day anew."

—from the *Book of Hamil, the Seabound*

CHAPTER SEVENTEEN

Vi

Nothing I'd read could have prepared me for the reality of Ilor. The air was thick and damp, like breathing through a wet cloth. And the heat! The heat flat took my breath away. Somehow, in that moist oven of a land, plants grew with a fervor I'd never seen at home. They sprouted from the ground with enormous, wild enthusiasm. Flowers, like ladies in bright silks, sprang up from every patch of dirt and hung from every branch.

I did my best to distract myself from the overwhelming anxiety blossoming in my gut by spending every waking second out of doors. I studied the outrageous birds that mimicked folks' voices and giggled at the antics of the small, funny monkeys with long fingers and furry yellow cheeks. Mal said that great big cousins of the mischievous fellows lived in the mountains, and I longed to see them. Sloth bears lived in the mountain hollows, too, smaller than the great gray bears that terrorized the northernmost parts of Alskad—gentler, too.

There were dozens of creatures here that I'd only read about, and even with the breakneck speed of Alskad's colonization, much of Ilor was still unsettled wilderness.

The Whippleston house was in the center of Williford, the largest of the port towns. There were three rambling floors, all rung round with covered porches. A huge walled garden surrounded the home, complete with a springhouse and burbling fountains. They set me up in a fine, wood-paneled room with a delicate net draped over the bed. A fan spun lazily on the ceiling, and its winding cord only needed to be yanked every half hour or so. Wide, slatted windows let in the jungle breeze, and the room opened onto the third-story porch. From there, I looked out over the town's roofs to the shining promise of the harbor.

Mal found the record of Sawny's and Lily's contracts before I'd even unpacked. They'd gone to Phineas Laroche, the man with the amalgam wife. Never in my life had a piece of luck felt more like fate. As the days passed, and I grew increasingly anxious about who might purchase my contract, Mal tried to tempt me with flowers and fruits I'd never seen before. He told jokes and read to me from novels set in Ilor, but none of his distractions could stop me from worrying. I'd hung all of my hopes on the slim possibility of being reunited with Sawny and Lily, but I didn't even know if they'd be happy to see me when I arrived. I couldn't manage to think of anything except the uncertainty of my future, and the dreamy reminders of the kisses I'd shared with Quill.

I hardly saw Quill at all during the day; he and his uncle, Captain Hamlin, were kept busy negotiating contracts for the other workers who'd come over from Alskad, making preparations for their new business office in Williford and arranging interviews for me. But every night, long after darkness fell and the chorus of cicadas started outside my windows, Quill tapped softly on my door. He sat on my bed and told me everything he knew about Phineas Laroche and his amalgam wife. I was determined to mold myself into the most appealing candidate possible.

When I was done peppering Quill with questions, we found our inevitable way into each other's arms, and together, we discovered all the ways a person could be kissed. Our time together was vastly and horribly limited, but that wasn't enough of a reason for me to stop kissing him. I didn't think anything could make me want to stop kissing Quill Whippleston.

On the morning of my interviews, I woke to a cacophony of birds jabbering outside my window. I lay in bed, wanting desperately to suck every last drop of pleasure from the feather bed and the cool white sheets. But if I was to be honest, I would admit that I was scared. Scared of diving headfirst into unknowable waters, scared of losing my heady new connection with Quill.

I sat up and scrubbed my hands through my snarled curls. I couldn't afford to go down that gloomy road on a day already so fraught with emotion.

As if he'd read my thoughts, Quill suddenly bounded into my room, limbs flying.

"I can't believe you're still in bed," he cried. "We've got so much to do. You've got to bathe and wash your hair, and then we've got to get you dressed. Do you remember what you're to say?"

"At least let the poor girl have breakfast and a cup of tea before you start in on her, Quill." Mal followed his brother into the room, smiling. He carried a tray laden with tropical fruit, a mound of pastries and a glass pitcher of creamy tea beaded with condensation. The housekeeper, Noona, kept big jars of water, tea and fruit juice in the springhouse so there was always something cool to drink, a true luxury in the oppressive heat.

Quill made a face at his brother, and Mal set the tray down on a little table. "You look like you've been sucking on limes, brother mine. Careful your face doesn't stick that way."

I snorted and tried not to laugh. I'd tried to eat one of the sour little fruits the day before and had spent the next ten minutes spitting and scowling at Mal, who'd howled with laughter.

"Don't you have business that wants tending?" Quill asked. "Maybe a friend to see in town?"

Mal rolled his eyes at Quill. "I do have to run, but good luck today, Vi. I can't wait to hear how it all turns out. Just remember to be yourself and choose the person who'll treat you with the most respect."

When the door closed behind Mal, Quill stuck out his tongue and made a rude gesture, sending me into peals of laughter.

"He's always been too serious," Quill said. He waggled his eyebrows and handed me a tall glass of strong, milky tea. "Are you ready for this?"

I grinned at him. "Ready as I'll ever be."

The rest of the morning passed in a blur. I took a long, cool bath, and the housekeeper's freckled, redheaded twin, Ophenia, told me stories in her lilting accent as she washed my hair. I sat in the garden, wrapped in a bright cotton robe, and listened to the little monkeys chatter as my curls dried in the sun.

The scent of unfamiliar spices wafted out of the kitchen and made my stomach growl. Frustratingly, when I finally sat down to lunch, I was too nervous to eat more than a bite of the spicy fish stew. Captain Hamlin stomped around the house, directing servants as they cleaned and arranged vases overflowing with tropical flowers. Mal and Quill's father, Jeb, had absented himself almost as soon as we arrived, and I hadn't seen him since.

Noona did her level best to help me dress, but I'd done for myself for so long that I felt like a fool even letting her try. I'd kept the trunk of clothes Mal had given me, but most of them were impractical to the point of foolishness, having been made in Alskad with its dreary gray chill in mind. There were a handful of light silks that might have been made to work, but Quill insisted that I have something special for the occasion, so he'd brought a seamstress in to rush a dress for the auction.

The dress was a loose, sleeveless style that Noona claimed was popular in Ilor. I didn't have much practice wearing dresses, and I hated the pale pink, tissue-thin fabric Quill had chosen. He claimed it would highlight my blushes becomingly. I'd knocked him hard in the arm for that one, face reddening all the while. Noona chose a bright orange shift to complement the pink, and she helped me tie the garment in place. I stared at myself in the mirror. The dress had a straight collar that fell just under my clavicle, and a scant inch of cloth covered each of my shoulders. The sash was tight around my ribs, and the full skirt fell loose to the floor. My dark curls wafted around my shoulders, and I suddenly felt an overwhelming surge of sadness. Hideous pink or no, this was the first garment I'd ever owned that hadn't been handed down to me—and it would be the dress that I wore on the day I said goodbye to Quill.

As I studied my reflection, I couldn't help but picture Lily and Sawny getting themselves ready to meet Phineas Laroche, just as I would in a few short hours. Lily would have fussed over Sawny, her nervous energy sending her flying around the room. I could almost see his slow, tolerant grin as he waited for her to settle. Just like them, I was being prettied up for an uncertain fate, and I could only hope that I would find a way back to my friends.

Noona saw the tears welling in my eyes and patted my cheek. "It won't be so bad, dear. There are many who find good placements, and sign contract after contract with the first folks who hire them. You needn't be nervous."

I sniffled and grasped for a lie. "Thank you, but I'm not so worried about the contract. There's naught I can do about that, is there? I suppose I'm overwhelmed."

"Oh, you poor, dear little bug. No one's ever been even half-decent to you, have they?" She wrapped me in her arms and squeezed. "Be kind to the folks you come across who aren't so fortunate as you, eh? Though I think you'll have a hard time finding any."

I hugged her back, hard, and did my best to choke back the tears. There was a knock at the door, and Quill slipped in.

"No, no, no!" he exclaimed. "I won't have you all red-faced and weepy! Today's the day that the bright, shiny part of your life starts."

Noona ducked out of the room, leaving me alone with Quill.

"Do you want to take it back?" Quill asked. "I can go down there and tell them all to go away if you want."

"No," I lied. "I've no desire to turn myself over to the temple now. Not after we've both put so much into this. It'd only bring you to their attention, and neither of us wants that."

"You don't have to do either," Quill said. "Ilor is a big country. You could start a new life."

I laughed through the tears, but I didn't let myself dwell on the idea for even a minute. "I am starting a new life. And if you do your part and negotiate well for me, I'll be wealthier than I could've ever imagined."

Quill wrapped his arms around me, hugging me close to his chest and tucking his chin on top of my head.

"You are going to be amazing. I'll come to bring you down in half an hour."

I rubbed the tears out of my eyes, blew my nose and went over my mental notes about Phineas Laroche one last time. *If ever you wanted to intervene with the gods in my favor, Pru,* I thought, *now would be the time to lend me a hand.*

I knew Quill would see me well settled, no matter what, but I wanted to make sure that I did everything in my power to see that Phineas made an offer. To make certain sure that I found my way back to Sawny and Lily.

CHAPTER EIGHTEEN

Bo

After spending an uncomfortable night waiting, at Gerlene's insistence, in a fleabag inn near the wharf, it was a relief to be shown to my cabin aboard the *Adelaide*. Despite her initial protestations, Gerlene had eventually stopped trying to convince me to change my mind and booked a first-class passage for Bo Abernathy on the next ship leaving for Ilor. The pseudonym had been her idea—Abernathy was Ina's surname, so I supposed I had a better claim to it than I did to Gyllen. More importantly, though, it was a name that linked me to Vi.

She'd asked, over and over, if I wanted to go back to the house in Esser Park and say a final goodbye to Claes, despite the danger such a venture would present. I'd nearly gone, but the fury and betrayal overwhelmed everything else I'd ever felt for him. I didn't want to give him a chance to explain—I knew what he'd say, and I had no interest in his excuses. The Claes I'd loved was really and truly gone, if I'd ever known him at all. Everything I'd understood about him, about us, had been ripped away when he told the Suzerain my secrets.

Gerlene would tend to the running of my estates until I returned. She'd provided me with a handful of *drott*, a small sack of *ovstri* and a larger pouch of *tvilling*. It was as much money as she could gather quickly without raising eyebrows, though it didn't seem like much to me. She also gave me letters that would allow me to withdraw funds from the bank in the town closest to the land my mother owned. I would travel under the guise of an assessor, hired by Gerlene to check on my mother's holdings in Ilor.

Lost in my thoughts and unaccustomed to answering to the name I'd assumed, I didn't hear the steward call me at first. "Mister Abernathy," he repeated. "Your room is down this hall to the right."

He unlocked the door and handed me the key before showing me in. The room was quite small, its furnishings outdated, but it was well equipped enough to serve. The steward gave me a map of the ship. He pointed out the first-class decks, dining halls, exercise room and parlors, as well as other amenities, such as a swimming pool and cards room. Then he said, "If you'll give me your tag, sir, I'll bring up your other bags."

I blinked at him for a moment, not understanding. When he gestured to my rucksack and the valise Gerlene had given me, it dawned on me that most of the other passengers would have a great deal of luggage being loaded from the wharf, and the tag he mentioned must be a way of organizing those bags. "Oh, eh, this is all I've brought, actually… What was your name?"

The young man's face split in an incredulous grin. "Schaffer, sir. Would you like me to send up the tailor? He'll have you a whole new wardrobe by the time we see land again, he will. But you've got to get to him quick-like. The other gents always have him booked up after their first night winning at the tables."

I pressed a gold *drott* into his palm. "Yes, thank you, Schaffer. That would be lovely." Considering for a moment, I gave him another. "There'll be two more when we dock if you'll bring my meals up to me."

Schaffer gave me a firm pat on the back. "They aren't so superstitious in the Ilor colonies," he said. "You'll do fine."

It was an odd statement, and I wondered what he was insinuating, but thought better of asking. "Thank you, Schaffer. Will you bring up a pot of kaffe when you've got the time? After you see the tailor, please."

Schaffer left with a bobbing bow and eased the door closed behind him. I'd no sense of what these kinds of clothes would cost me, but it would be worthwhile to leave the ship with a wardrobe appropriate to the climate and fashion in Ilor. The last thing I wanted was to stand out.

I ran my hands through my hair and thought of my sister. I wondered if she looked like me, like Ina. I couldn't think of her as my mother, no matter how I tried, but I wanted to know everything about Vi—what she liked and didn't, what sorts of things made her laugh, what frightened her. I promised myself that I would do everything in my power to make up for the circumstances of her childhood.

I spent much of the two-week journey pacing the ship and trying to distract myself from the guilt and grief that washed over me in waves. I hated myself for the anger that had kept me from saying a final farewell to Claes, who was surely gone by now. Every corner I turned reminded me of him. He'd so loved the enormous sunships and had always talked of our traveling to Denor or Ilor together one day. In some moments, I wished desperately that he could've been here, leaning over the railing and watching the dolphins with me, but in the blink of an eye, I went right back to hating him for going to the Suzerain with my secrets. I wondered if he knew that his betrayal could end with my death as well as my sister's, or if he'd only been thinking of the dictates of the temple and the lessons we'd been taught about the superiority of the singleborn.

The tailor came to deliver my new wardrobe and collect his payment late one afternoon. I counted the money into his palm, silently cursing myself; for when it was done, the whole endeavor had drained most of my reserve. Sniggering silently in the corner, Schaffer did his best—and failed—to hide his mirth.

"Spent a bit more than you expected, sir?" He grinned at me. "What if after the tea's all delivered, I come back and show you up to the library. Gentlemen like you love to read, and all them books are just gathering dust as it is. No one ever goes up in there, except to clean. Even has its own deck, the library does. You can take the sea air and get your head off this ship for a bit. It's restlessness and boredom from being too far from your twin. Turns your mind all crooked, sir. Can't be without that other hand what to stay your own." Schaffer clapped a hand over his mouth. "Forgive me, sir," he said. "I let my mind run off with tongue. I meant no offense, really."

I laughed, finally realizing that he'd thought that I was one of the diminished all along. "It's fine, Schaffer. In fact, I'm on my way to my twin as we speak."

Schaffer heaved a sigh. "That's good to hear, sir. Truly it is. Terrible thing to be apart though, ain't it? That's what happened to you, then. Can't make a right decision with my Selah too far off. She keeps me even. I took a job without her once, when she was growing a babe, and I spent my whole pay on a bottle of bubbly for a girl over in Williford. Didn't even think on it 'til she downed the last sip. That's when I realized I'd have naught to eat for the week we was ashore before our return trip. Why'd you let him go, if you don't mind me asking?"

"She'd business to attend, and I couldn't get away." I gave him a long, appraising look. Perhaps he was right. Maybe the impulsive decisions I'd been making since my birthday and my mother's death could be attributed to Vi's departure. The timing was certainly right. I said casually, "I've never heard that before. Were you irrationally peevish, as well?"

"You mean was I touchy and quick to use my fists? Aye! I was, now that I think on it. Most folk don't ever leave their twins, so they don't talk much on it."

I turned that over in my mind. He was right. No one in the Alskad Empire ever went more than a hundred or so leagues from their twin, and even that was rare. Odd. Very odd. "I think I would like to see that library, Schaffer," I said. "Will you show me the way?"

When we landed in Cape Hillate, Schaffer pointed me in the direction of an inn he called "not at all awful for the price" and said they'd be able to direct me to a livery. Heaving the strap of my newly acquired valise onto my shoulder, I took a deep breath and set off down the gangplank. As soon as I stepped off the ship, a wall of heat, like that from a potter's kiln, hit me. I gasped, filling my lungs not with crisp sea air, but with a substance that felt more liquid than gaseous. I wanted to take off my jacket, to roll up my sleeves, but I couldn't. Not without revealing the telltale gold cuff on my arm.

The docks swirled with activity. Women and men in loose trousers and sleeveless shirts hefted ropes as thick as my forearms and carried crates off ships. Fisherwomen flung insults back and forth as they hawked their wares. Other folk ambled through the crowd in loose linen suits and long, flowing dresses, their expressions insouciant and paces distinctly unhurried.

I marveled at the colors as I made my slow way off the docks. The ocean water was turquoise and clear in a way I'd never expected. The trees were rich with enormous leaves in every shade of green. Flowers erupted from the rich, dark earth. At the edge of the water, sailors crowded outside taverns, their faces slicked with sweat and eyes blurred with alcohol.

"Look, ladies, that pretty Alskad orchid's crumpling up and dying, and him not even having touched Ilor's soil yet."

My face burned with blushes. Nervous sweat trickled between my shoulder blades.

"Watch out, gents. This one's gone so red, he might catch fire any minute."

I cringed and did my best to brush past them, back straight, but my breath caught in my throat and my legs went weak. "How does anyone survive in this heat, much less choose to settle here?" I muttered to myself.

"You get used to it, bully," a deep voice said from beside me as a big hand clapped me on the back.

"Excuse me? What did you call me?" I glanced at the man as I spoke. He was just my height, but where I was slim, he bore broad, muscular shoulders and arms like a blacksmith's. His green eyes twinkled with laughter, bright against his tanned, freckled skin. His sun-bleached hair was tied back in a tail that drew attention to his square jaw. He was beautiful. Not like Claes, with his perfectly arranged black hair and high cheekbones, but a livelier, less polished beauty.

I pushed Claes out of my head and did my best not to gape into this young man's gorgeous green eyes.

"Bully," he repeated. "It means friend."

A brawny man, whose sharp nose and beady eyes made him look like a bird of prey, strode up to us and shoved my newfound companion. He stumbled backward a step.

"What'd you do that for?" the beautiful young man asked, pouting.

"You know why," the hawkish man snarled. "Get out your purse, Swinton."

I took a step back—I had no desire whatsoever to find myself in the middle of a dock brawl. Another step backward bounced me off an iron wall of a person, who'd evidently come to watch the impending fight with several of his largest friends.

"Watch yourself," he snapped.

"Pardon me." I hefted my valise and tried to make my way through the crowd.

"Not so fast," the hawkish man called, reaching for my valise. He threw a sly look at the handsome young man he'd called Swinton. "What do you say I just take this one off your hands, and instead of breaking your knees, I'll give you a week to pay up."

Something tickled my nose, and I rubbed it, irritated. "I don't even know this person. I really must be going—"

But before I could finish, one of the onlookers shoved me between the two young men.

"I'll tell you what," Swinton said. "I'll come on by and talk this through with your pretty sister. I'm sure she and I can settle this between us. We all know you don't have a head for figures." He turned to me with a grin. "Come along, bully. We'll be on our way." Swinton moved behind me, but the hawk-like man stepped toward us and grabbed for Swinton over my shoulder.

Suddenly, unable to contain it for another minute, I sneezed, and my head hit something, hard. Pain flared across my forehead as I fumbled for my handkerchief, and laughter rose around me like a swelling wave. Looking up, I saw that our harasser was sprawled out on the planks of the dock, his nose streaming blood.

Swinton took my arm and pulled me through the crowd as it dispersed, grinning and nodding at everyone who caught his eye. When we finally broke free and made our way off the dockside boulevard, I was short of breath and sweating profusely.

Swinton patted me on the back and gave me a broad, white grin. "Thanks for getting me out of that one, bully. And to think, I was about to lift your wallet."

"You were about to what?" I asked, aghast, rubbing the tender spot on my forehead.

"Don't look so put out. You're an easy mark. Not that I'd let anything like that happen to you now. You saved my skin back there."

He offered me his hand, which I shook, warily. I said, "I'll be going, then."

"I can't let you go off by yourself in a city like Cape Hill-ate, not with you a newcomer, and me owing you a debt. Let me take you to an inn, at least."

His trousers were bright orange linen, slightly rumpled— though what else could one expect from linen in this heat?— and faded along the seams from regular ironing. His creamy cotton shirt was unbuttoned past his clavicle. Rather than proper shoes, he wore leather sandals. Disreputable as he looked, though, Swinton made a good point; I didn't want to be robbed of my last few coins. I fumbled my valise from left to right hand and pulled a scrap of paper from my waist-coat pocket. "I'm looking for an inn called the Traveling Bluesman. Do you know it, Mister...?"

"Just Swinton. How's about I walk you over there, and you can tell me what brings you to Ilor."

I told him the story I'd concocted with Gerlene, the true bits—that I was looking for a young woman about my age, with dark, curly hair and a Penby accent. I said she was a by-blow of my father's, a dimmy, who'd come to serve a labor sentence with the temple. And then came the lies—that I'd come because our father had remembered her in his will, and my employer had given me leave to bring my sister her in-heritance, so long as I checked on my employer's estates in the meantime.

The papers, bank drafts and letters of introduction Gerlene had provided for me backed this story, and—in a less than amusing twist of fate—my meager stock of remaining coin made it even more plausible. Swinton made agreeable noises and nodded as he steered me through the crowded, swelter-ing streets of Cape Hillate. I finished my story as we stopped in front of a two-story building, its wooden shingles gone gray from years of exposure to the salty ocean air. A sign, black script on white, swung over the door: The Gilded Vole.

"This isn't the Traveling Bluesman," I said dumbly.

Swinton opened the front door and waved for me to go first. "I couldn't take you to a hole like that in good con-science. It's full of rats, and the beds are more bugs than feath-ers. My auntie runs this place. She'll take good care of you."

"I don't know. I appreciate the thought, but my valet recommended the Traveling Bluesman. I'm certain he wouldn't lead me astray."

"And I'm sure he takes a cut from the Bluesman for every rich fool who pays for a dirty room and a bad meal. You seem like a nice young fellow. Let me do you a favor."

I searched Swinton's twinkling green eyes for a sign that he might be less than sincere. Finding none, I took a deep breath and walked through the door he held open.

CHAPTER NINETEEN

VI

I clutched Quill's arm in a white-knuckled grip that was sure to leave bruises as we walked together into the parlor. The nonsensical babble of birds wafted in on the breeze as we entered the room. Aside from myself, Quill and Hamlin, there were two women and two men, all dressed in light fabrics cut in elegant, unfamiliar styles. The women wore elaborate hats with wide straw brims. Both men wore shirts cut long over their hips and closely tailored linen trousers. One of the women wore a blue striped dress similar to mine, while the other sported loose cotton trousers and a sleeveless blouse made from thin Samirian silk.

Hamlin stood by the hearth, a sweating silver cup clutched in one big hand. His bright grin glowed in the dark of his skin. He elbowed the portly man next to him. I took all my prospective employers in one by one, assessing, calculating. Quill laced his arm through mine and leaned down, reminding me to smile under his breath.

"Ladies and gentlemen, it is my great honor to introduce to you Miss Obedience Violette Abernathy. Vi is a sixteen-year-old from the capital of our empire. Each of you are here because you've expressed interest in hiring one of the diminished in the past, and now we, the Whippleston Exchange Firm, would like to offer you that opportunity for the first time in the history of Ilor. Vi has been among those unfortunates some call dimmys for near on sixteen years, and in that time, she's shown nothing but good judgment and piety. Vi's contract will last for ten years, and the bids for her salary will start at two hundred and fifty *drott* per year."

I felt my eyes widen slightly and shot a quick glance at Quill. He'd said that they'd make a fortune off my contract, but I had no idea it would be *that* much. Quill's face remained pleasant and welcoming as he said, "Please avail yourselves of the refreshments we've provided and take some time to interview Vi. She is a lovely young woman with a number of interesting, erhm, talents that would be an advantage to any household in Ilor."

Quill pried my fingers away from his arm and gave me a little shove into the center of the room. I bobbed a slight bow to cover my stumble and glared back at him, but he was already moving toward the door. The men and women hoping to bid on my contract surrounded me like flies to a piece of half-rotted fruit. I twitched, but Quill had warned me about this; I needed to bear it as politely as I could.

A middle-aged lady with a round face and tiny hands lifted a curl off my neck and peered at my skin. Mehitabel. She was the godly one. I simpered at her, playing the part she expected of me.

"She's quite pale. That milky, freckled skin they have in Northern Alskad. She'll burn like Gadrian himself, Phineas.

You won't be able to take her out riding, and we all know how much you and Aphra enjoy your horses. Best leave her to me."

Ice shot up my spine, despite the heavy heat in the air, and I turned to look at him, plastering the friendliest smile I could manage on my face. Phineas circled me, appraising my swimmer's build and long muscles. He was a big man, with a thick barrel of a chest and arms as wide around as my legs. His glossy brown hair was laced with gray, and he had creamy skin tinged gold from the sun.

"You're wrong, Mehitabel. She's pale, but tough. She'd do fine on my estate, riding and all. Do you like the outdoors, child?"

"Very much, sir," I said, smiling.

The portly man—he must've been Luccan—patted me on the waist, looking through me as though I weren't even there. "A little full in the hips for my taste, perhaps."

I seethed.

"Too bad about the nose," red-faced Constance said, taking a crystal flute from a passing servant's tray. "If it hadn't been broken, she might be nearly pretty."

I did my best to tamp down my surging temper, but when a hand squeezed my bottom, I whipped my head around and spat, "Excuse the piss out of me! Where exactly do you think you get off, you—"

Hamlin strode across the room. "Excuse us for a moment." He yanked me out of the room by the elbow. "Control your temper, girl. It would be a grave mistake to insult the people who will determine your quality of life for the next ten years. A contract like this is nearly impossible to get out of once signed. We can play that last off as a charming show of sass, but do not—I repeat, *do not*—offer these people insult. Do you understand me? If you behave nicely and manage to gain their favor, your life will be comfortable. If you do not, well, Dzallie protect you, for I won't be able to."

When we reentered the parlor, I managed a fair approximation of an apology to the woman who'd taken a handful of my ass, Constance. Luckily, she laughed it off. I spoke briefly to Luccan, who seemed more interested in the Whipplestons' wine collection than in hiring me, and sat on the couch between Mehitabel and Phineas.

"I do hate these virtue names that we have, don't you, child?" Constance tittered. "I keep hoping they'll go out of style, but they seem to be here to stay. Tell me, do you have any talents or training at a craft?"

"Well, ma'am," I said, "I used to dive for pearls, and I'm quite good at cheating at cards." Quill'd told me that Phineas and his brother were known throughout Ilor for the days-long gambling parties they threw. I winked at Phineas.

Constance and Phineas burst into laughter, but Mehitabel's expression grew sour. *Perfect.*

"It's true." I turned to see Quill coming through the door. He smiled at me before turning to Phineas. "She took more than thirty *ovstri* from me on the journey here. I didn't even know she understood brag until I'd lost more than half my purse. She's a canny one, though I can't attest to her skills as a diver."

"Ah, Quill, you're back. Let's get down to the meat of it, shall we?" Constance suggested.

Phineas nodded, and Mehitabel said, "Yes, let's. Our time is valuable."

Hamlin seemed to have disappeared with Luccan. Everyone in the room looked to Constance, who said, "We've all come here because we're interested in hiring one of the diminished. We all have our own reasons, which, I assume, we would rather not divulge. But I assume we all need to know about her history."

Mehitabel piped up. "And, of course, her devotional practices."

They all nodded, and I tried not to twitch. This was all very strange and very personal. More personal than they knew. Quill gave me an encouraging smile.

Phineas said, "I'll start. Have you ever committed a violent act against another person or an animal?"

I furrowed my brows and debated how to answer for a moment. "I've thrown a punch or two, but never unless I was hit first," I admitted. "As for the other, I'd never hurt a beast." I thought of what Mehitabel had said earlier about how much Phineas loved riding. "I love all animals, especially horses."

"No need to get defensive, child. You must understand why we have to ask," Constance said. "Now, have you ever stolen anything?"

I bit the inside of my cheek. "Nothing I didn't need more than the person I stole it from, ma'am. I've done a bit of pickpocketing, lifted a few loaves of bread, a few pieces of fruit. Nothing substantial." A blush crept over my face. It wasn't an outright lie. I just happened to see my pearls as my property, where the temple saw them as theirs. I glanced up, guarding my expression, but for the barest hint of a smile. Quill'd said she was paranoid. I wanted her to feel a tinge of worry that I might make off with her jewels. Just enough to stay her hand.

Mehitabel cleared her throat. "Are you faithful?"

I thought of the hundreds of hours I'd spent at adulations in the haven hall in Penby, the years I'd scrubbed the flagstones in front of the temple's altars and the thousands of times the anchorites had implored me to find solace in prayer. If the women who raised me could have given me one thing, it would have been faith, but the stories about the gods and goddesses had always seemed like that—stories.

I decided to give an honest answer. "I was raised in the temple in Penby and schooled by the anchorites, but theirs was never my calling."

Let them chew on that, I thought to Pru. I had to be bright red now, like one of the strange talking birds in the trees outside.

Quill clapped his hands onto his knees. "I think that'll do it. Vi, if you'll retire? Ladies, gentlemen, this way." He ushered them toward the study, glancing at me over his shoulder. That may not've gone as he'd expected it, but I crossed my fingers, hoping my answers would push the folks who'd make bids for my employ to do as I wished.

I paced my room for more than an hour and a half before Quill burst in, grinning. He swept me up in his arms and twirled me around in a circle. But when he set me down and leaned in close, I pulled away, anxious.

"Well?" I asked.

"We did it, Vi!" he declared with a laugh. "Phineas and Constance did their best to outbid each other. They were practically foaming at the mouth to get you."

"So, who is it?" I asked, heart beating in my throat.

"You'll go with Phineas—Master Laroche—to Plumleen Hall in New Branisford. You get to be with your friends, Vi. And it's only a half day's ride south of here. He agreed to eight hundred *ovstri* a year for your salary." I sucked in a shocked breath as Quill continued excitedly. "Even less our ten percent, that's a fortune for you! Better still, Luccan has agreed to an exclusive shipping contract for our wine. You've just secured a future for Mal and me."

Quill put a gentle hand on my cheek, pulled me into his

arms and kissed me. And for a moment, the whole world melted away. Everything was sparks and light and the warm comfort of his arms around me. All I knew was his lips on mine, his arms around me and the insatiable need to kiss him back.

When we finally, reluctantly pulled apart, I slumped on the edge of the bed. It was like the wind had been knocked out of me. I'd done it. I'd actually managed to pull it off. Eight hundred *ovstri* a year. I couldn't imagine that kind of money, much less someone having that sum to throw away on a servant.

I took a deep breath, my heart racing. In a few short hours, I would see Sawny again. Excitement ran through me like a bolt of lightning, leaving shocks of nervous joy in its wake. I couldn't wait to see the look on Lily's face when she saw me.

I wasn't blind to the risk I was taking. I'd heard the rumors of unrest, the stories of contract workers horribly mistreated. I knew that I'd sold ten years of my life away—ten years of being trotted out at parties and gawked over, being Phineas Laroche's most recent badge of bravery. But I'd done it for the simple possibility of a bit of happiness, a little more time with my best friend, and I couldn't bring myself to regret it.

"I've heard nothing but good things about him, Vi," Quill said, kneeling before me. "We never would have done business with him otherwise." He tucked a curl behind my ear, suddenly solemn. "I'm sorry, but Phineas wants to leave at once. Can you ride? We'll lend you a horse for the journey— gods, we'll *give* you a horse!"

I scoffed. "Of course I can't ride, numbskull. What, you think the Suzerain bought me a pretty white pony when I was a girl? The closest I've been to a horse is the back of a tatty cart. I can walk, thanks." I couldn't help the acid on my tongue, despite everything he'd done for me. Despite everything I felt for him.

Quill and I stared at one another for a tense moment, and he burst into laughter.

"But you told them that you loved..." He trailed off, grinning. "I'll see about a gentle horse for you, then. Maybe find something a bit more practical to wear?" As I moved to my trunk, glad for a reason to shed the dress and its layers of billowing fabric, Quill said, "I know that you made this decision with open eyes, Vi, but there're some practical things you ought to know. It's not getting any easier for contract workers, and every one of the laws favor the wealthy. Mal and I'll do whatever we can for you if aught goes wrong, but it'll be to your advantage to try to gain favor with Phineas and his wife. The more they like you, the easier your life will be."

I grimaced. "I'll do my honest best, but the truth is I'm about as likable as a nest of rats in the bedsheets."

"Vi, please. I'm trying to look out for you." He cupped my cheek in his hand. "I care about you. You're wonderful."

I rolled my eyes, but didn't pull away from him.

"Well, you're wonderful when you aren't attacking folks with the sharp side of your tongue and rolling your eyes at them."

I bit my lip, trying not to blush. Having cleared the first, impossible hurdle—having found a way to Sawny—I was suddenly overwhelmed. I needed time, a quiet moment to collect my wits. "Can't we wait for a minute? I haven't packed. I haven't said goodbye to anyone."

Quill arched one of his eyebrows, raising it nearly to his hairline. "No reason to pack everything now. Just take what you'll need for a few days. We'll send your trunk along sometime this week. I'll send Mal up for a goodbye if I can find him."

"What about you?" I asked.

"What about me?"

"Are we going to say our goodbyes downstairs in front of your uncle and Master Laroche and everyone?"

A smile, like a ray of sun breaking through rain clouds, passed over Quill's face, and he folded me into his arms. I shouldn't have let him, should have pushed him away, but nothing in my life had ever been quite so wonderful as letting Quill hold me tight to his chest. I let myself savor the moment, knowing that I would be stuck at Plumleen Hall for the next ten years, and this would likely be the end of our brief, blissful romance.

Quill kissed me, one hand tracing the line of my jaw, the other around my waist. He laid a row of feather-light kisses down my throat and across my clavicle. When he was done, and I was nothing but ocean spray and the unrelenting warmth of an Ilorian sun, he took my face in both his hands and fixed me with his golden stare.

"There's no need for us to ever say goodbye. We've only just begun to explore this thing between us. We have all the time in the world."

Just then, Noona strode into the room, carrying a pair of heavy leather saddlebags. I sprang back from Quill, blushing. There were a thousand questions on the tip of my tongue, and while I desperately wanted to believe that this wasn't goodbye, I knew better. Even if Quill wanted to labor under the illusion that we could maintain this thing between us, I had to be realistic.

"I packed some food for you." Noona set the bags down by my steamer trunk and shooed Quill away to envelop me in a hug. "You be well, Vi. Tell the boys if you need anything. I wrote down our address here, as well as the new office. Remember what I said. Be kind to those around you, hear?"

"Thank you," I said, tears welling in my eyes.

"You're welcome," she said. "Phineas told me to say he was leaving in half an hour, and you with him. Best hurry."

Quill said, "I'll go see if I can't find my brother," and ducked out of the room with a playful wink at me.

My chest was tight, and I couldn't catch a breath. Noona flew into action. She helped me strip off the filmy pink dress, and I pulled on the light cotton shirt and pair of trousers. When I had dressed, I knelt in front of my trunk, digging around for my pouch of pearls. I slipped the cord over my head and tucked it into my shirt while Noona's back was turned. I exchanged my thin sandals for soft leather boots and stuffed the sandals and a few changes of clothing into the saddlebags. Noona folded all the diaphanous layers of my pink dress into a bundle and tucked it in on top.

"That's all that will fit. Everything else will have to be sent along. Now, you take care of yourself, hear me?"

I nodded and hugged her one last time. As I trudged down the stairs, weighed down by the saddlebags, I felt a wave of sadness wash over me. I had so badly wanted to say goodbye to Mal. He'd become a friend, and a dear one at that. His laugh lit me up, and I didn't want to go the rest of my life without hearing it again. I hated that he wasn't here to see me off.

Phineas was waiting in the foyer with Hamlin and Quill. There was a large, iron-banded chest that had not been there when I went up, and my new employer was tapping a riding crop against his boot.

"Well, Vi, Quill here tells me that you don't know how to ride. No time like the present to learn, eh? The wife and I are great riders. In the stable morning, noon and night. You will be, too, soon enough." Phineas's accent carried the lilting music of the Ilor colonies, but none of its relaxed pace. He clipped many of his words short, racing for the next one.

"I'm to be a stable hand, then?" I asked with a mischievous smile. "I think you may've overpaid a bit, sir."

The Whipplestons cast sidelong looks at Phineas. I watched, too, trying to gauge his reaction. Phineas studied me for half a moment, then chuckled.

"I'd be a fool if that were the case, my dear. No, no, no. Your contract is a surprise for my wife. She…" He paused, pursing his lips. "Well, you'll see. Come along, then."

His wife. That piece of the puzzle fell on me like a stone block. His *amalgam* wife. Shit. I'd entirely forgotten about her. I wondered if everything I'd been told about the amalgam was true. *I certainly hope not, Pru,* I thought, shuddering.

Hamlin took my bags from me and clapped me on the back. "Be well. My nephews have spoken quite highly of you. I wish you all the best in your new home."

He and Phineas led the way outside. Quill pulled my arm through his as we walked out onto the porch. On the front lawn, a big, gold-colored horse was being led in great prancing circles by a stable hand. Phineas strode across the lawn, took the reins from the girl and whispered to the horse before swinging into the saddle. Hamlin threw my saddlebags across the broad back of a dull brown horse, who stood patiently while he fastened them.

"That's Beetle," Quill said. "Uncle Hamlin bought her when he first started trade in Williford. She's old as sin, but gentle and patient. Don't pull on her mouth, keep your weight in your heels, and you'll be fine. Beetle will take good care of you."

Quill hoisted me into the saddle, and Beetle snorted and

shifted below me. I grabbed her mane in panic. Quill laughed and Hamlin handed me the reins, patting my leg reassuringly.

"We'll go slow until you get your bearings. Remember, heels down," Phineas said. He loomed over me on his elegant gold horse. "We'll be home before supper."

He nodded to the Whipplestons and started off across the lawn. Beetle jolted into action, swaying beneath me like the ocean beneath a ship. My heart raced, and I twisted in the saddle, calling to Quill. He jogged to catch up.

"Tell Mal goodbye for me. Please. And take care of yourselves." Tears washed down my cheeks. "I'm going to miss you."

Quill reached up and squeezed my hand. "We won't be far, and I promise—we'll check on you soon."

Phineas turned onto the main thoroughfare, and as Beetle followed, I looked back over my shoulder at Quill, waving now from the wide porch. I blew him one last kiss before Beetle's plodding steps took me away.

CHAPTER TWENTY

Bo

The delectable smell of roasted meat and unfamiliar spices drifted out of the inn's kitchen, quelling most of my reservations. Swinton ambled in after me and gestured to a table. Grateful for the breeze generated by the fans overhead, I set down my bags and took a seat. Swinton reappeared a moment later carrying two big, green spheres. A stout woman in the odd sleeveless style of dress that seemed to be popular here followed him, smiling broadly.

Swinton handed me one of the rough orbs—it was surprisingly heavy and appeared to be some sort of fruit—and set the other on the table.

"Auntie Kelladra, this is Mister..." He coughed and gave me a pointed look.

I put the fruit down beside Swinton's, rose and bowed politely over the woman's extended hand. "Bo. Bo Abernathy. A pleasure, madam."

"Would you look at the manners on this one!" She pulled

out a chair and sat, gesturing for us to do the same. "So, Mister Abernathy. What can I do for you?"

As she spoke, Kelladra stabbed the tops of the fruits on the table with a queer, triangular knife. She handed one to me and the other to Swinton, along with thin, metal tubes.

"Thank you, madam. I need a room for the night and the name of the nearest livery, if you please."

"Drink up," Swinton said. He'd put the tube into the fruit.

I followed suit and sucked briefly on the metal tube. Cool, salty-sweet liquid filled my mouth like moonwater. "What is this?"

Swinton and Kelladra laughed, deep belly laughs, and she said, "Coconut. Better than water in this heat. Now, as for the room, you can share for ten *ovstri*, or have one to yourself for twenty. A bath is two *tvilling*, and meals are the same. As for the livery, well, Tueber must be smiling on you. I run carriages from my stable out back. Where're you headed?"

"I'm not entirely sure yet. I'm looking for someone, and I haven't yet learned where she's landed."

"No trouble there. My Swinton's got his ear to the ground. I'm sure he'd be happy to help you find what you're looking for. His day rate as a guide is—what, ten *ovstri*? Any idea where you might start?"

I stared at my shoes, completely at a loss. "I do need to get to Southill at some point."

"You want a carriage? That'll be…" She considered for a moment, counting on her fingers. "Four *ovstri*, plus ten *tvilling* for food. Less if you can find folks to share with you."

I gulped, unable to hide my shock. That would eat up nearly all my money, leaving me nothing at all. "And what to buy a horse?"

"I've a hardy little mare I'm willing to part with for two

ovstri, but you'll never get anywhere without a guide, you not knowing the countryside and all. Swinton, dear, fetch me something stronger while I think."

Swinton rose and disappeared through a slatted door at the back of the room. I fidgeted nervously while Kelladra fanned herself with a yellow silk fan that matched the trim on her dress. She was a handsome woman, and she bore more than a passing resemblance to her nephew. They shared an air of cunning mirth that was both charming and worrisome. Swinton reappeared a moment later with a tall glass of startlingly orange liquid, which he handed to his aunt before resuming his seat.

Kelladra and I soon came to an agreement—one that left me with only a few small coins jingling in my pocket. Swinton would help me learn what I could in Cape Hillate, and he would serve as my guide in Ilor—for a fee. I would pay half the cost of the horse and guide services when we left, and half when Swinton and I parted ways. I headed upstairs to stow my bags in my room and bathed rather hurriedly in the slat-walled outdoor shower. Once I was dressed, I went back downstairs to meet Swinton for a late supper and some reconnaissance.

I found him waiting for me in the common room, flirting with a young woman with dark brown skin whose head was shaved bald. Her eyelids were painted gold to match the embroidery on her sleeveless dress.

"All set?" Swinton asked, springing to his feet. He kissed the girl on both cheeks and whispered something in her ear that made her eyes crinkle delightedly at the corners.

My stomach lurched. The disappointment that coiled through me when I saw Swinton flirt with the young lady unsettled me, but I certainly didn't want him to know that.

It didn't seem right, even given his betrayal, to be so attracted to someone else so soon after Claes. Swinton's charms only brought my imagination to life, though, and I couldn't help but consider how it would feel to kiss him.

I forced the thought from my head, and said in what I desperately hoped was an unconcerned voice, "I am if you are, but I don't mean to take you away from something important."

"Aw, Lalia will wait for me, but if she's otherwise engaged when we get back, I can see her sister, Alzabetta, right?"

Lalia slugged him hard on the arm and said, "We ain't interchangeable, you scoundrel. Get gone, and don't you come crawling back to me later." But her grin belied her tone, and Swinton returned it, winking at me.

He blew her a kiss as he steered me out onto the street. The onset of darkness had done only a little to lift the damp heat, and sweat glazed my temples even as we walked. The tree-lined streets buzzed with the rasping shrieks of seven-year beetles.

"I thought we'd head to a little tavern I know. It's a shade nicer than the dockside hells, and the cook sets a damn fine table."

We passed a group of women lounging on a porch. One sang an aching ballad in a sweet, low voice. The others picked out a tune on twangy stringed instruments and kept time on a steel drum. Swinton tossed a *drott* onto the porch, and the women smiled at him, but kept playing.

When the music had faded behind us, I asked, "Why not go to a hell? Wouldn't we have more luck finding information about someone just arrived and headed for a temple in a place where sailors drink? She'd be fairly distinctive, wouldn't you think? A dimmy traveling alone?"

Swinton laughed, stopping in the middle of the street to pound his knees and gasp for breath.

"It isn't that funny," I said, irritated.

"Not funny?" Swinton hooted. "Not funny! Little lord, you might be nothing but a low-rent clerk, as you claim, but you walk and talk like you piss streams of gold. I'd put good money on that valet of yours setting you up to get robbed blind, and if I take you to a hell, there's no hope of us making it a step—much less all the way home—with our purses intact. At least in midtown, folks will take your money honestly while they pretend to believe your lies."

I gritted my teeth and silently thanked the gods for the darkness that hid my reddened face, saying nothing. What could I say, when he was so obviously right?

"You're right about one thing, though," he said. "If your dimmy landed anywhere on this coast, we'll hear about it. Not every day a captain'll agree to take a dimmy on board."

Swinton led me through a maze of alleys that eventually emptied into a square. Tangles of moss hung from the branches of the stunted, gnarled trees that edged the center green. A statue of the first Queen of Alskad loomed in the middle, her shape familiar even in the darkness, and dim lamps lit the signs that hung over the squat buildings' doorways. The air felt close and thick with humidity and stank of meat smoke.

Swinton darted up a set of unswept stairs and eased a door open, gesturing for me to enter. There were twice as many women as men in the tavern, and most bore the weathered, leathery skin of the maritime life. Many of the patrons' arms were tattooed from shoulder to knuckles, beautiful and terrifying pieces that made me want to stare. One woman turned from her seat to gesture at a serving lad; I gasped when I saw the lines of blue ink snaking up her neck and across her face.

I'd never seen tattoos on someone who wasn't one of the Shriven. Swinton elbowed me in the ribs.

"Don't be a fool. Stop gawking and find us somewhere to sit. I'll get drinks."

I nodded, and he slid toward the bar. I edged around the room, trying to ignore the low whistles directed at me as I passed through the crowd.

"You can come sit on my lap, sweetheart," a rasping voice called out behind me.

I bit my lip and scanned the room for an empty table, pretending not to hear the woman. I spotted one littered with glasses, but the stools around it were empty. I darted through the crowd, anxious to sit somewhere, anywhere, out of the way.

A hand reached out and squeezed my bottom. I yelped and whirled around to face a table of women. All in their middle age, their faces were tanned, skin tones ranging from light fawn to dark russet brown. Their eyes were ringed in dark makeup, and dozens of silver rings marched up each of their ears. The woman closest to me sported another silver ring in her nostril. She grinned at me, her teeth dazzlingly white, and patted the stool next to her.

"Come have a sit, pretty. Let Baya buy you a pint."

I channeled the Queen and looked down the full length of my nose at her, saying, "I'll thank you not to touch me again, madam."

A muscular arm wound round my waist, and my stomach rose to my throat.

"Sorry, bully. He's with me." Swinton kissed me on the cheek, and shivers raced down my spine. I absolutely shouldn't be excited by kisses from this rapscallion, not after I'd seen him cozying up with someone else not an hour before, especially not with the memory of Claes still looming over me—and most of all, not when he was in my employ. But a part of me couldn't help it. Something about Swinton set my heart racing.

"What say we buy you all a round to drown your sorrows? Sit down, sugar."

I glanced at him, confused, but he pushed me onto an open stool and snatched another for himself. When the barman arrived with our drinks, he ordered more for the table. While Swinton made easy conversation with the sailors about the tides and trade prices, I kept my mouth shut and watched. Swinton had a way with people. He seemed to slide seamlessly into the conversation, and within minutes, the rough sailors acted as though they'd known him their whole lives. They trusted him, and I found that I did, too. Whatever he was up to, he had a good reason.

Eventually, the conversation turned to the temples, and I saw an opportunity to ask about my sister.

"I wonder if—"

Swinton cut me off, giving me a sharp look and shaking his head just once. "Let's have another. What do you say?"

Several hours and a half dozen of my small coins later, Swinton was deep in conversation with the women. I'd stopped listening some time earlier. Instead, I watched the people in the tavern flow in and out like the tide and considered the plethora of human faces. The great variety of wealth and cleanliness alone was something to gawk at, but even more interesting was the range of styles and fashion. Unlike in Alskad, it seemed that no one style dominated in Ilor, and everyone simply dressed however they wanted. There were people in trousers and dresses, in leather and lace and linen, dyed in raucous colors and patterns. There were people with hair in every imaginable shade from gray to white, gold to black. The woman behind the bar had hair dyed indigo. It was her I was watching when Swinton dug his elbow into my ribs.

I turned my head. "I'm sorry. I didn't hear you."

"I said that you had heard the rumors about a captain bringing a dimmy across the Tethys, but you didn't believe a word of it. D'you remember the captain's name?" Swinton gave Baya a disarming smile.

I took a deep breath to calm my nerves and tried to play along. "Don't waste their time, Swinton. No one is idiot enough to confine themselves aboard a ship with a dimmy. Certainly not long enough to cross the Tethys."

Swinton had cautioned me about betraying any interest in Vi herself—that would only cause trouble. If we could find the captain, we could find Vi.

Baya picked at her teeth with a bone from the pile in front of her and spat on the floor. "Believe it, love. Whippleston's his name. He sails between Penby and Williford. He's navy, but he's in shipping, not military. There're rumors about him—all kinds of things, but I do know he moves goods for the navy and books passengers, too. Does a nice trade in wine and exports, and his nephews do some recruiting of contract workers. Man's got to be richer than Rayleane. Heard he brought a dimmy across not long ago. I think his nephews arranged for her contract in Williford. Made quite the profit off his cut alone, or so I'm told."

"He must have nerves of steel," Swinton said.

"Or a death wish," one of the other women added.

"He's one of the only men to make captain in Her Majesty's navy. He's a lot of things, but he ain't cracked," said Baya. "I sailed with him when I was a lass. Man'll do damn near anything if it'll give him two extra coins to rub together.

Brave as spit, he is. I wouldn't bring a dimmy over, not for any kind of money."

"Why would anyone want to give a dimmy a contract?" I asked, baffled. A part of me hoped it was true. The farther she was from the eye of the temple and the Shriven, the better off she'd be. "Most people back in Penby can't get far enough away from them."

"You ain't been in Ilor long, have you, son?" Baya asked.

I shook my head.

"It's still half-lawless here. The temples don't have the kind of power they have in the rest of the empire. There ain't more than two dozen of the Shriven in the whole of Ilor. Some folks with strange predilections and bizarre ideas come to settle here for just that reason. Rich folks get off on proving to each other who's got more guts by collecting that what scares them and showing off to their pals. After what happened before, well…folks need contract workers for labor, and they've found a market for the more…exotic, as well."

I started to ask what she meant, but Swinton interrupted me. "Isn't that the truth? Speaking of, we've a long day tomorrow, and I'm eager to get this one home, if you know what I mean." He gave the women an exaggerated wink, which sent them into howls of laughter and me into a deep red blush.

We made our way outside, and when we were away from the dim glow of the square, Swinton clapped me on the back.

"Williford," he said. "I'd put good money on your sister being there, or close by. I don't know Captain Whippleston himself, but I know his nephews. Better, I know where they like to drink. Not too bad for a night's work, is it?"

"How far is it to Williford from here?"

"From here? A couple of days by ship, less than a week by horse." He reached out and rapped on a porch's wooden railing. "So long as we don't run into a herd of aurochs or a band of thieves, it shouldn't be a hard ride."

"What that woman said back there..." I trailed off, hesitating. "About what happened before. What did she mean?"

Swinton swung an arm around my shoulders, sending shivers up my spine. "It's old news. Nothing to worry your pretty head about, little lord. I'll tell you as we ride, if you'd like."

I thought of Lalia, the beautiful girl Swinton'd been kissing in his aunt's common room. "You don't mind being gone so long? I don't want to pull you away from your sweetheart."

"You can't mean Lalia? She's not my sweetheart, just a friend. We have a bit of a flirt sometimes, but it isn't serious. I'm a free man, and my tastes vary widely." Swinton laughed and gave me a wink that threatened to melt me. "I'll go with you, bully, and happy to. You've got secrets I plan to learn, and it wouldn't hurt for me to get away from the folks under the impression I owe them money. Plus, can't pass up an opportunity to help out a fellow dimmy, can I?"

CHAPTER TWENTY-ONE

VI

I slid off Beetle's back in the stable yard of Plumleen Hall, so sore and exhausted I could hardly walk straight. Phineas— he'd told me to call him by his given name—had explained during our ride what he'd meant about my contract being a surprise for his wife. Her birthday was less than two weeks away, and until then, I would be hidden away and receive training from the butler and other staff. He'd been more than clear that I was not, under any circumstances, to be seen by his wife, lest I ruin her gift. I wondered if Mal and Quill had been pulling my leg, or if the woman really was an amalgam. I certainly wasn't going to ask Phineas.

I wanted him to like me, but I also desperately wanted him to stop talking. He'd hardly shut his mouth since we left the Whipplestons', and the more he talked, the more my nerves knotted with anticipation. I was so close to seeing Sawny and Lily.

Somewhere in the jungle, about halfway through our ride

to Plumleen, I'd realized that, for the first time in my life, I had almost everything that I wanted. Up until that moment, all my energy had been focused on convincing the Whipplestons to help negotiate my contract and making certain that it was Phineas who won it. I hadn't given much thought to what would come next, what I would do when I was finally happy.

"Lucky for you," Phineas said, interrupting my thoughts, "our master of horse has recently been let go, and I've not had time to replace her, so her apartments are empty."

He clapped me on the back, a little too hard, and steered me toward a door that led off the barn's main hallway. A passel of dogs in all sizes and colors yipped at his feet, but he hardly noticed them.

"It isn't lavish," he continued, "but you won't have to share with anyone while you get used to the way things are run here at Plumleen. Of course, after the party, you'll move into the manor house, so Aphra can have access to you at all times."

Access, I thought, my stomach sinking. I hadn't dared hope for any kind of privacy once I started my work, but that word slammed into me. Though the grounds and barn had hardly registered in my mind's eye until now, his words jolted me out of my daze, and I finally began to take in the details of my new space.

The rooms Phineas showed me were almost enough to make me forget my aching body and nerves. Almost. A wooden door opened off the barn's main hallway into a tiny mudroom equipped with hooks for jackets and shelves for shoes. We removed our dusty boots, and Phineas showed me into what he called the great room. It was as big as my whole cabin onboard the *Lucrecia* and boasted a wide sandstone hearth. The room was sparsely furnished with old-fashioned, though well-maintained pieces—a couch, an armchair, a bookcase with shelves that sagged from the weight of too many books, a table with four mismatched chairs.

Phineas gestured to the door by the hearth. "Through there is the bedroom and washroom. There's hot water for bathing, so long as the boiler's not gone out again. Get some rest, and I'll see that one of the kitchen lads brings you a bite. Tomorrow Hepsy and Myrna will start your lessons."

"Thank you, sir," I said. "This is all very generous."

"The rules here at Plumleen Hall are simple, Vi, and if you follow them, you'll do well. Many of our servants have chosen to stay on past their initial contracts. First, you must never leave the property unless my wife or I give you permission. Second, you must never refuse a direct order from a member of my family or the managerial staff. And, most importantly, you are expressly forbidden to speak about my wife's condition. Not to her. Not to me. Not to any of the other servants. Do you understand?"

I nodded, though my mind seethed with questions. What kind of orders were these folks giving that following them had to be laid out so plainly? And why was Phineas so concerned about his wife's so-called condition becoming a topic of conversation? I wondered if Mal had been right, and the lady of Plumleen was an amalgam.

Just then, one of the stable hands brought my bags into the apartment. Phineas introduced her as Myrna, and she smiled at me. I returned the smile, grateful that at least one of the people who would be training me seemed friendly. Phineas wished us a pleasant night before gliding out of the room.

Myrna looked to be no more than five or six years older than me. While she might've been as pale as I was had she lived in Alskad, the sun had turned her skin nut-brown and bleached her hair to nearly white. It hung in a long, pale gold braid over one shoulder, and her wide smile took over her whole face—even her eyebrows crinkled.

"You look like you could fall asleep standing up," Myrna said kindly. "You get yourself into bed. I'll wake you come morning. If you need anything, our rooms are over yours. Stairs are around the corner by the hay. Can't miss 'em. Sleep well."

I thanked her, and she gave me a rakish grin before leaving me alone in my new home. As the door closed behind her, I resolved to ask her to help me find Sawny and Lily as soon as I could manage it.

Myrna hauled me out of bed when the sun was still a distant promise of lavender streaking up the horizon. I felt like I hadn't yet been asleep for more than a minute—despite my aching weariness after the ride from Williford, trying to sleep in the unfamiliar bed had been like trying to climb an ice-slicked roof. Every time I was close to sleep, I'd startled myself right back to wakefulness, excitement about seeing Sawny and Lily pulsing through my veins with every heartbeat.

I pulled on the trousers, boots and shirt I'd worn the day before and darted into the apartment's main room, where Myrna was waiting for me with a giant glass of cold, milky tea and a thick slice of ham tucked inside a soft white bun. She shoved the sandwich into my hand and started toward the door, already talking at breakneck speed.

"Phineas said you're to learn to ride, but that you've not had any practice at all—which, frankly, doesn't seem at all possible to me, but I left Alskad when I was still a brat, so what do I know?"

I gulped down the tea and followed Myrna into the barn, sleep-addled and barely tasting the sandwich as I chewed.

"You're going to be getting quite the education in all things Plumleen these next few weeks, so say a prayer or whatever works for you, because you shouldn't expect to sleep much. Every morning you'll help me feed the horses and muck stalls, and I'll give you a riding lesson. From there, you'll go to my horrible twin, Hepsy. She's the butler, and she'll be boring you to death with lessons in household protocol. You'll serve the evening meal for the staff, then the same thing all over again. Aphra's birthday's in less than a month, so you'll be running yourself near to death between now and then. Are you ready?"

She thrust a pitchfork into my hand, not waiting for an answer. If I was to serve the evening meal to the staff, that would be my chance to find Sawny and Lily. I couldn't wait to see the look on Lily's face when I passed her grub to her.

"Because I'm the most wonderful friend a girl could have, I've already fed the horses and put them out to graze. All we have to do now is muck stalls. Have you ever..." She trailed off, shaking her head in answer to her own question. "Of course not. You can't ride, stands to reason you can't muck a stall, either. I'll show you."

Three backbreaking hours later, I'd hefted and tossed and wheelbarrowed, calling on muscles I didn't even know I had. And all that before I'd even climbed onto Beetle's back. I'd gone through my whole life believing I was strong, hauling oysters and diving for the temple, but nothing could've gotten my body ready for this kind of work.

The riding lesson was another hour of Myrna shouting at me to keep my heels down, my toes pointed in and to flow with the horse, whatever that meant. When it was finally all over, Beetle untacked and released into a field, I collapsed onto a hay bale in the barn hall, my legs gone to jelly, my stomach growling so loudly I was sure to spook the horses.

"I don't think I'll ever walk again," I moaned to Myrna. Laughing, she offered me a hand. I batted it away.

"You're going to have to. You've only got an hour to clean yourself up and grab a bite before you're to meet Hepsy in her office."

I moaned. "I can't do it. I can't move. I accept the consequences of my fate. You can tell her I said so."

"I'm not telling my sister squat if I can help it, and I'm not going to let you lie there and get yourself in a world of trouble on your first day. Up you get."

Reluctantly, achingly, I accepted her hand and groaned to my feet. Myrna patted me on the back.

"Better run. Hepsy doesn't accept excuses, and she can't stand lateness. You don't want to find yourself on the sharp side of her tongue."

As I bathed—quickly, thanks to years of growing up with fifteen or more other brats sharing the same bathroom and not nearly enough hot water—I wondered why Myrna and her sister didn't get along. It wasn't that twins were always the best of friends, but I couldn't see how anyone could manage not to get along with Myrna. She was one of the cheeriest, kindest people I'd ever met. *She never even mentioned the fact that I'm a dimmy, Pru.* She treated me like any other normal person.

As I dashed out of the bathroom, tying a bit of string around the end of my wet braid, I saw that Myrna'd brought me lunch, bless her. There was a flatbread piled high with roasted squash and caramelized onion and strung through with bits of soft blue cheese. Rayleane's cheeks, I could kiss the woman. I folded the flatbread in half and stuffed it into my mouth as I jogged toward the manor house. Following the directions Myrna had given me earlier that morning, I raced down the steps and into the basement servant's entrance.

Hepsy was waiting for me outside her office, arms crossed over her chest. She and Myrna were identical, or had been at one point. Where Myrna was tan, Hepsy was pale. Where Myrna's hair was long, Hepsy's was cropped just beneath her chin. Where Myrna was plump and muscular, her sister was rail-thin. The two women could not have been more different.

Hepsy eyed me up and down disapprovingly. "You're three minutes late, you have food smeared on your cheek and your hair is wet."

"Ma'am—" I started, but Hepsy cut me off.

"We've no time to waste. I assume you, being diminished, know nothing about etiquette or how to behave in a properly run household?" She didn't wait for me to answer. "No. Of course you don't. Follow me. We'll start with the basics."

For the next five hours, Hepsy lectured me on a thousand things—how to properly fold a napkin, open a bottle of wine, remove a plate unobtrusively from a dining table. And that was just to prepare me to serve the staff meal that evening. In those five hours, I didn't utter a single word. There was no space for it. While Myrna was quite the talker, she, at least, was jovial about it. Hepsy seemed to be so irritated by the fact that she and I had to exist in the same room that she filled every moment with endless instruction, making no little effort to assure me that she wasn't pleased in the least to be the one tasked with my education in etiquette.

I could hardly contain my excitement as Hepsy led me into the kitchen. Surely, given his experience and training, Sawny would be peering into an oven or stirring together some sort of delectable sauce. The kitchen was not one room, but three, and as Hepsy nattered on, I studied every person who walked through the door, searching for Sawny's familiar features.

Steady me, Pru, I thought. *I feel like I could explode.*

Hepsy turned to me, her voice sharper than any kitchen knife. "Are you listening?"

"Of course," I lied.

"Let's get you an apron, then. The Laroches won't be pleased if their dinner's delayed because ours runs long."

As the servants streamed into their dining room, I carried platters of crisp-skinned duck and charred ears of corn, huge bowls of salad and tureens of creamy, delicious-smelling soup to the pair of long tables, scanning the room for Sawny and Lily all the while. As the room filled and folks started eating and chatting, I was nearly shaking with anticipation. My friends were nowhere to be seen. As I circled the table, re-filling the tall water glasses and replenishing the bottles of chilled makgee, I listened for their names.

Perhaps Sawny and Lily were occupied in another part of the estate—maybe their work had kept them late. But surely someone would mention them. There were more than fifty people in the room: folks with dirt beneath their fingernails that hinted at their work in the kaffe groves or gardens; those dressed in kitchen whites or neat, dark household uniforms; a group clustered around Myrna who clearly worked with animals. But as they finished eating and drifted out of the room, my heart sank. No one had said a word about Sawny or Lily.

When Hepsy finally dismissed me, she said, "Tomorrow, tell my sister that you simply must arrive to your lesson on time. The least she could do is respect, for once, the importance of my work. And make sure your hair is dry. We're going to begin your understanding of caring for Madame Laroche's clothing, and it wouldn't do for your dripping hair to spot her silks."

I trudged back to the barn, pausing inside my door for a

moment to greet the puppies I'd found living in my apartments. The tumbling balls of golden fluff wagged their whole
bodies as I scratched their ears. I fished in my pocket for the
scrap of ham I'd secreted off a dinner plate as a bribe for the
puppies' mother and looked up to greet Myrna. My heart
leapt when I saw that she was sitting on the steamer trunk
Mal had given me.

"You didn't tell me you had a beau," Myrna said, pouting. "And he's deadly good-looking, too. What's worse, you
didn't tell me you were flipping rich."

My eyes darted around the room, searching, I supposed,
for Mal or Quill. I didn't know which of the two I'd rather
see, but I desperately hoped they'd waited. Myrna grinned.

"He left before sundown. Said he had to get back to his
business in Williford."

A weight settled in my stomach and disappointment must
have clouded my face, because Myrna burst into gales of
laughter.

"Don't look so downtrodden, pet. He left a note."

Myrna pulled an envelope from behind her back and waved
it in front of me. I reached for it, but she hopped onto the
trunk and held it over her head. The puppies yipped and ca-
vorted around us, and their mother bayed a single long note
before putting her head back on her paws.

"No, ma'am," she said. "This has to be an equal exchange.
You tell me all about your handsome beau, and I get to go
through your trunk. Then you can have your precious note."

I stuck my tongue out at her. "Come on! He left it for me,
not you," I said, her contagious laughter catching in my throat.
"Nothing in there is worth a damn in this heat, anyway."

"I saw silks and velvets when your beau got the paper. I

just want to know what kind of work you thought you'd be doing to need such fine things."

"They were a gift," I said. "And he's not my beau. Now give me the note. You can have anything you want out of the trunk. Really. It's yours."

Sighing, Myrna handed me the envelope. "He certainly seemed like a beau, the way he asked after your happiness and health and all."

She hopped off the trunk and dove into its contents, flinging sweaters and trousers around the room gleefully. The puppies bayed and tottered around the room, soaking up as much excitement as each of their wiggly bodies could hold. I settled down on the floor next to their mother and opened the note.

Vi,

I waited as long as I could in hopes of seeing you, but I have to be back in Williford tomorrow. I'm sorry that I've had to leave without speaking to you. Keep your head up. I'll see you soon.
Cheers,
M

Nothing from Quill. I could have kicked myself for the shameless yearning that raced through me. My face was hot, and when I looked up, Myrna was watching me with a quizzical expression of amusement.

"Not your beau?" Myrna asked, grinning.

I threw a pillow at her. "Can I ask you something?"

"Surely."

"Two of my friends from back in Penby, Sawny and Lily Taylor, took contracts here about a month ago, but neither of them were at dinner tonight. Do you know where I might be able to find them?"

Myrna's face paled, and she went still, her hands knotting in her lap.

"What is it?" I asked, and I could hear the fear raw in my throat.

"I hate to be the one to tell you this, but your friends..." She stopped and cleared her throat. "From what I understand, Lily noticed an error in the estate's account books. She was helping with the bookkeeping, see? And rather than telling Phineas, she brought it to Aphra. That sent Phineas spinning."

One of the puppies pawed at my knee, whining, and I pulled her into my lap, grateful for the sweet, soft warmth as my heart turned leaden and heavy in my chest. I couldn't make sense of what she was telling me. "What do you mean, 'spinning'?"

"I was going to wait a beat to warn you. Phineas—" Myrna's lips tightened, and she let out a long, slow breath. "Phineas is a monster. When he found out what Lily'd done, he hauled her out of the house by her hair and beat her bloody."

My jaw was clenched so tight I thought my teeth might shatter. "Where are they now?" I gritted.

"Vi, I'm so sorry. Lily died that night, and Sawny the next day. They're gone."

I sat there, the puppy wriggling in my lap, numb for a solid minute before I fell entirely to pieces. Tears flooded my cheeks, sobs wracked my throat, and Myrna held me as I cried until I could cry no more.

CHAPTER TWENTY-TWO

Bo

Swinton and I traveled well together. On our first evening in the jungle, when a roar in the distance sent me shooting to my feet, panicked, he managed not to laugh.

"It's a wild dog, bully," he yawned.

"You say that as though it should make me feel better."

I couldn't see anything past the dim ring of our fire's light, but I heard the horses, hobbled in the clearing with us, stamping and snorting.

"They don't come down out of the mountains hardly at all, and they're too afraid to get close to anyone with a fire. Don't worry about it. Get some rest."

I sat, pulling my knees in close to my chest and staring into the fire. Nothing in my life had prepared me for this. I thought of Runa, of her endless lessons on the monarchy and behavior and the history of Alskad. All information that would surely be useful to me someday, but here, in the half-wild jungle of Ilor, none of it was helpful. None of it was at all relevant.

Swinton cracked open one eye and looked at me across the fire. "What's giving you trouble, bully?"

"Nothing. I don't mean to keep you awake. Go back to sleep."

Swinton pulled himself to a sitting position and stared me down, a hint of amusement tugging his lips up at the corners.

"If you're not sleeping, I'm not either. After all, you did hire me to keep you company on the way to Williford."

I fought the urge to scrub my hands through my curls. "I hired you to show me the way, not to act as my nanny."

Swinton *tsk*ed at me and waggled one finger back and forth admonishingly. "If you refuse to sleep, then I'll need something to occupy my time. Entertain me, little lord."

"I'm not—"

"Buh, buh, buh," he said, grinning. "No negatives. Only positives. Tell me about yourself."

He dug into his saddlebags and pulled out a thin cotton sack of caramels wrapped in waxed paper. He offered the sack to me, and I took one, peeling off the paper and popping it into my mouth.

"You go first," I said through a mouthful of sticky caramel. The thought of how Mother would've reacted if I'd done the same at home flitted across my mind, scoring a thin line of pain through me, like stepping into salt water with a cracked heel. "What was it like growing up in Ilor?"

Swinton's easy laugh was like balm. "I've nothing to compare it to. What was it like to grow up in Alskad? What was it like to grow up rich?"

I wanted to blame the heat in my face on the fire, but

I knew—and Swinton knew—that he'd made me blush. I shrugged and threw my wrapper into the fire.

"Have anything to drink over there?"

Swinton pulled a bottle out of his bag and came to sit beside me on my bedroll. I wanted desperately to ask him about his casual admission that he was one of the diminished, but I couldn't manage to find a way that didn't feel horrifyingly rude.

"So, little lord. Tell me. What prompted you to travel all the way across the Tethys to meet this sister of yours? Generosity, or curiosity?"

"Both?" I laughed. "Neither? It seems so odd that I could have a relative I've never met, especially a sister."

"And your twin?" Swinton asked. "What's he got to say about this adventure of yours?"

I panicked for a moment, realizing that the story I'd so carefully constructed with Gerlene hadn't included my having a twin at all. But the memory of Gerlene fluttering around that awful room at the inn by the docks flashed through my mind, and I decided that she was as good a stand-in as anyone. "She's a planner, and I sort of sprang the idea on her at the last minute. Let's just say she wasn't best pleased."

We talked until the moon set, plowing through the caramels and the bottle of fizzy fermented tea. Swinton was as captivating as he was surprising, and it was easier for me to talk to him than anyone else I knew. I felt like I could be myself with him—the real and honest part of me that I'd always kept shielded from my family, for fear of their disapproval.

My initial terror of traveling with one of the diminished wore away to nothing as we made our way to Williford. Swinton wasn't someone I needed to fear. In fact, in his company,

I felt as safe as I ever had in my life, wild dogs and other dangerous jungle beasts be damned. He made me laugh, really laugh, in a way I never had before. I was thrilled to be on an adventure with him. Swinton's bright moods shone like the sun, and though a sour-tinged sadness curled in my belly when memories of Claes flashed through my mind, each time Swinton shot me a devilish grin or rested his hand on my thigh for a second too long, giddy currents of joy rolled up my spine.

As we entered the crowded streets of Williford, leading our horses, I indulged in a brief fantasy about a hot bath and a comfortable, long night in my bed at home. The nights I'd spent curled on the rocky ground, listening to the strange symphony of jungle sounds and barely dozing, had left me ravenous for a solid night of decent sleep.

Swinton nodded at a squat building set back from the street a ways. In the growing dimness, I couldn't make out the words on the sign.

"Looks like that's our best bet. Shall I see if they can put us up for the night, or do you want me to wait with the horses?"

I gave him a wry look. After a vendor in Cape Hillate had laughed me out of his shop when I tried to buy supplies for our trip, I'd agreed to let Swinton do our negotiating from then on. While I had a good idea of what it cost to maintain my household in Alskad, and the currency was the same, I'd not the foggiest clue what everyday items ought to cost in Ilor.

He reappeared a few minutes later. "She's all full, but for one room. Nice lady, though. Offered to stable our horses for the cost of grain and said she'd give us a bottle of makgee if we buy supper. What do you say? We can flip a *tvilling* for the bed." Swinton smiled playfully at me, waggling his eyebrows.

I laughed. "Whose coin would that be? Yours? I can't seem to remember you paying for so much as a cup of kaffe since

I met you." The thought of kaffe made my mouth water. I hadn't even smelled it since I left the ship, and though the headaches I'd had the first few days had now faded, I would have done just about anything for a cup of that particular nectar. "Do you think she has kaffe?" I asked.

It was Swinton's turn to laugh. "You can't wrap your head around the costs of things, can you, little lord? There ain't been a soul stay in this inn who can afford kaffe, well, ever."

We led the horses around back to the stables and surrendered them to the grizzled old man we found there.

"But kaffe is grown here," I whined, unwilling to give up the argument.

Swinton held the back door open for me, saying, "And most of it is shipped to the heart of the Alskad Empire for lords like you."

"I'm not a—" I tried to protest, but was interrupted by an enormous woman who crushed me to her bosom.

"Welcome to Bethesda's!" she boomed. "I'm Bethesda, and I'm so pleased my boy's brought you to see me."

The pressure of her arms released for a moment, but before I could step back, I found myself nose to nose with Swinton, who'd also been pulled into her tight embrace. He grinned at me.

"My Swinton's never brought anyone home to meet his mama." She let us go and swatted Swinton, whose face turned red.

I raised an eyebrow. Swinton shrugged, and his mother said, "After Taeb, I kept waiting to hear…" Bethesda paused, and her genial expression flicked briefly. She twitched her apron, but when she looked up, a smile was once again plastered on her face. "No matter. You're both here now. I am sorry that I don't have two rooms for you, but business is good." She elbowed Swinton. "Can't complain about that, can we? Now tell me, how is my waif of a sister?"

★ ★ ★

After unpacking our saddlebags, bathing and putting on clean clothes, Swinton and I made our way down to the common room of the inn. I headed toward the only open table in the large, slat-windowed room, but Swinton pulled me to a long trestle table in the corner. Two women and a man sat around a nearly empty platter. Half-full glasses of milky white makgee and a number of empty bottles littered the table.

Swinton's hand closed around my elbow, and his breath tickled my ear as he said, "I don't let it get around that I'm a dimmy, so keep your mouth shut of it, aye?"

I gave the barest nod, and Swinton clapped an arm around my shoulder.

The man stood when Swinton and I approached. His collar was open and his sleeves rolled up, revealing deep brown skin and the ropey muscles of his forearms. As we crossed the room, I saw his golden brown eyes pass over me, taking in everything from my shoes to my dark, messy curls and dismissing me, all in a matter of moments. When we reached the table, before introductions could be made, the man grinned and enveloped Swinton in a hug.

"Good to see you, bully. How've you been?" he asked.

Swinton leaned across the table to kiss each of the women on their cheeks, and sat, gesturing for me to do the same. "Billa, Rue, Mal, this is my good friend, Bo."

I climbed over the bench and took a seat next to the two women. A serving boy bustled over with a pair of glasses and two more bottles on a tray. He and Swinton spoke for a moment in hushed tones, and he hurried away.

"So, Mal," Swinton said. "When did you get back?"

I poured makgee into everyone's glasses, hastily tucking my cuff up into my sleeve before I reached across the table to pour for Swinton. Nevertheless, I saw the glint in Mal's eyes. He'd clearly seen the gold around my wrist.

"Almost a month ago, and just in time, too. Billa was about to run off with a paneller and break my poor heart."

The woman next to me chuckled, and the other—Billa, I assumed—reached across the table and cuffed Mal on the ear. He grinned.

"How long are you staying this time?" Swinton gave me a significant look and explained. "Mal's from Penby, but his uncle is one of the only male captains in the navy—perhaps you've heard of him? Hamlin Whippleston? Mal and his brother, Quill, are apprenticed onboard, though by all accounts they're both terrible sailors."

My heart raced, but before I could open my mouth to ask about Vi, Swinton kicked my shin, rather harder than was necessary. He shook his head ever so slightly and poured more makgee for Mal.

Mal nodded his thanks and continued, all joking conviviality. "We aren't so bad as all that. We have loads of admirable qualities."

"Only one I can think of," Billa quipped. "You're awful pretty. Too bad you're both denser than knotted wood."

Mal pouted, and everyone at the table burst into laughter. When the mirth was more or less contained, Mal said, "I'm surprised you haven't heard. Quill and I are here permanently now. You're looking at the proud co-owner and operator of the Whippleston Exchange Firm."

The serving boy reappeared with an enormous platter and a basket, which he sat between Swinton and me. The tray was heaped with food—there were salads of roasted beets and pickled onions, potatoes in creamy green aioli sharp with the scent of wild garlic and shaved summer squash piled with capers and anchovies. Dumplings in a variety of colors were arranged alongside the salads, all piled atop a thick, spongy-looking crepe. And all around the tray, small copper tureens were overflowing with stewed and potted meats, chutneys and savory jams. The complex, unfamiliar scents made my mouth water, but even still, I was anxious to get to the point.

"What do you import?" I asked Mal.

"I import wine and liquor and export a variety of things—kaffe, cloth, sugar, tafia and the like. My brother brings over contract laborers."

"It might be that you could help me, then," I said, doing my best to sound casual. "I'm looking for a young woman called Obedience. She's from the capital, a dimmy. She may be calling herself Vi."

Mal's eyes narrowed. "Not saying as I do know her, but why are you looking for her?"

Swinton closed his eyes slowly and shook his head, but I plowed ahead.

"She's my half sister," I said. "A by-blow of my father, and it seems he remembered her in his will. I'd heard that your uncle brought a dimmy across the Tethys not too long ago and wondered if it might be the same girl."

Mal's face contorted into an expression of shock, and he stared at me for a long moment before he managed to collect himself and look down into his glass. Swinton glared at me.

"I don't have much interaction with the passengers. I'm sorry, but I don't think I know her."

Swinton raised an eyebrow. "Have a heart, Mal. He's looking for his sister. All he's wanting is to meet the girl and give her a bit of money. You sure you don't remember a girl named Vi? She might've been one of Quill's contracts. Probably earned him a mint. We'd heard a rumor… We're trying to find where she's gone."

"Can't say I know her, bully. My apologies. I can ask around for you, if you'd like. Anything special about her? Memorable?"

"She's one of the diminished. I'd imagine that would stick out in just about anyone's mind. Especially on a ship."

"Didn't Quill tell me—" Billa started, but Mal interrupted her.

"If I know my brother, I'm sure he was far into his cups, and like as not there wasn't a lick of truth to anything he said to a pretty girl like you. Now, speaking of drinks, shall we have another before we're off?"

The women agreed, and Swinton amiably called for another bottle of makgee. I laughed and made jokes about the differences between Alskad and Ilor, but beneath the surface, I was stewing. By the time Mal rose from the table, beckoned to the two women and we made our goodbyes, I could hardly contain myself.

The moment the slatted door swung shut behind him, I looked at Swinton and said, "He was lying, Swinton. I know it."

Swinton rolled his eyes. "Was he, Bo? Was he really? How could you tell?"

"No reason for you to be nasty about it. You know he was lying. Why wouldn't he tell us the truth?"

"He lied to you, not me. I'm not the one who asks idiotic questions."

I sniffed. "That's helpful. Thank you so much for your insight."

Swinton refilled my glass. "He doesn't trust you. You were blushing the whole time. He knew there was something you weren't saying. I'm going to race to his house and see if I can't beat him there. Perhaps if I can talk to his brother, I can clean up the mess you made. You stay here and finish your supper. Have another glass of makgee. Don't talk to anyone."

I groaned. There was a part of me that thought he was right. I should stay behind. After all, I had managed to make a terrific mess of my only tie—however loose it might be—to my sister.

"How will you find him?" I asked.

"Thought I might start with his house."

"I'd like to come. I promise to do my best not to bungle things any more than I already have done."

Swinton stared down at his empty glass, frowning. I pressed my hands between my thighs to keep my fingers from dancing an impatient jig on the tabletop. The din of the inn's common room might as well have been the empty silence of a ticking clock as I waited for Swinton's answer. I desperately wanted him to trust me. To like me.

When he finally glanced up, the stern look he gave me was belied by the twinkle in his green eyes. "You can come, little lord, but you'll agree to my terms first, hear?"

I nodded, doing everything in my power to contain my glee.

"First, you'll do your best to follow my lead. I think Quill will be more easily persuaded with a bit of cash. There's more to your story than you're giving away, and that's all well and good. But when you get on with your poor try at a straight face, you look like a half-wit fox what thinks he can masquerade as a hen in the henhouse. Don't do that. Unless you're ready to spill the whole story, you keep your trap shut. Agreed?"

Swinton's insults stung, but I saw the truth in what he was saying, so I did as he asked and gave my silent assent.

"Second, money'll open doors not even my silver tongue can unlock. What do we have to work with, cash-wise?"

I considered. If he connected the truth of my relationship to Vi to the gold cuff on my wrist and the crown, and thought to sell that information to the right people, my troubles would become far more unmanageable than they already were. However, if I lost Vi because I was afraid Swinton might learn my secrets, I would hate myself. I would have to walk a careful line and play my cards close to the vest.

"I've got a line of credit at a bank in Southill. Bribe away, I suppose."

CHAPTER TWENTY-THREE

Vi

My responsibilities and tasks didn't let up just because my heart was broken, but Myrna, at least, let me sleep late the next morning. She shook me awake with just enough time to ready myself to face Hepsy—and the fact that the whole of the estate had turned itself upside-down in preparation for Aphra's birthday celebration as I was mourning the loss of my best friend.

Serving dinner that night was particularly horrible. Every moment was a reminder of how excited I'd been the night before, and how quickly that single moment of happiness had been ripped away from me. Before I could take my own meal back to my rooms, Hepsy pulled me aside and spent a torturous hour—through which my stomach groaned and yowled resentfully—detailing every aspect of the coming celebration, from the fireworks to the appetizers.

"This party," Hepsy said threateningly, "will be attended by every person worth knowing in Ilor. So when you are pre-

sented with the rest of Mister Phineas's gifts, you will not—
do you understand me?—*you will not* embarrass me."

That night, as I lay in bed, staring up at the dark ceiling,
surrounded by sleeping puppies, I prayed to Pru to help me
find a purpose, somewhere to put all the anger and grief and
pain that was welling up inside. I was scared, more terrified
than I'd ever been, that Sawny's death would be the thing to
break me. I'd made it through sixteen years as a dimmy, but
this loss felt like more than I could bear. I wished for a sign,
something to show me the way out of all this sadness. But
even after the moons dipped below the horizon and sleep finally overtook me, nothing came.

When I sought Hepsy out for my lesson the next day, she
scowled and flapped her hand. "I'm too busy to tend to you
now. Find somewhere else to be."

I glared back at her. "What am I supposed to do, then?"

Hepsy looked at me like I'd grown a second set of ears.
"You're to do whatever anyone asks of you, dullard. Make
yourself useful. Now, off with you."

I went to look for Myrna. I was used to feeling like I was
a nuisance, but the bustling, prickly servants at Plumleen
had a way of making me feel like not only was I in the way,
I smelled like rot, had stolen their breakfast and spent every
free moment trying to make their lives more difficult. The
only place I was comfortable was in the barn with Myrna
and the animals.

The sun was high overhead when I found Myrna barefoot and knee-deep in the manure pile, holding a pitchfork.
"Well, well, well, has old stone-eyes given you the afternoon
off?" she asked.

Once again, I wondered about the rift between Myrna and

Hepsy. I'd seen siblings fight, but I'd never seen such a thorough and unrepentant loathing between two people whose connection ought to've been strong. I nodded.

"Good. You take the next load, Vi. My heart's fit to explode in this heat, and some exercise might do you good. Distract you."

"Next load of what?" I asked, and then I saw the handcart, half full of manure, and cringed. "Oh. Good. Have anything else that needs doing?"

Myrna let out a loud, cackling laugh, and dipped her hand into the bucket of well water beside her and splashed it on her face. "The gardeners showed up this morning, demanding manure for all the flower beds by the end of the day tomorrow. This load is going to the jasmine on the back lawn. Do you think you can manage, or are you too much of a delicate Alskad flower to haul a handcart?"

I scowled at her, faking irritation. The truth was, I liked working in the barn with Myrna, and she was right. I needed something to fill the time, to keep me from wallowing in my dark thoughts. I admired her strength, and somehow, her teasing never felt weighted by truth. I didn't mind the actual work, either. In fact, I reveled in the idea of developing some new muscles, different from those I'd cultivated swimming or with the exercises I'd learned in the temple.

"I bet I can do it twice as fast as you, and for twice as long," I teased.

Myrna heaved a last pitchfork load of manure onto the heap in the handcart and said, "Have at it. Do you know where you're going?"

I nodded and pulled a scarf from my belt to tie back my wild curls. It took a great deal of heaving to get the single wheel of the handcart out of the muck behind the barn, but once I had it on the lawn, the going got easier. The grounds at Plumleen Hall were unlike anything I'd ever encountered in Alskad. The wild jungle plants native to Ilor were cultivated and carefully tended here; their oversized leaves shaded stone walkways, and flowers sprang up and hung like vivid, gaudy decorations from every plant. The vast expanses of lawn were carpeted in hardy, emerald-green grass that sprang up to meet my footsteps.

Birds sang and chattered in the trees, a far more pleasant sound than the ceaseless hum of adulations echoing through the temple's halls. It smelled better, too. There was no stench of rotten fish or unwashed reek of too many bodies all crowded together at Plumleen. It was all green growing things, the dusty musk of horses and heady floral perfume.

I cut a wide path around the manor house, so as to avoid being seen by Hepsy, who would surely find some fault in my hauling manure for her sister—or Phineas, who might be displeased that I wasn't studying with Hepsy. When I finally reached the bed of jasmine, sweat trickled down my face and chest, and my arms were shaking with effort. I hadn't met any of the gardeners who helped me unload the manure, but when I said hello, they turned the other way, muttering about dimmys. I bit my tongue. Some things, like good-for-nothing foot-lickers showing their stripes, never changed.

A bucket of water hung from a thick tree limb in easy reach, but when I moved toward it to get a sip, the gardeners blocked my path, arms crossed over their chests. Cart empty, I trudged back toward the barn, my throat dry and a familiar, lonely gloom curling in my belly like a snake. I'd guessed that folks in the colonies would be more concerned about surviving all the awful diseases and terrifying animals I'd read about than about one teenaged dimmy. But folks like those silent, glaring gardeners made it clear that once again, I'd guessed wrong.

As I wound my way back through the gardens, I found myself lost in memories of Sawny and Lily. With them gone, I was once more adrift, purposeless. I'd committed myself to a life at Plumleen, at least for the next ten years, and I had to make every day count for something. I had to find a way to channel my anger and grief, to keep it from consuming me. My fury was quickly shaping itself into an arrow directed at one person: Phineas. He was the reason Sawny was dead. He'd destroyed my last tie to Penby, to my childhood, to the only person who'd never been afraid of me.

I wanted revenge. I knew, from the newshawkers back in Penby and the warnings the Whipplestons had impressed up on me, that there was some kind of rebel group fighting back against cruel people like Phineas. I wondered if there might be a way for me to find them. Help them.

And if they might, in turn, help me avenge Sawny and Lily.

Halfway back to the barn, I heard hoofbeats and glanced around, wondering who it might be. People came and went on horseback all the time, and there'd already been scads of deliveries for Aphra's birthday celebration since I arrived at Plumleen. Suddenly, a horse I recognized rounded the corner, and I gasped. My head spun, and, not sure what else to do, I dove into the clump of bushes closest to me, leaving my cart abandoned.

I must look like quite the fool, Pru, I thought, but even as I thought the words, I felt fear coursing through my veins, remembering Phineas's warnings. I watched from between the leaves as Aphra's horse, a lovely sorrel gelding, cantered by with a woman on his back. The woman, who could've been no one but Aphra, rode like she was part of her horse. She wore her hair in a low coil, strands of red and gold knotted together and covered by a wide-brimmed hat. She, like me and the stable girls, wore tight breeches and a sleeveless blouse, though her breeches were impeccable, glowing white, and her blouse was light and dark green striped silk.

After she disappeared, I stayed crouched behind my bush for a long while. I'd never imagined that I would see an amalgam, and I was as afraid of her and the stories I'd grown up with as I was terrified of what Phineas would do to me if she saw me. I kept myself hidden until I thought enough time must have passed for her to get back to the barn and tend her horse herself. Not, of course, that the lady of the estate would have enough time to do a chore like that, but I wanted to be safe.

Myrna was walking the big sorrel gelding, Riker, into his stall, still a little damp from having the sweat washed off him, when I finally wheeled my cart back into the barn. She slid Riker's halter over his ears and gave him an affection-ate scratch on his forehead. She caught sight of me as soon as she closed the stall door. "Rayleane's teeth! Where have you been? You decide to take a nap in one of the hammocks on the way back?"

"I saw her," I panted.

"Saw who?" Myrna asked. She dipped a ladle into a bucket of well water kept for the stable hands to drink and handed it to me. I drank gratefully and splashed a little on my face. She eyed me up and down, plucking a leaf from my hair. "Where've you been hiding? I've taken three carts myself since you took yours, and the gardeners said you left near abouts an hour ago."

"I did," I said, and told her about seeing Aphra in the gar-den. By the time I finished, all the color had drained from

Myrna's face, and her mouth was compressed into a thin, hard line.

"Did she see you?" Myrna asked.

"I don't know. She was moving along at a right smart clip—that Riker's faster than my Beetle by half—but I wasn't exactly sly. I left my cart right there on the lawn when I dove into the bushes."

"Dzallie's bosom," Myrna spat. "This is all my fault. I should have kept you well out of sight."

"How bad would it be if she saw me?"

Myrna pursed her lips again and glanced at her boots. "Breaking one of Phineas's rules is bad enough on a good day. But with the stress of this celebration, and the fact that Singen arrived this morning... Magritte's nose," she swore. "Let's hope she didn't see you, or if she did, she forgets all about it."

"Why does it matter so much? Surely she doesn't know every servant at Plumleen."

"You wouldn't think so, would you? No, if she got even half a look at you, she'd know you were new. She knows everybody on this estate, for better or worse. Let's hope she doesn't ask Phineas, not while Singen's here."

"Who's Singen?" I asked.

"Singen is Phineas's twin. They—well, you know how some twins make each other better? Push one another to be nicer or more pious?"

"Of course," I said.

"Well, the Oxfeld men—that was their name before they married—they bring out the worst in each other. Singen's servants say that he hardly drinks when he's at home, but when he's here, he swills liquor like it's water," Myrna explained. "And Phineas is strict, but usually fair. The minute Singen shows up, anything might be enough to earn his ire. Singen was here visiting when..." She trailed off.

I winced, realizing she was referring to the incident with Lily.

Myrna bit her lip and paused for a long moment before she finally said, "It wasn't just Lily that time, either. Phineas gave one of the houseboys fifteen lashes for eating an apple too loudly. He happened to walk by when the boy was having his snack, and the next thing any of us knew, the boy was tied to the fence, screaming his lungs out. Cracked two ribs and only just got back to work. He got two days added to his contract for each one he missed."

My stomach turned and twisted, coiling into a heavy knot in my belly. It didn't seem possible. It couldn't be legal. But I remembered the warnings Mal and Quill had given me, everything they'd told me about the unfair balance of power and the law. Fury was well on its way to replacing my grief now. If I could manage to do anything with my life, I wanted to put an end to this kind of injustice. The problem was, I had no idea where to start.

"All that for eating an apple too loud?" I asked. "How are you supposed to eat a damned apple?"

Myrna chuckled grimly. "Far, far away from Phineas. He hates to hear anyone chewing. There's always a musician in the dining room. Always. It's the only way he can eat in the same room as anyone else."

"What does Aphra say about all this?" I asked.

"She won't take a whip to any of us, but I've never heard of her stopping him. It seems like she indulges him in everything. Never mind about that, though. There's nothing to be done now. I need to get the herd fed and turned out for the night."

"Can I help?"

"No," Myrna said, taking me by the shoulders and steering me toward the door to my rooms. "You any good with a needle and thread?"

"I'll do," I said cautiously.

Myrna grinned, opened my door and gave me a gentle shove. "Good. I've got a heap of saddle pads what need mending, and we should probably keep you out of sight for a while."

I sighed and closed the door behind me, turning over the day's events as I absently greeted the dogs. I wished Madame Laroche hadn't gotten her eyes on me, but a part of me was glad I'd seen her at last. My glimpse of her assured me that she didn't have green skin or a second head, but as I sat down to repair the pile of saddle pads my mind churned, wondering how I might coax more information about Aphra out of Myrna. That, I supposed, was better than the alternative, because thinking about Phineas made my skin crawl, and I'd almost certainly begin to weep if I spent another moment dwelling on Lily and Sawny.

CHAPTER TWENTY-FOUR

Bo

Where Cape Hillate had been a rabbit warren of twisting paths and secret squares, the lamp-lit, cobblestone streets of Williford were laid in a wide, spacious grid that extended out from the harbor and stopped within a hair's breadth of the jungle. Even late in the evening, long after the sun had fallen below the horizon, heat still oozed from the earth and sweat prickled my neck as I tried to keep pace with Swinton. His long strides ate up distance with an ease and grace that totally escaped me.

When we finally stopped, I was drenched and heaving. Swinton led me across a wide lawn to a three-story, porch-ringed house set far back from the street. A line of lamps glowed along the front porch rail and the high garden wall. Two windows on the lower floor shone with the warm light of solar lamps, as did the glass-paned front door.

"Ready?" he asked. Before I could answer, he rapped on the door and whispered, "Remember to follow my lead."

A lithe, middle-aged woman with fiery red hair and laugh lines around her freckled mouth swung open the door, took one long look at Swinton and flew at him. I drew in a quick breath and squeezed my eyes tight shut, steadying myself against an attack. But laughter rang through the thick night air, and I looked up to see Swinton twirling the woman in a circle, their heads thrown back in glee.

"Whenever did you get back to Williford, pet?" she asked. Her musical voice carried the lilt of Ilor and was backed by a rasp like nutmeg in a spice mill.

Their questions came fast, toppling over each other like eager puppies.

"When did you leave my ma's place?"

"What're you doing here then, and at this hour?"

"Your brother still making those cocoa cream rolls? I'm hungry just thinking of them."

"How's your Auntie Kelladra?"

When the barrage of questions finally ended in more laughter, Swinton said, "It's right good to see you, Noona, and I'm that sorry to trouble you so late, but I'm here looking for Mal and Quill. Might I speak with them?"

She swatted him with a towel she'd had draped over her shoulder. "And look at you, forgotten all your manners as soon as you got grown and out of your ma's house? Who's this, then?"

Swinton glanced over his shoulder at me, grinned and dropped into an overly elaborate bow. "My dearest Noona, it is my great and profound honor to present to you Mister Bo Abernathy of the Alskad Empire, newly arrived in our great colony of Ilor. Mister Abernathy, the woman who is responsible, if not for my good looks, then at least for my excellent manners and brilliant education, Missus Noona Booker-

Hirsch. My ma hired Noona when I was wee to help care for my brother and me."

A shadow crossed Noona's face at the mention of Swinton's brother, but she took my hand and gave it a firm shake, studying my face with narrowed eyes. "A pleasure. You come on in. Mal's still out, but I'll see if Quill can't come down and have a chat with you."

Noona ushered us into the house and deposited us in a comfortable sitting room before bustling up the stairs. She returned a moment later with a young man, presumably Mal's twin, Quill. He was identical to the man I'd met earlier, but for the hair. His tied back in long locks rather than the short curls Mal sported. Swinton stood and grasped Quill's elbow, drawing him close and clapping him on the back. Both of them were beaming when Swinton released him.

"It surely is good to see you, bully. Quill, this is Bo. Bo Abernathy. He's hired me to help him find his sister. We think you might be set up to lend us a hand."

Quill looked over Swinton's shoulder at me, and took a step back, fumbled his way to a chair and sat with a loud exhalation. "Abernathy, is it?"

Swinton raised an eyebrow at me encouragingly. I sat in a chair opposite Quill and tugged my sleeve down over my cuff in a swift, practiced motion. It'd become habit at that point, to tuck the telltale gold into my sleeve. To keep it hidden. I bit the inside of my cheek, wondering how close to the truth I might tread. "My mother's name is Abernathy, as is my sister's. We'd hoped that you would know her. We think she may have crossed the Tethys on your uncle's ship."

Quill's face had turned impassive. I looked to Swinton, hoping a touch of his confidence might bolster me. He squeezed my hand.

"Look," I continued, a pleading note in my voice. "We'd heard your firm made an enormous commission on her contract. I'm trying to find out if the girl you worked with was my sister."

Quill's tawny gold gaze locked on me, and he seemed to choose his next words with a great deal of care. "I don't discuss other folks' contracts. Even if I did remember your girl, I wouldn't be able to help you. Bad for business, see."

"You'd remember this one," Swinton said. "She's a dimmy. Vi Abernathy, by name."

"And why, exactly, are you looking for her? Not saying as I know her or not, but if she's taken a contract in Ilor, she'll not be going anywhere for quite some years."

Swinton gave me a long look and nodded. I steeled myself and plunged closer to the truth than was necessarily comfortable. I hoped that sympathy—or if not that, then gold lust—would convince Quill to help me. "I only recently learned of Vi's existence. It seems that my father had an affair with her mother that led to the birth of Vi and her twin. He left a large estate, and, well, it seemed only fair…"

I cleared my throat. Before I could go on, heavy footsteps on the front porch interrupted my thoughts, and a moment later, the door was flung open. Mal stormed into the house, shouting for Quill. He slammed the door shut, and the windows rattled in their frames.

"Quill! Haul your gods'-damned arse out of bed." Mal's thunderous steps started up the stairs and stopped abruptly. "Oh. Noona. I'm sorry. I hope I didn't wake you. Have you seen my brother?" His voice took on a chastened, almost boyish tone, and Quill looked as though he was struggling to hold back a smile.

"Might be if you took a moment to look around before

you came hollering, you would've seen your brother in the sitting room." She lowered her voice into a dramatic, though still-audible, whisper. "With guests."

I managed to get to my feet as Mal barreled into the room. Mal took Swinton and me in with a single glance and shot an accusatory stare at his brother. Noona followed him, clucking with irritation, and set a tray of pastries and a pitcher of milky tea, beaded with condensation, on a low table.

She patted Quill on the shoulder, pinched Mal's arm and said, "I'm off to bed now. No more shouting, or else I'll wake my sister and set her on you."

Once Noona left the room, Mal demanded, "What're you doing here? I told you before I don't know anything about the girl you're looking for."

"We didn't think to trouble you with it again," Swinton said, charm oozing from his smile. "I'd thought your brother might know more, him being the one who handles contract work and all. We're happy to pay you for any information you care to pass along."

Quill raised an eyebrow and shrugged. Mal shook his head, scowling.

I tried a different tactic. "My only wish is to meet my sister and see that she receives the inheritance she's due. I've no desire to disrupt the life she's chosen for herself."

Swinton narrowed his eyes at me. "What Bo means to say is that if you do, in fact, know where his sister is working, he'll do nothing to jeopardize your relationship with your customers."

I caught the thread of his argument and ran with it. "Actually, I may even be able to help grow your business. My employer has an estate here in Ilor that she's asked me to look in on. I believe the majority of the work there is done by contract laborers. It wouldn't be outside the realm of possibility for me to make some kind of arrangement with your exchange firm in return for your assistance."

"That's all well and good," Mal said. "But we don't know the girl, do we? Now, I hate to be rude, but it's awfully late and—"

"Mal, don't be—"

"Enough!" Mal said firmly. "Now, I'd like for these gentlemen to leave so that I can find my bed." He extended his hand to Swinton. "If you find yourself in these parts again soon, I'd love to have a game of brag with you, yes?"

Our window was closing, and I couldn't imagine how I'd manage to find Vi without the help of the Whipplestons. I needed them to see how dire her situation would soon become, even if it meant breaking my agreement with Swinton.

"Please," I said, a desperate note in my voice. "I need to find her. The Shriven are, even as we speak, looking for Vi. I've no idea how long it will be before they manage to track her down, but if I've found you, they certainly will, and there's no telling what they'll do to her. I'm begging you— please help me."

Swinton's face turned to stone, and within a moment, Mal was steering us through the door and onto the porch, closing it decidedly behind us. The lock thudded into place, echoing like distant thunder, and inside, heavy footfalls mounted the stairs. We stood silently on the porch, side by side. I moved to leave, my heart crumbling to dust in my chest, but Swinton caught my hand and gave it a gentle squeeze.

"Wait," he said, and his lips curled in a sly smile. "We're going to have a talk about your little outburst, but just you wait a moment."

Even though my throat was as tight as if I were being

choked, and I felt as though I'd flayed myself open and left my heart beating in that entry hall, I was comforted by Swinton's touch. As his thumb absently drew circles on the tender skin of my wrist, I closed my eyes and breathed in the cool night air. It smelled so green, so fresh. I thought I could actually smell the new growth as it shot out of the ground. I inhaled the salty ocean wind, too, carrying its deep secrets. It was, however, Swinton's scent that captivated me—musky, pine-scented soap overlaid with smoke and makgee, and below that, something uniquely his own. A scent I would, even after such a short time with him, recognize anywhere.

"Do you trust them, Swinton?" I asked.

"Enough," he said, and brought my wrist to his lips, asking a silent question that sent delicious shudders all down my spine. It wasn't until our hands dropped back to our sides and the gold bracelet—the symbol of my place in life—fell heavily back into place, and my heart with it, that I realized what Swinton might now suspect about who I was.

We couldn't have been on the porch for more than a few minutes, my heart beating like a hummingbird's wings as my thoughts raced to match, before the front door opened once again and someone stepped out onto the porch. Swinton let go of my hand, and my treacherous stomach sank. We turned, and Quill stepped into the circle of lamplight where we stood. I scrubbed a hand through my hair, waiting for him to speak.

"How did you connect Vi to the temple?" he asked.

"I've told you the truth. I'm her brother. I just want to see her safe. If I can find the people who bought her, maybe I can offer them enough to buy out the rest of her contract. See her well and truly safe."

"Are the Shriven really looking for your sister?"

I let out my breath in a slow exhalation. "They are. I don't know how much they know, or how soon they'll find her, but you know as well as I that the Shriven don't fail when they have someone in their sights." I hesitated, then hurriedly said, "I'd see you well compensated for your help."

"We'll find a way to do this so as your business isn't affected. If you agree, that is," Swinton added.

Quill nodded his head slowly. "We'll help. Not for the money—I wouldn't see her in the hands of the Shriven. But you'll need quite a sum to buy her contract off the people who hired her, and even still, it might not be an easy thing. Her contract's meant as a birthday gift, and you'll have a far better chance of convincing them if we manage to negotiate before the celebration. You'll need cash in hand in less than two weeks' time."

"Can we get to Southill and back in that time?" I asked Swinton.

"We'll have to make tracks, but we can do it."

I ran a hand through my hair and nodded at Quill gratefully. "Thank you for your help."

"You're welcome. But, Mr. Abernathy, if you make one wrong move—if I for one moment think you don't have her best interest at heart—I'll make it my business to find out the truth about the cuff you wear."

I froze, taken aback. I didn't think he'd seen it.

"You look like her, you know," Quill said, suddenly amiable. "The same eyes, the same blushes, the same hair. She even has that same tic you do—ruffles her hair so it stands on end when she's anxious."

I compressed my lips and waited, feeling the heat of a blush curl up my neck.

"It isn't that Mal's callous. I think he's just mad we got her into this position in the first place. I'll bring him around to the idea. Just give us a bit of time to plan. We can't trot you onto the estate, visitors for the servants being frowned upon and all, but with a little luck, I might be able to sneak you in to see Vi. You'll want to see her and let her know the plan, yes?"

My heart leapt at the thought of seeing Vi for the first time, and my voice shook as I replied. "I can't tell you how much I appreciate this."

Quill eyed my wrist pointedly. "I believe you. It looks like you have a lot to lose."

Quill clapped both Swinton and me on the shoulder and headed back into the house. Before the door was fully shut, I flung myself into Swinton's arms. Laughing, he hugged me tight and released me, skipping down the porch's steps.

"I do believe you owe me a drink, little lord," he said. "A drink, and a raise. I'll play along with this little farce of yours as long as you like, but I'll get the truth from you at some point."

I wanted to tell him everything in that moment. The truth about Vi, the Queen, every secret I'd held so carefully guarded since I left my house in Esser Park. But I forced myself to hold my tongue, at least for a little longer.

CHAPTER TWENTY-FIVE

Vi

Sweat slicked every inch of my body and dripped, stinging, into my eyes. The sun had only just risen, but the blasted sunbeams were already beating relentlessly down on me, burning my once-pale, freckled skin and heating my dark curls past bearing. All I wanted was to be off Beetle's jostling back, to let go of the reins and lift my heavy braid off my neck, to stick my whole head in a bucket of cool water. Instead, I did my best to focus on staying in the saddle and making at least some of the seemingly endless corrections Myrna shouted at me from the back of her delicate chestnut mare.

"Shoulders back," Myrna called, the reminder a familiar refrain. "Heels down."

I obliged, my breath ragged and heaving. It was beyond understanding that I could hold my breath for minutes at a time comfortably beneath the cold Alskad waves, but here in Ilor, each hot, wet breath I managed to pull into my lungs came with a fight. Despite Myrna's assurances, I didn't think a body could ever get used to this kind of humidity. Not really.

After one more jolting trot around the flat field, Myrna slowed her mare to a walk, and I, gratefully, did the same. Reins in one hand, I lifted my heavy braid off my neck with the other.

"You're getting better," Myrna said. "Now all you need to do is stop being so terribly scared."

I laughed. "I'd hardly say I'm scared. Just sensible. I'm a tiny scrap of a thing compared to Beetle here, yet somehow, I'm to convince her that I'm in charge? Seems unlikely at best and right stupid at worst."

Myrna laughed, and we rode toward the barn in companionable silence for a few minutes before she drew her horse to a halt. She peered down the hill. "What's that, then?" she asked. "A bit early for deliveries, wouldn't you say?"

I followed her gaze down the hill to the drive, where a wagon loaded with casks and trunks was winding its way toward the manor house. Two figures sat on the back of the wagon's bed, their feet dangling off the end, and two more on the wagon's seat. They were still a bit too far away for me to make out more than their shapes, and it would take them a couple of minutes or so at least to get to the barn at the pace they were going.

I wiped the sweat from my brow and looked at Myrna. "Think we ought to go down and lend a hand?" I asked.

"You're just looking for an excuse to cut your lesson short," Myrna said with a cackle. "All right, then. We'll go on down, but if you want me to go easy on you, you'll have to beat me there."

Without another word, Myrna urged her horse into a gallop and went flying down the path. I gritted my teeth, tapped Beetle's sides with my heels and gave the little mare her head. Beetle took off after Myrna's chestnut. I clung to the reins and her mane and pushed my weight into my heels, holding on for all I was worth. By the time Beetle skidded to a halt outside the barn, my sides were heaving nearly as hard as hers, but Myrna had already dismounted and loosened her horse's girth.

"I'd no idea the beast could move that fast," I gasped.

Myrna gave me a sardonic look. "Hates being left behind, that one." She hefted the saddle and blanket off her horse in one swift movement and set it on a rack. "Now you hop off so we can get these horses wiped down and turned out before our visitors get here."

I'd just managed to get Beetle settled and eased myself, aching muscles screaming, down onto a stool when the creak of wagon wheels and hooves came to a stop outside the barn.

Myrna smacked me lightly with a crop as she streaked past. "Up you get. There're horses to tend." She paused and turned back to look at me. "Not even noon, and you're soaked through. How does a person so fair turn so very red?"

Groaning, I heaved myself to my feet and trudged after Myrna, muttering curses. I stopped at one of the water buckets hanging by the door to splash cool water on my face. When I looked up again, I found her beaming at me expectantly.

"What?" I asked. "What is it?"

"Come see for yourself," Myrna said.

Sunlight silhouetted the figures in the barn door, and it wasn't until I stepped outside and shaded my eyes that I saw who our visitors were. I whooped with surprise and joy and sprinted toward them. Mal turned in time to catch me in his arms, and a moment later I felt Quill wrap himself around us, too, joining our happy embrace. I breathed in the smell of salt air and pine-scented soap and their own clean sweat, fighting back the tears that threatened to cascade down my cheeks. After bearing so much sorrow in the wake of learning about Sawny's and Lily's deaths, I was beyond grateful to seek comfort in their arms.

A cough behind us reminded me that we weren't alone, and I quickly let go of the twins. Quill kept hold of my shoulders and held me at arm's length, looking at me.

"Are you well, Vi?" he asked. "Happy enough? Eating enough? You look thin."

I crushed him into another hug. "I've gotten some bad news, but I'll do. Don't worry yourself. I'm so happy to see you."

"It would seem our Vi has lost hold of her manners entirely," Myrna said. "I met your brother before, but I don't believe we've had the pleasure. I'm Myrna."

Suddenly, I remembered the other two people in the wagon and broke away from the Whipplestons, my smile only slightly abashed. One man was occupied with unhitching the horses from the wagon. The other, a slouch hat pulled low on his brow, sifted through the wagon bed.

Quill nodded to Myrna. I spotted a tiny, mischievous twitch at the corner of his mouth and eyed him carefully. "Lovely to meet you. Our companions unloading the wagon there are called Swinton and Bo. Think you might offer us a place to cool off and wait? Mal's got some business to attend to in the manor house."

"I have some work I've got to see finished. But Vi doesn't really have anything in the way of duties. She can entertain you while you wait. It's hotter than an oven out here." Myrna winked at me. "She's as red as I've ever seen a body, and that fellow there doesn't look much better. Take them inside and give them something to drink, will you, Vi?"

Glowing with excitement over seeing Mal and Quill again, I said, "I suppose I wouldn't mind that." I turned to Mal. "Will you come say goodbye before you leave?"

"Of course." Mal gave my hand a squeeze and went to the wagon, where he took a box from the man in the bed with a terse nod. Quill, arm still wrapped around my waist, was beaming down at me. My cheeks hurt from grinning.

"Not your beau?" Myrna asked.

I shot her a baleful look and slid out of Quill's arms with an apologetic smile. Myrna's laughter rang out through the morning air.

Shaking my head, I led the young men into my rooms.

"Sit, eat," I said, gesturing vaguely at the table, where some leftovers from breakfast still lay. My hands shook and sweat beaded my forehead, despite the cool breeze of the ceiling fans. I'd no idea what'd come over me. I needed to breathe. I needed to be alone.

I headed for the washroom, thinking I'd splash more water on my face. "I won't be but a minute."

I noticed Quill's odd expression just before he caught my arm. "Vi, wait." Inexplicably irritated, I glared at him and tried to jerk my arm free, but his grip was too strong. "We want to keep this quiet. There isn't much time."

"Time for what? Keep what quiet?" Anxious energy flooded through me like ice water.

"I've brought your half brother here to meet you. Let me introduce you."

His words sounded like gibberish. I didn't have a half brother. What was he talking about? I took a quick step away, suddenly feeling faint.

"Vi, wait."

Something in that voice stopped me in my tracks. It was familiar. Comforting. A sound I'd been waiting for my whole life without ever knowing I'd been missing it.

"My name is Bo. My father was your father."

The floor creaked and wheezed as Quill moved away from me. I knew I'd have to turn around eventually, but the pounding in my chest and the nonsense racing through my head would have to slow down before I was ready to face whatever reality stood behind me. I exhaled, long and slow.

"Vi, will you look at me? Please?"

A hand touched my shoulder tentatively. I whirled around and found myself looking into gray eyes achingly like mine. I swayed and went cold. He—Bo—took my arms and guided me gently into a chair. He knelt in front of me, put his hands on my knees and smiled a shy, blushing, familiar smile.

"It's nice to finally meet you. I've come a long way to find you."

I grasped for something to say, but there was only one word in my head. A single word spinning, gaining speed like a wave flying toward the shore, threatening to drown me.

Twin. Twin, twin, twin. TWIN.

"Dammal Traegar's your da, too?" I sputtered.

Bo shook his head. "It makes sense that your mother would have hidden it, him being married and all, but no, Dammal Traegar isn't my father. Nor is he yours. My father had an affair with your mother before she ever married, when she worked on my family estate."

My mind raced in circles around my memories, conjuring moments with my da. It was like someone was telling me the moon had never split when I'd seen its halves dancing across the sky every night of my life.

This was absurd. I pushed Bo's hands off my legs, glaring. The honesty, the sincerity, the love came off him in waves, and fury blossomed through my veins. I didn't want to believe him. I didn't even want to be *near* him.

"What proof do you have?" I asked.

"Have you never looked in the mirror, bully?" The other man, the beautiful one who must be Swinton, said. "You're as alike as twins. Your father's blood must've been right strong to stamp you both so."

I took in the lovely cloth and careful tailoring of his shirt and trousers, his fine leather boots. The quiet, regal confidence of his gestures. Bo's life had been easy, comfortable. He oozed a sense that people would go out of their way to take care of him. Every jeer, every dirty look, every bloody nose and bruise of my childhood welled in the banks of my memory and threatened to pour out in waves of tears.

I surged to my feet, knocking him out of the way. "I don't know what kind of cruel game you're playing, but I want you out. All of you. Get out." I pointed to the door. "Get. *Out.*"

Swinton and Quill stood frozen. I scowled at them.

"Vi. Just listen…" Bo scrambled to his feet, but held his ground.

I shoved him toward the door, but he loomed over me, and his lean ropes of muscle made him as immovable as a boulder. My body shook, hot with rage. It was an uncontrollable force, rising like fire through my veins. Bo clenched his jaw and scrubbed his hands through his hair. The gesture was so familiar, so my own, that it knocked the breath from my lungs. The anger washed out of me as fast as it had ignited.

I studied him carefully. His nose was the nose I would've had if mine hadn't been broken so many times. His dark curls matched my own. The square line of his jaw was stubbled with the promise of a beard, but the wide, full mouth looked as right on his face as it did on mine. I read a range of emotion in his gray eyes that hadn't touched my own in time beyond remembering.

Twin, I thought again.

I sank back into the chair, my head spinning. Bo pulled another chair out from the table and settled himself in front of me.

"How?" I heard myself ask.

The story he told was something out of a tragic novel. My ma, a young maid, caught between a cold, guarded mistress and a sad, lonely master, both desperate for a child and distanced by repeated loss. A moment of tenderness and sympathy that got a set of twins on her just before the mistress fell pregnant herself. Ma'd been whisked away to the city to avoid a scandal, but Bo's father—my father—had remembered us, Prudence and I, in his will.

As Bo spoke, the still water of my own history whirled and muddied. Something in his story felt wrong, and though I pushed it away each time it rose up, that one word kept ringing in my head. *Twin.*

"What was he like?" I asked. "Your father?"

"*Our* father." Bo smiled, a sad, longing smile. "He loved to read. He was funny. Silly. Mother was always scolding him for not behaving properly in front of the servants. He swam, even in the dead of winter. It was like he was impervious to the cold. He was the best horseman I've ever met."

Ma's decision to give me to the temple throbbed like a scar newly reopened, and my heart ached, realizing that the man I'd thought was my father, who'd visited and defended me even when Ma wouldn't come near me—the only one of my relations who'd ever cared a whit for me—wasn't even blood kin. I hadn't given him more than a passing thought since setting foot in Ilor, but now, sitting with Bo, I yearned for my da.

I shook my head and bit my lip, trying everything in my power to stave off the furious disbelief that threatened to drown me. I couldn't stop looking at my hands. They looked so strange, as if my body, my whole life didn't really belong to me.

Bo put a tentative hand over mine. "It's a lot to take in, but we don't have much time. There are other things we should talk about, Vi."

It was then that I noticed it. The sadness in his eyes. An ache that was at once mine and not mine.

"I've got money. Our father was very wealthy, and my mother's work increased that wealth exponentially. It's all mine now. I can bring you back to Alskad, set you up in a house there."

I gaped at him, tempted, for a moment, by the idea of running away from Phineas. But I couldn't think of Phineas without remembering what he'd done to Sawny and Lily, and I steeled myself against the idea. I would see him pay for his violence, for the murder he'd done, no matter the cost to me. "Oh. Our father was wealthy, and now you can rip me out of a life I chose and whisk me away? Play the hero? That's it, is it? If it was our father's money, then what he left me is mine and mine alone. I can take care of myself."

"I only meant..." he spluttered. "I told Mal and Quill I came to the colonies to give you the money. I thought it would be easier if..."

"Your life has been nothing but finery and flowers, and mine's been shit and scars." I spat the words at him, hoping he'd feel the sting of my hurt. "All you know is easy. You haven't got the foggiest clue about right."

Bo sat back, looking stunned, and the shards of pain— again, not my own—pricked at my brain. I glared. He wasn't telling me the whole truth. How could I possibly trust him if he started out with lies?

"Vi, think sense, just for a minute," Quill said. "If you walk up to Phineas with a handful of cash and demand to be allowed to buy out the rest of your contract—" He put up a hand to stop the protests burbling up in my throat. "Don't say you'll be subtler about it. You're about as subtle as a pod of whales. If he didn't have you arrested for stealing, he'd laugh you out of his office. Best case. You need help."

"What if I don't want to go? What if I'm fine where I am? I did choose this, after all," I snapped.

"Oh, certainly," Bo said, voice dripping sarcasm. "As though you would've done this if you had any choice at all. Stop being so damned stubborn."

I glared, but part of me knew he was right. This was a way out of the hell I'd bought for myself, a way to live what was left of my life—

I stopped myself. I didn't believe for a gods'-damned minute that the man standing in front of me was my half brother. He was my twin. I knew it in my bones. And he was offering me a way to live the rest of what could be a long life—a fact that took my breath away—however I wanted. I could find the rebels. Help them. I could do something important, something *useful* with all the anger and grief I'd locked away for so long. I could see Phineas pay for what he'd done.

I turned to Quill. "Then you do it. You take his money and buy out the remainder of my contract."

The agonized look Quill gave me sliced into me like a knife. "Vi. That would ruin me. Ruin the business I've just started to build. If we're to do this, we need to do it with great finesse—and like it or not, you need your half brother's hoity-toity manners and piles of cash. No offense, bully," he said to Bo.

Swinton nodded his agreement. "Your contract is to be a present to the mistress of the house, right?"

"He's going to give me to her at her birthday celebration," I said. I gritted my teeth and avoided Bo's eyes. If he wasn't interested in telling me the whole truth, I wasn't interested in him at all.

"It'll be a lot easier to get this done before Phineas makes a spectacle of Vi," Quill said.

Bo looked at Swinton, and I could feel the desperate grasping for reassurance that radiated from his questioning eyes.

"We'll be back in time, Bo. I'll make sure of it."

There was a brief knock at the door, and Mal padded in a moment later. His broad smile wavered and faded as he took in the tension-filled room.

"Introductions go well, then?" he asked.

Quill shook his head at his twin, an uneasy twitch of a smile hiding in the corners of his mouth. "How'd it go with Phineas?"

"Well. He's taking most of the wine we brought, and wants us to try and find a few more things for the party. He asked if we could lay hands on fireworks. Can you?"

Quill grinned, anxiety melting away at the prospect of a challenge. "You know me. Anything for a customer."

Mal quirked an eyebrow at Bo, but refused to meet my eyes. "If you're planning to be back in time for this party, you should get on the road this afternoon. We'd best be going. I'll get the horses hitched." Mal jerked his chin at Swinton. "Ready?"

Swinton nodded and followed him to the door. When he reached it, he turned to me with a last discerning stare that seemed to see straight to my bones. "We'll be seeing each other again soon, bully. You take care, now. Try not to get into too much trouble."

I stood and walked past Bo, who sat as still as one of the statues in the garden, and went to Quill, head spinning. He wrapped his arms around me. I reveled in the stillness of his embrace, breathing in his scent, my own heartbeat slowing to match his.

"I wanted more time with you," I whispered.

"There'll be time enough soon," he said, bending to kiss my cheek. "If I give you a minute alone with your brother, will you promise me you won't gut him?"

I scoffed and tried to pull away from Quill, but he held on. "Don't pretend like it's not crossed your mind. You looked about ready to go for a knife when you first saw him."

"I did not!"

"You did, and you know it. Promise you won't hurt the poor boy. He'd never be able to hold his own against an imp like you."

Righteous indignation welled up in my throat, but I pushed it down. I stole a quick glance over my shoulder and saw Bo, standing rigid, jaw clenched. I smothered the urge to smirk.

"All right. I won't do anything to him," I said, squeezing Quill's hand.

Quill's expression was serious as he released me and moved to leave. "You'll be able to start a whole new life soon, Vi. Be thinking about how you want that to look."

The moment the door clicked closed behind him, Bo started talking. "I'll have to go out there soon, so please hear me out. I'm not your half brother. I'm your twin. I'm sorry I couldn't tell you before. It's got to stay a secret, for both our sakes."

I stared at him. "I knew you were lying. I could feel it. I can feel everything you feel. Can you...?"

"Yes. Look, I'm so sorry about the lies. I promise I'll tell you everything as soon as we get you out of here. Will you trust me for now?"

"How can I? I've only known you for half an hour, and

all you've done is lie to me. How can I possibly trust you? I thought…" I stopped, embarrassed. "I thought my twin was a girl."

"I thought I was alone. All these years, I thought I was all alone." There was pleading in his eyes, and his hurt swirled around me. "Everything I said was as true as I could manage. Please, Vi. Being around you… I feel like I've found a part of myself I didn't know I was missing. I wanted this to be a happy meeting, and I've gone and bungled the whole thing."

The door squeaked open, and Quill's voice shouted in. "Let's go already! Time's wasting. I'll look for you at the party, Vi!"

Bo took my hands. "Be careful, Vi. Promise me. There are people looking for you, and they mustn't, under any circumstances, learn who you really are. I'll be back for you. I'll prove myself to you, I promise, but please, please be careful in the meantime," Bo said, and the ache in his heart was as real to me as the pain in my own.

I looked at him and bit my lip. I'd spent my whole life battered and bruised by the word that followed me around: *dimmy*. How had he been allowed to skate through life so whole, so unscathed? Tears welled in my eyes, and I turned away from him, silent. I refused to open myself to his pain when my own was as deep and vast as the ocean.

The door closed a moment later, and I couldn't tell the difference between his sadness and my own. I hadn't asked anything about him. Not why he'd thought he was alone, not why he'd finally come to find me after all these years. Nothing. I hadn't even asked which of us was older.

I sank to the floor, my back against the cool, stone wall, and I wept for everything I didn't know and for everything I did.

CHAPTER TWENTY-SIX

Bo

At dusk, we set up camp in a clearing carpeted with dense, springy grass. I looked after the horses while Swinton set about making a fire. Not for heat—that was oppressive enough—but to keep the animals away. When the fire was crackling and the horses were hobbled and munching contentedly on their grain, Swinton and I unrolled our blankets and stretched out, our heads propped on our saddles, bottles of cider at our sides.

It had been hard not to give up as we rode away from Plumleen and Vi. She'd as much as said she had no interest in my help, in knowing me, in learning what it was to be twins. She'd ripped my heart right out of my chest when she'd turned away from me, her words and thoughts full of venom. But as the door had closed behind me, I'd felt the rending in her own heart and the sadness that welled from deep within her. If not for that strange, miraculous connection of our twinness, I would have gotten on the first ship back to Alskad.

It would take time to make this right. Time, and stubbornness—if nothing else, it seemed we had enough stubbornness between us to deny the moon had ever split whilst gazing up at its halves in the night sky.

I spotted those halves of the moon, mere slivers in the sky through the tree branches, and sighed deeply.

"A question, little lord," Swinton said. "Why do you pretend that you're a clerk?"

"I am a clerk," I lied, fighting the teasing tone that threatened to creep into my voice. "Whatever gives you the impression that I'm not?"

"Oddly enough, I'm fair perceptive. Among a host of other clues, you've a terrible head for figures and haven't got the foggiest idea what anything ought to cost a person who's not dripping with *drott*. We needn't even touch on the 'half sister' who's as like you as a girl could possibly be. Plus there's that cuff on your wrist."

I blanched. He hadn't mentioned the cuff since Quill pointed it out. I had hoped that he had forgotten it. "Don't be ridiculous," I protested, trying to hide the panic in my voice.

"How much did our supplies cost?" Swinton asked. I'd bought the necessary food and drink for our journey in Williford while Swinton exchanged the horses we'd borrowed from his aunt for sturdier, faster mounts. We needed to ride quickly to Southill, with a brief stop to rest at the land my mother had bought halfway between the two cities on the way there and back.

"Four *ovstri*."

He cackled wickedly. "If you paid four *ovstri* for this lot, you've paid that merchant's bribe to the temple for the year."

"Weedy, boil-brained flap-dragons," I cursed. It had seemed like such a reasonable price.

"You curse like a lord, too. And walk like one, and eat like one. I've never seen a man take such delicate bites as you. Tell me, what's the truth in your story?"

I chewed on my lip. I wanted to trust him with every secret I'd ever kept. I wanted to lay my head in his lap and pour my every hope and happiness and fear and anxiety into his arms and offer myself—in all my wretched imperfection—to him. In truth, I didn't just want to tell someone—I wanted to tell him particularly. I wanted to share the burden of his secrets along with my own, even though I knew that I shouldn't tell anyone in Ilor about the crown I would someday wear. Couldn't, really. I hadn't even told Vi.

Instead, I said, "Tell me about your twin, and we'll see."

I waited, listening to the howls of monkeys, the rasping screams of cicadas and the raucous quiet of the jungle, until Swinton finally cleared his throat.

"Taeb was the good son. My parents didn't stay together long after they made us. Mama's a fighter, and Papa, well, he'd rather do about anything than yell. Nevertheless, they were cordial after the split, and each did their part in raising us, though it was clear from day one which son they favored. Taeb was sweet and thoughtful, always bringing Mama flowers, helping Papa in his shop.

"The gods and goddesses of the Alskad Empire hadn't quite caught on here when we were coming up. Most of the folks who'd settled Ilor were adventuring types who didn't have time for worship. The temple folk didn't start coming until folks like my grandparents had tamed the land a bit. But when we were ten, an anchorite moved to town and began to build himself a haven hall, one stone at a time. Curious brats that we were, we followed him around for a while, asking questions. He told us tales of the power of the goddesses and gods and tried to convince us to open our hearts to them."

Swinton took a long drink from his cider and stared into the fire for a bit before continuing. "Having little patience for being preached to by teachers or anchorites, I wandered off right quick and found something else to occupy my time. Taeb, though. Taeb fell in love with that young anchorite's stories, started following him around, waiting for the next word to drop out of that man's mouth. By the time we were thirteen, the anchorite's little haven hall was finished, and more had come to join him. Taeb came home one night and declared to me and Mama that he had decided to join the anchorites. He'd be moving into the temple the next day and would have to take a vow of silence until he was fully inducted into the fold, so anything we had to say to him, we'd have to say it right then."

"Was your mother happy?" I asked.

"Happier than I thought she should be. She cried a bit, of course, but then she started telling him how proud she was. She even dragged Papa out of his shop to tell him the news. Got to the point that I couldn't bear to watch them congratulate him any longer. I couldn't fathom why they were so proud. It wasn't as though he was studying to be a merchant or a builder or something that could actually earn some money. Taeb had decided to join a religion they didn't practice, one that would condemn them to eternal darkness as nonbelievers."

I whistled. I'd never thought of it that way. Growing up with the temple so much a part of our lives, I had always assumed that the only nonbelievers were people in the outer reaches of the Alskad Empire, too stubborn or too stupid to see the truth taught by the anchorites. It had never occurred to me that there might be intelligent people who had simply chosen not to follow the temple.

"What did you do?" I asked.

"I kept quiet as long as I could. Like I said, Taeb was the good son. He'd always kept me out of trouble—stopped some of my more harebrained schemes from crashing down on my head. But eventually, I couldn't stand it anymore. I raged at him, called him an idiot, told him he was betraying me and worse. He sat, listening and nodding until I ran out of curses to yell at him. Then he took my hands in his and told me that he would always be my brother first."

Swinton went quiet for a moment and sipped his cider again. I poked the fire and added another chunk of wood. I wanted to go to him, to pull him into my arms, but I was frozen by my own fear that my comfort would be unwelcome. That *I* would be unwelcome.

"I spat on him. I said he was no brother of mine and stormed out of the house," Swinton said, tears glimmering in his eyes in the light of the fire. "Those were the last words I ever spoke to him. He was dead before we turned fifteen. The anchorites claimed he'd caught a summer flu when they brought Mama his ashes." He seemed to deflate, as if this intensely personal story had rushed out of him and stolen his form in the process.

"I'm so sorry," I whispered.

"So am I. Sorrier than I can ever say. He's been dead these four years, and no amount of wishing can take those words back."

"Are you scared?" I asked, thinking of Vi.

"Of being a dimmy?" Swinton sighed and rolled away from the fire. "There's not much that could be worse than the waiting, knowing I may hurt someone I love. But as hard as that is, there's naught to be done about it." He yawned.

"Best get some shut-eye, little lord. Don't forget, you owe *me* a story now."

I reached out and found his hand, sliding my fingers between his. His hand tightened around mine, and we fell asleep like that, fingers intertwined.

The next morning, the fog burned away from the tops of the trees, and the sunlight reached the jungle floor. After riding and sleeping damp from a rain that swung from miserable drizzle to perilous, lightning-studded downpour with hardly a moment's notice, the sight of the sun was a relief. Just as the trees gave way to fields of blossoms, we spotted a wooden sign carved with the name *Gyllen*—my name. We'd found the right place.

The red-dirt road carved a curving path in front of us, bordered on either side by rolling hills carpeted in bushes heavily laden with cream-colored flowers. The bushes were planted in neat rows, close enough to one another that their glossy emerald leaves reached across the rows to caress each other. Two big, black birds circled over the fields, the only part of the scene before us that was less than idyllic.

"Do you smell that?" I asked. A blanket of perfumed air fell over us as soon as we left the canopy of trees.

Swinton scowled, his mood suddenly dark. "As you can see, I do have a nose."

"I've never seen plants like this, but the scent's familiar. Do you know what they are?"

"They're philomenas, though I've no idea why a body would plant so damn many of them."

I sniffed the air and closed my eyes, trying to conjure the scent in my memory. It came to me like a bolt of lightning, and a wave of grief along with it. "It smells like the perfume my cousin Penelope wore."

"Tell me more about this Penelope of yours," Swinton said, his voice full of mischief. He hadn't given up trying to pull the truth of my heritage from me any more than I'd given up trying to glean what it meant that he was one of the diminished. I'd yet to see any wildness, any violence in him. If anything, he was more cautious than I tended to be.

Dogs barked in the distance, and my dun mare's ears twitched. "Did you hear that?"

The barking was getting closer by the moment, and suddenly a pair of horses, their riders carrying rifles, crested the hill before us at a brisk trot.

"I think we may've stumbled upon our destination, little lord."

I reined my horse to a stop and said, "Please, Swinton. Try to remember that I'm a clerk, not a lord."

He winked. "Whatever you say, your lordship."

The riders, a man and a woman with the same wan complexions, gangly limbs and mousy hair, came to a stop directly in front of us, tipping the broad brims of their hats up and leveling their rifles at us. A pack of enormous, wiry-haired hounds circled our mounts, sniffing and snarling.

"State your business," the woman said, her high, thin voice cutting through the morning stillness like a knife.

I raised my hands so that they could see I held nothing but my reins and shot a glance at Swinton, hoping he'd do the same. He lounged in his saddle, hands on the pommel, an indolent expression of disinterest on his face. I grimaced.

"Lower your weapons, if you please. My name is Bo Abernathy," I said. "I've been hired by Gerlene Vermatch to assess the progress of operations on this estate. I would like to be taken to the manager of the property—Fredricks, I think it is."

The man lowered his rifle a scant inch and glanced at the woman next to him. "I can't say I know a Gerlene Vermatch. Do you, sissy?"

"I know that the Lady Myrella, whose place this is, gave some pretty strict orders about visitors. Do you recall what those were, brother?" The woman kept her rifle trained on me.

"Shoot 'em," he said. "Throw the bodies in the jungle for the wild dogs and catamounts."

"Reckon we ought to follow orders."

"Wait!" I cried. "Gerlene Vermatch is Lady Myrella Gyllen's solicitor. I am certain that if you take me to the person in charge, I can prove the veracity of my statement."

"Veracity means truth, dunderheads," Swinton said.

"That is not helpful," I hissed.

The riders lowered their weapons and removed their hats, using them to shield their faces from us as they whispered back and forth.

"I suppose if I get shot today, there's little chance I'll go on a killing spree tomorrow," Swinton mused. "Not a total loss, then."

"If you keep talking, I might be the one taken by a murderous impulse," I whispered.

Swinton beamed at me, eyes sparkling.

Settling their hats back in place, the pair—I could see they were twins now, with the same thick eyebrows and muddy eyes—slid their rifles into holsters that hung from their saddles.

"You'll come with us," the woman snapped. "But one false

move, and I'll have a hole in your gut sooner'n you can say a prayer to your god."

Swinton grinned at me. "Today's coming up aces, ain't it, little lord?"

I glared and kneed my horse into motion.

The rifle-toting guards led us to a rambling, shingle-sided mansion that possessed an air of dilapidated elegance. Under careful supervision, we tied our horses to a hitching post and climbed the front stairs. The woman told us to wait on the porch, which was shaded by tall trees, their limbs all hung with lacy, gray-green moss, while she fetched the overseer. Her brother settled himself in a wicker chair and propped his rifle against his knee. It was an excellent firearm, nicer than most I'd seen in the colonies.

"Y'all go on ahead and sit down," he said. "Makes me antsy watching you stand there."

"Thank you, I will," I said with as much dignity as I could muster, and sat gingerly on a swing.

Swinton perched on the porch's railing, as casual as you please. "What's your name, bully? I do hate to have my life threatened by a man whose name I don't know, even when his weapon's as nice as that one there."

The other man narrowed his already small eyes and pursed his lips, like remembering his name was a nearly impossible task. "They call me Hoss. Hoss Dickle. I'm the luckiest man in Ilor to be employed here at this nice place with the kind of boss we got ourselves. Woman knows her way around a weapon, that's for damned sure."

I snorted.

"You got a problem with my name?" Hoss snarled.

"That can't possibly be your real name," I said.

"Don't be too sure," Swinton said, tone serious. "I've known a number of great men named Hoss in my time. Dickle, you say? Any relation to the Lakehead Dickles?"

I shook my head in astonishment. Swinton could charm the embroidery off a merchant's coat and be paid for the favor, no doubt.

"They're my mother's folks. She came up here 'round about…oh, I'd say near on forty years ago now. Right after she took up with my pa. He was a Munn, see. You heard about the Dickles' feud with the Munns, I'll warrant. Folks weren't best pleased when Ma took up with Pa, so they decided to ride on up out of there."

"Well, I'll be. I was just telling—"

The screen door slammed open, and Swinton's monologue cut off abruptly. Hoss's sister stalked out of the house. Her sour expression twisted up even more when she saw her brother, elbows on his knees, grinning at Swinton.

"Hoss, I swear. I'm going to wring your neck for you one of these days. What do you think you're doing?" She smacked her brother on the back of the head, and he rose, rubbing his scalp and looking perturbed. "Boss'll see y'all now. Best come on ahead afore she gets her toes twisted."

We followed her into the cool, dim foyer, past a broad staircase and into an elegantly appointed study. The rugs were silk, the bookshelves crammed with rich, leather-bound books and the furniture elegantly appointed. The woman gestured to a pair of wing-backed chairs. "Sit. Boss'll be here in a minute."

Swinton raised an eyebrow at me. "Nice stuff for a backwoods farm manager, wouldn't you say?"

"I was just thinking the same thing."

A well-dressed woman swept into the room, her attention focused on the folder she carried. "Excuse me. I'm sorry to have kept you waiting. Clem says that you're a clerk sent by Gerlene Vermatch. Is that right? Why Myrella would involve her solicitor is simply beyond me. We've been following her instructions to the letter. Is this to do with the last shipment?"

I gaped. "Aunt Ephemella? What…what are you doing here?" I stammered. The one thing I had been counting on—my anonymity—shattered around me like a crystal glass dropped on a dance floor.

"Ambrose?" She fumbled the folder, and papers floated gently to the floor. Her tan face paled above the high-cut neck of her long, Ilorian-style linen tunic, and her tiny hands fluttered around her face. "What are *you* doing here? It's the twins, isn't it? Oh, Dzallie preserve me."

My heart sank. Ephemella wasn't technically related to me—she was Penelope and Claes's mother's twin—but I'd always known her as Aunt Ephemella. She'd been as close to them as their parents before they decided to immigrate, and she clearly hadn't heard the news about them and Mother yet.

I crossed the room and stilled her hands, leading her to a chair. "I'm so sorry, Auntie," I said. "I thought you were at your estate in northern Ilor. The letter I sent…"

Swinton knelt on the carpet and collected the papers that had fallen there. Tears gathered in the corners of Aunt Ephemella's dark eyes. She'd grown stouter in the years since I'd seen her last, and her rounded cheeks did away with the hawkish quality she'd had in the past.

"Don't keep me waiting, darling!" she said in her high, timorous voice. "Tell me why you're here."

I eyed Swinton over my aunt's shoulder. He appeared to be completely absorbed in one of the papers he'd bent to retrieve. "After Mother's death—"

She interrupted me. "Myrella is dead? What happened? No, tell me about the twins. What's happened to them?"

"I'm so sorry," I said awkwardly. "I wish you had gotten my letter. There was an accident at the mill. Mother and Penelope were there on business. I'm afraid there was nothing to be done."

"Was it murder?" Ephemella asked. "Was it Rylain? I never trusted that old horror's supposed shyness and seclusion."

My back stiffened. "If it was murder, I've seen no evidence of it. I'd hardly suspect Rylain would be the one responsible, though."

"And Claes?"

"I suspect he's gone by now. He didn't seem to have much time left when I left Penby."

Ephemella's chin trembled, and her eyes filled with tears, but she did not weep. "What possessed you to come all the way here?"

Something wasn't right. Ephemella should have been running her own estates, miles and miles away. "I needed to get away from Alskad for a bit," I said hesitantly, "and when Gerlene told me that Mother held land here, I thought I might come to see it for myself. After all, Ilor is part of the empire." I paused, and asked, "Why aren't you at your estates? Where are Uncle Rudell and Aunt Limina?"

Ephemella waved her hand dismissively. "They're looking after things at home. You can't mean that you've suddenly taken an interest in the management of your affairs? Runa surely can't have approved of this trip."

Swinton continued to study the paper he was holding, but he tensed at the mention of the Queen's name, and the muscles in his jaw tightened.

"I've always been interested. That's the reason I've taken it upon myself to understand the extent of my holdings."

"I'm sure that Runa wants you back in Penby as soon as possible. And she'll need to find you a new match. You can't be left unmarried. It wouldn't do," Ephemella rambled.

"Runa gave me permission to come," I said, gritting my teeth in irritation. "Why don't you tell me about this estate? What's grown here? Where is the overseer that Mother hired?"

"Philomenas," Aunt Ephemella said with a sigh. "Your mother entered into a farming contract for this land, and when her manager fell through—well, I was close and willing to do her a favor. There wasn't any reason that you should have known. I split my time between the two estates, and Clem and Hoss take care of the place when I'm gone."

Swinton gasped. My aunt twisted in her chair and caught sight of Swinton, papers bunched in his hand. He stuck his index finger in his mouth and smiled apologetically. "Apologies, ma'am. I got me a paper cut," he mumbled around his finger.

"I'm the one who should apologize." I stood, smiling at my aunt. "Aunt Ephemella, may I present my friend and guide, Swinton. Swinton, this is the Lady Ephemella Brace, Duchess of Ablemarlis and Kinsingmore, Marchioness of Oysells."

Ephemella extended her hand, which Swinton bowed over. She smiled and said, "A pleasure to meet you. You will stay with us for a time, won't you? I'll have the servants make up rooms for you both." She glanced at the papers in Swinton's hand. "Oh, do set those on the desk. They came earlier, and I haven't had time to sit down and puzzle them out. Tell me, Swinton, do you read?"

"No, ma'am," he said.

That was a lie. He could read. I'd seen him. I wondered what he was up to.

"It really is too bad about the horrible educational system here, isn't it?"

"Surely is, ma'am. If you'll excuse me, I'd like to see about our horses." Swinton bowed obsequiously, and as he left the room, I saw a flash of white paper slip into his shirtsleeve.

"Wherever did you find a strapping young man like that? I believe he might be taller than you!"

I laughed. I'd forgotten how charmingly straightforward my aunt could be. She was so unlike her shrewd, secretive sister.

"Now tell me, child, where did you find this Swinton fellow? I would hate to see you taken advantage of." Her eyes were narrowed, and insistence crept into her voice, reminding me that this was a noblewoman I was dealing with. Someone accustomed to games and deceptions. I needed to sharpen my tactics and go forward warily.

"He's been incredibly helpful. No need for you to worry about him."

Aunt Ephemella nodded, and an affectionate smile spread across her face. "You look a mess, my dear. I'll see that the servants prepare rooms for you and your companion. You'll both want to get cleaned up before we eat. Dinner at seven?"

My heart was in my throat as I left the study. The lies and half-truths I'd told Swinton swirled around my head. He had looked furious as he'd stalked out the door, and more than anything, I wanted to make it right with him. He was the only person I'd ever known who seemed to like me based on nothing but my personality. At this point, he was the only person who actually knew the real me—who I was behind the crown and the cuff on my wrist that shackled me to the throne.

I didn't want that to disappear.

CHAPTER TWENTY-SEVEN

Vi

I woke to an earsplitting scream in the middle of the night. A crash followed, like a sack of grain being thrown down the barn's steep loft staircase. I sat up in my bed, fuzzy headed and heavy lidded, wondering if I'd dreamed it. I'd had a lot of nightmares since leaving the temple, but they didn't often wake me.

Another shriek came from outside the barn. I sprang out of bed, the sleep washed from my limbs in a rush of fear, and hurriedly pulled on a pair of trousers. I slid my feet into sandals as I ran out of my rooms. The cries continued, but curiously, I didn't hear the women who shared the loft room above my apartments scrambling to get out of bed.

The barn was usually quiet after sundown, but for the occasional snorts and crackle of hay as the horses shifted their weight in their sleep. Tonight, though, the yelling had woken the sleeping beasts, and they stirred restlessly in their stalls. Riker, Aphra's big sorrel, pawed at his stall door, and Phineas's palomino whinnied in the stall next to him. I wished that I could do something to comfort them, but the screams coming from outside were human, and whoever it was needed help more than the horses needed soothing.

I snuck down the stall-lined hallway and eased through a crack in the back door. The twin halves of the moon were just slivers that night, and clouds curtained the stars, blocking their light. I tiptoed along the outside of the barn, careful not to make any noise. Flickering firelight outlined the edge of the building, and when I peeked around the corner, my eyes went wide. I didn't even have the presence of mind to stifle my own yelp, though screams covered the sound.

Those awful, blood-curdling wails came from a woman, stripped to the waist and lashed to the fence posts. Her long hair hung in knotted ropes that spidered across her welted back and over her shoulders, trailing blood. Two men, silhouetted in the torchlight, swayed with their backs to me. They were of a height, with the same sloping shoulders and thick waists, and they each held a whip in one hand. One other person stood in the circle of torchlight: Hepsy, her face carefully impassive.

The whips cracked once and again, and two more red stripes appeared on the woman's back. One man turned, laughing, to face the other, and I saw clearly then that it was Phineas, his pale skin turned red in the firelight. The two men weren't identical, but the similarities in their hard faces were striking. Phineas, whose jaw was squarer, clapped the other man—his nose much sharper than his twin's—on the shoulder, and over the sobs and moans of the woman, I heard him say, "What do you think, brother? Has she had enough?"

"She ruined your surprise, Phin. Didn't she? Give her ten more." He turned to Hepsy. "You wouldn't let her get off so easy, would you, Hepsy? You're tougher than aurochs' hooves."

Her lips compressed ever so slightly, but then Hepsy smiled. "Thank you ever so much for the kind compliment, Mister Spivey. I'm sure you know better than I what's for the best."

"Call me Singen, won't you, dear?"

Phineas barked a laugh, which was matched by his brother. "Five more lashes, Singen. Then we'll have a nip and turn in."

The woman moaned and twisted in her bonds, trying in vain to get loose. Her sun-bleached hair fell away from her face, and I saw the upturned line of Myrna's nose. As Singen and Phineas lifted their whips, all I could see was Lily. Her sharp face contorted in pain. Her sleek black hair damp with her own blood, and Sawny forced to watch. Before I had a chance to talk myself out of it, I ran from my hiding place, shouting one word over and over again.

"Stop. Stop it! *Stop!*"

Phineas's arm dropped to his side, and the whip coiled by his leg. It wasn't until he turned to look at me, his face contorted in a furious grimace, that the weight of what I'd done settled on my shoulders like an iron mantle. For one endless moment, the world stood still, and the only sounds were Myrna's sobs, the crackling of the torches and the orchestra of our collective breathing.

"I think that girl gave you an order, brother mine," Singen said.

Myrna groaned and sagged against the ropes that held her, blood and sweat rolling over the welts on her back. Phineas glanced from her to me and back again. A slow smile blossomed over his face.

"You tell me to stop, Vi, but you are as much to blame for

this as she is. But it's good you came out here. I should have thought of this beforehand."

"String her up, too. I'd warrant a few stripes would be becoming on skin like that." The lustful, untamed violence in Singen's eyes sent a panicked need to flee screaming through my veins, but I remained rooted in place, held by some invisible force. This scene was so blindingly, infuriatingly wrong. I didn't know how it could've happened. How it could've even started. I just knew that I had to make it stop.

"Get over here," Phineas ordered. "See what you've done."

I didn't move. I'd spent my whole life keeping my head down, working to keep the grief from breaking me and not knowing my own twin was close at hand the whole time. I'd kept my mouth shut when I saw other dimmys harassed, beaten. I'd watched the cruelty of twins equal anything I'd seen from even the worst dimmys.

I was done with shutting up. Done with holding my tongue. I wouldn't let anyone else die at Phineas's hand.

"I'm not the one with a whip in my hand," I said coldly. "I don't see where you get off claiming this is my fault, you pathetic, horrible little man."

Phineas started toward me. "I gave you one simple task," he said, beating a steady cadence against his thigh as he slowly closed the distance between us. *Thump, thump. Thump, thump.*

"Can't let them mouth off like that. You've got to show her who makes the rules," Singen slurred.

My heart raced in my chest, screaming for me to run. *Thump, thump.*

The rabid fury in Phineas's eyes hypnotized me. I couldn't move. Couldn't speak. But there was something else, too. My own rage grew like a fire in my chest. I'd spent my whole life tamping down that anger, and now, standing in front of me was a person so insecure, so unstable, that he'd decided he could use another person's pain to fuel the fire of his power. I wouldn't let this moment pass without taking revenge.

For Lily. For Sawny. And now, for Myrna. The thought of it was sweet on my tongue.

"I told you to keep out of Aphra's sight," Phineas growled.

I glared at Hepsy, but she assiduously avoided my gaze. Phineas was less than a pace away. I wanted to break his nose. I wanted to feel it crunch under my fist. I wanted to do to him the same violence he'd done to my friends.

Thump, thump.

"But wouldn't you know, after dinner tonight, my darling wife said something that took me quite by surprise. What did she say, brother?"

"She said she'd seen the strangest thing. She saw a girl she didn't recognize dive into the bushes when she rode by the other day. She has the irritating habit of learning the name of every servant who sets foot on this estate." Singen's voice was thick with disdain.

Phineas loomed over me. "I can't whip you and give you to Aphra bruised and striped. What would the guests at the party think? But Hepsy said she told you to find something to do, and Myrna admitted that she sent you into the gardens when she knew Aphra was out riding." He paused, and a wicked smile spread across his lips. "Now, Hepsy and I have an understanding. She'll see her wages docked these next few months, and that's punishment enough. But Myrna can still do her job with a few stripes on her back, and she should have known better. Isn't that right, Hepsy?"

"It is, sir." Her voice came from over my shoulder, but I was too frightened and furious to look away from Phineas's eyes.

"And I can make Vi watch, can't I, Hepsy?" Phineas asked.

"You can, sir. You're the boss."

I clenched my jaw and did everything in my power to keep the fear off my face. My fists were knotted by my sides. If I hit him with his brother right there, it would be the last thing I did. I'd lose my chance for real revenge.

Self-control was a whisper-thin net holding me back.

"Do you know what I can make you do, Vi?"

I glowered in response.

"I can make you mete out your new friend's punishment."

My mouth dropped open. He couldn't be serious.

Singen cackled. "Oh, Phin! That's too good."

I growled a single word. "No."

Phineas grabbed my jaw in one hand. The crushing force of his fingers brought tears to my eyes. "Now you've broken two rules, girl. You do not say 'no' to me. Not ever."

Terror flooded my body, and my knees went wobbly. Phineas grabbed me by my hair and dragged me, stumbling and cursing, to stand next to his twin in the circle of torchlight.

"What's the count, Hepsy?" he asked.

"Myrna's had twenty, sir."

"I was going to stop at twenty-five, for the number of years my dear wife has been alive," Phineas said. "But for your edification, Vi, we shall up the count to thirty."

A low moan rose from Myrna's slumped form, and she started to wail. I was going to be sick. Phineas opened my balled fist and closed my hand around the hard, braided leather handle of the whip.

I wanted to turn it on him instead.

"Ten, please. And if Singen or I think you're going too easy, we'll add two more lashes each and dock you a month's pay."

"You'll need to step into it to make it really count," Singen said wickedly, and handed his brother his own whip. "Put your weight behind it."

Between gritted teeth, I said, "You can't make me do this."

In a flash, Phineas's hand was tangled in my hair. He yanked my head back and leaned over me. Pain radiated from my skull. His eyes glowed in the torchlight, and he raised his other hand, the one holding his brother's whip. "You're a dimmy. *My* dimmy. And you'll do as I say."

I howled, as much with anger as with pain. The whip cracked behind me, and a flash of pain seared the backs of my legs. I fell hard onto my knees. The whip cracked again, and Myrna whimpered.

A new voice, one I did not recognize, rang out across the stable yard, clear as silver bells. "What in the names of Rayleane, Dzallie and Magritte do you think you are doing?"

Phineas let go of my hair, and I swiped a hand across my eyes to clear away the tears. My chest heaved, and I fought hard to keep the sobs that robbed me of breath from devolving into wails. A soft, cool hand cupped my elbow and brought me to my feet.

"Untie Myrna, Hepsy, and take her to the old stable master's quarters. Tend to her wounds. I'll discuss this with you later. Goddesses' sakes, she's your sister."

"Aphra, please. If you'll let me explain," Phineas whined.

"I can't even look at you right now," she snapped. "Singen, I want you out of my house before luncheon tomorrow. You are no longer welcome here."

The two men looked at her dully for a moment. Aphra stamped a booted foot and, in a dangerous tone, demanded, "Get out of my sight."

Phineas and Singen turned on their heels and fled into the

darkness. My legs shook as I watched them go. Aphra took my chin in her hand and gently turned me to face her.

"Let me see you," she said. "You're new. What is your name?"

My eyes widened, and it took every grain of self-control I possessed to keep from screeching when I saw her full face. Her right eye was grassy green, while her left was violet. The skin on her right was peppered with freckles, like mine, and on her left, it was clear and pale. Her hair was parted in the middle, the right side a bright, fiery red; the left, pale gold. She looked like two separate halves of two distinct people had been stuck together.

Seeing my expression, Aphra gave me a wry smile. "Don't worry. You can look. Phineas thinks I'm far more sensitive about it than I actually am. Will you tell me your name?"

"Vi, ma'am," I whispered. "Obedience Violette Abernathy."

"Obedience? Was that wishful thinking on your mother's part, or is your twin's name something like Piety?"

I returned her smile. Her forthright kindness set me at ease. "My twin was called Prudence. Ma called the others Patience, Remembrance, Amity, Clarity—you get the idea."

Her smile disappeared. "Was? Oh, I see now. You're one of the diminished. Where's Phineas been keeping you?"

I didn't correct her. My anger at Bo still smoldered beneath my skin, but there was something else there, buried deep—loyalty. Irritating, illogical love. He'd said it was important to keep quiet about our being twins, and I'd do it—at least until I got the explanation I was owed.

"In the barn, ma'am. In the old stable master's quarters."

"Shall we go inside then, and have a chat? It's too late to wake someone for a cup of tea, but I know where Torsha kept a bottle of tafia stashed."

I bit my lip. "Ma'am, I…" I stuttered, trying to find the right words.

"I won't let Phineas do anything to you. Let me guess. You were supposed to be a present for me. For my birthday."

"Yes, ma'am."

"Well, then, we should get to know one another. Come in out of the heat. I'm being eaten alive, and I think we could all use a drink."

We found Hepsy in my washroom with Myrna. Myrna held a bottle of tafia in one hand and steadied herself against the counter with the other. The air was stuffy and hot, and the room smelled of alcohol, herbs and metal. Bloody rags littered the floor, and Hepsy's attention was focused on the stripes crossing Myrna's back.

Seeing my concerned face in the mirror, Myrna bared her teeth at me in a semblance of a smile. "Don't worry, Vi. It's just a few stripes. Soon they'll be scars, and all the men'll be swooning."

Aphra coughed behind me, and the young women both paled.

"Excuse my sister, ma'am," Hepsy said, snatching the bottle away from Myrna, who'd just taken a pull. "She's had a little too much to drink."

Aphra came into the room holding another bottle, which she offered to Myrna as she perched on the edge of the tub.

"Don't be absurd. After a beating like that, I'd want to numb myself, too. I feel I owe you an apology," Aphra said, her face full of regrets. "I had no idea that he'd gotten this bad again so quickly. After Singen's visit last month, well…" She pursed her lips. "He's usually so much more reasonable. I know I can't take back blows already dealt, but we'll see if I can't make things a bit better."

"Thank you, ma'am," Myrna said softly.

"Hepsy," Aphra said, "may I speak to you outside? Vi, if you'd finish tending to Myrna's wounds and see her settled, I would greatly appreciate it."

Hepsy rose and followed Aphra out of the room in silence. When Myra's wounds were cleaned and bandaged, I gave her one of the soft nightshirts out of my trunk. It didn't take much to convince her to spend the night in my big, pillowy bed rather than the hammock she used in the upstairs loft. Though it was late, I wasn't the least bit tired anymore. Not after what I'd seen. Myrna would certainly make better use of my bed than I could that night.

I settled on the couch in the front room and pulled Mal's note from the drawer in the side table. I'd already unfolded and refolded it so many times that the creases were worn, but the scratchy handwriting and familiar words comforted me.

I jumped when the door creaked open. Aphra emerged from the mudroom, her expression grim. "It's just me," she said. "Is Myrna still awake?"

I shook my head.

"Good. I wanted to have a word alone with you." She went to the cabinet and retrieved two glasses. She handed one to me and picked up the bottle of tafia from the table where I'd left it. "Care for a drink?" Aphra asked.

"No, thank you. I don't have the taste for it."

"Nor do I, usually, but after a night like tonight..." She trailed off. "So. Vi. Tell me how it is that you came to be here."

As I told her the story, she nodded and took sips from the bottle of tafia. When I finished, I tucked my hands under my legs and bit my lip, waiting for her to respond.

She looked at me thoughtfully for a few moments and finally asked, "How much is he paying you?"

"Eight hundred *ovstri* a year, less the Whipplestons' commission."

Aphra paled. "Please tell me I misheard you. Eight hundred?"

I nodded.

"That bloody fool." She sighed. "His need to be seen as powerful and fearless is infuriating. It's the only reason he married me—to show me off, and show others how much power he has. Everything he does is about power. How little he thinks he has. How out of control he feels. He wants to be brave, but he's nothing more than a worm."

"Brave?" I asked. It was better than the real question that was spinning around and around in my head. The question I knew I couldn't ask.

Aphra arched her red-gold eyebrows at me. "You can ask, you know. One of the two people in my marriage is scared of it, but it's not me."

I looked away, and she laughed. It was a bitter sound.

"You want to know what I am."

I pursed my lips, not meeting her different-colored eyes. I didn't really need to ask. I knew. She was a fearsome story come to life. She was powerful, dangerous, two-faced. She was an amalgam. She was magic.

Amalgam were the stuff of nightmarish stories told to children to make them behave. Some stories said they were oracles, while others claimed they could control the minds of those around them and use that power to destroy whole nations. I'd even heard that they were the ones who'd split the moon and nearly wiped out our ancestors. The anchorites insisted that they'd been eradicated by years of worship and toil on the part of the faithful.

"We're called amalgam, people like me," Aphra said, echoing my thoughts. "But you would have grown up with the stories, of course. I imagine you know what it's like, to exist in a world where everyone fears you."

Aphra gave me a wry smile and offered me the bottle of tafia once more. This time, I took a sip, letting the sweet, fire-bright alcohol slide down my throat and burn in my belly. I grimaced.

"I do. But you…" I paused. "You must've felt so alone."

"Most times, when a child's born with two different eyes, the Shriven come to get them and they disappear."

"I wish I could say I was surprised," I said. "But I grew up in the temple. I know the kinds of horrors the Shriven commit at the bidding of the Suzerain."

"I suppose I could call myself lucky," Aphra said thoughtfully. "Lucky that my parents were wealthy. That they cared enough to save me from the Shriven." She looked out the window, staring at the broken pieces of the moon. "My mother and father hid me long enough to sell their businesses and estates in Alskad, then booked us passage here. They gave up everything to protect me.

"Mother died in childbirth when I was still quite young. My siblings, twin girls, went with her, and it was just Father and me until I was nineteen. When he passed, I was left without protection from the temple. For years, Father had bought their silence with extraordinary tithes and gifts to the anchorites here in Ilor. But when I tried to send the tithes on my own, the anchorites came calling. That was when the threats started. Unsigned letters, underhanded implications from the anchorites, from people I'd once called friends. I knew it was a matter of time before the Shriven showed up."

My jaw tensed, and I couldn't help but picture the tattooed, white-clad Shriven hauling Aphra off her horse and away from her home. She was right—one person alone could disappear without much effort on the part of the Shriven. A body needed at least one other person—if not a whole community—to keep them safe.

"Phineas started coming around at just the right time, and when he made it clear that he wanted a marriage, I was at my wits' end," Aphra said. "With his family and connections, I knew he could keep the Shriven at bay." Shaking her head, she took another swig from the bottle of tafia. "I wish I'd known then that he's the real monster in this marriage. He was so charming, so tender with me as I grieved for my father, and the moment we were married, the anchorites stopped visiting, stopped threatening me."

Though she wore no visible bruises, it wasn't hard to see that she'd not escaped her marriage unmarred. As we continued to pass the bottle back and forth, Aphra told me more about her life. Her parents had left her a great deal of money and land, which lent weight to the strange, dangerous appeal that drew Phineas to her like a fly to honey. Plumleen Hall belonged to Phineas's family, but he'd bungled the management of the estate so badly that he was near about destitute by the time Aphra agreed to marry him. Her money and management had pulled the estate back toward its past glory.

As the moon's halves sank below the horizon, Aphra fixed me in her startling, mismatched gaze. "You, my dear, have managed to go an entire night without asking me a single question about what it means to be an amalgam. Not many people last more than five minutes without asking me if I can read minds or do magic or see the future."

I looked down, blushing. There were so many things I wanted to ask, but those questions, each and every one, boiled down to rumors and myths that had sprung out of fear. The person sitting in front of me was just that—a person. And one who'd trusted me with her story. My curiosity hardly mattered in the face of everything Aphra had faced in her life.

I woke at midmorning, disoriented from the few hours of sleep I'd had on the couch. It had been nearly dawn when Aphra left my rooms, and my mind still reeled from the glut of information she'd shared. I eased myself off the couch, joints crackling. Just outside my door, I found a basket and a pitcher of tea.

I unpacked the basket. Inside, there were thick slices of sweet nut bread and a covered bowl of fruit for breakfast, a jar of salve and an envelope with a note from Aphra.

Vi,
Phineas has agreed to go on as though nothing has happened. He will present you to me at the party. In the meantime, see if you can't pick Myrna's mind about the inner workings of the estate. She might be able to see that you don't find yourself in a situation similar to last night's again.
—A

When Myrna emerged from the bedroom, her eyes still bleary with sleep, I poured her a tall glass of tea and slid the note across the table for her to read. The puppies and their mother came tumbling out of the bedroom behind her, all wagging tails and joyful yips. It was as though the night before had never happened, at least not for them.

"How do you feel?" I asked, and winced, knowing the answer couldn't be anything good.

Myrna scanned the note and snorted. "Like I got the skin whipped off my back last night. Just wonderful." Then her eyes softened. "Thank you for giving up your bed last night. My hammock would have been right awful."

"Stay as long as you'd like. Please. It's my fault you got those stripes."

"Hogwash," Myrna said. She crammed a whole slice of nut bread into her mouth. Mouth full, she said, "Singen and Phineas are the only ones who can shoulder the blame. You hear?" She poked me. "Get it? Shoulder?"

I groaned. "That's not even a joke."

"What did Aphra tell you last night?"

"She told me what she is and explained to me about her and Phineas. She said he wasn't so bad when they got married." I tried to work myself up to asking what Aphra meant in her note. After what I'd seen the night before, I was even more determined to see that Phineas never hurt anyone again. But to do that before Bo went about executing some half-cocked scheme to get me free of my contract, I'd need help. I'd need someone to rely on.

I took a deep breath. "There's got to be something to be done about him," I said. "He can't be allowed to keep hurting people. Isn't there some kind of rebel group here fighting to stop people like him?"

"I never thought I'd see Aphra go off at him like that," Myrna replied, stepping around my question.

"Why wouldn't she say something before? Why wouldn't she do something?" I asked. "It's her estate as much as it is his."

"She needs him," Myrna said, simply. "And the contract she signed is even harder to break than yours or mine." She narrowed her eyes at me, seeing that I was clearly still waiting for an answer to my earlier question. She sighed and said, "You've heard the rumors about the resistance, then?"

"Some," I said carefully. "I know it exists. I'd like to know more. I'd like to help."

Myrna deposited the puppy on the floor, went to the door and checked the lock. She returned to the table and sat back down. "The resistance gives aid to mistreated workers," she said quietly. "They're doing their best to end the temple's protection of the folks who ignore common decency and abuse the terms of their contracts. But their goals extend well beyond what I know."

"Are you part of it, then?" I asked.

Myrna nodded, and hesitated briefly before speaking again. "So is Aphra. She's been funneling a big chunk of the estate's profits to the resistance for several years now."

"What?" I nearly leapt out of my chair in alarm. "How do you know? Does Hepsy know?"

Myrna smiled and slid a knife from her boot, thumbing the edge. "I know because I'm Aphra's contact. And my sister? There's not a chance." She studied me closely. "You really want to make sure this doesn't happen again?"

I swallowed, loudly enough to feel self-conscious. I couldn't imagine a way this could possibly end well for me. I'd wanted this—to find the rebels, to stop Phineas—right up until the moment that it became real. Now fear washed over me like an enormous, drowning wave. While the rational part of my mind cried out all the reasons I shouldn't get involved, a bigger part of me was already screaming, *Yes! Yes! I'll help, yes!*

"I do, but..." My voice trailed off.

"Don't you want to be free?" Myrna poured more tea into our glasses.

"I'll be free when my contract is over. Free and wealthy." I chewed the inside of my lip, hating the taste of the lie in my mouth.

Myrna sighed. "*If* you're paid. I wouldn't count on it. Phineas will strip away a month's wages for no reason at all. You saw that last night. You've not been here long, and of the people you've met, we're the lucky ones. We're young and strong enough—or pretty and well-spoken enough—to be given positions on the estate proper."

I wouldn't have called Myrna lucky by a long stretch, after what had happened, and she must have seen the doubt on my face.

"Do you know where most contract workers end up?" she asked, an edge in her voice.

I shook my head.

"Almost all of the men and every woman not qualified for estate service wind up working kaffe. It's backbreaking. The overseers can extend the already brutal work hours on a whim. No one out there eats enough, and when they get sick—which they all do—they have to wait until temple day to see a healer," Myrna said, anger simmering in her voice. "More than half of them die before their contracts are up. The rest of them are stuck picking kaffe for pocket change until they die, unable to afford anything better."

"But aren't they supposed to be given tools to start a life? Aren't they saving their wages?"

Myrna scoffed. "Don't need more than a basket and a knife to pick kaffe, and they don't get paid half what they're promised."

"I don't know what I can do to help," I said. "I don't have

any real skills, other than diving and what you've taught me about horses."

"We've been looking for a way to get one of us close to Aphra for ages, but Phineas is in charge of the staff, and it would look strange if she were to take an interest in someone all of a sudden," Myrna explained. "All we'll need you to do is pass her letters and the money she gives you on to me. It makes more sense for you to seek me out than it does for her. She's taken to hiding notes in Riker's stall and dropping coins into his buckets a couple at a time." She paused, and asked, "How are you at climbing trees?"

I shrugged. "I've climbed up more buildings than trees. Not too many trees in the capital, and a roof is a good place to hide. Why?"

"You're going to be even more useful than we thought."

I grinned at her. "When do I start?"

Phineas came into my rooms late that evening, looking as dapper and well-rested as the first time I'd seen him in Hamlin's parlor—the complete opposite of the wild, furious person I'd seen in the stable yard. Myrna froze the moment he stepped through the door, and she watched him with wary eyes. I started to stand, but he waved me back into my chair. He took a seat on the edge of the couch and looked at the cards spread over the table.

"I certainly hope you aren't betting real money," he said. "She cheats."

Myrna threw her cards down and kicked my shin. "Dzallie's eyes!" she exclaimed. "You best give me my money back."

I tried to gauge Phineas's mood, but I must've stared too hard. He glanced at me, and for a moment, he let his cool mask slip, and I saw the irritation in his eyes.

He clapped his hands and said, "Ladies, ladies. I'll only take a moment. I've come to apologize for my behavior last night. There are times when one twin can bring out the worst side of the other. Singen and I tend to exacerbate one another's faults." He took a deep breath. "Myrna, I know you had no way of predicting that Aphra would see or notice Vi. I'll give you all the time you need to recover, and as an apology, I'll even allow you to keep your wages for time lost."

Myrna rose, wincing, to her feet and bowed deeply. "I'm extremely grateful for your generosity, sir."

"Would you, perhaps, give me a moment alone with Vi?"

"Of course."

When Myrna'd closed the bedroom door behind her, Phineas turned to me and reached out to rest his hands on my shoulders. I tried to flinch away from him, but his grip was like steel.

"I'd like to offer you an apology as well, Vi." He spoke loudly enough to be heard through the door. Then he hissed, "If you ever cross me again, dimmy, I'll lay your head on Tueber's harvest altar and boil your bones to feed my kaffe pickers. Now say thank you."

Phineas's grip on my shoulders was sure to leave bruises, and he held his face so close to mine that the sharp reek of kaffe on his breath enveloped my head in a cloud of the foul stench. Cold sweat trickled down my spine, but I wasn't frightened.

I was furious.

Determined to stay calm, I took a deep breath. I knew he had the upper hand now, but I wouldn't be forgetting this anytime soon. "No need to apologize, sir. I knew better. I shouldn't have put your surprise in jeopardy just to get some actual work done."

Phineas narrowed his eyes, but he released my shoulders

with a final ferocious shake. His voice once again a tad too loud, he said, "Lovely. I'll have the seamstress come and fit you for clothes for the party in the morning. In the meantime, you'll continue your riding lessons and your work in the stables, but you'll have no more lessons with Hepsy. Instead, you will report to me for training every day. I'll expect you in my study after the luncheon hour. Is that clear?"

"Yes, sir," I breathed.

"First lesson." Lightning fast, Phineas reached out and grabbed my ear, twisting it viciously. "You must speak audibly."

Despite myself, I whimpered. Anger beat away the fear that raced through me, and in the deadly calm of fury, I steeled myself. I was going to stop this man. Someday, he wouldn't be able to hurt anyone any longer.

He gave my ear a last hard yank, and the room swam before my eyes. I gasped when he released me, slumping down in my chair. He patted my cheek. As he headed for the door, he called over his shoulder. "I'll expect you tomorrow. Good night, Obedience."

CHAPTER TWENTY-EIGHT

Bo

I barreled into Clem on my way out of the study and bounced off her, jostling a spindle-legged table and upsetting a vase of bright purple flowers. The woman was sturdier than a Willand pony.

She glared up at me. "You best see to your friend afore I shoot him. I done had enough of this nonsense."

"Where is he?" I asked.

"Out yonder." She pointed vaguely in the direction of the front door. "Seems he's set to kick over every bush in that near field afore the sun sets." I groaned and started for the door. "You get him under control. If the boss says to fill him full of lead, I ain't giving him more than one chance to quit."

"I understand. Thank you, Miss Clem."

As the screen door slammed behind me, she yelled, "I'm no miss. Just Clem."

I rushed out into the fading afternoon and found Swinton in a field of philomena bushes. They were awash in the red light of the setting sun. Their flowers, normally creamy white, looked as though they'd been dipped in blood, and Swinton's white shirt glowed crimson. He took hold of a bush. Yanked. Waxy leaves and petals flew through the air, but the plant's roots held firm.

"Swinton." I approached him the way I would a spooked horse—slowly, speaking softly the whole way. "Swinton, come inside. It'll be dark soon."

He silently continued his assault on the bush.

I took a step. Another. When I got close enough, I laid a hand on his shoulder. And then I was on my back, staring at the flame-licked sky, its pinks, oranges and reds more vibrant, more real than any sunset I'd seen before. Air rushed back into my lungs as the door to the house opened and lanterns were set out on the porch. With the light came the pain. I gasped, took several shuddering breaths. Something tickled my ear, and Swinton's face appeared above mine.

"Are you planning to lay in the dirt all night? I want to be well away from this place before the moons set."

Taking my hand, he hauled me to my feet.

"Do you plan to apologize?"

"No."

"Fine," I sighed. "But it doesn't make any sense to leave tonight. Aunt Ephemella will give us dinner, a bath, a bed. A real bed, Swinton. Plus, it's been years since I've seen my aunt."

Swinton's face went blank. He spun on his heel and strode toward the house.

"We can leave tomorrow," I said, dashing to catch up.

He whirled on me. "You may do whatever suits you, lit-tle lord. I'm not staying under that woman's roof. Not for a minute. I've fulfilled my obligations to you. Pay me what you owe, and I'll be out of your hair."

"What do you mean? I thought we were going to South-ill together. I thought..." I trailed off, remembering falling asleep with his fingers wrapped around mine. "Was it something in the papers you took?"

"You saw that, did you?"

He shoved a handful of loose papers at me. I glanced around and, finding no one in sight of the field, tilted the papers to catch the light of the setting sun. The top page was some sort of ledger. Names ran down one side, and neat columns of numbers and symbols filled the rest of the space. I couldn't make heads or tails of it. There was a letter addressed to my aunt, acknowledging her request for additional contract laborers for the coming harvest. On the bottom of the stack of papers, a letter bearing the official seal of the Suzerain gave specific instructions for the infusion and distillation of a tincture of philomena blossoms. The letter was signed simply "C & A."

Swinton watched me as I read, shadows gathering in the furious lines of his face. In all the time we'd spent together, I'd never seen him so mad.

"I don't have any idea what all this means. It looks like what my aunt said—that she's running the farm as a favor to my mother to fulfill a temple contract."

"Never mind that you've been lying to me about who you are. We both knew very well that was the case. But this is too much to be borne. The contract is with the Suzerain, Bo." He snatched the papers away from me, found the ledger and waved it in my face.

I batted it away. "So? They're making something for the Suzerain. What of it?"

"What do you know about philomenas?" he asked.

"Nothing. Why?"

"About fifty years ago, someone got the bright idea to use philomenas for perfume. They smell remarkably similar to the karlenias that grow in Samiria, but they're much hardier plants. Cheaper to maintain. They planted acres and acres of land with the flowers and built several perfumeries. They imported the latest solar-powered distillation equipment and trained staff from all over Ilor to work in the perfumeries." He looked at me, his mouth set in a hard line. "You've really never heard about this?"

I shook my head.

"Everything turned upside down. The unlucky souls who'd been hired to pick the flowers turned on each other, on themselves. It was the bloodiest disaster in the history of Ilor. The people who worked in the factories died. All of them, within just weeks of beginning their work. The managers were able to destroy the essential oils they'd produced and keep the perfume from being exported to the rest of the Alskad Empire, but the investors from Alskad lost scads of money and thousands of people here died."

"Why didn't you say something when we were riding up?" I asked, horrified. "You knew what these flowers were then, didn't you?"

"What was I going to say? I thought you were just checking up on someone else's investment. I didn't know this was all yours." He took a deep breath. "There's more, Bo."

My breath caught in my throat. "Do you know what those marks mean?"

"I have an idea."

I waited.

"I recognized one of the names on the list." There was a

hitch in his voice. "When the priest came with Taeb's ashes, there was a young man with him, an initiate who'd been studying with Taeb. He wanted to tell us what a good friend Taeb had been to him. His name was Basel Felp. I got word last month that he died in an accident, and here he is, on this list. There's an X by his name, and it's dated a month ago."

"All these Xs, by all these names... You don't think..." I trailed off.

"I don't know why, but I think the flowers your aunt is growing here are connected to my brother's death. I think the temple is testing whatever it's making from these flowers on children. Ilor's children."

I caught sight of Clem and Hoss standing on the edge of the field. Their shadows stretched out before them, specters in the growing darkness. I didn't want to be a part of any of this. Maybe I should have stayed home with my books and my horses and my endless, tedious lessons. I'd gone my whole life without knowing I even had a sister. There was no reason I should have felt compelled to go halfway around the world to find her now.

Even as I thought it, I knew it wasn't true. Every day I'd spent away from home, I'd learned more about myself. I'd grown stronger and smarter, and learned more about the people I'd someday rule. There was no way I could walk away from this now. Just knowing that my money, my land was a part of whatever it was the Suzerain were doing made me complicit.

The weight of the cuff was heavy on my arm, reminding me of my promise to the empire. I had to do something. Had to stop this. Had to free Vi. Had to take charge of the empire I was born to lead.

Still, doubts filled my mind. "You don't know for sure

that's what killed your brother," I said hesitantly. "He might have died of the flu, like you said."

Swinton glared at me and shook his head.

"What?" I asked. "What is it?"

"I know he didn't. I think I've always known."

"How? How could you possibly?" I wanted to reach out and help him through this old grief, but he stood just out of arm's reach.

"No one at home died. No one in Williford even got sick."

I didn't want to face the implications of what he was saying. I needed there to be a different explanation. "Swinton, be reasonable. Taeb was at the temple. He was an initiate in training, wasn't he? It makes perfect sense that the disease didn't affect you in Williford. He was far away."

Swinton's fists clenched. His shoulders tightened. "If you could take your head out of your own ass for a minute, you might understand. The school was *in* Williford, down the road from my house. But only the boys there got sick. No one else, not even the anchorites. They claimed they'd kept it contained. They said it was the will of the gods, but, Bo, I could feel him. He wasn't sick. He lost some essential part of himself, and I nearly lost myself, as well. I could *feel* his terror, his rage before he died."

"Gods save us," I breathed.

"They can't," Swinton said. "They aren't real."

I stared at him. "You don't believe in the gods?"

Swinton sighed. "Never mind. It doesn't matter."

My head spun, and I looked across the fields. "If the anchorites and the Suzerain know that these flowers are so dangerous, why would they continue to farm them? To produce these distillations? And why would my aunt have that list?

You think the temples are actually using this substance for some…nefarious purpose?"

"Open your eyes, Bo!" Swinton said in frustration. "It's obvious that they are. I don't know why, but I do know that the people who died in that first accident—the laborers, the factory workers? They acted like the diminished do when the grief finally takes them."

I shuddered at the implications of what he was saying. His grief, his fury, was written all over his face. I stepped forward and laced my fingers through his, looking deep into his eyes. "I'll make you a promise, Swinton. The moment that Vi is free of her contract and away from Plumleen Hall, I'm going to do everything in my power to learn exactly what is going on—and I'm going to stop it."

The weight of everything I'd learned in the last few months hung heavily from my shoulders, dragging at me, pulling me toward a future full of conflict I didn't know if I wanted. But the one thing I knew I did want was Swinton. His forgiveness. His hand in mine.

He nodded jerkily and looked away. I let my hands drop to my sides and decided to ask the question that had been weighing on my mind since he first told me he was diminished.

"Have you ever felt like…like you might…" I trailed off, unsure of how to frame such an indelicate question.

"Like I might lose myself?" Swinton asked. I dipped my head in assent, and he sighed deeply. "Every morning when I wake up, I expect that it will be the last time I see the morning light unfiltered by mindless rage. Every evening, I am grateful I've lived another day without the grief taking me just because I lost my brother. It's been years since he died, and still, I mourn his loss every day. But despite all the grief and the fact that I could shatter at any moment, I go on living, because that's all I can do, really."

Clem and Hoss disappeared down the path toward the house when Swinton and I stopped talking. We stood together, silent, as darkness filled the sky. When the stars began to twinkle, overwhelming what was left of the sun, I took Swinton's hand.

"I'm sorry I didn't understand," I said.

He squeezed my hand, and the ice in my gut melted. I'd never felt this way about anyone, not even Claes. I'd longed for his approval. I'd welcomed his kisses. But I'd never needed Claes the way that I needed Swinton in that moment.

"Can I tell you a secret?" I asked.

The night was full of buzzing insects and the distant calls of jungle creatures. Taking his silence for agreement, I began. "Vi…she's not just my sister, Swinton. She's my twin."

"You must be joking," Swinton said, his voice tinged with mocking, sarcastic shock. "I never would've guessed, seeing the two of you standing next to each other."

"Would you listen?" I huffed. I was terrified that this would be the last thing I told Swinton. That after he learned the full breadth of my lies, he would walk away and never speak to me again.

"Fine."

"My full name is Ambrose Oswin Trousillion Gyllen. Just over a month ago, Queen Runa named me the official heir to the throne of Alskad." I looked at him, expectantly, waiting for some kind of reaction.

Swinton blinked rapidly, his brows furrowed, opened his mouth as if to say something, and closed it again.

"I'm sorry I didn't tell you. It's just…" I let out a long, slow breath, staring at the toes of my boots. "It's a lot."

Swinton remained silent for so long that I finally looked up to gauge his reaction. To my shock, his face was full of mirth. "I suppose I should've been calling you 'little prince' rather than 'little lord' this whole time," he said, teasing. "Go on, then. Out with the rest of it."

Relief and warmth flooded me in equal measure. It felt so good to tell someone. To tell *him*. To not be alone with my secrets anymore. I left nothing out—my father's infidelity, my birth and adoption, the successions, the deaths that had set me on this road, Gerlene finding Ina, the trip to the Ilor colonies. Everything. As I talked, we walked through the fields, away from the well-lit path.

When I was finished, I waited for him to say something, anything. He didn't breathe a word. The starlight rinsed the gold from his hair and skin, and in that gray-white ancient light, the stark lines of his face were the most beautiful thing I'd ever seen. On a sudden impulse, I leaned in and pressed my lips to his. He froze, and I pulled away, embarrassed. I dropped his hand.

"I'm sorry..." I stammered. "I didn't mean... I just..."

Swinton smiled. A bright, dazzling thing. He wrapped his arms around me, drew me in and kissed me back. I closed my eyes, and nothing in the world existed except that kiss. His lips melted into mine, and he pulled me close, our chests twin planes made to match. Our tongues flickered and danced, and everything in the world disappeared except our bodies and my endless, aching need for him.

When he pulled away, sound and light came rushing back in a dizzying wave. "Oh," I said stupidly.

Swinton winked at me, but behind his smile, he looked sad. As sad as I'd ever seen a person. "I'm glad you told me, Bo. I'm glad you trust me."

"So am I," I breathed. I looked back toward the house, weighing our choices. "We can leave in the morning. I don't know what to do about this place, but there'll be time once we get Vi free. Is that all right with you?"

He nodded.

"I'm sure that my aunt will understand if you'd rather eat by yourself. I actually think that might make this easier. I can see if she'll have something sent up to your room."

Again, he nodded. "Be wary, Bo. I wouldn't trust that woman for a minute."

"I don't. Not for a blink." I squeezed his hand. "And to think, she's one of the less vicious members of my family."

The stark, bleak nighttime light smoothed the imperfections of the rambling house into a beautiful lie: the chipped paint and weathered shingles disappeared, leaving the elegant lines and trailing vines that belied the viper that lived inside those walls. We walked back through the poisonous, destructive bushes, hand in hand, lit only by the stars and the slivers of the broken moon rising over the horizon.

CHAPTER TWENTY-NINE

Vi

The study was empty when I arrived the next day. Always hungry for a new book, I scanned the shelves that lined the room for something that might not be missed if it happened to find its way into my pocket. While most of the books were rich, leather-bound classics, I spotted a row of cheap paperbound books on a bottom shelf in the corner. I'd just squatted to get a better look when Phineas swept into the room leading a pair of anchorites, unmistakable in their sunset robes.

I hopped up and immediately sank into a low, proper bow.

"This is the diminished girl?" a deep, feminine voice asked over my bowed head.

"She is." Phineas's voice was doing more bowing and scraping than I was. "You may stand, Vi. Say hello to Anchorite Mathille, Anchorite Tafima and Shriven Curlin."

I started and looked up, seeing the white-robed figure enter behind the anchorites. It wasn't a coincidence—it was actually Curlin, *my* Curlin, smiling triumphantly at me. Her long, straight nose was bisected by the black paint of the Shriven, and a new tattoo crept up her neck. A scream rose in my throat, and I quickly swallowed it. If she'd not shaved her head, I would've wanted to rip her hair out. Now all I wanted was to break that long, straight nose of hers. She, more than anyone else, was responsible for my present situation.

I took a deep breath, searching for calm. "Magritte's blessings upon you," I said.

"My," the younger of the anchorites exclaimed. "She's practically docile, especially for one of the diminished."

"We are working hard toward that end, Anchorite Tafima," Phineas reassured her. "I hope our little excursion today will bring her fully into the mind-set she needs to be of use to my dear wife."

The eldest of the three, a middle-aged woman whose yellow robes clashed horribly with her sallow skin, shot a thin-lipped smile at Phineas. "If it does not, nothing will. Shall we be off?"

Phineas handed the anchorites and Curlin into their waiting carriage while I mounted Beetle and wiped my sweaty palms on my breeches. We rode down twisting jungle roads, taking so many turns and switchbacks that I eventually lost all sense of direction. The cries of wild animals echoed through the air, and bright birds swooped around us, unafraid. Great gnarled trees, their branches hung with gray-green curls of moss, loomed over the wide road. Their canopies blocked the sun, so when we finally emerged, I found myself blinking furiously in the late afternoon light.

The carriage creaked to a halt. Beetle slowed her plodding pace without even a twitch of the reins on my part. My eyes widened at the sight of a stone wall rising out of the jungle, at least twice my height, with nasty iron spikes shooting from its crown. A massive iron gate eased open, and I filed in behind the anchorites' carriage and Phineas on his big palomino mare.

Once inside the gates, a swarm of servants in neat gray uniforms descended on us. One took Beetle's reins from me. Another wrapped his big hands around my waist and pulled me out of my saddle. My heart raced, and I kicked, fighting with all my strength. My booted foot made contact with something soft, and the man dropped me, cursing. I landed on my feet and shifted into a fighting stance, hands up and feet wide. A wave of the gray-clad servants rushed toward me, but a gravelly voice rang out across the courtyard, stopping them.

"The girl is a guest here today. She won't be staying."

"Thank you, Anchorite," Phineas said, his voice cold. "You see why I thought this visit necessary?"

Embarrassed, I offered my hand to the man I'd kicked. "Sorry about that, chum. Guess I'm a bit jumpy today."

He snarled, showing black gaps in his mouth where he'd lost teeth.

"This way, Obedience," the orange-clad anchorite said. "Phineas, would you allow us to take charge of your servant for the rest of the afternoon? Anchorite Mathille will have kaffe for you in the Ancients' parlor, if you please."

Nodding, Phineas led the way to a brick building that looked oddly familiar to me, followed by the trio of women. As we got closer, I realized this was an exact replica of one of the anchorites' houses in Alskad.

How absurd, I thought, *for them to build something like that here.*

The building had tiny windows to keep out the cold winter air in the heart of the Alskad Empire, but here, the lack of air circulation would undoubtedly make the interior stifling. I eyed the chimneys dotting the roof and realized they must've added the traditional hearth to every room, as well. All those fireplaces would be useless in the heat of Ilor.

Phineas and Anchorite Mathille split away from the other two women and me in the foyer. I followed Curlin and Anchorite Tafima down a pristine, well-lit hallway and into a library. The anchorite sat at a broad desk, and Curlin stood behind her, motioning me toward a hard, ladder-backed chair. I sat, and for several long, uncomfortable minutes, the anchorite peered at me critically. Curlin poured a glass of juice from a crystal pitcher and handed it to me. Surprised, I took the glass and sipped, thirsty from the ride. The room reeked of some heavy perfume. Knowing from long experience with anchorites that I'd have my head bitten off if I spoke first, I waited, the cut crystal of the glass leaving marks on my palm.

"Obedience Violette Abernathy, daughter of Xandrina Fleet Abernathy. Diminished. You've mostly sisters, I think—just two boys in your mother's whole brood. Given to be raised by the temple as an infant. You were meant to be here, laboring in service of the temple, as I'm sure you know." The woman glanced down at the neat stack of papers on the desk in front of her. "But as you're now engaged in service to one of our most loyal worshippers, and Mister Laroche has most generously offered to increase his tithe to compensate for our labor loss, I suppose we'll do with you what we can."

A memory of Bo's face rose like bile in my throat, and I narrowed my eyes at her. I wondered what her game was. I'm sure it wouldn't be long before I figured it out—scams and grifts were a way of life in the End. If a body let their guard down for a minute, they'd be missing every shiny button from coat to boot.

The anchorite made a disgusted face and said, "You've been

brought here to learn a lesson in deference. Ironic, given your name. Are you ready?"

She stood, and Curlin glided to open a door at the back of the room, her head bowed. She'd been so still that I'd almost forgotten she was there.

"This way," the anchorite commanded.

I followed her down a stairwell dimly lit by solar lamps. Curlin's white robes swished behind me, and when I glanced over my shoulder, I saw that she held a metal-tipped staff across her body. It nearly touched the stone walls on either side. There'd be no turning back now.

We stopped in front of a heavy door at the bottom of the stairs. The anchorite pulled a key from a long chain around her neck and unlocked the door. The space beyond the doorway was shrouded in darkness, but the anchorite walked into it with the ease of long familiarity. I paused and bit my lip. Sweat rolled down my back, though the basement was cool.

"Come." The anchorite's voice echoed out from the darkness. A moment later, the smooth heel of Curlin's staff pressed into my lower back, like the promise of pain to come. I walked forward into the dark. Before I had taken three blind steps, I heard the familiar scrape of steel on flint, and a flame gave shape to the dingy room. The anchorite handed it off to Curlin, and she moved between lamps hanging at even intervals along the stone walls, lighting each of them. Steel bars enclosed a number of alcoves, still bathed in shadows. As the room grew brighter, groans and whimpers rose from what I now saw were cells.

It wasn't until the rough wooden door scratched my shoulder blades that I realized I'd been backing up. Someone slammed into the steel bars next to me and cackled. A skeletal hand reached toward me. I recoiled, my skin prickling. The hand was missing two fingers and its thumb.

"They're perfectly secure," Curlin said, disdain coloring her prim accent.

"What is this place?" I stammered.

"These are the diminished of this region of Ilor, those who have undergone the change," the anchorite said. "Your employer gave a generous gift so that you might see what happens to the diminished who misbehave here in the Ilor colonies. Take a good look."

Numb, I walked behind her, glancing into every cell along the way. The people behind those bars looked past me with blank eyes. Some wept. Others shouted curses. I hated myself for the relief that flooded through me, knowing now that I would never be one of them.

A voice echoed down the stairs. "Anchorite, you're needed in the parlor for a moment."

The anchorite huffed and went to the staircase. "Show her, Curlin."

Curlin nodded respectfully, and the anchorite swished out of the room. The second the door thudded closed at the top of the stairs, Curlin turned to me with a wicked grin.

"Follow me," she said.

"What are you doing here?" I seethed.

Curlin, a full head taller than me, took me by the arm and whipped me around to face her. "They're watching," she whispered. "We've never met. You and I cannot know each other. It's for your safety. Got it?"

I tried to jerk away from her, but she'd grown stronger since joining the Shriven, and her tattooed fingers held me like a vise.

"Come on, girl," she said in a loud voice, haughty and full

of venom. "I'm going to show you what happens to dimmys like you."

Staff heavy on my back, and her hand wrapped viselike around my arm, Curlin pulled me into the next room. My heart sank in my chest when I saw a boy and a girl, one dark-skinned, the other pale and ruddy. Neither could have been a day over ten. They were strapped to upright planks that were the same light pine as the table in the temple kitchen where I'd eaten almost every breakfast until so very recently.

Curlin locked the door behind us and went to a table where two half-full glasses waited.

"It's so sad," Curlin said, her tone equal parts threat and delight. "You could have been one of us. No one sees a dimmy when they look at me. All they see is power, control. Now that I'm Shriven, I can do no wrong." She turned to look at me, her face grim. "Watch."

Curlin had grown steadily nastier after she joined the Shriven, but this wasn't like her. Something in her had snapped, and she'd become more like one of the horrible green tree vipers of Ilor than the adventurous, bossy girl I'd grown up with. I did as I was told, my eyes fixed on the children. They were gagged, but their eyes flicked from side to side like caged insects, taking in everything in the room.

"Dimmys," Curlin explained, "are as common as rats in the wilder parts of this country."

I saw her dismissive gesture out of the corner of my eye and, fists clenched, asked, "Why've you brought me here? What are you doing?"

"You were supposed to be coming to the colonies to labor in the service to the temple, but you've wormed your way out of that nicely, haven't you? Now, on the one hand, we could leave you where you are. Phineas contributes a great deal to the temples, mainly so we'll turn a blind eye to his amalgam wife. I imagine he'd give more to keep his pet nearby." She paused, and her gaze turned predatory. "On the other, we could snatch you away from Plumleen. I believe we need someone to mop up after us down here. Unless, of course, you choose to cooperate."

Curlin took one of the glasses from the table and approached the boy. She whispered something in his ear before removing his gag.

"Tell us your name, child," she said.

"My name is Tobain, Shriven."

"Your age?"

"I'm nine." His voice shook with fear. "Please don't beat me. I'll be good, I swear."

My throat clenched.

"I know," Curlin cooed. Her voice was calm and soothing. "Now tell me the truth, Tobain. Have you ever hurt anyone? Played with fire? Killed an animal?"

He whimpered. "I wrung a chicken's neck for supper once. But Ma made me! I hated it! I'll never do it again, I promise!"

"How long ago did your twin die?"

Tears ran down his round cheeks. "Three years." He sniffled.

"Very good, Tobain. Now, I want you to drink this medicine. Will you do that for me?"

Tobain nodded, and the girl next to him screamed behind her gag. His eyes went wide, but the glass was already pressed against his lips. He struggled against the strap that bound his head to the board, tried to press his lips tight together, but Curlin held his nose. When he opened his mouth to breathe, she poured the liquid down his throat. I watched, grinding my teeth, as his throat constricted and he swallowed. Curlin stuffed the gag back into his mouth.

"Watch carefully, Vi," Curlin said. "This is his fifth dose. You've already had two."

"What do you mean, I've had two?" My muscles tightened, and my hands clenched into fists. "Two of what?"

"The records say you had one dose of the same medication I've just given this boy when you were back in Penby. I gave you another upstairs, and you had no idea. Watch and see how it works. See what five looks like."

The boy shook. His eyes rolled back in his head, and he shook violently. Horror and confusion boiled in my brain. I couldn't watch this child die right in front of me.

Just as I started forward, he stopped moving, and his eyes fluttered shut.

Curlin put one hand up. "Wait. Watch. Unless, of course, you want the little girl to be next. Her name is Clarity, like your little sister. The same age, too. What a coincidence."

The boy's eyes flew open, and he wrenched at his bonds with such ferocity that I worried he might break an arm or a leg. Gingerly, Curlin pulled the rag out of the boy's mouth and backed away.

Tobain cackled. The hysterical, maniacal sound swelled and echoed in the stone room. He locked eyes with me and stopped suddenly. In a cold, distant voice, he said, "I'll wear your ears on a string around my neck. I'll rip your toes off one by one. Your pretty, long fingers will make me good bracelets…"

I sank to my knees as his rant continued. A vise closed around my chest. My thoughts swam, and I tasted the sweet echo of the juice Curlin had poured for me earlier.

For the first time since I'd met Bo, I wanted to reach out

for Pru. I'd known, all those years I'd spent talking to her, praying to her, that it was all just my imagination. Bo—the complicated, difficult reality of my twin—had driven Pru from my head until now. Tears welled in my eyes. She may've just been in my head, but I felt her loss deeply, and for the blink of an eye, I was as exposed as an oyster ripped from its shell, pearl-less and fragile.

Clenching my jaw, I forced myself back into the small, dank room. There'd be time to mourn imaginary losses later.

"Do you see, Vi?" Curlin asked. "Do you understand? It used to be just some of us that were lost to the grief. One in a hundred would survive the death of their twin, and one in five hundred would become violent. One in five hundred would become a dimmy. But now the temple has the power to choose. We control who the people fear. And when they are afraid, they turn to us. With fear comes faith, and with faith, power." She smiled triumphantly. "The Suzerain have more power now than at any point in our history. They have people everywhere. In every town, in every house. They can command you to be dosed again at any time. You have to do as we say, or you'll be next. You'll be lost just like all those countless others."

Hand on the cool, stone floor, I heaved, wishing I could rid myself of the foul poison I'd swallowed earlier, but nothing came up.

"Shall I show you with the girl? It's important that you fully comprehend the lesson."

Though the room was spinning, I managed to shake my head.

"I need you to tell me, Vi. What do you understand?"

"You control the change," I gasped, barely audible over Tobain's rant. "You're the ones who make us go bad," I stammered, knowing that no one would ever believe me if I told them. "You dosed me. You poisoned me."

Curlin's laugh swirled around me, filling my ears, my mouth, making the ground shake.

"It was only a little. Not enough to do much. Not now. It has to build up, you see. But it's not the first, and it certainly won't be the last."

The room spun, and the boy's rants grew dimmer as everything around me faded to black.

I woke up some time later to see Curlin's disapproving glower hovering over me. I lay on a lumpy couch in the library. The glory of a fiery sunset streamed through small, slatted windows, painting the room in stripes of gold, orange, pink and crimson. The beauty of the late afternoon clashed so completely with the growing pit in my stomach that I wanted to curl into a ball and wait for the world to change.

"She's awake, Anchorite," Curlin called.

"Thank you, Curlin." Anchorite Tafima glided over and sat in a chair opposite me. "Now, Curlin tells me that was quite a dramatic display down there, child. Do try to warn me if you feel faint again."

I stared at her, flabbergasted that she would show any concern for my welfare. But, naturally, it didn't last.

"While we were waiting for you to come around, I had a quick look at your records," she said. "It seems that the anchorites in Alskad had other plans for you. Plans that you upset when you so brazenly wiled your way out of your punishment and took a contract with Mister Laroche."

My jaw clenched, and I thought of the women who'd raised me, of the trips I'd taken to see other dimmys with Anchorite Lugine, the hours I'd spent studying under Anchorite Sula's watchful eye. I wondered what they'd been preparing me for. I'd imagined that they'd saved me out of the goodness of their hearts, but that clearly was not the case—they must've needed me for something.

"Nevertheless, you've managed to place yourself in such a way that we can still make use of you. Shriven Curlin suggested you might be of use for a task we need done."

"I'm not going to help you!" I blurted. "What you did down there, what you're doing... It's horribly, horribly wrong. Unforgivable."

"You don't have a choice," Anchorite Tafima said with a sneer. "Dimmys are dangerous. They must be locked up. Wherever you hide, the Shriven will find you. You have neither the resources nor the knowledge to get very far. We have absolute power over you, and though you might be of use to us, we won't hesitate to lock you up if you prove...difficult."

My mind reeled, trying to make sense of it all. When had I been drugged? As a child? Who'd done it? How? Before I could begin to answer my own questions, I felt something stronger than curiosity. Loss. Something had been taken from me. Just a nip and a nibble, but something, nonetheless. They'd altered my personality. They'd changed who I was meant to be and outright robbed countless others of their lives. And now, here I was on the edge of freedom, only to see it ripped away once more. Even if Bo managed to buy out my contract, the Shriven would find me.

They would always find me.

"What do you want from me?" I twisted my hands together in my lap, and made myself stop. I needed to be stone. I couldn't afford to give up anything more to them.

"It's quite simple. Your employer means for you to serve as a maid to his lady wife. We need someone to watch her—

someone inside her household. She is an amalgam, and therefore cannot be trusted. You will report any unusual activity to us, as well as her dreams."

"Her dreams?"

"Yes." The anchorite gave me a look that brokered no arguments.

"Rayleane's teeth! How could I possibly discover what she dreams about?"

Curlin gave a derisive huff, but the anchorite only studied me. Calculating. Weighing. "You're a clever girl. I'm sure you'll think of something."

"I still haven't agreed to help you," I said stubbornly.

"You don't have a choice. If you choose not to cooperate, I will personally guarantee that you will never see the sun again."

Curlin gave me a pointed look over the anchorite's shoulder. I bit the inside of my cheek, but I couldn't see a way around it. The anchorite was right. I didn't have a choice.

"Curlin, please go tell Mister Laroche that we are nearly finished here."

Curlin stalked out of the room, and the anchorite turned back to me.

"Your reports are to be written in a legible hand, using lemon juice in place of ink between the lines of another letter. Maybe to a sweetheart, or some such nonsense. You will place one report each week in the blue birdhouse next to the pond at Plumleen. If you miss a report, you'll be warned. After one warning, there will be consequences." The anchorite adjusted her sleeves and laid two pious fingers on her brow. "Do not try to escape. We have people everywhere. You will be found."

My mouth went dry, and the backs of my arms prickled.

Having grown up in the temple, I knew all too well how true that was. If the Suzerain wanted to find a person, there wasn't anywhere on this earth they could go to hide. Their resources were nearly limitless, and the Shriven were nothing if not persistent. Curlin would fit in well here.

"Do you understand your instructions clearly, Vi?"

I nodded, and as she pursed her lips, I anticipated her. "I'm sorry. Yes, ma'am. I understand. When is my first report due?"

Curlin peeked her head into the room. "Anchorite, may we come in?"

She entered without waiting for a reply, followed by Anchorite Mathille and Phineas. I glowered at Curlin, who smiled sweetly at me. Phineas clapped me on the back, all humor and good cheer.

"Was it an educational visit for you, Vi? I've come away with a whole new sense of piety. May even build a haven hall at the estate. What do you say to that?"

"Wonderful idea, sir," I gritted, my back stinging where his hand had smacked me.

"We should be going, then," he said. "If you'll excuse us, I'd like to be back for supper."

I trailed after him. Our horses waited in the courtyard, strangely placid. We rode away in silence, and Phineas's false joviality disappeared as soon as we were out of sight of the looming iron gates. My thoughts spun round and round, searching for a way out of all the darkness surrounding me.

CHAPTER THIRTY

Bo

When I entered the dining room, a blush crept up my neck and spread across my cheeks. Next to Aunt Ephemella, whose formal blouse and trousers shone with gold embroidery, I was a veritable ragamuffin in my shirtsleeves and cleanest trousers. I could've at least put on a waistcoat and jacket, even in this damnable heat.

I'd given her the advantage, and she knew it. I would have to be extraordinarily careful about what I said over dinner.

"My apologies, Aunt. I didn't realize we were dressing for dinner. Please go ahead without me while I change."

She laughed, a sound that bubbled like sparkling wine. "No, no, no. Don't go, dear. Oh, I'd somehow forgotten your sweet blushes. Do sit down."

"If you're sure you don't mind." It was clear she'd meant to throw me off balance.

She waved my words away and took a seat at the head of the long table, gesturing for me to sit next to her. As a servant poured water and wine, Aunt Ephemella said, "I'm such a silly thing. I haven't properly expressed my condolences for your loss. To lose both your mother and your cousins in the space of a week... You must be in shock."

The real shock had been learning that so much of what I knew of my history was a lie, but I couldn't say that, so I said simply, "Thank you, Aunt Ephemella. That's very kind."

"I hope your tutors have been a comfort to you." She took a sip of her wine as a servant laid the soup plate on the table before her. "I'm surprised they didn't accompany you."

I waited for the servant to retreat back into the corner, and dipped out a spoonful of the soup. "This is divine, Aunt. My compliments to your cook." I took another bite before answering her remark about my tutors. "Thamina and Birger were so supportive through the trial of the last month, so I wanted to give them some time with their family while I traveled. I have come of age, after all."

"You're lucky to have found a companion so loyal in such a short time in the colonies. Do your tutors know you've hired a guide?"

"As I said, my tutors are spending time with their family. I've chosen not to bother them with the details of my journey," I said, waving a hand dismissively. "As for Swinton, he ought to be loyal, given what I pay him." I thought of Hoss's expensive rifle and the way he'd talked about my aunt. Ephemella was no stranger to buying a person's loyalty, and my next veiled insult might just put her at enough ease to drop the subject. "But you must know how that is, I'm sure."

Her look told me I'd made my point. We made polite conversation as we finished our soup. When the servant whisked out of the room with our plates, I said, "The wine is very good. Is it Denorian?"

Aunt Ephemella arched an eyebrow at me. "Thinking of visiting Denor on your holiday, as well?"

"Not this time, Aunt. Though I've heard it's lovely in the summer."

"Perhaps I can convince you to stay with me for a time? It does get so lonely here."

I coughed. I needed to leave in the morning, but the last thing I could tell my aunt was the truth about why. "I wish that I had more time, but I have leagues of traveling to do yet, and the Queen will become impatient if I stay away too long."

Aunt Ephemella pounced on the subject of Runa. "What has the Queen told you of her plans for your marriage? It would be a shame to break the family alliance. Perhaps one of my daughters..."

Though I'd anticipated the question, the blunt way she addressed it surprised me, and I nearly choked on my sip of wine. I coughed, drained my glass of water and, finally collected, smiled sheepishly at my aunt. The servant appeared with the fish course and refilled our glasses. I cleared my throat and said, "The Queen has not discussed a new match with me. There hasn't been much time...since..." I trailed off, staring at my plate.

She reached out and patted my hand. "I'm surprised Queen Runa allowed you to travel alone, given her plans for the succession."

I simpered, hoping that my mawkish behavior wasn't too absurd. "I was so wrapped up in my grief, I just wanted to get away. When I saw the opportunity... Well, I took it. The Queen didn't seem to mind too awfully much. I'd heard that Lisette traveled throughout the empire when she came of age, and I thought the idea was marvelous."

Aunt Ephemella smiled at me, and I was grateful that Limina wasn't at home. She'd always seen right through my play-acting. "She did visit, not five years ago. I hosted her myself."

"Oh, I would so love to know what her itinerary was while she was here. I couldn't possibly return without having outdone her." I leaned in conspiratorially. "For the sake of the stories, you know."

"Of course." She paused while the servant laid slices of roast lamb alongside heaps of creamed corn and dark, vinegary greens on the china plates before us. "I believe I have a copy in the office. I'll make sure to find it for you in the morning."

By the time dessert was served, I had exhausted myself by nattering on about fashion and other meaningless nonsense. But at least Aunt Ephemella seemed to believe I was a witless ninny with no idea that she was telling me lies.

When my soft knock at Swinton's door went unanswered, I slipped into the room that had been prepared for me next to his and undressed. I flicked the solar lamps off and, head still swimming from the myriad revelations of the day, opened a window and curled up in a chair beneath it. Stars shone bright in an unclouded sky, the droning buzz of insects filled the air and the heady perfume of the philomenas drifted in on the breeze. I reveled in the quiet noise of the jungle, willing my own thoughts to still.

My mind was a cacophonous tangle of secrets and treachery, of anchorites and poison, of perfumers killed by their own creations. Ephemella's assumption that Rylain had been the one responsible for the accident at the mill was a burr I couldn't shake, but there was nothing to be done about it while I was still in Ilor. I toyed with the cuff on my wrist, remembering my vow to Runa, to Alskad. I'd promised to serve the empire, to be its conscience. Though the circumstances that had led to that vow may have been shrouded in lies, I'd made those promises with a clear head and honest— if reluctant—intent. And now, here in this wild colony, I'd stumbled across a cause I was bound to serve. A mystery I was compelled to unravel.

Just as soon as my sister was freed.

My body was slow and heavy with sleep and my eyelids had begun to droop when I heard voices outside my window. I went to lower the sash, but then I recognized the slow, tenor drawl of Hoss's voice, clipped short by his sister.

"Boss said she wanted them dead by morning, so that's what we'll do. Or don't you like having a roof over your head and food to eat?"

"It ain't that. I just… They seem like nice boys. That Swinton fellow knows our kin."

"Then take comfort in the fact that he'll have folk to talk to in hell. Come on."

I strained to hear more, suddenly wide awake, mind racing, but the voices trailed off into the dark night. Of course Ephemella would want me dead. With Penelope gone, there was nothing to tie me—or my money—to her anymore. Since I was unmarried and uninterested in her own daughters, and her sister's husband my closest living relative, she'd assume that everything I had would go to them at my death. I wondered briefly if she'd always been so ruthless, but of course she must have been. The nobility always sought power by any means necessary. They were knife-edged brutality dressed in silk.

I struggled into my clothes as fast as I could manage and stuffed my boots into my saddlebags, not wanting my footsteps to be heard in the quiet house. Ear to the door, I listened for movement in the hallway. I had to get Swinton out of the house before Hoss and Clem made it upstairs. I had no weapons, and my training in hand-to-hand combat had been summarily abandoned when, as a ten-year-old, I not only showed no aptitude for the craft, but also refused to take my tutor seriously. I hadn't thought it a skill I would ever use.

I could have throttled my ten-year-old self in that moment. *Not*, I thought, *that I would even know how.*

Saddlebags over my shoulder, I slipped into the empty hallway, lit by the dim glow of solar lamps turned down low. I eased Swinton's door open and found him in a chair by the window, pulling on his boots. He gave me a sardonic look. "You, little lord, are as loud as a herd of aurochs. Perhaps more so when you're trying to be quiet. Ready to go, are you?"

"They're going to try to kill us."

"Obviously," he whispered. "Best put your boots on. I assume you've no idea how to defend yourself?"

"I'm a very good shot," I said, tugging on my boots.

Swinton opened the window, and the wet smell of coming rain flooded into the room on the back of the heady scent of philomena blossoms. "That's a useful skill with the heaps of guns we've got lying around."

"I could do without your sarcasm."

Swinton's voice rose to something between a shout and a whisper. "And I could do without the headache of trying to keep your incompetent, evasive backside alive, but we all get what we sign up for, don't we?"

He tossed his saddlebags out the window and reached for mine. Footsteps echoed in the foyer and started up the stairs. I handed Swinton my saddlebags, and he sent them flying out the window. They landed with a thud in the grass of the lawn.

"Look, bully. Do your best not to get hit." He cast around the room, and darted to the fireplace, coming back with an iron poker and brush. "I'll manage the twins. Get our bags and tack up the horses as fast as you can. Wait for me behind the screen of trees in front of the house. Don't you dare leave me behind, hear?"

I nodded, gripping the iron brush with tight knuckles. The stairs creaked under someone's weight, and I heard a hissing curse.

"If they get too close, go for the soft spots. Eyes, throat, balls and joints. Hit their knees hard enough with that iron rod, and they'll shatter."

Swinton crossed the room, wrapped an arm around me and pressed his lips hard against mine. Despite everything, my insides turned to jelly, and my heart raced even faster.

"Good luck, bully," Swinton said, positioning himself inside the door, poker over his head.

A moment later, the door crashed open, and Swinton brought the poker down hard onto Hoss's head. He staggered back, knocking into Clem, and I raced through the door, barreling past them into the hall. I swung over the bannister and onto the stairs, but lost my balance and fumbled for the rail in a panic. I managed to catch myself, turning an ankle and cursing as pain shot up my leg.

Heart pounding so hard it seemed to drown the sounds of the struggle on the landing, I started down the staircase as fast as I could. Something caught my collar and yanked me back, unbalancing me. I whirled around on my good ankle to find Hoss, blood streaming into one eye, on the stair above me, holding tight to my shirt. Instinctively, I swung the iron brush up with all my might. It connected with his jaw in a sickening crunch. Hoss's eyes opened wide, then fluttered shut. All at once, his knees buckled, his grip on my collar relaxed, and he tumbled toward me.

I flung the iron brush down and reached for the stair rail

in a vain attempt to stay on my feet, but when Hoss's limp form careened into me, my bad ankle gave way, and I went toppling down the stairs. Hoss landed on top of me, knocking the breath from my chest. When I finally managed to suck in a gulp of air, I heaved him off me and limped for the door, not waiting to see who had been aroused by the noise of our scuffle.

I raced, wincing and hobbled by my already-swelling ankle, for the barn, pausing only to scoop up our saddlebags from the grass where they'd landed outside Swinton's window. I found our horses, their tack flung carelessly outside the stalls where they stood dozing, and cinched saddles onto each of their backs. I buckled the saddlebags in place, slipped their bridles on, and led them quickly out of the barn. Holding Swinton's horse's reins in my hand, I mounted my own and rode to the screen of trees where I was to meet Swinton.

My breathing slowed as I waited. The minutes crept by, and each muffled sound from inside the house pushed me closer to going back to help Swinton. Just as I kicked my foot free of the stirrup, the front door of the house banged open.

Swinton yelled my name, and I urged the horses toward the house as smoke billowed from the windows on the second floor. I gaped at the sight of the bright flames in the doorway. Swinton ran from the house, grabbing the oil lamps from either side of the porch. He flung them to the ground, and the philomenas went up in a whoosh of oily flame. Swinton swung into the saddle with a grim look back at the burning house and kicked his mount into a gallop.

I followed suit, and in that moment, I desperately missed the horse I'd left behind in Alskad. Laith, with his long legs and boundless energy, would have delighted in a predawn gallop, but the borrowed mount I rode now seemed reluctant, at best, to keep up with his companion.

We rode at a bone-jostling pace into the jungle until the thick branches overhead blocked the dim glow of the sun inching its way toward the horizon and we were forced to slow. My ankle throbbed more each time one of my horse's hooves struck the hard-packed trail. By the time we stopped, tears of pain streamed from my eyes.

As soon as I'd managed to choke the tears out of my voice, I asked, "Why? Why would you set the house on fire? Have you…" I stopped myself.

"Have I lost control?" Swinton snapped. "No. And I'll thank you never to ask me that particular question again, dimwit. What was I to do? Let them poison more of my people? I shouldn't think you'd care for folk who'd tried so hard to murder you."

I wanted to kick myself for hurting him, but I had to press. I had no desire to be an accomplice to murder, especially of innocents. "What about the servants? They didn't know any better."

"The servants have quarters well away from the house," Swinton reassured me. "But, Bo, your aunt tried to have you killed. Living around philomenas like that for so long… She and Clem and Hoss were all tainted. A bit off-kilter, and none of them a stranger to violence. It's better this way. At least they can't hurt anyone else now." He sighed. "I'm sorry for biting your head off. You were right to ask if I'd lost my grip. You've got to keep yourself safe, little lord. Are you in one piece?"

He rode up beside me and reached out to squeeze my hand. I pressed his in return and nodded. "My ankle's twisted, but it'll heal in a few days, I think. I'll do. Though a lesson in hand-to-hand combat might not go amiss. I don't want to leave you to do all the fighting for me. How far to Southill?"

"We'll be there tonight if we ride fast and the horses last." He hesitated for a moment, clearly conflicted. "Do you want to go back?" he asked, his voice soft. "We can if you'd like."

"No. As you said, it's better this way." I shook my head and kneed my horse around to follow Swinton deeper into the moonlit jungle.

CHAPTER THIRTY-ONE

VI

The morning of Aphra's birthday celebration, I was sunk deep in furious contemplation when a sharp knock broke the stillness. I opened the door to find Hepsy, holding a large basket and wearing an expression I'd never seen on her face before. Her mouth was screwed up and her brows knitted together, but her red-rimmed eyes plainly showed she'd been crying.

She shoved the basket into my arms. The breeze that came through the open door was warm enough to send a shiver down my spine.

"Well," she said, "are you going to invite me in?"

I nudged the door all the way open with my foot and nodded for her to enter. "Myrna's still sleeping," I cautioned.

Hepsy stepped inside and glared at me. "Wake her up, if you please."

"I will not," I spat. "After what she went through the other night, she should sleep as much as she can." I set the basket on the table.

There was a fire in Hepsy's eyes as she said, "I'll take off my belt and beat you over the back of that couch if you don't do as I say, girl."

"I'd like to see you try," I snapped.

Hepsy stepped menacingly toward me. I planted my feet and took a deep breath, readying myself for her to lunge. Just as Hepsy went to unbuckle her belt, the bedroom door swung open.

"Dzallie's toes! What's going on out here? You two look like a couple of dogs fit to tussle!"

Myrna stepped between us and shot her sister a look.

"Why're you here?" Her voice was icy, though polite.

"I've come to bring you your breakfast, as my mistress asked me to do, and to ask if you'll help ready Vi for the celebration tonight. Mistress Laroche knows you're skilled with that sort of thing, Myrna." She jerked her chin at me. "This insolent dimmy refused to follow my orders."

Myrna scowled. "I heard. She was only trying to help me."

"Don't you think you can take a tone with me just because the mistress took pity on you. I've coddled you more than you deserve."

"Shove it, Hepsy. You've coddled me about as much as a turtle looks after her eggs."

Hepsy sniffed and turned back to me. "As for you, little Miss Nose-in-Everyone's-Business, your time in the manor house promises to be mercifully short. Mark my words, you'll be on the mountain, breaking your back in the kaffe groves, before year's end."

I gritted my teeth. There was a battle raging between the side of me that begged me to be cautious and the part of me that didn't take well to being insulted by a self-important besom like Hepsy. The reckless side won, to no surprise. "I guarantee you that won't happen, you wicked old goat."

I didn't let my eyes leave Hepsy's irate face. Myrna whistled, long and low.

After another long minute, Hepsy turned on her heel and stalked out of my rooms, slamming the door behind her.

"Well, that may be the stupidest thing I've ever seen a person do," Myrna commented. "And I once watched a woman cuddle up to a cottonmouth because the anchorite in her town claimed that if she was faithful, the goddesses would keep her safe."

"Hailstones in a handbasket, but that woman makes me so mad," I said. "I'm sorry. I know she's your sister."

Myrna shrugged. "When we turned destitute after Ma died, Pa packed us onto the first ship out. Sold our contracts, and us not yet ten. We've coped in different ways."

"How much time do you have left on your contract?" I asked.

"Because we were only little brats, Phineas wouldn't take us for less than twenty years. That, plus time added for getting sick and the like? We should be done when we're a bit past thirty. Only ten more years or so."

"Magritte's tongue," I breathed.

"It's been no worse than it would have been an orphanage. Plus, if everything goes as planned, you and I'll both be out of here long before that. Now, I'm starved. Let's see what's in that basket, and you can tell me about your day with Phineas."

"Go on. Have a look. I think you're finished." Myrna patted me on the shoulder. "You look so pretty!"

I blushed and smoothed the thin, diaphanous silk over my hips. "It's not too dark?"

Phineas had sent the seamstress to me alone, and—still smarting from his cock-and-bull chicanery—I'd picked a fabric I knew he'd hate. The seamstress grumbled about the rush to get the dress done in time for the party, but the garment had turned out beautifully. Dark gray silk, the color of thunderheads, fell in a swirling cloud from my shoulders to my feet, cinched tight at my waist by a beaded belt. I wore a bright blue underdress, and the color flashed at the hem and in the slits the seamstress had made beneath my arms to my waist.

"Not a bit," Myrna said. "Go look!"

A spiderweb of cracks splayed in one corner of the mirror, which was probably the only reason it wasn't still in the manor house. One crack, the biggest, ran up the side of the glass, and darted across, breaking my body into two disjointed halves, an oddly fitting image. I studied the girl staring back at me and thought of Bo. I'd heard not a word from him or Quill, and time was slipping away. Not that it really mattered. Even if he could buy out my contract, the anchorites would find me and rope me back in somehow.

"Well?" Myrna asked.

She was right. Despite the imperfect reflection, I was pretty. The gray silk deepened my eyes, ringed in dark lashes, and complemented my pale, freckled skin. Myrna had tamed my curls, pinning them into elaborately constructed braids and twists that sat atop my head like a crown.

"How'd you do that with my hair?" I asked, amazed.

For once, I wasn't the one who turned pink. "I've always liked playing with hair," Myrna admitted. "There's a part of me that hoped Aphra might choose me to be her personal maid, but my fate, unfortunately, seems fair well chained to these horses."

"You're awfully good at it. I've never seen hair like this outside the rich folks in the haven hall."

"There's more," Myrna said. She pulled two knives, shaped like arrowheads and wickedly sharp-looking, from a drawer and handed them to me. "You know how to use them?"

I slid the hilts between my fingers and gave a few experimental jabs. Knives like these were favorites with thieves. Easy to hide and all. "Enough to be trouble. How did you manage?"

Myrna grinned and untied the belt from around my waist. She took the knives from me and slid them into well-concealed sheaths, leaving only the flat handles showing. She raised one eyebrow, smiling. "The seamstress is a friend. I've got a thigh sheath, too, if you want. Never know when you might need a knife."

"Is there something I should be worried about?" I asked as Myrna tied the belt back in place.

"Never know when you might find yourself alone with someone particularly nasty," Myrna said, her face drawn and set in hard lines. "Never know when a knife might come in handy in the middle of the night, what with guests here, and drinking, and no one keeping track of servants."

My mind flashed from Bo, working to free me from this hell—the hell I'd chosen for myself—to the people I'd be leaving behind. The people here who might very well suffer the same fate as Sawny and Lily. I dashed into my room, dug through my trunk and emerged a moment later with my small pouch of pearls. I took Myrna's hand and poured half of my wealth into her palm. "By way of a thank you. Maybe it'll help a bit."

Myrna stared at me, open-mouthed. Just as she started to speak there was a knock at the door.

"Don't say a word. Just take them," I said, looping the pouch over my head and tucking it beneath my dress.

Myrna shoved the hand into her pocket and gave my shoulder a squeeze with the other.

"It's probably Hepsy again. I'll get it. Just keep a sharp eye out and your wits about you," Myrna whispered, and in a louder tone said, "I hope she's brought some food. I'm starved."

There was no way I could eat. My stomach had twisted itself into knots hours ago and didn't look to settle anytime soon.

"Well, well, well," Myrna's voice came from the mudroom. She poked her head into the great room. "How are your nerves, Vi?"

My heart started to race. "Fine," I said, slow and wary. "Why?"

"Better sit down anyway. I'll be forced to throttle you if you spoil your hair by fainting."

I sat, but as soon as the door swung open, I sprang to my feet again. Mal leaned against the doorjamb, grinning. He held a small, neatly wrapped parcel in one hand and his boots in the other. I watched him, dumbfounded, as he put his boots down and walked toward me. A part of me—larger than I wanted to admit—was disappointed that he wasn't Quill, but I didn't want to hurt his feelings asking after his brother first thing.

Myrna let out a long, low whistle. "Good to see you again, handsome."

"Treats for the puppies," Mal said, looking bashful and setting the parcel on the table. "You look amazing, Vi."

Myrna chuckled and imitated Mal's deep, sonorous voice. "It's nice to see you as well." She switched to an exaggerated, high-pitched voice. "Thank you, Mal. So rare to see a young man with such good manners."

"Don't mind her," I said with a laugh.

Myrna gave me an exaggerated wink and herded the puppies toward the bedroom. "You two catch up. I just need to see about, um…something in here." Before she closed the door, I saw her grinning at me, making lewd gestures behind Mal's back.

I rolled my eyes and called, "You're a bloody nuisance, Myrna."

Mal crossed the room and hugged me.

"Is Bo with you?" I whispered as soon as he let go.

He leaned against the back of the couch and grimaced. "Not so much as a hello, then?"

I blushed and looked down at my feet. They were small, like my mother's, but I had long, knobby toes that were unlike anyone else's in my family. When I was a little girl, I'd spent the brief visits with my family soaking in every detail of their appearances, their personalities. Even though they held me at arm's length, and it was clear that those visits were more duty than pleasure, I had always tried to imagine what it might be like if Pru hadn't died, if my family had actually loved me. Now I had a brother—a twin—bent on getting me out of the contract I'd shoved myself into, and my asking about him clearly touched a nerve with Mal, who'd become as dear to me as any brother. The thought carved a hollow space in my chest.

Mal reached out and touched my cheek. "Where did you go, Vi? Are you all right?"

I shook my head. "I didn't mean to hurt you with the asking. It's just that…"

"I know it's important. He's here," Mal said reassuringly. "Join me for a stroll?"

"Better not," Myrna called through the door. "Hepsy's sure to be back any minute."

I pursed my lips. "She's right."

"There are things you need to know. Quill's here, and Bo made it back, too, but if we can't wrangle a meeting with Phineas in time—"

The outside door squealed, and we froze. I didn't know what Hepsy would do if she found a man in my rooms, but I was certain sure it wouldn't end well for me. I put a finger to my lips, eyes wide and heart pounding, and grabbed Mal by the arm. I pulled him to the bedroom, flung open the door and, after Myrna tumbled out, shoved him inside. When Hepsy bustled into the great room a moment later, we were both red-faced and standing by the hearth.

She gave us an odd look, but said, "They're ready for you in the manor house, Obedience." Eyeing her sister, she said, "Someone left a pair of rather large boots in the mudroom. They look like Haskell's spares. See that he gets them back, Myrna."

I gritted my teeth. Hepsy's habit of calling me by my given name infuriated me. As I followed her out, my stomach turned somersaults. I knew my part—curtsy and smile. Don't speak unless spoken to. If I'd been the praying type, I'd be on my knees begging Dzallie that Bo would find himself alone in a room with Phineas before I'd been presented to Aphra. Tension was thicker than the humid air at Plumleen, and I suspected that nothing this night would go as easily as I hoped.

Hepsy led me to one of the tiny sitting rooms off the great room. There were four of these little rooms, all kitted out with potted plants to perfume the air, small tables to hold drinks and love seats for canoodling. One door led into the great room, the other down a short staircase and into the garden. Hepsy drew a long key from her skirt pocket and locked the garden door.

"You make a peep before I come to collect you, and I'll make sure you don't sit down for a week," she hissed.

I stepped toward the love seat, my face a placid mask. Every word out of her mouth made me want to do just the opposite of what she said.

"You will answer me when I address you, girl. Do you understand me?"

I gave her an exaggerated nod, but before I was out of her reach, she pinched my arm so hard I yelped.

"You said to keep my trap shut!" I cried.

"Don't you get saucy with me. And don't sit down. I don't want you wrinkling that dress more than you already have." She clucked as she turned to enter the great room. "Gray. What were you thinking?"

As soon as I heard the key turn in the lock, I plopped down on the sofa.

I listened to musicians tuning their instruments, servants chattering and glasses clinking as the final preparations were made on the other side of the door that led into the great room. I shifted my belt, irritatingly aware of the knives' hard pressure on my waist. I hadn't been able to stop thinking about Curlin and the way she'd acted in the jungle temple since I'd left. It'd been as though she didn't know me, hadn't known me since we were grubby brats. I couldn't parse it, and it looked as though I never would.

Not if Bo got his way. I wanted the freedom Bo had promised me, but I wanted to use it to make a difference to the people I'd met—people like Myrna and Aphra, who'd accepted me without prejudice or fear. I didn't know how I could do that if I left with Bo and went back to Penby. There was also a part of me that was tempted to abandon Ilor and all its problems so that I could get to know Bo. I wanted to learn everything about him, and more than that, I wanted desperately to explore what it was to be a twin.

I went round and round with myself as the music started and the coarse accents of the servants were replaced by the genteel tones of the guests.

A soft knock at the garden door brought me to my feet. I shook out my skirts quickly, but the door stayed shut.

"Vi," a soft voice called through the door, and I was flooded with anxiety and anticipation not entirely my own. "Vi, can you hear me?"

I didn't know yet if I'd forgiven him for lying to me. Didn't know if I trusted him. All I knew was that he was my twin, and he was going to help me out of this mess, like it or no. I knelt and put my ear to the dark wood. "Bo? Is this a good idea? There are people everywhere. Someone will be coming for me any minute."

"Can you let me in?"

"The door's locked."

"Did Mal find you earlier?"

"Yes. Manage to sort things out with Phineas yet?" I whispered.

"No. He's rebuffed every attempt Quill has made to schedule a meeting. We're going to have to wait until the party itself."

"Rayleane's pounding hammer," I cursed under my breath.

"Look, if you can't manage to get me out of this mess, it'll be all right. I chose this life, after all."

He hushed me. "Vi, the Shriven are looking for you. For my sister. If they haven't found you here yet, they will soon, and I'm not going to let that happen to you. Call me selfish, but I can't lose you. I want to know you. I want to have a chance to be your twin, and I won't let the Shriven snatch you away from me."

My throat seized, and my stomach dropped to my ankles. "What?" I croaked, mind racing. *Dzallie bless me*, I thought. He'd said before that people were looking for me, but he hadn't said it was the Shriven. I knew what they were capable of, what they did to people in the name of the temple. If they knew that I was Bo's sister, there was nothing in the world that would keep them from finding me. And I could only imagine what they'd do once they got their hands on me. If I'd known it was the Shriven, I would've run. I wouldn't be here.

Curlin's face came to me like a punch in the gut. I was done for. She'd only need to see a portrait of Bo to know the truth.

"Vi, don't panic." He must've felt it coming off me in waves. "We're going to get out of this. Together. And then, I promise, I'll explain everything."

The other door swung open, and I leapt to my feet.

"Obedience, get yourself together this instant. They're ready for you."

I brushed my skirts into place. "Bows tied? Gift neatly packaged?"

Hepsy sighed, heavy with aggravation, and pulled a curl loose from the nape of my neck. "There. Pretty as a picture. Just try to not talk. It'll ruin the effect. We'll have to do something about that accent of yours sooner or later."

I rolled my eyes, doing everything in my power to cover

the terror I felt at learning the Shriven were looking for me. Hepsy led me out into the great room, where we cut left behind a line of potted plants. Tiny solar lights twinkled overhead, reflecting the faint stars that shone through the many skylights in the ceiling. Lilting reels and jigs drifted across the crowd and smoothed the edges of the fractured conversations that filled the room. Through the leaves of the ferns, I ogled the bright silks spinning around the Laroches' guests as they danced. Other folks sat, displayed like prized orchids, on the couches that lined the walls.

Hepsy yanked me to the side of the small platform where the musicians were playing and hid me behind a carved screen. "Wait here until Mister Laroche calls for you. It shouldn't be long."

After she left, I scanned the room for Quill, but he was nowhere to be seen. Servants dressed in somber black livery moved through the crowd, carrying tall glasses of jewel-colored drinks on trays held high over their heads.

Phineas and Aphra skimmed across the dance floor. Her copper-gold hair whipped out behind her like a flag. Aphra's dress was gold, slashed with violet, and he wore a shirt and waistcoat to match, with a cream-colored jacket and trousers. They laughed so convincingly as they circled around the room in one another's arms that, if I hadn't seen their fight over Myrna's bloody back, I'd have almost believed they really loved each other.

When the music stopped, the musicians set down their instruments and turned to Phineas expectantly. Phineas whispered in Aphra's ear, and she shook her head, frowning. He kept his smile firmly in place, but even from my hiding place behind the screen, I could see the good humor drain from his eyes. He snatched two glasses from a passing servant's tray, handed one to his wife and raised the other.

"As you all know, tomorrow is the twenty-fifth anniversary of the birth of my beloved wife, whose grace, wit and beauty do great honor to my ancestral hall, where we stand tonight." He raised his glass to Aphra, who bowed her head to him. "And," he cried, "in two days, we celebrate the anniversary of our marriage!"

Cheers rang through the great room.

He went on. "But tonight, on the eve of the anniversary of her birth, we honor Aphra with music, gifts and dancing."

I tensed. My moment would likely be coming soon.

"Join me in raising a glass to my dear Aphra, who cools my days and lights my nights. To Aphra!"

Aphra inclined her head, the picture of grace. She raised her glass to her husband, the crowd and then the musicians, who picked up their instruments and began to play once more.

Phineas hushed them with a wave of his hand, and the strings screeched into silence. "I know I may be getting ahead of myself, and my lovely wife will likely scold me, but I cannot keep this surprise to myself for another moment. Obedience, will you come out, please?"

Cold sweat ran in rivulets down my back. Soon, my dark gray silk would be patched with black where the sweat soaked through my shift. I did everything in my power to keep myself from touching the handles of the knives at my belt as I stepped out from behind the screen.

The crowd's murmuring quieted as Phineas began to speak again.

"Obedience is one of the diminished. I was able to offer her a contract, thanks to the good fellows at the Whippleston

Exchange Firm in Williford. I believe they're here tonight. Quill? Mal? Would you raise your hands?"

I bit my lip and scanned the crowd, looking for the twins. Fear ringed the eyes staring back at me. I saw muscles tense and hands reach for knives left at home for such a formal occasion. I caught a glimpse of Curlin, her arms crossed over her robes, and I wanted to smack the smirk off her face. I wanted to scream the truth into the crowd—tell them it wasn't me they should fear, but the anchorites, the Shriven, the Suzerain. Even as I tried to calm myself down, to convince myself that it was all out of my hands, my heart picked up its pace and fluttered madly in my chest.

Phineas went on. "My dear wife has long been without a well-trained lady's maid of her own. Therefore, when the opportunity came along to offer a contract to one of the diminished—a young woman as unique, if not as beautiful, as Aphra herself—I couldn't bear to say no. I've spent the past weeks training Obedience to be the perfect servant for my darling and, hopefully, to live up to her name. Obedience, if you will make the proper courtesies to your new mistress?"

Panic clenched my throat, and even as my own good sense slipped away, waves of calm and comfort washed over me. Bo was in the room. My twin was nearby.

I couldn't afford to dwell on all the horrible possibilities that swirled around in my head. Phineas would refuse to sell my contract to Bo, or he wouldn't. I would be dosed again, or I wouldn't. The Shriven would find me, or they wouldn't.

But I knew better. The Shriven would always find me. Perhaps they already had. My eyes settled on Mal and Quill at last, Bo standing right next to them with Swinton at his side. Bo nodded at me and raised his hand to his waist, waving his fingers. That boy needed a lesson in subtlety, and quick.

I passed through the crowd and sank into a deep curtsy in front of Aphra. Aphra offered me her hand and pulled me back to my feet before raising her glass to the crowd, her smile tight and false.

"I've no idea what I've done to deserve such a husband," she said. "Now, please. Enjoy the party. Drink! Eat! Make merry!"

With a wave of Aphra's freckled right hand, the musicians leapt into song. The cacophony of the guests' conversations rose around me once more. Folks started to dance, and servants snaked through the crowd. Light-headed, I watched the dancers' colorful silks swirl under the warm glow of the solar lamps for a moment. I blinked and looked eagerly for Bo's dark curls in the sea of people.

A cold hand closed around my arm.

"Look at you. You've sweat straight through your clothes," Hepsy scolded. "Come on, then. We're to move your things up to your new quarters. Master Laroche wants you all settled by the time Madame Laroche makes her way upstairs tonight."

"But—" I tried to protest, but she was already dragging me by the arm toward the door.

"Good thing, too," she snickered. "You look a right mess."

I cast one last look into the great room as she yanked me through the door. I found Bo searching the crowd for me. Our eyes met, and he put his hand to his heart, mouthing the words, "Trust me," before the door shut between us.

CHAPTER THIRTY-TWO

Bo

Threads of Vi's outrage wound into me, twining around my own emotions, distracting me. Finding her, calming her became preeminently important. The whirling dancers and laughing guests were no more than obstacles between my seething twin and me. I worked my way to the door she'd been dragged through, excusing myself mechanically as I shouldered through the crowd. When I finally tried the handle, I found it locked.

I automatically tucked my gold cuff into my too-short sleeve, scanning the room. Swinton had cobbled together our formal wear from a trunk of clothes found in the attic of his mother's inn. The odds and ends we wore had been forgotten over the years, and while each piece was horribly out of fashion or obscenely garish on its own, the end result was dazzling.

I eyed the cluster of richly dressed anchorites in the corner. One anchorite bent her head in conversation with another, more ancient anchorite, whose brows furrowed as she scanned the room with rheumy eyes. The youngest of the anchorites, in wide yellow skirts, was attended by an old man wearing a dour expression.

The sight of them brought to mind the list of dead children's names Swinton had found in Ephemella's study, and my skin prickled to gooseflesh. These people, directly or not, were complicit in the abuse of the citizens of the empire I was sworn to protect. I couldn't tell if Vi's rage was feeding mine, but the anger welling up inside me made my already tenuous hold on my temper slip.

Jaw clenched, I started toward them. Swinton sidled up next to me, put his hand on my arm and slipped a cold glass of something yellow and fizzing into my hand.

"Pull yourself together, bully," he murmured. "You need to focus on one thing at a time, and barreling through the room like a scent-drunk hound won't do anything to convince Phineas to give up his prize."

I took a sip and let the sweet, fruity liquor fizz down my throat. "Nothing has gone according to our plan. I need her to know that I'll get her out of here. I'll get her free."

"Bo. Look at me." Swinton adjusted my collar and caressed my cheek. "You spoke to her earlier. If ever a young woman could take care of herself, it's Vi. Do your part and stop worrying about her."

I nodded. "Fine. What's our next move, then?"

"You need to ingratiate yourself with our host. Get him to like you. A house like this says the man's got money, but it's new. Maybe his daddy's. Old money families don't show it off so much. You can impress him with your fancy family and your royal manners." Swinton raised an eyebrow at me.

I stood a little straighter, and Swinton squeezed my hand.

"You, of all people, were born to make sniveling, grasping ne'er-do-wells like Phineas Laroche grovel at your feet," he said. "You'll impress him and make him want to impress you, in turn."

I bit the inside of my lip, blushing. "I think you may be misunderstanding the role of the King, my dear. That said, political maneuvering is not outside the realm of my experience. Is there anything you know that might be of use? Any sore spots I can lean on?"

"The majority of the money is hers now, but apparently this is his family's estate, built by his parents," Swinton explained. "If I'm right, they took advantage of the first wave of colonization and trade, leaving them quite wealthy. His idiotic mismanagement of the place had him nearly bankrupt by the time he married Madame Laroche. Her family is old Alskad Empire nobility. They moved here when she was born." He raised an eyebrow. "For obvious reasons."

I drew myself up to my full height and gave him my most imperious look. "New money? Power-hungry? Next time, let's try and find a challenge. This is a game I was born to play."

Swinton covered his mouth, eyes wrinkling with laughter. He looked like he was about to have a fountain of the fizzy gold cocktail he'd been drinking come streaming out his nose.

I grinned at him. "Let's track down Mal and Quill and see if they'll make our introductions."

Some time later, we approached the Laroches where they sat receiving guests in an alcove. Mal and Quill stood on either side of Swinton and me as we waited in the receiving line. Despite having started on a sour note with the twins, I'd found that I liked the Whipplestons. They both seemed to care deeply about Vi and her happiness.

On our way to Plumleen Hall, they'd regaled me with tales about the journey across the Tethys with Vi. In Quill's stories, she came across as a trickster, a great one for jokes and pranks. Mal told me about her sharp wit and the way she seemed to always put the welfare of others before her own. He went on and on about her compassion and how hard her childhood had been, while Quill talked about Vi like she was a complex, dynamic woman—someone he admired. I didn't presume to know Vi really at all yet, but the young woman I had met seemed like she was all those things and more.

The line moved quickly, and soon there were only a few people in front of us. Beside me, Swinton drew in a sharp breath and grasped my wrist. I craned my neck and saw the woman on the couch, whispering into her husband's ear. She turned, and I saw why Swinton had gasped. She was an amalgam. I hadn't noticed the couple while they were dancing earlier, having been scanning the room for Vi. Never in my life had I imagined that I might come face-to-face with an amalgam.

Her hair, parted in the middle, was copper on one side and golden on the other. Half of her pale skin was dappled with freckles, the other creamy and unblemished. Strangest of all, one of her eyes was green and one violet. Despite the terror that came with seeing an amalgam in the flesh, I had to admit Madame Laroche was one of the most beautiful women I'd ever encountered. Her features were delicate and well-defined. Her eyes were large and arresting, her lips full.

Quill leaned close and hissed, "The husband is incredibly sensitive about her. You mustn't react."

I nodded, and heard Mal whispering a similar warning to Swinton. He remained stiff at my side, but relaxed his grip on my wrist, and before long, we stood in front of our hosts.

Mister Laroche rose, clapped Quill on the back and shook hands with Mal. "And who are these handsome gentlemen you've brought with you this evening?"

Before Quill could say anything, I bowed and kissed Madame Laroche's hand, allowing my cuff, the emblem of the royal house of Trousillion, to slip out of my sleeve. "Ambrose Oswin Trousillion Gyllen, madam. At your service." I gestured to Swinton. "This is my esteemed companion, Swinton."

The Laroches gasped in unison, and I caught the barest hint of an approving smile on Swinton's face as I straightened. Mal and Quill both looked astonished, as well. I hadn't been sure that I should risk using my real name—most everyone in the Alskad Empire surely knew the name of the successor to the throne, and it could put me in a vulnerable position—but uttering it clearly had the intended effect.

Mister Laroche folded at the waist and said, "Phineas Laroche, Aphra's husband. Your Highness, you must allow me to welcome you to Plumleen Hall. I was unaware of your presence in the Ilor colonies."

Leaning in close to him, I whispered, "I haven't made my presence well known, and would appreciate it if you kept the truth close to the vest. I have adopted a sobriquet for my travels, but I simply couldn't lie to a man so prominent as yourself." Aphra moved as if to stand, but I stepped back and motioned for her to stay seated. "I wouldn't dream of taking you away from your guests any longer, but perhaps we could find some time to chat later in the evening? I was extremely impressed with the present you gave your wife. Only a bold man would have the nerve to allow one of the diminished to wait upon the person he loves the most in the world. I admire that kind of confidence."

"Please make yourself welcome in our home, Your High-ness." Aphra's dazzling smile stopped at her mismatched eyes, which seemed to be weighing me and finding me inadequate.

Phineas gestured at a servant in dark livery. "See that these gentlemen want for nothing this evening. Open a bottle from my private cellar for them—ask Hepsy to choose something appropriate for a prince."

After concluding our courtesies, we moved away from the Laroches and found a cluster of empty chairs in a corner of the room.

"That seemed to go fairly well," Swinton said.

"A prince," Quill breathed. "You didn't tell us you were a bloody prince."

I blushed. "I didn't tell much of anyone. This errand required a bit of secrecy on my part. The Queen would be furious if she found out about my father's infidelity. I trust that you'll honor my wishes to keep this under wraps?"

Seeing the matching looks of calculation on the twins' faces, I shot desperate eyes at Swinton.

"He'll pay, of course—"

A scream cut through the din of the party. The musi-cians' instruments squealed to a discordant stop. Like a herd of horses, our heads all snapped in the direction of the scream, and for the briefest moment, there was silence.

"What's going on?" I whispered to Swinton, but before the words had left my mouth, I caught the smell of some-thing burning. Not a moment later, I saw a cloud of black, billowing smoke drift toward the ceiling, chased by flames. We were on our feet in a moment.

Chaos erupted through the great room. Men and women shrieked and bolted for the doors. Mal and Quill exchanged significant glances, and each drew a knife from sheathes hidden in their boots.

"The Laroches," Swinton said, pointing. "They're heading this way."

Aphra had pulled Phineas to his feet, and they were moving toward us.

"What are they doing? We're nowhere near a door. They should be leaving. *We* should be leaving," I said.

"Keep in mind that they've got Vi's papers," Mal said.

"So?"

"So, even if the house burns to the ground, Vi's contract will still be theirs. You need them to sign over her contract to you."

I grimaced. "Then they're coming with us. It's time to drop the subtlety. We're going to have to make him sell Vi's contract to me."

The moment they reached us, Swinton grabbed Phineas by the collar.

"Unhand me, sir!" Phineas's voice was pitched high.

Smoke curled around the solar lamps, dimming the room. Servants and guests rushed past us, bright silks flying behind them. I bit the inside of my cheek and looked at Swinton. "What do we do?"

"Something's blocking the doors. I say we take this one and get the hell out of here." He eyed Aphra. "The lady can come, too, I suppose."

He was right. There were masses of people around the doors, but the crowds were growing, not shrinking. Phineas moaned, burying his face in his hands. Aphra's jaw tightened, and she gave her husband a hard look. The screams at the eastern door grew louder by measurable degrees, and the people at the back of the crowd turned and ran back into the great room, looking for another way to escape.

Aphra narrowed her eyes at her struggling husband. "We'll go. Careful, now. Panic's setting in quickly, and a mob like this can be unpredictable. No telling what's started the fire."

Mal and his brother exchanged a series of indecipherable looks before Quill nodded and took off his jacket. "It's the rebels. They've been doing this all over the region. Look sharp—this promises to get ugly."

The air was thickening with smoke, and sweat pricked at my neck. I took a deep breath, trying to focus on the people in front of me rather than the terrified chorus of voices swimming around us. This was all happening far too fast.

Mal and Quill positioned themselves on either side of Phineas, and Swinton came to stand by me, giving my arm a reassuring squeeze. It looked like it was taking all of the twins' strength to keep Phineas on his feet. Quill jerked the man upright and slapped him hard across the face. "Where do you keep your servants' contracts?" he demanded.

Phineas snorted and spat, missing Quill's face by a hair's breadth. "That's none of your concern."

Swinton glanced over his shoulder at the door. I followed his gaze and saw a number of silk-clad guests staggering away with shocked looks on their faces and hands pressed against bloody gashes.

Aphra's unsettling eyes landed on me. "Swear on the future of the Alskad Empire and in the name of your chosen god that you'll get us out of this room."

Jaw tight, I held her gaze and nodded. "I swear. On my honor as the heir to the throne of the Alskad Empire, I'll do everything in my power to get you out alive. Your husband, too. You'll sign over Vi Abernathy's contract to me in exchange."

"What do you want with the dimmy girl?" Phineas asked, looking confused.

"That's none of your concern."

Aphra offered me her hand. "It's a deal. The papers are in my husband's study on the other side of the house. Second desk drawer on the left. Mal and Quill know where it is."

Mal nodded and said, "We'll have to split up. Go out a window, and get to the barn quick as you can. I'll get Vi's papers."

"I'm going with him," Swinton said. "Get the Laroches out of here."

"The papers won't do anyone any good if Vi's locked in a room somewhere. We have to get her out," I said.

"I'll find her for you, Bo."

It broke my heart to admit it to myself, but I knew he'd be faster, stealthier. He'd see her out in one piece. "Where should we go?"

"Do you think you can find my mother's place?" he asked. I nodded.

"Go there. She'll see you taken care of." Swinton cupped my cheek. "Watch your back. I'll bring Vi to you safely."

I took his face in both my hands and kissed him, quickly, before he slid into the crowd.

Figures in gray, their faces covered, darted into the room. They brandished the long, peculiarly curved knives used to harvest kaffe, but as one of them passed, I saw the tattoos streaked across his fingers and the paint blackening the skin around his eyes.

These weren't rebels. They were the Shriven. I steeled myself against the panic and started searching for a way out. They'd surely come to collect Vi, and I had no intention of letting that happen.

CHAPTER THIRTY-THREE

VI

Hepsy kept her trap firm shut as she pulled me up a back staircase and through a rich suite of rooms I barely had time to see. We paused in a closet as big as my bedroom in the stable, its walls lined with shelves of clothing and racks of gowns hanging in shimmering waves to the floor. My mind raced. I needed to get back to the party. To Bo. If the Shriven were looking for me, if they knew where I was, they'd waste no time. Bo wasn't safe, and neither was I.

Hepsy pulled back a curtain to reveal a small door and riffled through the ring of keys she kept on her belt. I reached out to touch a dress made from gold cloth, thinking. I needed to find a way to escape from Hepsy and get the people I cared about out of that room.

Hepsy smacked my hand away. "Don't you touch that. Not with your filthy, sweat-soaked hands."

Her reprimand snapped me out of the riptide that threatened to drown me in my own head, and I quipped, "Oh, so you do remember how to speak."

Glowering, Hepsy fumbled open the door and shoved me in, ducking to follow. Inside the room, moonlight streamed in through a small, round window, a hair bigger than a serving platter. The washed-out moonlight shone on a small, oak-framed bed covered in a ratty quilt. The only other furniture in the room was my trunk. It would serve double duty as storage and bedside table.

"Don't think you can be wandering off while we're all busy downstairs. This door here'll be locked until Madame comes up tonight, hear me?"

Before I'd time to squeeze in another word, Hepsy bustled out of the room and closed the door behind her with a heavy *thunk*. The key scraped in the lock, and like that, I was alone. I slumped onto the bed. It felt good to be off my feet, but I was more than ready to be out of this sweaty dress. I couldn't afford to waste any time.

I needed a plan. And I needed to find a way out of this locked room.

The dress, though unwieldy to get into, dropped to the floor as soon as I tossed the belt onto the bed and untied the knots at my shoulders. I pulled the pins out of my hair, letting it fall in a heavy tangle down my back. Basking in the relief that came with shrugging out of those uncomfortable clothes, I bent to pull a more practical getup from my trunk. Determination flooded my veins, steeling me against the exhaustion and anxiety that hounded me. I would be ready to face whatever the night held in store for me.

I pulled the knives Myrna had given me from their hidden sheathes in my belt. Last, I touched the pouch of pearls hanging around my neck. I didn't know how this night would end, and if Bo managed to buy my contract from Phineas, there might not be time to come back for my things. Bo'd told me plain there'd be money for me, and plenty of it, but I planned to keep the rest of my own meager stash. No matter how small it was next to the inheritance from Bo's—our—father, what was left of the wealth I'd made beneath Penby's waves would stay with me.

Once again clad in my everyday breeches, blouse and boots, I made slits in the double-thick crown of leather around the tops of my boots so that I could safely carry the two blades. Twisting my hair into a thick braid, I climbed on top of the trunk to peer out the window. The halves of the moon lit the sky, and though it was nearly as bright as day outside, the world was washed in gray. A mountain range of roofs crowded my view, but I could just make out the skylights in the great room, twinkling with solar lamps. Something about the light looked strange to me. I peered through the window, doing my best to get a closer look, but the wavy glass made it difficult.

The window was fitted with a lock, like the door. Lucky for me, two of my hairpins, bent straight, made short work of the lock. For a few uncomfortable breaths, the window tight around my hips, I was sure that Aphra was going to walk in after the celebration later and find me wedged half in, half out of the window. But I wiggled, cursed and finally crashed out onto the roof tiles.

I'd never been good at staying in locked rooms.

I scrambled, trying to balance as I slid toward the open air at the edge of the roof. I finally found my footing, then froze. A rumble of voices arguing in quiet whispers and the scrape of boots on gravel several stories below drifted up toward me. If I could hear them, they could hear me, whoever they were. For the first time, I found myself glad I'd spent so much time hiding from miserable brats bent on bloodying my face. Long experience treading lightly in soft-soled boots'd made me quieter than a seal slipping through the water.

I crept to the edge of the roof and lay flat on my belly, peering over the edge. Shadowy figures in head-to-toe gray swarmed the garden below. The black paint bisecting their faces and their shaved heads made it all too clear who these people were.

The Shriven. They'd found me.

The house was surrounded by them. Fifty or sixty folks at least snaked through hedges and across the lawn. The Shriven, their dark clothing blending into the shadows, slid into place all around the house, pulling knitted caps low over their brows, hiding the telltale signs of who they were. They had disguised themselves, but why? They wouldn't be punished for anything they did. That was what it was to be Shriven. They could do no wrong. There was nothing to forgive. Nothing to hide from.

One person, stout and short, stood on the marble mounting block in the center of the garden. It was carved in the shape of an aurochs, head down and horns forward, as if about to charge. "Take your positions. The great room will catch at any minute, and I don't want to see a single person come through the doors."

It was a woman's voice, and though it was familiar, I couldn't place it. What did she mean, "catch"? What were they planning? The gray figures below raced toward the great room at her direction, and I wriggled back from the roof's edge. I got to my feet and flattened myself in a shadow against a wall.

I took a deep breath. The perfume of the night-blooming flowers filled my nose, along with the green of new-cut grass and pit smoke. The air in the Ilor colonies was cleaner by a league than the rot and smoke that we breathed in my neighborhood in Alskad.

The End. Something in the air brought the End rushing back to me.

I sniffed again. It was the smoke. The smoke tickling my nose—it wasn't the clean branches of green wood or slow burning knots of a pit roast. It smelled like burning trash. Rot and wood and the tangy smell of hot metal. It smelled like the End in the desperate part of winter before the thaw, when folks got low on tinder.

Blood like ice water racing through my veins, I looked out over the mountain range of the roof. There, behind the great room's glass ceiling, a pale gray cloud drifted up in a slow dance toward the moonlit sky.

I watched the trickle of smoke billow upward, taking with it all the careful planning that'd been done to set me free. This was a tide far stronger than me and my plans. And then I remembered—the resistance had targeted wealthy landowners with large numbers of contract workers. Estates burned to the ground. No survivors among the owners or guests.

The Shriven were going to burn Plumleen to the ground and blame it on the resistance.

I felt sick. I had to do something, but I couldn't very well rush in against fifty of the Shriven out for blood. Even as I tried to worm my way out of getting involved, the cold realization gripped my throat like a fist.

Bo. Bo was in the great room, with Mal and Quill.

I took off across the tiles, racing toward the great room, where the skylights were clouded with smoke. The roof was nearly flat, which made it easy to dash from one peak to the other. Long instinct and practice kept me balanced, and a good thing, too, because my mind was spinning. As I got close to the great room, the panicked screams of the Laroches' guests pierced the air. Flames licked up the side of the building, and the fiery glow was garish in the washed-out landscape of the moonlit estate.

By the time I knelt next to the nearest skylight, the view into the great room was totally obscured with thick, black smoke, and the glass was hot to the touch.

"Dzallie's teeth," I cursed, slamming my fist against the roof's cool tiles. I had to get down there. I couldn't let all those people fend for themselves, and me twiddling my thumbs like a half-drunk bear.

Two choices loomed up in front of me. Either I'd sprint back across the roof, through the tiny window and pick the bedroom's lock before sneaking through a house full of vigilant and possibly rebellious servants—or I'd take the easy route, and shimmy down three stories of drain pipe, praying to whatever goddess, real or not, who'd listen, that I'd make it down in one piece.

I gritted my teeth and crawled to the edge of the roof once more.

The only pipe nearby was skinny, smaller than three of my fingers around, made of steel pitted with rust. A thin strip of metal and a pair of bolts every five paces was the only thing holding the pipe to the side of the house. I cast about, hoping for a less hair-raising choice, but I didn't see another way down.

This far away, I'd no sense of what Bo was feeling, but I hoped that he—or if not him, Swinton—had had the good sense to keep his head down and get the hell out of the great room.

I swung my legs over the side of the roof, grappling for

a hold with the toes of my boots. Slowly, I edged my way down, gripping with my knees and toes. The muscles in my legs screamed, and the roof tiles were slick under my sweaty palms. Quick as a darting fish, I shifted one hand to the pipe. In a tight-eyed moment of terror, I let go of the roof with the other hand and found myself clinging to the slatted side of the mansion, high above the ground. I took a deep breath and let my body take over. I'd climbed up and down buildings higher than this—and in worse shape—dozens of times.

By the time I reached the second story, my arms trembled with the effort and half my toes'd gone numb in my boots. The smoke stench grew stronger with every passing second. I sped up. Just before I reached the top of the first-story window, my boot slipped, and I crashed into the side of the house.

I heard a loud pop, and before I'd a moment to realize what was happening, shooting pain sparked down my body and I tumbled backward. I hurtled through the thick branches of the bushes that lined the house and landed flat on my back. The wind rushed out of me in a gush. Lightning strikes of pain raced from my neck to my right hand and back again. I lay there, stunned and breathless, chest searing for a few long seconds before I gasped and gulped air like a beached shark.

Slowly, still flat on my back, I took stock of the damage. Bruised from head to toe, I'd ache for days. The bushes had left deep scratches in my cheeks and arms and rents in my clothing. The worst part, though, was my shoulder. My arm lay limp at my side, and it burned with a fire that could only mean one thing. I'd pulled it out of place.

I gritted my teeth and tried to stagger upright, but froze when I heard voices.

"You hear that?"

"Hear what?" The second voice sounded like a woman, though it was rough and scratchy with age.

"Over there. In the bushes."

I held my breath.

"I didn't hear nothing."

My shoulder throbbed, and the pain threatened to drown me. I breathed, slow and shallow, and let the agony wash over me, focusing on the rough voices next to the bush.

"I did. Gadrian's flames. Ain't we supposed to be watching for folks getting out of that great room?"

"Hamil's drowning glory, but I do hate this island. Can't hardly breathe, and now we've gone and added smoke. I'll be glad to get back to Penby, that much I'll tell you."

The footsteps faded away, and I screwed my eyes up in relief. Taking shallow breaths, I counted to a hundred before scrambling to my feet. I didn't think there was much time left. I'd seen enough buildings go up in the End to know that if the fire made it to the roof beams, no one inside would stand a chance.

There had to be a way for me to distract the Shriven and get everyone out of the burning room at the same time. I needed to cause a ruckus big enough to overwhelm the fire and confusion inside. If my throwing arm weren't totally useless, thanks to my goddess-blasted shoulder, I'd smash the great room windows. Give the poor folks trapped inside an escape and distraction all in one. But a stone thrown with my left arm'd be weak at best, and it'd make the other shoulder worse.

I needed a better plan. Something big and splashy.

It came to me in a flash. Fireworks. Quill'd been meant to find fireworks for the celebration tonight. If he'd done it— and I prayed he had—they'd be in the cellar.

I edged along the side of the house holding my limp arm

close to my body with my good hand. I hoped the tall rhododendron bushes would screen my movements, but if anyone was watching carefully, I was shit out of luck. I'd need to move fast and hope no one noticed.

The cellar door was around the corner. Hepsy'd sent me down into the maze of rooms below the house a handful of times to fetch this or that for the cook or to find a bottle of wine Phineas wanted with his supper. If Phineas'd ordered something rare or dangerous and meant to be a secret, it was sure to be down there.

I peered around the bushes, looking for the Shriven. Seeing nothing but the long shadows of moss-draped oaks, I turned the door's handle. It stuck.

"Dzallie's hair," I hissed. "Don't do this to me now."

I jiggled the knob. Nothing. Someone'd locked it. I let out a long stream of low curses. Picking locks was a job for someone with two working hands. There was no way I'd be able to get it open on my own.

"Vi?"

I whirled around, pulling a knife from my boot with my good hand, and saw a familiar face. My head swam with the sudden movement, and the few bites I'd eaten that afternoon rushed back up. When I'd finished emptying my stomach into the bushes, I wiped my mouth and looked up at the two figures looming over me, outlined by moonlight. Still woozy, I narrowed my eyes at them.

"What've you done to your arm, Vi?" It was Mal. And next to him, all broad shoulders and curly hair like spun bronze, was Swinton.

My shoulder throbbed, my mouth tasted like bile and my head was spinning. A part of me was blazingly happy to see Mal, but with the pain and the imminent threat of becoming a real dimmy, the best I could manage was a grim smile. "Where's Bo?"

Mal grimaced. "He's with Quill. They'll be out of that mess in there in no time flat."

My throat tightened, and my heart quickened. "Why're you here?" I fumed at Swinton. "Why aren't you with Bo? He's so soft, he'll melt if someone looks at him wrong. He needs protecting." I wiped sweat off my forehead with the back of my hand, still holding the knife. Noticing Swinton's eyes on my knife, I slid it back into my boot.

Swinton glared at me. "He's stronger than—"

I interrupted him. "Nothing for it now. You say Quill's with him. That'll have to do. Can either of you pick a lock?"

Swinton took my hairpins, and as he worked the lock, he told me that they'd swiped my contract from Phineas's office and run around the outside of the mansion to bypass all the confusion inside. While Swinton spoke, Mal inspected my shoulder, muttering to himself.

"You've pulled your shoulder out of the socket. I can set it, but it'll hurt like nothing you've ever felt."

"I doubt that very much," I said.

Mall unknotted the silk cravat from around his neck and quirked an eyebrow at me. "Ready?" he asked.

I nodded, gritting my teeth. He took my arm, and in a flash of gut-rending, star-spinning pain, heaved my shoulder back into place. I bit my lip hard, willing myself silent, but tears streamed down my face. In the blink of an eye, my arm went from bone-grinding pain to totally normal. I blinked, stunned.

Before I'd gotten my breath back, Mal'd tied my arm tight to my body with his cravat. Swinton whipped the door open and waved us in. He'd popped the lock near as fast as I could've myself. I muttered my thanks and followed Mal into the basement, gripping the rail with my good hand.

I heard Mal fumbling for a switch at the bottom of the stairs.

"There aren't any solars down here," I said. "There should be a lamp and a box of matches in a nook on the right."

After another moment's cursing, a match sizzled and struck, and the warm glow of the oil lamp bathed the room. I took the lamp from Mal and started down the corridor.

"This way. We've got to hurry," I said.

"Do you have a plan?" Swinton asked.

"Something like that."

Two wrong turns and an empty room later, I found the door I was looking for and nodded for Mal to open it. I slid past him into the room and nodded, a grin spreading across my face. The dusty room was stacked with large, wooden crates, all painted in bold black letters with one word: FIRE-WORKS.

Swinton whistled, eyebrows raised. "That'll do."

CHAPTER THIRTY-FOUR

Bo

We stood in a huddle in the eye of the screaming hurricane that swirled around us. Mal and Swinton had disappeared into the panicked mass of people rushing from one end of the room to the other. I forced myself to think. We needed to find a way out of the ballroom as quickly as possible.

A small group of the Shriven, disguised as members of the resistance, entered the great room and menaced their way through the guests, shouting for the Laroches. I swiped at the sweat beaded on my forehead and wished that I'd taken the gaudy decorative knife Swinton had offered me. Standing over the dusty trunks in his mother's attic, the idea of wearing a weapon encrusted with fake gems—even if they were good fakes—had seemed absurdly unnecessary. I promised myself that I'd take Swinton's advice from now on.

Quill eyed the flames creeping toward the beams that held the glass roof of the great room. "It'll be the smoke or the ceiling that'll get to us before the rebels."

Wild-eyed, Phineas squeaked, "They'll want my head on a pike. It's all that will matter to them. You have to get me out of here."

"They'll be coming for me, too, I suppose," Aphra said, disconcertingly calm. "The windows may be our only option."

I forced my face to stillness. They'd no reason to think otherwise. No reason to be anything besides self-involved. I scanned the room, looking for the nearest window. Quill nodded toward the row of potted ferns that lined the room, creating a concealed path for the servants. Aphra eyed the disguised Shriven as they herded the guests away from the doors and into the center of the room. They hadn't made their way to us yet, but it was only a matter of time.

The closest window was a dozen feet away, but a bevy of Shriven loomed in our path. Quill tapped my shoulder and pointed to another that stood unguarded on the other side of the room.

"If we can get behind the potted plants, we might just make it. Keep close, and try not to draw attention," Quill said, giving Phineas a pointed look.

Aphra drew a knife from somewhere inside her gown and nodded. "I'll keep his mouth shut."

Phineas paled, and we edged toward the plants. Aphra and Phineas led the way, and I followed close behind, keeping one hand on Phineas's shoulder. Quill brought up the rear. His height gave him the advantage of seeing over the heads of most of the people straining to see what was going on.

"Watch your left." Quill's breath was hot on my ear, and I twitched, but my arm came up in time to stop a corpulent man from knocking me over as he fainted.

"Thanks." My voice came out in a hoarse whisper.

A flash of gray to my right caught my eye, and I froze. One

of the Shriven pushed an admiral in full regalia and a man who must've been her husband to their knees. Tears streamed down the man's face, and he blubbered, begging for mercy. The Shriven slowly drew the wickedly curved blade she held along his cheek. Blood welled and trickled into his blond beard. The admiral's face was pale, but she kept an impassive expression.

"Tell me your darkest secret," the Shriven growled. "If it's entertaining enough, I might let you live."

A hand closed around my wrist and yanked me forward. Aphra hissed in my ear, "We can't stop them. We need to get out of here *now*."

I followed her as she slid through the crowd like a snake through water. Moments later, we darted behind the large fronds of a potted fern and scurried around the corner. Aphra stopped in front of an absurdly small window.

I threw my full weight up into the window's sash and, muscles screaming, managed to wrench it up.

A commanding voice boomed through the smoky air of the great room. "Listen close, you indolent pigs. None of you will survive the night. None of you—except the soul who produces the dimmy girl."

I froze. Vi. They *were* here for Vi after all. I took deep breaths, trying to stay calm. I had to trust that Swinton would find her and see her safe.

Before I'd even managed to step fully away from the window, Phineas was halfway out, his legs flailing like a newborn colt as he wriggled through the tiny opening.

"Where's Quill?" Aphra asked.

"He was right behind me." I looked over my shoulder, but could see nothing over the ferns and the bobbing heads of the screaming guests. "He should be here any second."

I eyed the tightly clad rear end of the master of the house,

laid a boot squarely on the seat of his trousers and shoved.
Phineas popped through the window and, a moment later,
stuck his head back through.

"Was that truly necessary?" he sputtered.

I ignored Phineas and offered Aphra my hand. "Your turn."

Aphra shot me a determined smile, gripped the window
sash and slid through, landing easily on the ground outside.
"I don't see anyone," she hissed. "Come quickly. We might
just get off before they notice we're gone."

I compressed my mouth into a thin line. "You two go on.
Get off the property. I'll be right behind you."

Aphra pulled herself back through the window and glowered at me. "Certainly not. I won't leave you here on your
own. Who knows what these people will do?"

I bit my lip. "I can't leave Quill behind."

"I've known the Whipplestons for a long time." Aphra
scowled. "They're resourceful. Quill will find his way out.
Come on. We've got to go."

I took a deep breath and scrambled through the open window. I landed clumsily and fell to my knees in the damp mulch
behind a clump of bushes.

"Hush!" Aphra hissed. "There are a group of them around
the corner."

"We have to head to the barn and get our horses," Phineas
whispered. "We'll never outrun them on foot. It'll take hours
to walk to the next estate."

"We're not going to another estate," I said, grasping for a
lie. I couldn't afford to let the Laroches learn that Vi was the
reason for the chaos on their estate. "If the servants are rebel-
ling here, there's a good chance that there'll be more of the
same on other estates. We'll go to Williford. I know a place
we can hide."

"We'll still need horses," Aphra said. "They think everyone is inside. I imagine they've left the stables unguarded. If we can get across the lawn, we'll be safe."

"They'll realize I'm not in the great room soon enough. We've got to hurry," Phineas whined.

Aphra led the way down the outside wall of the great room, away from the growing flames. The overgrown inner branches of the bushes scraped my face and hands and tore at my cobbled-together finery. I tried to step as lightly as I could, remembering all the times Claes had admonished me to think about where I placed my feet while we were hunting, but Phineas's muttered curses and the twigs he snapped soon rendered my efforts pointless.

"Could you try to be a little quieter?" I snapped. "I'd rather not learn what the rebels do to people who assist in the escape of their quarry."

Aphra whirled around, a finger to her lips. She pointed emphatically at the corner of the manor house, ten paces in front of her, and mimed drawing the knife she held across an invisible person's throat.

I shook my head and slipped in front of her. Killing another person, even one of the Shriven, simply to get away from the violence that had overtaken this house was unacceptable. I only saw one guard, a lanky man lounging against the corner of the building.

In a moment, I was behind him. I slid an arm around his neck and held him firm, as my fencing instructor had taught me so long ago. He slashed weakly at me over his head, but he was already slowing enough that dodging his knife was easy. Soon, the man's eyes fluttered, and he lost his grip on the knife. I checked to make sure that he was still breathing, and, seeing no one else around, dragged him through the bushes.

I laid him behind a bench in the garden, well away from the house, in case the fire spread. He would have a sore throat and a headache when he woke, but at least he would wake.

The barn loomed in the gray-white light of the moon, across the lawn, and I waved for Aphra and Phineas to hurry. They scurried across the grass and crouched beside me.

"It would've been safer to kill the poor fool," Phineas said.

"For what?" I asked. "Standing outside a burning house? He was hardly more than a boy."

Phineas sneered, and Aphra tilted her head, considering me quizzically. She said, "You surprise me, my lord. I wouldn't have imagined your sympathies falling with the rebels."

"I do not condone unnecessary violence, especially the murder of my own subjects, no matter who they are or what they've done. I'm not a judge, and I refuse to play the executioner. Let's get you out of here before we begin debating philosophical matters, shall we?"

"If we get out of all this, we'll owe you a great debt, Your Highness," Aphra said.

"Signing over Vi's contract will be plenty repayment, but there'll be time for all that once we're well away, and not a moment before," I said. "Follow me."

I sprinted across the lawn, not realizing that I was holding my breath until I flung myself through the barn doors and collapsed, heaving, against the rough wood wall. Aphra flew through the doors a moment later. Phineas burst into the barn last and fell to his knees.

"I haven't run like that since I was a boy," he gasped.

Before he managed to rise, Aphra was suddenly beside him, hauling him up. Just as Phineas regained his footing, I felt a cold blade pressed into the thin skin of my throat.

"Don't move a muscle." Aphra's voice was hard, and as she

spoke, a gag was stuffed into my mouth. It tasted like it had been drenched in perfume. "I'm sorry to drag you into our domestic squabble, Your Highness, but I can't let you take my husband off the property."

In no time, my wrists and ankles were bound up in a lead rope. I'd kept my joints stiff, hoping to be able to wriggle free like the hero in a novel I'd read long ago, but Aphra's companion obviously had a great deal more practice tying knots than I had getting free of them.

I looked up to see Aphra standing behind her husband, holding a knife to his throat. Her strange, halved face was hard to read, especially in the dim light of the moons, but I thought I saw a twinge of pain behind the triumph in her mismatched eyes.

"Why?" Phineas's commanding voice had crumpled into a child's whine. "Why would you let them destroy our home?"

I was surprised that Aphra hadn't gagged him, as well.

"I only wish that I'd managed to coordinate a thing like this. What you see, my dear, is luck, plain and simple. And really? *Our* home?" Wry humor colored Aphra's words. "This is no more my home than one of the moon's halves would be, and twice as lonely. I'll be happy to be rid of your shackles, thrilled to know you can no longer leave a trail of pain and destruction in your wake. Rayleane's eyes, man, you think I haven't seen the scars left on Myrna's back? You think I don't remember that girl you whipped to death? Her name was Lily, Phineas. And you killed her. For sport."

"Where will you go? I sheltered you, Aphra. Without me, the Shriven will come for you. They'll lock you up and throw away the key."

Aphra smiled. "As if they could. For having lived with me these six years, Phineas, you hardly know me at all."

Phineas gaped, as though trying to digest what she'd said.

Aphra took a deep breath, knife glinting in her hand, and before I had time to react, drew the blade swiftly across his throat. A dark line appeared, his eyes went wide and blood gurgled, nearly black in the moonlight, down the collar of his jacket. His bound hands scrabbled at his throat, and I lurched back, only to knock into the figure behind me.

Aphra looked on stoically as her husband collapsed in a puddle of his own blood. Silence, but for the uneasy shifting of the horses in their stalls, hung over the barn. I was sickened, horrified, and I saw no escape. I would surely die here.

Explosions burst through the silence and shook a sprinkling of dust loose from the barn's beams. The horses screamed and panicked in their stalls. Aphra and her companion—whom I now recognized as Vi's friend, Myrna—started and dashed outside.

I inched awkwardly toward a stack of hay bales against the barn's wall. In every barn I'd ever visited, there had been a dull knife hanging by a bit of string on the wall, used to cut baling twine. Sure enough, a steel blade swung from a nail on the wall. I struggled to my feet and plucked it from its place, refusing to look at Phineas's corpse.

I sawed desperately at the ropes holding my wrists, working as quickly as I could. Once my hands were free, I pulled the gag from my mouth, spitting to rid myself of the foul taste of Aphra's perfume. More explosions boomed through the sky, and this time, they were accompanied by screams from the direction of the great room. I had to get away, but the thought of Vi tugged at me. What if she was still in the house? And could I really leave Swinton behind?

I crept to the barn door and looked outside.

Fireworks blossomed dangerously close to the elegant manor house. People in soot-smeared clothing streamed from the windows and doors of the great room, and in the chaos, I couldn't tell the guests apart from the Shriven. The acrid, oily smell of the fire filled the air, and a cacophony of breaking glass erupted from the great room. I watched in horror as the roof collapsed.

The two figures took off running away from the house, and I fought the urge to do the same. The thought of Swinton, Mal, Quill and Vi froze me in place. Were they all inside? I sent a fervent prayer to Gadrian that none of them were still in the great room.

Two choices lay before me. I could join in with the crowd, searching for them, or I could stick to the plan. I knew what Swinton—and likely Vi—would tell me to do.

Stomach in knots, I turned my back on the chaos and retreated to the barn.

I chose a horse in the farthest stall from the door, a nervous chestnut who looked ready to run. In mere minutes, I'd saddled the horse. I left it in its stall and sped back down the barn aisle.

Horrible though Phineas had been, I couldn't leave his corpse lying in the middle of the barn where it might be trampled or worse. I dragged the body into an empty stall, gasping at the weight of him, and threw a blanket over him. As I closed the door, I said a quick prayer and wiped my hands on a saddle pad hanging next to the stall.

I flung open each of the stall doors, releasing the horses one by one. It would slow down Vi, Swinton and the Whippleston twins, but it would make it that much harder for Aphra or the Shriven to pursue me, as well. When all the horses had been freed, I led my chestnut out of the stall, mounted and galloped away from the burning house.

CHAPTER THIRTY-FIVE

Vi

Fireworks had always looked large in the sky, but when they burst on the ground, the great shower of sparks was enormous and destructive. We shot a round at the far end of the house, forcing the knot of Shriven blockading the doors to scatter. Soon, folks started streaming from the windows and doors of the great room. It was working. In no time at all, the entire great room would be empty.

Relief flooded over me as the first groups of coughing guests tumbled onto the lawn. I watched for Bo and Quill, searching for their faces among the soot-smeared crowd, but I didn't see them. Mal laid a gentle hand on my shoulder, like he could feel the anxious energy exploding inside me. If they weren't in the great room, where were they?

"Could they've gotten out?" I asked Mal.

"They were on their way out when we left. We've got to assume they're already gone," Mal said.

Unease writhed like eels in my belly, but I kept moving,

setting the fireworks and hopping back to let Swinton and Mal light the fuses. Flashing, unnatural hues of firework sparks lit the stream of folks flooding across the lawn. The tide had slowed, but the danger wasn't over yet. Even as the crying, silk-clad guests did their best to flee, the Shriven kept appearing, blades in their hands as they slinked from between the trees and jumped out of windows like beetles. I hoped Phineas was in among the crowd—a cringing, cowardly part of me was glad that my plans for revenge had been interrupted, that it might not have to be my hand that ended his life.

I hated myself for that cowardice.

The Shriven were everywhere. My reckoning was way off—they'd more than doubled since I'd counted them from the roof. They were coming from the house, from the trees, from all around us. We'd hidden ourselves behind a screen of bushes, but I knew it'd only be minutes before they found us.

"I've got to go find Bo," I whispered.

Mal looked up at me, his face illuminated by the fuse he'd just lit. "You can't. You've a hurt wing, and we don't know how soon the whole house will go up. It looks fit to blow already. They'll be fine."

He was right, in a way. The fire'd spread to the wing of the house closest to the great room. The flames danced behind windows filling fast with smoke. A windowpane on the first floor burst in a scream of shattering glass as I watched. The house's stone walls were the only reason it could have possibly lasted this long. I scrubbed a hand through my hair, thinking.

"I promised your brother I'd see you safe out of here," Swinton said. "Bo can take care of himself."

So can I, I thought. But rather than wasting my breath arguing, I set the last firework and darted back to squat by Mal. "What now?"

Mal snorted. "I thought you were the one running the show here."

I cuffed him with my good fist. "This isn't the time for jokes."

"I haven't seen them," Swinton said. "Have you?"

"Not yet."

"Come on then," Swinton said. "Quill and Bo must've already made it out. Let's find our horses and get gone. We'll meet them in Williford. I told Bo to meet us at my mother's."

His domineering attitude stirred up an overwhelming urge to argue in my gut, but I stuffed it down. Being obstinate wouldn't do anyone any good. I led the way through the wooded edge of the garden, taking a roundabout route to the barn. So many of the Shriven had poured out of the woods to surround the folks on the lawn—I hoped we'd be safe if we kept out of the open.

We'd nearly reached the barn's long shadow when I tripped and fell. I landed hard on my knees, but my good wrist squished into something soft. Whatever I'd landed on let out a low moan. Strong hands, either Swinton's or Mal's, yanked me to my feet by the elbows, sending riots of pain shooting through my hurt shoulder. Spots of color crowded my eyes, and I did everything I could to keep the bile from rising in my throat again. The minute we got safe, I was going to give those boys a tongue-lashing they'd never forget.

"Hamil's ass. It's one of them," Mal said.

"She's covered in blood."

My vision cleared, and I saw Swinton crouching next to a crumpled pile of muddied gray silk, which, apparently, was one of the Shriven.

"She's alive?" I asked. I knew the answer. I'd heard her, felt her warmth under my hand. My shoulder throbbed, and

I wanted to get the hell away from this place while we still could.

Swinton turned her over, and I was startled to see that it was Curlin. Luckily, she was out cold.

"Gods and goddesses all be damned," I swore. I poked her leg with my toe. "Is that all her blood?"

"Her arm's been slashed fair bad, but if the bleeding stops, she'll live."

"Will it stop on its own?" I asked. No one but the Shriven had been armed—I wondered who'd given her such a nasty cut.

Swinton gave her a critical once-over. "Might. Might not. No great loss either way. She's one of them. Stop wasting time. We need to go. Now."

Beneath the bloody, mud-spattered robes...under the tattoos, the painted face, the shaved head...the girl whose life was draining into the dirt knew me better than anyone else in the world. Better than my own twin. Despite the betrayal and the threats and the horrors she'd no doubt committed since joining the Shriven, I couldn't let Curlin bleed to death in the woods by herself.

I looked at Mal. "Can you carry her?"

Swinton's anger cut through his words like ice. "Let her die."

"I've known her my whole life. I can't."

"There isn't time to argue. Let's get her bandaged and get the hell out of here," Mal said. He bent and scooped her up in his arms. "Come on."

"Magritte's tongue. I'm going to regret this," I muttered, but led the way into the barn.

The stalls were nearly all empty; their doors stood open. I hurried into my old rooms, leaving Mal and Swinton to follow me. The main room was dark but for a single lamp on one of the side tables. Before my eyes had fully adjusted to the dimness, I saw movement in the bedroom.

"Bo?" My voice trembled. If it was anyone else, I didn't know what I'd do.

Swinton and Mal froze behind me.

"Vi?"

The old plank floor shook, and a familiar figure came toward me. In a moment, I was wrapped up in Quill's arms. One hand laced through my hair and freed my curls from their braid. The other wrapped around my waist, and his mouth found mine. A rush of hot, frantic relief washed over me, and I let myself sink into his embrace. He was safe. I was so gods'-damned grateful that he was safe.

I pulled myself away, realizing what he'd done.

"What the damn hell were you thinking, staying here?" I snapped. He reached out to me, but I put up a hand to stop him. "Dzallie's toes! Why would you stay? The place is crawling with Shriven. And where's Bo?"

"I left him to come find you. He was nearly out of the great room." Seeing my glare, Quill's eyes went wide as he tried to explain. "With the fire and the Shriven... I needed to make sure you were safe, Vi. Surely you—"

I cut him off. "I can take care of myself, thanks. I don't know if I can say the same for that pampered and privileged ninny."

"Enough. The both of you, honestly. Are we taking this one with us or not?" Mal snapped. It was the first time I'd ever heard anything close to ire come out of his mouth. "Because if we are, we need to get her wrapped up."

I nodded, and Mal carried Curlin inside. She whimpered, still mostly unconscious, when he set her on the sofa.

Irritation curled through my body like smoke. I didn't quite know why I felt the need to be so protective of Bo. Despite the fact that he was my twin, I didn't even know him. All the years I'd spent talking to Pru flashed before me, and I suddenly realized that the connection I'd felt—the thing that had steadied me all these years—was Bo. Neither of us had known it, but we'd had each other all along.

"So my brother is still trapped in the great room? With the Shriven?" I demanded.

"He'd gotten to the window, Vi," Quill said, trying to reassure me. "He was fine. I'm sure he's already halfway down the road."

"How do you bloody know? Did you not see what's happening out there?" I couldn't keep the fear out of my voice. I didn't even try. "What if he's lying on the ground somewhere, bleeding to death like she was?"

I jerked my head at Curlin.

"He's got a better head on his shoulders than you're giving him credit for, bully," Swinton said softly.

"I'm going to look for him," I said, the weight of it settling on me like a curse. I didn't want to wade back into that bloodbath, but I wanted Bo. I wanted to see him. To feel him nearby.

That thought hit me like the shock of an eel. I couldn't feel him anymore. He'd been there earlier in the evening, but now he was gone. Suddenly, I was on the verge of panic, but with the estate full of Shriven, I didn't have much of a choice. Somehow, I had to trust that he'd made it out. That he was still alive, and safe.

Swinton and Quill exchanged a look, and Swinton reached for my hand. "He'll meet us at my mother's place. We need to stick to the plan, Vi."

"Fine. See if you can't find us some horses," I said with a sigh, knowing they were right.

Swinton, his jaw tight, left the room with Mal.

A huge part of me wanted to leave Curlin to fend for herself. The malicious ninny'd caused me more grief than one person should bear in a lifetime. But the old loyalty I felt to her was stronger than my resentment, and we didn't have much time. I heaved a sigh.

Curlin woke with a scream when I poured tafia onto the slash on her arm. Quill clapped a quick hand over her mouth as I glared at her.

It'd occurred to me that Curlin might be the key I needed to get out of the mess I was in with the Shriven. She'd kept our relationship a secret in the basement of the temple—she'd even warned me. Though of what, I'd no idea. It didn't feel like a coincidence that she'd turned up at Plumleen tonight, though. Certainly didn't feel like a coincidence that she—one of the Shriven—had turned up with a slash on her arm when the only folks who'd been armed were the Shriven themselves.

I wasn't going to let her out of my sight until I found out the truth. The whole truth.

"You'd best keep quiet if you want to get out of here in one piece," I told her. "It won't hurt me a bit to leave you here praying Rayleane'll care enough to save your sorry hide. Are you going to shut your trap, or do I need to knock you out?" I asked.

Curlin studied me through slitted eyes. She'd seen the calculations whirring through my brain. Truth was, she didn't have much of a choice.

She nodded her head.

I handed Quill a strip of the bandage I'd been using to wrap up her arm. "Gag her. We shouldn't take any chances."

★ ★ ★

Dawn flooded the lavender sky with streaks of red and orange and pink as we rode into town. I held one of the pups, curled and asleep in my lap. The others were snoring in our saddlebags, and the mama dog walked beside my horse. I'd insisted on bringing the dogs, not able to stand the idea of leaving them behind to fend for themselves in whatever was left of the estate. Despite the danger, despite the exhaustion that seemed to drag at my core, despite my aching shoulder and my worry over my brother, I was strangely calm. I was free of Plumleen Hall, free of my contract, and I had Curlin—she could fill in the rest of the picture.

She would. I would make her.

The others in our party were quiet as we entered Williford, following Swinton. When he drew rein in front of a squat stone inn, he and Quill tumbled off their horses, relief clear as day in their bloodshot eyes. They took the pups from their saddlebags, and I couldn't help but smile as they tumbled around their mama, yipping and wagging their little bodies.

Quill helped Curlin down from her perch in front of Mal's saddle, and she stood straight-backed as ever, cradling her bandaged arm. Despite the bloodstained, mud-spattered remains of her robes, and the black paint trailing down her face, she still managed to cut quite an intimidating figure. If I hadn't known her my whole damn life, I would've been as wide-eyed as the stable hands gaping at us from across the yard. A gesture from Swinton brought one of the girls sprinting over, and Quill handed her his reins. Not to be left out, the other girls darted across the yard and gathered the rest of our mounts. Quill took firm hold of Curlin's uninjured arm.

"Just this way," Swinton said, leading us through the cobblestone courtyard, around to the back of the inn and its sprawling kitchen garden. He took a deep breath, squared his shoulders and opened the thick wooden door. I closed my eyes, willing Bo to appear when I opened them again. I thought I could almost feel his presence in my mind, but I couldn't be sure that my wanting wasn't the only real thing I felt.

"Swinton!" A woman as tall and twice as broad as Swinton himself barreled into him, wrapping him up in her arms and pressing his face into her ample bosom. "I've been beside myself with worry. Get yourself inside and tell me everything. Be quick about it."

It wasn't until she'd shuffled her son inside and went to close the door that she saw the rest of us standing by the garden gate. Shock registered on her face, followed closely by a wide smile. "You've got to forgive me. Come in, come in, and welcome."

Swinton's mother, Bethesda, sat us all down at the long plank table in the kitchen, which was groaning under the weight of enough food to feed a small army. After the initial surprise at seeing Curlin, Bethesda hardly looked at her. Instead, she busied herself pouring hot cups of tea for each of us.

I held my mug between my hands, jumping at every sound. I needed to see Bo. I had to know that he was in one piece.

"She'll need tending," Swinton said, nodding at Curlin.

"Surely, surely," Bethesda said. "Though I've no idea why you'd bring her here with the temple down the road."

"Don't worry yourself about it, Ma. Has Bo made it back?"

My heart quickened in my chest as I turned to look at Bethesda. Quill, sitting beside me on the long bench, squeezed my knee. I leaned into him, stealing comfort from his presence.

"I sent him upstairs for a bath and a change of clothes.

He'll be down shortly. Poor ducky looked half-starved, and I hadn't a thing ready to feed him."

I let out my breath, relieved. He was fine. He was *alive*.

"And you must be Vi, my dear." Bethesda shifted platters around on the table, making space for plates in front of each of us. "My Swinton and Bo've worked so awfully hard to find you. And you two, as alike as twins."

Curlin stiffened and sent a suspicious glance at me from across the table.

Bethesda shot her a strained smile. "I didn't happen to catch your name, dearie."

"I'm Shr..." She faltered and looked down at her hands. "I'm Curlin."

"Of course you are. Eat up, everyone. You've had a long night, by the looks of it."

Before I could say anything, boots clopped down the stairs. I clambered off the bench and to my feet.

He strode through the door, shirt untucked and dark curls dripping water. He'd made no effort to hide the gold cuff he wore around one wrist, shaped like the crown of the empire. Without sparing a glance for anyone else in the room, Bo went to Swinton and took him in his arms. They pressed their foreheads together, grinning at each other with their eyes barely a quarter inch apart.

"You're safe," Bo said, emotion choking his deep baritone. "Thank the gods. You're safe."

Swinton laughed, though the sound didn't seem jolly so much as relieved. "You didn't think I would let anything happen to me, did you? I'm far too wily to be taken down by a few ragers with knives, even if they are Shriven."

A noise burbled from Bo, half sob, half laugh, and a tumbling sense of love and relief and happiness tangled into my own anxious joy at seeing him whole. I wished I could see his face, but it was buried in Swinton's shoulder.

"I'm glad you got out of there, Bo." Swinton planted a tender kiss on Bo's lips. "I seem to've grown awfully fond of you."

Bo drew back, one arm still firmly wrapped around Swinton's waist, and caught my eye. He watched me, cautious, like he was bracing for a strike.

"You're well?" he asked.

I crossed the room and flung my good arm around him, crushing him to me. He may've been a pretentious, bumbling oaf who needed the whole truth beaten out of him, but he was mine. My twin.

He wrapped his arms around me, and hot, happy tears welled up in my eyes.

CHAPTER THIRTY-SIX

Bo

My breath caught in my throat, and had Swinton not been at my side, steadying me, I would have been knocked flat by the thundercloud of love and anger and pain and fear and happiness rolling off Vi. When she finally let go, I saw, to my great surprise, one of the Shriven in bloodstained robes at the table, staring blankly into a cup of tea. I automatically went to roll my sleeve down over my cuff, but stopped myself. If she hadn't already seen it, she would when I went to cover it. The scent of the philomena bushes came back to me in a rush, and with it, heartache as heavy as the golden net the Suzerain had settled on my shoulders so many weeks before.

"I've words to say to you," Vi said, a demanding note in her voice.

Her irritation cut through my memory, searing away my thoughts of the Queen and bringing into sharp focus the list of names Swinton had found in my aunt's study. "Why's there one of the Shriven here?"

"She needed saving. Is there somewhere we can talk?"

"What've you done to your arm?" I asked.

She waved her good hand dismissively. "Fell off a roof. That's nothing to do with anything. Stop dithering. Where'll we not be overheard?" she asked, turning to Swinton.

He looked at his mother questioningly, and Bethesda shrugged. "We're near about full. There's your room, and one other due to come empty 'round noon. If you're fussed about being alone, try the garden. There's not likely to be anyone about at this hour."

Vi jerked her head at the Shriven and addressed Quill. "See that one doesn't run off."

"As you wish, milady," Quill said, laughter in his voice.

Vi stared daggers at the grinning young man before stomping out the back door. I followed her, sparing a moment to kiss Swinton on the cheek.

"Watch your back," he whispered. "She's ferocious."

I found Vi in the farthest corner of the garden, perched on the fence, kicking morosely at the long weeds growing between the posts. The dawn had only recently broken, and dew still clung to the garden's explosion of plants. In her drab, dirty clothes, with that dark tangle of curls and smudges of sleeplessness beneath her eyes, she looked like nothing more than one of Gadrian's firebirds sent with a message to the garden of life. Fierce, misplaced, defiant.

"You owe me answers, Bo."

"I know."

Her eyebrows knit together as she studied me with her stormy eyes. I wondered briefly if I looked half so fierce when I was angry.

"Why don't you want anyone to know that we're twins?

Seems to me it would've been twice as easy to buy my contract off the Laroches if they knew I wasn't a dimmy."

I hefted myself onto the fence on her good side, half to give myself time to gather my thoughts, half to avoid seeing her reaction to the story I had to tell her. The smell of roasting meat drifted out of the inn's chimney, and I heard Vi's stomach growl. I wondered how long it had been since she'd had a meal.

"Spit it out," she said. "Your scheming and shuffling's loud enough to give me a headache."

"No one can know that I'm a twin."

Her kicking feet stilled, and she tucked one ankle behind the other. When she spoke again, she bit off each word, spitting them out as though every one was a bitter taste she wanted out of her mouth. "No one can know that you're a twin, or no one can know that you're *my* twin?"

"It isn't—"

Her fingers, the nails crusted with blood and dirt, reached out and brushed the cuff on my wrist. "It's to do with this, isn't it?"

A blush crept up my neck, and I forced the words out in an inelegant stream. "Almost everyone in the entirety of the Alskad Empire, with very few exceptions..." I paused and took a breath. "They know me as the singleborn heir to the throne. The crown prince. The only people who may not believe I'm singleborn are the Suzerain, and they've sent the Shriven looking for you. It's a horribly long story, but I believe that they plan to use you to control me when I sit on the throne. I don't mean to let that happen. I mean to wear the crown one day, and I mean for you to rule beside me."

Vi let out a long, low whistle. "Magritte's tongue. Why? Why d'you want a thing like that? Why d'you think *I'd* want a thing like that?"

I pushed through the waves of discomfort and doubt rolling off Vi. I had known this question was coming, and in the silences of my journey back from Southill with Swinton, I had shaped an answer as honest and whole as I could manage. I wanted... No. I *needed* to be completely honest with Vi. I would never tell her another lie.

"When I came of age, I swore that I would serve the people of the empire. I promised to put their needs before my own, to uphold justice. What I've seen here, Vi..." I shook my head. As if that could erase the list of dead children's names burned into my memory. As if shaking my head was enough to magically transport me back to the more innocent version of myself. "Until I find my way to the bottom of this mess, until I'm the King, you'll be safer if you're not my twin. Quill has agreed to help me arrange passage for us back to Penby on his uncle's ship. I'll see to it that you're safe, that you want for nothing. There's a house our father owned on the northern shore of Alskad. It's very beautiful—"

"Bo?" Vi took my hand in hers, and the energy she put into suppressing her frustration shocked me. Behind that, though, was love. Wave after wave of intense, bewildering, irritated, proud, complicated love. This, I supposed, was what it meant to have a sister. A twin. "Why, by Dzallie's teeth, would you think for a second that I'd be content to hide away in some forgotten cottage, waiting for you to save the world while I sit on my thumb?"

Birdsong and the nonsense chatter of the bright mimic birds filled the silence between us. In my own drive to find a way to fulfill my oath to the empire, to save my sister, to become the kind of man who ought to be King, I'd forgotten to consider what Vi might want. I hadn't thought that she, too, might want something more than a dull life.

"I didn't mean to hurt your feelings. I just thought…after everything you've been through…it would be nice for you to be comfortable. Safe. You can study, learn about the workings of the empire. Learn how to be Queen alongside me."

Vi's fingers squeezed mine. A rough chuckle, like ice over stones, came from beside me, and I turned to look at her. Tears were streaming down her cheeks and into the creases of her sad smile. I hopped off the fence and, biting the inside of my cheek to keep my own tears at bay, offered her my handkerchief.

"We'll have to save the conversation about my being a queen for a much later time, given that it's sure to end with a fight, and I'm not about fighting you as soon as I've found you." She gave me a wry grin and swiped at her face. "You know, up until a few weeks ago, I would've given my left arm for just what you're offering. Safety. A place of my own by the northern sea. But now…" She took a deep breath. "Tell me about this mess of yours."

I told her what I knew. About the philomenas growing on my estate, the deaths of the perfumers and the novitiate priests. I told her about Swinton's brother and my aunt's attempt to have me killed. Once I'd started, everything—my whole life— threatened to pour out of me. As I spoke, Vi's face betrayed nothing, though the tides of her emotions flooded over me.

I told her about Gerlene, about Claes and Penelope and their deaths. About my mother. About Queen Runa and her plans for me. By the time I'd finished, the sun had risen above the trees, and the air had gone from bearably warm to the heavy daytime heat that seemed to have shape and heft.

"Do you see?" I asked. "Do you understand why I must keep you secret? Safe? The empire deserves the truth, and that means someday, we'll sit beside one another, ruling together. But I need time to find a way to make it happen."

Sweat prickled my forehead, and I waited, anxious, for her response. She took her time, staring at the orange blossoms hanging heavy from the trees over our heads. Her lower lip was caught between her teeth, and I could almost see the thoughts spinning in her head.

Finally, she looked at me and said, "The Suzerain. The Suzerain and the anchorites, I mean. They aren't just killing folk for the joy of it. They've found a way to make us lose our grip on our tempers, to make us wildly, unstoppably violent. They're creating dimmys, Bo."

"Us? Vi, you're not one of them. You've never been diminished. It was all a lie."

Vi gave me a look hard enough to shatter diamonds. "We're twins, yes. I see that plain as the freckles on your face. But one doesn't take away the other. I've been a dimmy my whole life, and even if I didn't know that it was the temple making folk fear me, making me fear myself, I have been diminished, Bo. I am one of the diminished."

I took a deep breath, rebuttals already taking shape in my mouth, but she put up a hand to stop me.

"They made me a dimmy, but I'm going to make certain sure it stops with me."

"How?" I asked.

"I don't quite know yet," she said, and eased herself off the fence, cradling her bandaged arm. "But I think it's an awfully good thing my twin—" she stopped and winked at me "—I mean, my *half brother*'s set on being King." Her brows knitted themselves together, and a dark look shadowed her face. She didn't say anything about becoming royalty herself.

"Probably a good thing I didn't let Curlin die, either."

Vi took my hand and led me back toward the inn.

CHAPTER THIRTY-SEVEN

Vi

Back inside the kitchen, Curlin and Mal were bristled like
alley cats, stubbornly glowering in opposite corners of the
room. Swinton and Quill lounged at one end of the long
table, picking at the crumbs of what looked to've been a fair
substantial meal. The pair of them hardly paused their gab-
bing for a second when we came through the door. Swinton
looked up at Bo, a question on his face, and when Bo settled
on the bench beside him and squeezed his shoulder, Swinton
relaxed into him, smiling. I leaned against the door frame,
trying to decide which storm needed handling first.

Curlin's wound had been freshly bandaged, and half of her
face washed. She held a rag limply in her good hand. Mal
had washed away the soot and dirt of the night before, and
his tight curls clung damply to his dark, clean scalp. I took a
seat at the table, ravenous, but before I'd managed to swallow
my first bite of spiced duck pillowed inside a sweet roll, Quill
flourished a stack of papers in front of my face.

"What's this?" I asked, stuffing another bite into my mouth.

"Freedom," Bo said. "Quill had Phineas's signature on another document. Swinton traced it on to your contract, signing it over to me. I marked the term as completed, and Quill will file the documents with the proper authorities before the end of the day. You're free, Vi."

Curlin scoffed, and I shot her a hard look. For the first time in hours, I thought of the Laroches. "What happened to them? Phineas and Aphra?"

Bo's face tightened. "She killed him. Slit his throat."

A wave of cold raced through me, and I forced my face to stillness. "Not to say he didn't deserve it, but..." I took a breath. "You saw it?"

Bo nodded.

"And her? Where'd she go?"

"She disappeared after that. She left the barn, and I saw no reason to wait around to learn her fate."

"She was kind to me," I said. I was glad it had been her. Glad that Phineas's life had been taken by someone he'd hurt. I blushed. I didn't want Bo to see this side of me—didn't want him to see what a lifetime of fear and anger had made me. I wanted to be the best version of myself for him. "Murderer or no, I hope she's all right. I hope she finds herself a place in the resistance. She was helping them, you know."

Bo shot me a look so pointed, so expressive, that I knew he'd read every feeling that'd flashed through my mind. He smiled, and a little of the anger, a little of the hatred that'd followed me my whole life, melted away.

Quill laughed. "You've had the shortest contract on record, so far as I know, Vi," he said. "What'll you do with your new freedom?"

I touched the pearls in their pouch beneath my shirt and

looked at Curlin. Screams echoed in my head, the terrifying ranting of the little boy in the temple's basement. Tobain. I thought about the Shriven, dressed as rebels.

"Curlin, who cut your arm?" I asked.

Her chin trembled, and she refused to meet my eyes. Bethesda stood behind her and wrapped an arm around the shaking girl.

"Leave her be, Miss Vi. She's had an awful time of it. This one needs a bath and a rest, and then I'll see her back to the temple."

Curlin's good hand shot out and gripped Bethesda's hand. "No! No. You can't send me back there. You've no idea what they made me do. What they did to me. I'd rather die."

"The temple?" Bethesda asked, looking alarmed.

Swinton eased his ma into a chair, murmuring softly to her.

Bo shot me a questioning look. I could almost feel the pieces clicking into place in his head.

"What you showed me in the basement of the temple," I said. "Did you want that, or did they?"

"I didn't want to tell them, Vi. I know you won't believe me, but I did everything I could to keep your secret safe. Anchorite Sula and Anchorite Bethea made me swear before I came that I'd never tell a soul that we'd grown up together. They made me promise to watch out for you, Magritte only knows why. And I tried. I really did."

"But?" Bo asked. The single word held depthless menace.

Curlin looked at me, pain and tears clouding her eyes. "You saw. You saw what they can do. They've given me three doses that I know of. I only wanted to stop them watching me, stop them waiting for me to turn. I only wanted to be normal. They said that if I did as they said, I would be safe. That they'd keep me from losing myself."

I could feel Bo tensing beside me, and I put a hand on top of his.

"I tried so hard, Vi, but they saw me speak to you in the basement. They must've known all along that we'd come up together. I didn't tell them much, honest. Just your name. Your birthday. Where you'd said your ma was from. It was hardly anything, I promise," she said pleadingly. "But they brought me with them last night and made me confirm that you were the girl I'd been talking about. They promised if I did, they'd keep me safe, comfortable. They promised they'd keep me whole." Her hand sketched over the bandage on her arm. "But they lied. I'd served my purpose. Anchorite Tafima said it was time to be rid of me. She must've thought I'd bleed to death before anyone found me."

"What did she show you at the temple, Vi?" Swinton asked.

As quick as I could, I told them what I'd seen. Quill's lips pressed tight together, and Swinton looked fit to burst with rage.

"They killed my Taeb, didn't they, Swinton?" Bethesda's knife-edged voice was hard as steel.

"I've been saying so for years, Mama." Swinton took Bo's hand. "Whatever help I can give you, it's yours."

Bo's eyes lit with adoration, and he gave Swinton a swift kiss.

"It's not only that," Curlin said, giving Bo and me a pointed look. "The Shriven know who you are now. They know who you both are, and someone high up in the temple wants Vi captured in order to control you."

"Yes, I'm aware of that," Bo said grimly. "But putting aside our situation for a moment... The Suzerain are contracting estates to grow philomenas not for perfume, but to create an elixir that makes people lose themselves to violence, which they're using to turn people into the diminished. Do I have that right?"

Curlin nodded. "It's strategic. The dimmys are set to wreak havoc on neighborhoods or towns where folks aren't as devout as the Suzerain would like. The Shriven catch the dimmys and folks see the value of contributing to the temple's coffers. Not to mention the fact that the simple presence of the Shriven terrifies most folks. Makes them behave."

Bo twisted the cuff on his wrist absently. "I have to get back. I have to tell Runa what's happening. She'll never stand for this."

Swinton gave him a hard look. "You think she doesn't already know? She's the Queen. The most powerful person in the empire."

"I've got to find a way to stop it myself."

My heart glowed with pride. Perhaps he wasn't such a useless brat after all.

"Will you help us, Curlin?" I asked.

She turned to me, shock plain on her face. "After everything I've done to you, why would you even consider trusting me?"

I took another roll from the platter and bit into it, savoring the spicy, rich duck and soft, buttery bread. "Because you're a dimmy from the End, just like me. And the anchorites forced you into impossible situations, just like me. And I think somewhere under all that nose-in-the-air superiority, there's someone who doesn't want to stand by and let things happen to her anymore."

A slow smile lit Curlin's face, and for the first time in what felt like ages, I saw the girl who'd been my best friend once, long ago. "I'll help. I'll do anything in my power to stop them from hurting anyone else."

We debated for a long time. Bo had to return to Penby, and soon, and Swinton'd agreed to go with him with hardly a moment's hesitation. An adventure, he'd called it. A chance to see how the other half lived. Bo thought it would be best for Curlin and me to return with him, as well. We could hide on his estates until he sorted things out with the Queen. It made sense in a way, to get away from the place the Shriven were searching for me. But Curlin was adamant—and I agreed— that they'd kill us as soon as look at us if we were seen in Alskad. We finally agreed that Curlin and I would stay in Williford until our arms recovered, and we'd try to find our way to the rebel stronghold in Ilor's backcountry.

We all felt fair certain that we could buy our way into the resistance with my pearls, Bo's funds and Curlin's knowledge of the inner workings of the temple. The rebels had to be told about the Suzerain and their philomena poison. It seemed possible, too, that if Myrna and Aphra had escaped Plumleen, we'd find them with the rebels. I knew they'd vouch for me.

It promised to be difficult and risky. Bo especially hated the idea that I'd align myself with a dangerous and largely unknown rebel force, but of our choices, the resistance was, at the very least, working toward a goal we all believed in. Together, we might be strong enough to stop the Suzerain and put an end to the mistreatment of the contract workers who came to Ilor looking for a better life.

Mal and Quill had agreed to pass letters for Bo and me, secreting them across the Tethys on their uncle's ship and to Gerlene. The solicitor would deliver my letters to Bo and see that his got back across the Tethys to me by the same route. Bethesda offered Curlin and me safe harbor anytime we found ourselves in Williford, and Quill swore he'd keep me up to date on the royal gossip.

Before I'd time to wrap my head around it, I was standing on the docks, bidding Bo and Swinton farewell. Swinton hugged me tight and kissed me on the cheek.

"Promise me you won't let him do anything too reckless," I said.

Swinton's grin matched Bo's. "Promise. Try to keep yourself in one piece, bully. You hear me?"

I shrugged, smiling, and wrapped my arms around Bo. "I couldn't have asked for a better brother. Please take care. I'm not anxious to face the world alone again."

Bo made a sound into my neck, somewhere between a sob and a laugh, and pulled away and kissed me on the forehead. "I love you, Vi. We've each managed to conquer so much on our own—imagine what we'll be able to do now that we have each other."

I didn't know if I believed him, but I knew that I believed *in* him. I believed in us. I knew that I didn't need anyone else to make me a whole person, but the two of us together made something well worth watching.

A sob caught in my throat as the ship chugged out toward the open ocean, carrying my twin halfway across the world. And I caught sight of him, standing at the rail, waving his handkerchief at me. The sun beat down on me, and sweat prickled my skin, but the memory of Alskad's icy air and gray sea washed over me nonetheless. I pulled my own handkerchief from my pocket and waved back. Waved until I couldn't see him anymore. Waved until the last tickle of his love for me was nothing but a memory in my own head.

With that, I started inland. I'd seen a world of wrongs, and I was determined to do my part to right them.

★ ★ ★ ★ ★

ACKNOWLEDGMENTS

Writing this book has been an exercise in dualities—solitude and collaboration; tenacity and patience; research and imagination. I am deeply grateful to the legion of people who've supported me along the way, who've reminded me that I'm not alone, who've pushed me to keep pursuing this dream. It is deeply humbling to know that so many people believed in Vi, in Bo and in me.

This book wouldn't exist without my incredible, patient, brilliant agent, Brent Taylor. From that very first live Tweet, I knew it was meant to be. Thank you for always being there for me with smart answers to my illogical worries and solutions to every problem I encounter. I cannot imagine a better advocate for my career or a better friend, and I'm so happy to be walking through the wild world of publishing with you at my side. Thank you for your generosity, your humor and your brilliant notes. The Shriven wouldn't exist without you.

An ocean of gratitude to my wonderful editor, Lauren Smulski. This world came alive in your hands. Thank you for believing in me and the world of *The Diminished*. I am so grateful for your marvelous notes, which made this world and these characters sing, and for making my words so much stronger. Thanks for helping me sketch Penby on a cocktail napkin. Most of all, thank you for loving Vi and Bo just as much as I do.

To everyone at Harlequin TEEN who managed to turn my words into a real, actual book: You are my heroes. Thank you to Kathleen Oudit and Mary Luna in the art department, who broke the moon and made Penby real. A huge, warm thanks to Natashya Wilson and T.S. Ferguson for your unerring support and for always making me laugh. I am everlastingly grateful to Krista Mitchell, Bryn Collier and Evan Brown in marketing—thank you for making sure the world knew all about *The Diminished*.

I am lucky to call some of the most intelligent, unflinching editors in the world my friends. To Emily Thrash and Ashley Paige-Powers, thank you for slogging through the early drafts of this book and helping me find Bo. Huge thanks to Ashley and Nora Moser for asking me the hard questions, helping me clarify my timelines and making me think about the nitty-gritty details that make Alskad feel so real. I don't know that I could have gotten through querying or submission without Lana Wood Johnson and her constant support. A huge thanks to Daniel Felts for his incredible insight and for always being there to take the dogs on long walks. Thank you as well to Cale Dietrich, for being a great friend and for such insightful notes. I am so grateful to Anastasia Shabalov for our long discussions, her brilliant ideas and for reading oh-so-quickly. To Nena Boling-Smith, thank you for giving such great notes, for your generosity and for the long chats.

I have been given a great boon in the friends I've made along the way, and I wanted to say thank you and send big love to the following, in no particular order: Thalia Beaty, Elizabeth Kirkwood, Valerie Kelly, Natalie Parker, Julia Whelan, Logan Garrison Savits, Heidi Heilig, E.K. Johnston, Lauren Spieller, Sarah N. Smetana, Laura Lam, Jessica Spotswood, Bree Barton, Kelly deVos, Dana Mele, Rachel Lynn Solomon, Samira Ahmed, Kosoko Jackson, Alexa Donne, L.L. McKinney, Tara Sim, Traci Chee, Sarah Tolscer, Emma Higinbotham, Chandra Rooney, Troy Wiggins, Jason Barnett, Olivia Wilmot, Bob Arnold, Lauren Hales, Eva Beckemeyer, Tara Shaffer, Jen at Pop Goes the Reader!, the ladies of The Debutante Ball, the Class of 2k18 and my lovely Electrics. Thank you.

To the Fight Me Club: I honestly don't know if I could have made it this far without you. Thank you for everything, salt included.

To Whitney Gardner and Summer Heacock: Thank you for being the best agent-sisters and friends a girl could ask for. So much love for you both.

At certain points along the way, I found my way to teachers who believed in me enough to tell me that, yes, I could become an author. Thank you to Alice Holstein, Michael Knight, Marilyn Kallet, Rebecca Skloot, John Bensko, Carey Holladay and Carey Mickalites. See, I went and did it! I wrote a book!

Thank you also to the people whose critiques I hear in my head whenever I write: Michael Adams, Jenny Lederer, Jon May, Scott Carter, Courtney Santo and Tara Mae Mulroy. I think of you each time I use a gerund.

I couldn't have gotten this far without the support of my incredible family. To Mama and Dad: You have always cultivated my imagination and allowed me to be fearless and independent. My life has been full of adventure because of your hard work and the value you place on experiences over stuff.

Thank you for always encouraging me to take the big leaps. To Hannah: Thank you for sharing with me your overwhelming talent, your love of story and your friendship. You're the best sister anyone could ever have. To Pop: Thank you for telling me stories, and teaching me in turn to let my imagination soar. Thank you for sharing with me your love of history—it's the details I find in the annals of time that are always the most surprising. Love. Love. Love.

To my in-laws: Ronda and James, thank you for welcoming me so warmly into your home and your family, and for being so understanding and giving. Ed and Max, I will always appreciate your kindness, your generosity and your inclusion of me in your family. Katie and Dana, thank you for all the laughs and for being my sisters from the beginning. I love you all.

Though they're no longer around, I am deeply grateful to Iya, for my love of etiquette books and knowing when to break the rules; to Grandmother Patterson, for giving me a roof where I could read and escape; and to Pop and Grandma, for my sense of adventure and love of travel. I miss you.

To Cody: This book wouldn't exist without you. Thank you for being my best, first reader. Thank you for understanding me and loving me and for being the one person with whom I can be entirely myself. Thank you for being patient when I have to disappear into my writing cave for weeks at a time, for drying my tears when I spend too much time peopling, for making every day brighter and funnier, for enhancing my life with your art and for always taking care of me and our dogs. You are the kindest, most talented person I know, and I love you beyond all the worlds I can imagine.

Finally, thank you, reader, for picking this book up. It's a dream come true.